Praise for Debbie Macomber's
bestselling novels from Ballantine Books

Must Love Flowers

"A testament to the power of new beginnings. Wise, warm, witty, and charmingly full of hope, this story celebrates the surprising and unexpected ways that family, friendship, and love can lift us up."
—KRISTIN HANNAH,
bestselling author of *The Nightingale*

"Uplifting, warm, and hopeful. With her signature charm and wit, Debbie Macomber proves that the best relationships, like the perfect blooms, are always worth the wait. . . . This can't-miss novel is Macomber at the height of her storytelling prowess. I absolutely adored it!"
—KRISTY WOODSON HARVEY, *New York Times*
bestselling author of *The Summer of Songbirds*

"Debbie Macomber never fails to deliver an uplifting, heartwarming story. Whether you're just starting out, just starting over or anything in between, *Must Love Flowers* should be at the top of your summer reading list!"
—BRENDA NOVAK, *New York Times*
bestselling author of *Before We Were Strangers*

The Best Is Yet to Come

"Macomber's latest is a wonderful inspirational read that has just enough romance as the characters heal their painful emotional wounds." —*Library Journal*

"This tale of redemption and kindness is a gift to Macomber's many readers and all who love tales of sweet and healing romance." —*Booklist*

D0189743

It's Better This Way

"Macomber has a firm grasp on issues that will resonate with readers of domestic fiction. Well-drawn characters and plotting—coupled with strong romantic subplots and striking coincidences—will keep readers rooting for forgiveness, hope and true love to conquer all."
—KATHLEEN GERARD, blogger at
Reading Between the Lines

"Macomber keeps her well-shaded, believable characters at the heart of this seamlessly plotted novel as she probes the nuances of familial relationships and the agelessness of romance. This deeply emotional tale proves it's never too late for love."
—*Publishers Weekly* (starred review)

A Walk Along the Beach

"Macomber scores another home run with this surprisingly heavy but uplifting contemporary romance between a café owner and a photographer. Eloquent prose . . . along with [a] charming supporting cast adds a welcome dose of light and hope. With this stirring romance, Macomber demonstrates her mastery of the genre."
—*Publishers Weekly* (starred review)

"Highly emotional . . . a hard-to-put-down page-turner, yet, throughout all the heartache, the strength and love of family shines through." —*New York Journal of Books*

Window on the Bay

"This heartwarming story sweetly balances friendship and mother-child bonding with romantic love." —*Kirkus Reviews*

"Macomber's work is as comforting as ever." —*Booklist*

Cottage by the Sea

"Romantic, warm, and a breeze to read—one of [Debbie] Macomber's best." —*Kirkus Reviews*

"Debbie dazzles! A wonderful story of friendship, forgiveness, and the power of love. I devoured every page!"
—SUSAN MALLERY, #1 *New York Times* bestselling author of *The Friends We Keep*

Last One Home

"Fans of bestselling author Macomber will not be disappointed by this compelling stand-alone novel." —*Library Journal*

ROSE HARBOR

Sweet Tomorrows

"Macomber fans will leave the Rose Harbor Inn with warm memories of healing, hope, and enduring love."
—*Kirkus Reviews*

"Overflowing with the poignancy, sweetness, conflicts and romance for which Debbie Macomber is famous, *Sweet Tomorrows* captivates from beginning to end." —*Bookreporter*

"Fans will enjoy this final installment of the Rose Harbor series as they see Jo Marie's story finally come to an end."
—*Library Journal*

Silver Linings

"Macomber's homespun storytelling style makes reading an easy venture. . . . She also tosses in some hidden twists and turns that will delight her many longtime fans."
—*Bookreporter*

"Reading Macomber's novels is like being with good friends, talking and sharing joys and sorrows."
—*New York Journal of Books*

Love Letters

"[Debbie] Macomber's mastery of women's fiction is evident in her latest. . . . [She] breathes life into each plotline, carefully intertwining her characters' stories to ensure that none of them overshadow the others. Yet it is her ability to capture different facets of emotion which will entrance fans and newcomers alike." —*Publishers Weekly*

"Romance and a little mystery abound in this third installment of Macomber's series set at Cedar Cove's Rose Harbor Inn. . . . Readers of Robyn Carr and Sherryl Woods will enjoy Macomber's latest, which will have them flipping pages until the end and eagerly anticipating the next installment."
—*Library Journal* (starred review)

"Uplifting . . . a cliffhanger ending for Jo Marie begs for a swift resolution in the next book." —*Kirkus Reviews*

Rose Harbor in Bloom

"[Debbie Macomber] draws in threads of her earlier book in this series, *The Inn at Rose Harbor*, in what is likely to be just as comfortable a place for Macomber fans as for Jo Marie's guests at the inn." —*The Seattle Times*

"Macomber's legions of fans will embrace this cozy, heartwarming read." —*Booklist*

"Readers will find the emotionally impactful storylines and sweet, redemptive character arcs for which the author is famous. Classic Macomber, which will please fans and keep them coming back for more." —*Kirkus Reviews*

"The storybook scenery of lighthouses, cozy bed and breakfast inns dotting the coastline, and seagulls flying above takes readers on personal journeys of first love, lost love and recaptured love [presenting] love in its purest and most personal forms."
—*Bookreporter*

"Fans will happily return to the warm, welcoming sanctuary of Macomber's Blossom Street, catching up with old friends from past Blossom Street books and meeting new ones being welcomed into the fold." —*Kirkus Reviews*

"Macomber's nondenominational-inspirational women's novel, with its large cast of characters, will resonate with fans of the popular series." —*Booklist*

Starting Now

"Macomber understands the often complex nature of a woman's friendships, as well as the emotional language women use with their friends." —*New York Journal of Books*

"There is a reason that legions of Macomber fans ask for more Blossom Street books. They fully engage her readers as her characters discover happiness, purpose, and meaning in life. . . . Macomber's feel-good novel, emphasizing interpersonal relationships and putting people above status and objects, is truly satisfying." —*Booklist* (starred review)

"Macomber's writing and storytelling deliver what she's famous for—a smooth, satisfying tale with characters her fans will cheer for and an arc that is cozy, heartwarming and ends with the expected happily-ever-after." —*Kirkus Reviews*

CHRISTMAS NOVELS

The Christmas Spirit

"Exactly what readers want from a Macomber holiday outing."
—*Publishers Weekly*

"With almost all of Debbie Macomber's novels, the reader is not only given a captivating story, but also a lesson in life."
—*New York Journal of Books*

DEBBIE MACOMBER

The Perfect Holiday

That Wintry Feeling
and *Thanksgiving Prayer*

BALLANTINE BOOKS
NEW YORK

The Perfect Holiday is a work of fiction.
Names, characters, places, and incidents are the products
of the author's imagination or are used fictitiously.
Any resemblance to actual events, locales, or persons,
living or dead, is entirely coincidental.

2023 Ballantine Books Mass Market Edition
That Wintry Feeling copyright © 1984 by Debbie Macomber
Thanksgiving Prayer copyright © 1984 by Debbie Macomber

Published in the United States by Ballantine Books,
an imprint of Random House, a division of
Penguin Random House LLC, New York.

BALLANTINE is a registered trademark and the colophon is a
trademark of Penguin Random House LLC.

That Wintry Feeling and *Thanksgiving Prayer* were originally
published separately in paperback in the United States
by Silhouette Books, New York, in 1984.

ISBN 978-0-593-35986-0
Ebook ISBN 978-0-593-35987-7

Cover design: Belina Huey
Cover illustration: Alan Ayers, based on images by
Depositphotos (background and sky) and Dreamstime (couple)

Printed in the United States of America

randomhousebooks.com

2 4 6 8 9 7 5 3 1

Ballantine Books mass market edition: October 2023

Winter 2023

Dear Friends,

As you might have guessed, these two stories were written quite some time ago when phones were attached to walls and research was done at a library. In reading these stories again, the characters still capture my heart, even if they aren't texting each other!

I wrote *That Wintry Feeling* and *Thanksgiving Prayer* after my husband, Wayne, worked as an electrician in Alaska on the North Slope. He infused his love of the state in me, and years later I wrote several more books based in Alaska after I had a chance to visit myself.

Thanksgiving Prayer was one of the first books I wrote, and oh how I loved this story! I hope you will, too!

As an author, I have been blessed many times but never as much as when I hear from my readers. You can reach me through all the social media platforms. If you would rather write, my mailing address is:

P.O. Box 1458,
Port Orchard, WA
98366

Blessings,

Debbie Macomber

That Wintry Feeling

One

Cathy Thompson's long nails beat an impatient tempo against the Formica countertop as she waited.

"Yes, I'll hold," she said, and breathed heavily into the telephone. Her deep gray eyes clashed with Linda Ericson's, who sat at the table, a large newspaper spread over the top.

"Any luck?" Linda whispered.

A voice at the other end of the line interrupted Cathy's response, and she straightened, her fingers tightening around the phone. "This is Cathy Thompson again." The inflection of her voice conveyed the irritation. "Would it be possible to speak to Grady Jones?"

"Grady's in the air," a gruff male voice informed her. "Be with you in a minute, Harry," he said to someone who was obviously waiting in his office.

"When do you expect him back?" Cathy asked in her most businesslike voice.

A lengthy pause followed, and Cathy could hear the rustle of paper in the background. "Thursday afternoon. Will you hold the line a minute?"

Cathy's sigh was full of exasperation. Cradling the telephone against her shoulder with the side of her head, she pulled out a piece of paper and a pencil. As she looked up she happened to catch a glimpse of the school play yard. The sights and sounds of the last recess of the day drifted in through the open window. Her gray eyes softened as she unconsciously sought Angela Jones. A frown creased her narrow forehead as she discovered the pigtailed first-grader leaning against the play shed, watching the other girls jump rope. Angela always seemed to be on the outside looking in.

"Do you want to leave a message?" The harried male voice came back on the phone.

"I've already left four," Cathy snapped.

"Listen, all I do is take the message. If Grady doesn't return your call, it's not my fault." He hesitated. "Are you the gal from the school again?"

"Yes, I'm the gal from the school again." She echoed his words, doing her best to disguise her frustration.

"All I can tell you is that Grady is flying on assignment. I'll tell him you phoned."

The man wasn't to blame if Grady Jones didn't wish to speak to her, and Cathy's reply was less agitated. "Please do that." Gently, she replaced the receiver in its cradle.

"Well?" Linda looked up expectantly.

"No luck. It's the same as before. They'll take a message, but he won't be back until Thursday afternoon."

"What are you going to do?" Linda asked, concern knitting her brow.

Cathy shrugged. "Maybe it's time I personally introduced myself to the elusive Grady Jones. He'll have a hard time not talking to me if I show up at the airfield." Cathy had done her research well. The school information card had been sketchy. The card listed the father's occupation as pilot, employed by Alaska Cargo Company. No business phone number had been given, and when Cathy looked it up in the yellow pages she found a large commercial ad. The fine print at the bottom of the advertisement stated that Grady Jones was the company owner. The information card had stated that Angela had no mother. Cathy had found the comment an interesting one. How could any child not have a mother? It could be that Angela's parents were divorced. What Cathy couldn't understand was how someone as unconcerned and uncaring as Grady Jones could have been awarded custody of the child. Cathy had tried on several occasions to contact him at home, but the only adult she had ever reached was a housekeeper, who promised to give him a message. Cathy had stopped counting the times she'd left messages for him.

"After all the trouble you've gone through, I'd say that's about the only way you're going to get his attention."

"Believe me, I won't have any problem getting his attention. His ears will burn for a week."

"Cathy . . ." Linda warned, her large brown eyes worried. "Alienating Angela's father won't help her."

"I know, but I can't help but dislike the man."

The bell rang, indicating the end of recess. Emitting a soft groan, Cathy turned around. "Back to the salt mine." It had been another break wasted trying to contact a parent. Next time she'd pour herself a cup of coffee before making a phone call.

"Don't go yet," Linda called. "I want to read you this personal."

"Linda," Cathy said with a sigh, but she knew better

than to argue. Her friend would insist that she listen anyway. "All right, but be quick about it."

Rustling the paper, Linda sat upright and read. "Sincere gentleman seeking sincere lady for sincere relationship—"

"Only sincere women need apply," Cathy interrupted. "Dull, Linda, dull. If you insist on playing matchmaker, the least you can do is find someone with a little personality."

"Okay, here's another." She glanced up. "Man with large house, large cat, six kids. Cat not enough."

"Six kids." Cathy choked.

"That says a lot," Linda defended. "At least he's honest and forthright. He must like animals."

"That would make Peterkins happy, but unfortunately I'm the one who has to be satisfied. Six kids are out."

The shuffle of feet could be heard above the laughter as the children filed into the school building. The afternoon could no longer be delayed.

Two hours later, Cathy was about to unlock the door to her rental house on Lacey Street. She had rented a home so that Peterkins, her black cocker spaniel, would have a yard in which to roam. Steve had given her Peterkins, and the dog was probably the only good thing she had left of their relationship. In the beginning she had resented the fact that Peterkins had been a gift from Steve. Every time she looked at her floppy-eared friend she was reminded of a soured relationship. But Peterkins wasn't to be blamed, and there was far more than a dog to remind her of Steve. It was funny how many of her thoughts he continued to dominate. Yet it was totally, completely over. Steve was a married man. A knot twisted the sensitive muscles of her stomach. He'd been married for five months and six days. Not that she was counting. Bravely, she had attended the wedding, had been a member of the wedding party. The maid of honor. Her sister wouldn't hear of anything else.

Exhaling a quivering breath, Cathy turned the key in the lock and pushed open the door. Immediately Peterkins was there, excitedly jumping up and down. When she crouched down to pet him, he fervently lapped her hand with his moist tongue.

"Let me relax a minute, and we'll go for our walk," Cathy told him. Peterkins knew her moods better than anyone, Cathy mused while she changed clothes and sorted through the mail. Peeling an orange, she sat at the small circular table in her kitchen and leaned against the back of the chair.

Memories of Steve again ruled her thoughts. They'd quarreled. It wasn't any major disagreement; she couldn't even recall what it was that had sparked the argument. But something was different this time. Cathy had decided she was tired of always being the one to give in, apologize, change. They had talked about getting married on several occasions. If their relationship was to be a lasting one, Cathy had decided, then Steve must learn to do his share of giving. It would be a good lesson for him to admit he was wrong for once.

She pulled each of the orange segments apart and set them on the napkin, fingering each one. Her appetite was gone, and she scooted the afternoon snack away.

The whole idea of teaching Steve a lesson had been immature and foolish. Cathy realized that now. She gave a short laugh. What a wonderful thing hindsight was.

When Steve began dating her sister, MaryAnne, Cathy

had been amused. He wasn't fooling her; she knew exactly what he was doing. She had taken great pride in meeting him at the door when he came to pick up Mary-Anne for a date. With a cheery smile, she had proven she wasn't in the least bit jealous. He could date whom he liked. Twice she had arranged dates at the same time MaryAnne and Steve would be going out so that they would all meet at the apartment she shared with her sister.

The only one who had shown any concern over such foolishness had been their mother.

"Mom." Cathy had strived to brush off Paula Thompson's concern. "MaryAnne and I cut the apron strings when we moved out and got an apartment of our own. From now on you're only supposed to give advice when we ask. Remember?" Her words were a teasing reminder of what their mother had told them when they decided to move in together. Although her mother never mentioned a word again about MaryAnne and Steve, the question was in her eyes.

Six weeks had passed, and still Steve continued to play his game in an attempt to make her jealous. If she hadn't been so stubborn she would have seen what was happening. Twice MaryAnne had come to her.

"You don't mind, do you?" The gray eyes so like her own had pleaded. "I'd stop seeing him in a minute if our relationship was hurting you in any way."

Cathy had laughed lightly. "It's over," she said with a flippant air. "It was over a long time ago. There's no need to concern yourself."

Then one night MaryAnne had burst into the apartment and proudly displayed the beautiful diamond engagement ring. Cathy had been shocked. This was carrying things to an extreme. Steve had gone too far. She wasn't going to allow him to use her little sister like this for another minute.

The argument when she'd confronted Steve had been loud and bitter. They'd hurled accusations at each other faster and sharper than a machine gun.

All through the preparations for the wedding Cathy had expected Steve to put a halt to things. It was unbelievable that a minor disagreement three months before had been allowed to go this far.

Throughout the time they had prepared for the wedding, MaryAnne had been radiantly happy. A hundred times Cathy had to bite her tongue to keep from saying. "Listen, Sis, I'm not completely sure Steve loves you. He loves me, I know he does." Maybe she should have said it. The message was in her eyes; her mother read it the morning of the wedding. Steve saw it as she marched up the aisle preceding her sister. It was there when the minister pronounced Steve and MaryAnne man and wife.

The memory of those words seemed to echo, assaulting her from all sides. Urgently, Cathy stood and pushed her chair to the table. She needed to get out, away from the memories, the hurt.

"Bring me the leash, Peterkins," she said to her dog, who promptly stepped into the bedroom and pulled the rhinestone-studded strap off the chair. Cathy paused, fingering the red leather. The leash had been another gift from Steve. Would he continue to haunt her for the rest of her life? Would it always be like this?

For two months after the wedding Cathy had walked around in a haze of pain and disillusionment. This couldn't be happening to her. This wasn't real. It became almost impossible to hide her emotions from her family. She had to get away, to the ends of the earth. Alaska. The opportunity to work as a basic skills instructor had come as a surprise. Her application had been submitted months before. She had never intended to accept the job, even if it was offered to her. She had done it to tease Steve, telling him if he didn't proclaim his undying love she'd abandon him for parts unknown. Willingly, Steve had obliged. When she hadn't heard from the school district, Cathy was relieved. It had been a fluke, a joke. Now it was her salvation, a lifeline to sanity.

No one had understood her reasons for going—except her mother, and perhaps Steve. With a sense of urgency she had gone about building a new life for herself. Forming friendships, reaching out. It was only in the area of men that she withdrew, held back. Eventually that reserve would abate. A soft smile curved up the edges of her lips. Linda and those crazy personal ads she was always reading to her. If her friend had anything to do with it, Cathy would be married by Christmas.

She dressed carefully Thursday morning, the meeting with Grady Jones weighing her decision as she chose a dark blue gabardine business suit. The line of the suit accentuated the slender curves of her lithe form. Cathy was nearly five-eleven in her heels and secretly hoped to meet the man at eye level. She did with most men. Not once had she regretted the fact she was tall. In most cases, height was an advantage. Steve was tall. Her hands knotted at her sides as her resolve tightened. It was ridiculous the way her mind would bring him to the forefront of her consciousness. It had to stop, and it had to stop immediately. She needed to start dating again, meet other men. She'd do it. The troubled thoughts that had continually plagued her were all the convincing she needed. She'd answer one of those crazy ads Linda was always telling her about.

"Be a good dog, Peterkins." She ruffled his ears playfully. "You do like cats, don't you? What about six kids?" The large brown eyes looked up at her quizzically, and Cathy laughed. "Never mind."

Dawn was breaking as she parked her Honda in the school parking lot. Gracefully, she slid across the upholstered seat and climbed out the passenger side. As soon as she was paid she was going to get that other door fixed. She paused to watch the sun's golden orb break out across the pink horizon. There was a magical quality to an Alaskan sky that stirred something within her. The sky was bluer than blue, the air fresher, cleaner. Even the landscape that appeared dingy and barren held a fascination for Cathy. She hadn't expected to like Alaska but found herself mesmerized with its openness, enthralled with its beauty.

"Whew-yee." Linda whistled as she walked into the teacher's lounge. "You look fit to kill."

"I may have to," Cathy replied flippantly, as she poured herself a mug of coffee. "But that man's going to listen to me if I have to hog-tie him."

"Hog-tie him?" Linda repeated with a laugh. "Is that a little Kansas humor?"

Pulling out a chair, Cathy sat beside her friend. "It could be, but by the time I finish with Grady Jones, he won't be laughing."

"With that look in your eye, I almost pity the poor man."

Her long, tapered fingers cupped the coffee mug as she glanced at the paper Linda had placed beside her purse. "Without meaning to change the subject, are there any new ads today?"

"New ads. You actually want to look at the personals? As I live and breathe . . ."

The rest of what she was going to say faded away as she took the paper and opened it on top of the table so they could both read through the columns. Several of the listings were almost identical, with lengthy descriptions of their likes and wants. It was a small ad at the bottom of the page that captured Cathy's attention. It read, "Red Baron seeks lady to soar to heights unknown." It gave a post office box number for the response.

"This one looks interesting." Cathy pointed it out to Linda.

Her friend twisted the newspaper around so she could read the ad. She didn't comment on the contents. "Go ahead and write something, I'll put it in today's mail."

"Linda . . . I don't know what to say. Let me think about it awhile, then I'll—"

"No," Linda interrupted, her voice emphatic. "If you think about it you won't do it. There's paper here, and I've got an envelope and stamp in the office. Go for it."

Cathy's hand hovered over the paper while Linda left for her office. She chewed on the end of the pen and shifted her chin from the palm of one hand to the palm of the other. Finally she scribbled, *Interested in soaring. Heights negotiable.* She signed it *Snoopy* and gave the post office box where she collected her mail. She'd read the six-word message ten times and was ready to throw it away when Linda returned, snapped it from her hand, and placed it inside the envelope.

"I can't believe I'm doing this," Cathy mumbled. "There must be something basically wrong with me."

"There is," Linda confirmed. "You're lonely."

Cathy's responding smile was weak. It was a lot more than lonely, but she didn't explain.

Having made arrangements with the teachers earlier in the week, Cathy was able to leave the school before twelve. She was determined to speak to Grady Jones one way or another. Following the directions Linda had given her, Cathy arrived at the airfield promptly at noon.

Her car door slammed with the force of the September wind, shutting it for her. Another gust whipped her hair about her face and stimulated her cheeks until they were a rosy hue. She stopped to examine the buildings. A large hangar took up one side of the open field to the right of the runway. Directly beside the hangar was a smaller building she assumed must be the office. A large overhead sign read ALASKA CARGO COMPANY.

Checking her wristwatch, Cathy noted it was thirteen minutes after noon. Right on time. Her watch naturally ran thirteen minutes fast, which suited her since she hated being late. If Grady Jones hadn't arrived, she was prepared to wait. With her black leather purse tucked under her arm, she approached the smaller structure. As she neared the office a man dressed in grease-smeared overalls and a matching cap emerged from one of the hangars.

"Can I help you?" he questioned, his eyes surveying her with interest.

"I'm here to see Mr. Jones," she replied in a crisp business tone.

Something indecipherable flickered across the weathered face, but Cathy couldn't read him. She wondered if this was the man who'd answered her persistent calls. Had he recognized her voice?

"Grady's inside," the man replied, and wiped his hands on a rag that hung from his hip pocket. "I'll take you to his office. Follow me." He led the way, yanking open the office door. He was halfway through the entrance when he stopped as if suddenly remembering his manners and hurriedly stepped aside, allowing Cathy to enter ahead of him.

It took a moment for her eyes to adjust to the dim interior.

"Make yourself comfortable," he said, and indicated two worn chairs just inside the door. He disappeared behind another door around the counter. The office appeared to be divided into two areas. The outer room contained a long counter that was littered with papers, graphs, and charts. Behind it, the walls were papered by several maps. The two chairs were covered with old newspapers and dog-eared magazines. Cathy decided to stand.

When the mechanic returned, his eyes glanced over her appreciatively. "Grady will see you now." He held the door open as Cathy moved behind the counter.

Her heels clicked against the faded linoleum floor, and the sound seemed to echo all around her. Unconsciously, she held her breath and clenched her purse, as if to steel herself for the encounter.

Grady Jones was standing when she entered the room, and her eyes were instantly drawn to the lean, dark features of the strikingly handsome man. Curly chestnut-colored hair grew with rakish disregard across his wide forehead. His eyes were surprisingly blue, the same color as an Arctic blue fox's. They glinted round and intelligent. His full, almost bushy eyebrows were quirked expectantly, and Cathy realized she was staring. Nervously, she cleared her throat.

"Grady Jones?" she questioned briskly, disguising her shattered composure.

"Yes." His mouth twitched with humor.

This man was well aware of the power of his attraction, Cathy mused, disliking him all the more. If he thought he could disarm her with one devastating smile, then he was wrong. Leaning forward slightly, Cathy extended her hand over the cluttered desk.

"I'm pleased to meet you at last, Mr. Jones," she said with a trace of contempt. "I'm Cathy Thompson, Angela's basic skills instructor."

Grady accepted her hand, capturing it between two massive ones and holding it longer than she liked. Their eyes dueled, hers cool and distrusting, his deepening as they narrowed.

He dropped her hand, and it fell limply at her side. "Yes, I've heard quite a lot about you, Miss Thompson."

"You've heard quite a lot *from* me, too," she emphasized. "However, you've chosen to ignore my messages and phone calls."

"Listen, Miss Thompson, I'm a busy man. I've got a business to run. I can't—"

"Let me assure you, I'm just as busy," she interrupted

curtly. "But I believe Angela is important enough for us both to spare a few minutes."

"All right, I'll admit Angela's got problems."

Cathy had to restrain herself from saying that she thought most of the girl's difficulties stemmed from an uncaring father. "Angela's a sweet, sensitive six-year-old child with social and academic deficiencies," Cathy began. "But it's my guess that most of her academic difficulties are a result of dyslexia. I'd like your permission to have her tested."

"Dyslexia?" Concern furrowed the tanned brow.

"It's not as bad as it sounds," Cathy was quick to assure him. "It's a neurological disorder that affects one's ability to read, spell, and sometimes speak correctly. It's not uncommon for a girl to be dyslexic, but almost three times as many boys are as girls."

"Dyslexic." He repeated the word and slumped into a large rollback chair.

"Angela's in the first grade and has problems reading at the first-grade level, or printing her letters correctly."

"She's a lot like I was at her age," Grady murmured. "Only back then they called it *word blindness*."

"They have a name for it now," she said softly.

Grady looked up, and for the first time seemed to notice that he was sitting, while she was standing. "Sit down, Miss Thompson, please."

Cathy obliged. "Dyslexia affects three areas of learning. Audio, visual, and kinetic, which is the sense of touch or feel. Angela is affected in each area, but to what extent won't be known until she's been tested."

He drew in a deep breath. "You say there's a name for it now. Is there a cure?"

"No," she explained bluntly. "But there is help. Once my suspicions have been confirmed. Angela is going to need a tutor."

"It's done. Send me a bill."

Anger gripped Cathy. This man seemed to think everything could be solved with a signature at the bottom of a check.

"It's not quite that simple, Mr. Jones," she said, keeping a tight rein on her feelings. "It's not my responsibility to find a tutor for your daughter. I'll be happy to give you a list of those recommended by the school district. But finding the one who would work best with Angela is up to you." She spoke in a stiff, professional manner. "I'm also of the opinion that your lack of interest may be the cause of the emotional problems Angela has . . ." She stopped, clenching her hands tightly. Stating her feelings on the way Grady Jones chose to raise his daughter wasn't part of her job.

"That may be." The blue eyes became chips of glacial ice. "But I'm only interested in your academic impressions. I could care less if you think I rate a Father's Day card or not."

"I'm sure." Abruptly, she rose to her feet. "I won't take up any more of your time." She couldn't prevent the waspish tone. "After all, time is money."

"That's right, and you've taken up fifteen minutes already."

Fists balled at her sides with building outrage, she stalked from the office. He followed her out, opening the front door as if he couldn't be rid of her fast enough.

"I'll mail you the list of tutors," she said, in a way that

conveyed the message she would rather have communicated with him by means of the post office.

"You do that," he shot back.

His eyes seemed to bore into her back as she moved across the parking lot. Hating that he was watching her, she opened the passenger side of her car and climbed inside, scooting across the narrow enclosure. She couldn't leave the airfield fast enough, her tires spinning as she rounded the corner and merged with the street traffic.

Her fingers were trembling by the time she pulled into the parking lot at the school. If the meeting had gone poorly, it was her fault. She should have left her opinions out of it. Everything had been fine until she'd impulsively overstepped the boundary.

Looking at Grady Jones was like looking at her father. Not that there was any striking physical resemblance. Her father had died when Cathy was sixteen, yet she hardly remembered his physical features. She had a vague image of a tall, lanky man who drifted in and out of her life at inconvenient intervals. Donald Thompson had been a workaholic. Her mother had recognized and accepted the fact long before his death. And in reality little had changed in their lives after he was gone. He was so seldom home for any lengthy period of time that life went on as it had in the past.

Grady Jones showed all the symptoms. He was never home when she phoned, no matter how late. He worked himself hard and probably expected as much from those he employed. The lines of fatigue had fanned out from his eyes as if it had been a long time since he'd seen a bed. If he continued as he was, he'd probably end up like her father. Dead at fifty-five. Why the fact should bother her, Cathy wasn't sure. Personally, she didn't care for the man. Striking good looks didn't disguise the fact he was ambitious, selfish, and hard-nosed. She preferred a man who was kind, sincere, gentle. A man like—Her mind stopped before the name could form.

"You're back already?" Linda greeted her as she stepped into the school. "That didn't take long."

"I didn't imagine it would," Cathy said, the inflection in her tone voicing her sentiment. "Grady Jones is a busy man."

Linda nodded knowingly. "Relax a minute. There's no need to hurry back, Tom's taking over for you. I bet you didn't eat lunch."

"No," Cathy admitted, "I haven't."

"I could use a break myself. I'll come with you." A smile formed in Linda's large brown eyes. The two women had been instant friends. Although they'd met only two months before, it was as if they had known each other for years. The contrast between them was impressive. Linda was barely five feet tall, a cute, doe-eyed pixie. Her laughter was easy, her nature gentle. Linda had met her husband, Dan, through the personal column, naturally, and they had been happily married for seven years. The only gray cloud that hung over her friend's head was that Linda desperately wanted children. The doctors had repeatedly assured them there was nothing wrong and that eventually Linda would become pregnant. Once Cathy had overheard someone ask Linda how many children she had. Without so much as blinking, Linda had looked up and replied three hundred. By all accounts she wasn't wrong. As the school secretary, Linda did more mothering in one day than some mothers did all year.

"Do you want to talk about it?" Linda asked, as she sat at the table they had occupied that morning.

Cathy took the sandwich from the bag she'd brought with her that morning, examining its contents as if she had forgotten it was bologna and cheese. She knew that one look at her face and Linda knew everything had not gone as she'd wanted. "I blew it, plain and simple."

"He agreed to the tests, didn't he?"

Miserably, she nodded, shoving the bread back inside the brown paper sack. "He agreed to the tests, more or less, but I may have alienated him forever. I think it would be best if any future communication with Grady Jones were handled by mail."

"Don't be so hard on yourself. If he agreed to having Angela tested, you succeeded." The bell rang and students began shuffling out of their classrooms, jerking Linda's attention. "I better get back. Oh, by the way, I mailed your envelope."

"Great." Cathy's reply lacked enthusiasm. What kind of man did she ever expect to find through the personals?

Cathy spent Monday afternoon with Angela Jones. The child invoked a protective response in her. She was small for her age, her blue eyes as large and trusting as a baby seal's. She followed the directions carefully, doing everything that was asked of her.

"You were very good, Angela." Cathy playfully tugged a long brown pigtail.

"Daddy said I should be," she replied shyly, her eyes not meeting Cathy's. "You'll tell him I was, won't you?"

Cathy didn't have the heart to tell the little girl that she doubted she'd ever see her father again. "When I see your father, I'll tell him you were one of the very best."

Angela smiled, revealing that her two front teeth were missing. Cathy couldn't remember ever having seen the child smile. It was the memory of that toothless grin that buoyed her spirits as Cathy stopped in at the grocery store for a few items Monday after school. The store was directly beside the post office, which made it convenient if she needed anything. She was sorting through her bills when the boldfaced handwriting stared up at her. She nearly missed a step as she stopped cold. The envelope was addressed to *Snoopy*.

Two

Cathy glanced at her watch as she slid across the red upholstered booth in the restaurant. Eight-fifteen. Because
her watch was thirteen minutes fast she realized she was
almost a half-hour early. The letter had said eight-thirty.

A waitress came with a glass of water and a menu.
"I'm waiting for someone," Cathy told her hesitantly. "I'll
just have coffee until my . . . my friend arrives."

"Sure," the woman said with a distracted smile.

Cathy had chosen to sit in the booth that was positioned so she could watch whoever entered the restaurant.
At least that way she would recognize him the minute he
walked in the door. His letter said he'd be wearing a red
scarf. With unsteady fingers she opened the clasp of her
purse and removed the letter. She must have read it thirty
times, not sure what she expected to find. There didn't
seem to be any unspoken messages or sexual overtones.
The whole idea of meeting a total stranger was absurd. At
least he'd suggested a public place. If he hadn't she
wouldn't have done it. She wasn't quite sure what had
prompted her coming as it was. It was more than curiosity.

Cathy had dated a couple times the first month she
was in Fairbanks. It hadn't worked out either time. She

hadn't been ready to deal with a new relationship. She wasn't convinced now was the time, either, but she realized she had to try. Living the way she had been, with thoughts of Steve taunting her day and night, was intolerable.

Extracting the letter from the envelope, Cathy decided for the tenth time she liked the handwriting. It was large and bold, as if the man knew what he wanted and wouldn't hesitate to go after it. The message was direct, without superfluous words to flower the letter. It read, *"Snoopy: negotiations open. Meet me Friday 8:30 p.m., Captain Bartlett's. I'll wear a red neck scarf."* He hadn't asked her to identify herself. Cathy appreciated that. If he walked in the restaurant and she didn't like what she saw, she could leave. Somehow, she decided, it didn't matter what he looked like. In an unexplainable way, she liked him already. Certainly she wasn't expecting a handsome prince on a white stallion. Any man who would place an ad in the personals was probably unattractive, shy, and . . .

Her thoughts did a crazy tailspin as the restaurant door opened. Cathy saw the red scarf before she recognized the face. She swallowed in an attempt to ease the paralysis that gripped her throat. It was Grady Jones, Angela's father.

Grady's unnerving blue eyes met hers across the distance. He knew. A smile of recognition flickered over his mouth as he came toward her. Cathy felt trapped, her eyes unable to leave the muscular frame. Darn it, he was good-looking. He wore a dark wool jacket over a blue turtle-neck sweater. The sweater intensified the color of his eyes, making them almost indigo.

"Snoopy?" he queried evenly, resting the palms of his hands on the edge of the table.

Cathy gestured weakly, instantly conveying how unsettling this whole experience was to her. "Yes." The one word sounded torn and ragged.

"Do you mind if I sit down?" he asked, clearly struggling not to laugh.

She was glad he found the situation amusing. There didn't seem to be any other way to look at it. "All right," Cathy agreed, her voice somewhat steadier.

He slid into the booth, sitting across from her. The waitress came, and he turned over his coffee cup so she could fill it.

"Would you like a menu?"

"No," Cathy answered quickly.

"Yes, we would," Grady contradicted.

The waitress glanced from one to the other, unsure. "I'll leave two. Let me know when you're ready to order, but I have a feeling it's going to be a while."

Grady looked at Cathy. "Well, Miss Thompson, we meet again. I'll admit I'm surprised. You don't look like the type of woman who plays the personals."

"I don't . . . normally," she qualified, feeling defensive.

"What made you this time?"

"I have this friend . . ." she began, and paused. She couldn't blame Linda. She'd made the decision to go ahead with this idea herself. "I liked your ad," she told him honestly.

The bushy eyebrows quirked upward. "I liked your response."

"Did you get many?"

"A few."

Silence.

"You don't like me, do you?" There wasn't any derision in his voice. It was a statement of fact more than a question.

"I don't think I do. You're a rotten father, and you work too hard."

Grady shrugged. "I'm not sure I like you, either."

Cathy's short laugh was genuine. "I can imagine."

"You're opinionated, judgmental, and stubborn."

"Impulsive and quick-tempered," she finished for him.

"Not bad-looking, though."

She flashed him a wide smile. "And my teeth are my own."

Laughter crinkled lines about his eyes. "Would you like to order something?"

Cathy's gaze met his, and she shrugged. "Why not?" She hadn't eaten much dinner, her stomach uneasy over the coming meeting.

Grady signaled the waitress, who pulled a pad from her apron pocket as she approached.

"Are you ready?"

"I think so." Grady looked at Cathy, indicating she should order first.

"I'd like a piece of apple pie and a diet cola."

"I'll have the pie and a cup of coffee." As soon as the woman moved away from the table, Grady asked, "Do you normally order a diet drink with pie?"

Her eyes laughing, Cathy nodded. "It soothes the conscience somehow. I know I probably shouldn't be eating desserts."

"Why not?" Grady questioned. "It looks like you can afford to put on a few pounds."

It was the truth. She had lost weight before and after Steve and MaryAnne's wedding. Thoughts of them together caused her to look away.

When their order arrived, Cathy noted that he was studying her. They talked for a while about things in general, Alaska, and the coming winter. She told him about Peterkins and a little of her life in Kansas. She noticed he didn't mention Angela or talk about his job. In an hour there wasn't anything more to say.

"Well, I suppose I should think about heading home," Cathy said. "I hate to worry my dog."

"It's been"—he paused, as though searching for the right word—"interesting," he concluded.

Cathy quickly noted that he hadn't admitted that their time together had been pleasant. At least he was honest. If she had to find a one-word summary of their date, *interesting* said it well. She was glad he didn't suggest they meet again, because she wasn't sure how she'd respond. Probably with a no.

He walked to the car with her. "Thank you, Grady. As you say, it's been interesting." As she withdrew the keys from her purse, Grady opened the car door for her. When Cathy glanced up, her mouth opened, then closed. "How'd you do that?" she burst out.

"Do what?" He looked puzzled.

"Open that door," she demanded, her voice high and unreasonable. "It's broken. It's been broken for two weeks. I was waiting until payday because I couldn't afford to have it fixed."

Grady was laughing at her again, a lazy smile curving his mouth. "Sorry, I didn't know. If I had, I would have left it alone."

Her own mouth thinned as she scooted inside the car. "Curse you, Red Baron," she murmured, and slammed the door shut. Cathy could feel his eyes following her as she drove out of the parking lot. By the time she pulled into her driveway, she found herself smiling. But the amusement died when she attempted to open the door. It wouldn't budge. Ramming her shoulder against it as hard as she could, still it wouldn't give. Sighing, she shook her head in disgust and climbed out the passenger side.

Linda phoned at ten Saturday morning. "Well?" she demanded. "How was he?"

"Okay," Cathy admitted noncommittally. She felt strangely reluctant to explain that the man she had met was Grady Jones.

"That's all?" Disappointment coated Linda's naturally soft voice. "Will you be seeing him again?"

"I don't think so."

"Are you disappointed?"

Somehow it seemed important to Linda that Cathy have a good time. "No, I'm not disappointed in the least. It was an interesting experience." There was that word again.

"Want me to look through the personals for you?"

"I doubt if you'll wait for my approval," Cathy said, in slight reprimand. "But next time I think I'll revert to the more conventional means of meeting a man."

"Don't give up after one try," Linda pleaded. "I kissed a lot of frogs before I found my prince."

"I have no intentions of kissing anyone." She didn't, either. Not since Steve, almost a year ago. She was a healthy, reasonably attractive female. There had to be something wrong with her not to have been kissed in a year. She didn't even want to be kissed unless it was by Steve.

"I've got to go, Linda. I'll talk to you Monday." Cathy didn't mean to sound abrupt, although she realized she did. Replacing the receiver, she exhaled. Why did everything come back to Steve? Why couldn't she sever him from her thoughts as sharply and effectively as she'd cut herself away from her family and Kansas?

School went well the next week. Routine filled her days. She wasn't a regular teacher in a classroom. Her job involved working with the students who had problems with basic skills, such as phonics, reading, and fundamental math. In all, she worked with sixty students during the week for short periods of time in small groups. A great deal of satisfaction came as a result of seeing a child make strides in a particular problem area.

Linda continued to read her the personal ads every morning, but Cathy was successful in warding off any attempts to contact another potential relationship. The last week of September merged with October and the hint of the first blast of a frigid winter. Already the days had begun to grow short.

The letter caught her off guard. Although it was addressed to Cathy Thompson, Cathy recognized the handwriting immediately. Her heartbeat raced as she stared at the blunt lettering on the business-size envelope. The minute she was in the car, she tore it open. Normally, she waited until she was home and had relaxed a bit before sorting through her mail. Her bottom lip was quivering as she read the message: *"Interested in renegotiating heights. Captain Bartlett's Friday, 6:30 p.m. Grady."*

Cathy wasn't sure why she was so pleased. She didn't really like Grady Jones. He was everything she had accused him of being and more.

"I'm not going," she told Peterkins Friday after school. "It would be a waste of time for us both. We're not alike at all. I can't see furthering a relationship that won't go anywhere."

Peterkins raised his head from its resting position on her thigh, then lowered it again. Immersed in her thoughts, Cathy continued to run her hand down the dog's black coat.

"Maybe I should. I hate to keep him sitting there alone. It wouldn't hurt anything, would it?" Again Peterkins looked up at her, cocking his head at an angle. "All right, I'll go. But I'm going to make it clear this is the last time."

She changed clothes twice. First she chose a pale blue wool dress. One glance in the mirror and she realized she looked far too formal for Alaska. She didn't want Grady to think she'd gone to any trouble, or that this meeting was important to her. Designer jeans and a thick red cable-knit sweater seemed to satisfy her need to appear casual, along with her thick coat, knitted scarf, and matching gloves.

Peterkins lay at the foot of the bed, watching her movements in and out of the closet.

"Don't look at me like that," she mumbled irritably. "I know I'm being ridiculous."

Grady was already at the restaurant by the time she arrived, sitting in the same booth they'd occupied on their first meeting.

He didn't smile when she entered the restaurant, and Cathy had the impression he wasn't sure what he was doing there, either. Their eyes met and held for a moment as she paused before walking across the room.

"Hi." She felt awkward and slightly gauche as she slid into the seat opposite him. "You're early."

"No, I'm not," he immediately contradicted her.

She made a production of examining her wristwatch. "It's precisely six twenty-five," she said, showing him the digital face. "Your letter said six thirty, which means you're five minutes early."

Grady looked taken aback for a moment. "I don't think I want you to explain that."

"Fine. Just believe me, you're early." Without further comment, she picked up the menu, feeling the color invade her cheeks. *What an absurd way to start an evening, arguing over the time.*

"I hope you didn't have dinner."

"No, I was too busy deciding if I was going to show up tonight or not." She hadn't meant to be quite that honest.

Their eyes clashed above the top of the menu. He released her gaze by focusing his attention on her softly parted lips. "I was sure you would," Grady said, with complete confidence.

Deliberately, Cathy laid her menu aside. "I think you should know that the only reason I came is because my car door's broken again. I just wanted to see if you could open it a second time."

A smile twitched at the corners of his mouth.

Cathy couldn't keep from smiling herself. Every time she was with Grady she couldn't help but marvel what a handsome devil he was. Tonight he wore a smoke-colored sweater and charcoal-gray slacks. He was provocative, stimulating, and all male. If it weren't for Steve, she could see herself easily being attracted to him. When she realized she was staring, Cathy quickly averted her attention by seizing the menu.

"What do you recommend?"

"The crab's excellent."

"No." She shook her head, ruffling the brown curls. "I don't eat anything that walks sideways."

Studying the menu, Cathy was surprised to note that it catered to a full range of appetites. "I think I'll try the shrimp scampi."

Grady gave the order for two of the same to the waitress, who glanced from one to the other, obviously remembering them from the last time. "Glad to see you two agree," she murmured.

Cathy's fingers nervously toyed with the water glass. "I was surprised to get your message."

"I hadn't planned to see you again," Grady admitted. "I was flying into Deadhorse for one of the oil companies and—" He stopped. "You have a beautiful smile, Cathy."

She gave him one of her brightest. "A lot of men are impressed with my teeth." It hadn't taken her long to realize the only way she was going to be comfortable with Grady was if she could joke.

Their meal arrived. Cathy was surprised when Grady

began talking about himself. He explained how he had started out with one airplane and had built the company to its present holdings. The facts were stated without bragging or boasting. He didn't need to mention how much of his life Alaska Cargo Company had required. It had cost him a marriage already. If Grady was anything like her father, there were a lot more sacrifices to come.

"Alaska Cargo is important to me," Grady said, after pushing his empty plate aside. "But so is Angela. I realize I'm gone too much and too involved to be a decent father."

Cathy was surprised that he would openly admit to as much. "What about her mother? Perhaps it would be better if she lived with her."

"Pam's dead." The words were blunt and clipped.

Cathy lowered her gaze. "I apologize, Grady, I didn't know. I assumed you were divorced."

Without looking up, he said, "We were headed that way."

"Who cares for Angela while you're away?"

"Louise. She's the housekeeper, but she's retiring and moving to Seattle to be closer to her children."

"Who will care for Angela once the housekeeper moves to Seattle?"

He shrugged. "I don't know yet." He frowned. "Come on, let's go." He paid for their dinner and walked Cathy to her Honda.

Her car keys in her hand, Cathy stood beside the driver's side of the vehicle. "Well," she insisted, "go ahead. I'm waiting."

"Waiting?" A perplexed look widened his eyes.

"I want to see you open the door," she insisted.

He gave her a half-smile. With little difficulty and one fierce jerk, the door opened.

"I don't believe this," Cathy mumbled with an exasperated sigh.

"I'll admit it was a little tight," Grady said.

"A little tight?" she repeated loudly. "I've seen bank vaults with easier access."

"Come around tomorrow and I'll have Ray fix it for you."

"Ray?"

"My A-and-P mechanic, secretary, and all-around fix-it man," Grady explained.

The memory of the gruff-voiced man who had answered her repeated calls to Grady and the picture of the older man who had escorted her into his office came to mind. "Yes, I believe we've met."

"Can you be there about eleven?"

Tomorrow was Saturday, and she didn't have anything planned. "Sure." She hesitated, her fingers clenching the strap of her white purse. "Thanks for the dinner."

"The pleasure was mine." He took a step closer, and Cathy's heart skipped a beat. He was going to kiss her. A feeling of panic rose within her, and she moved to climb into the open car. A hand at her shoulder stopped her.

"Don't look so frightened." He sounded as though he was silently laughing at her. "My kisses rarely inflict pain. A few women have been known to like 'em."

Forced to meet his eyes, Cathy felt an embarrassed rush of hot color sweep over her features.

His index finger tilted her chin upward. As he lowered his mouth to hers, Cathy slowly closed her eyes. The lips that fit over hers were gentle, sweet. Gradually, the kiss deepened, and she slid her arms around his neck. The sky didn't burst into a thousand shooting stars; she didn't hear sky rockets, not even tinkling bells. The kiss was nothing more than pleasant.

When he lifted his head, his gaze searched hers. "You'll be there tomorrow?"

Cathy nodded.

"I don't know how else to describe it," she told Peterkins sometime later. "The kiss was"—she paused and laughed—"interesting."

She lay awake for a long time afterward, staring at the ceiling. When she kissed Steve, her body's response to him had been immediate. But she loved Steve, she was supposed to react like that. Try as she might, she couldn't recall what it had been like when she had been kissed by men she'd known before him. He had filled her life for so long it was hard to remember. Not that it mattered now, she reminded herself.

Sleep came several hours later, her mind battling her will, forcing out the memories. It was six months since the wedding now. *How much longer?* her heart asked. How much longer would it continue to hurt?

At precisely eleven-thirteen, Cathy pulled off Airport Way and drove toward the sign high above the building that read ALASKA CARGO COMPANY.

Wiping his hands on a rag, Ray sauntered out from one of the hangars toward Cathy. "Hello again."

"Hello, Ray." She'd washed her hair, curling it carefully. Grady hadn't said anything about seeing her this morning. Even if he had agreed to meet her, she wouldn't want him to think she'd done herself up for him. As if to prove something to herself, she wore her most faded jeans and an old sweatshirt.

"Grady said you'd be coming. He's waiting for you in his office."

"He is?" She hoped some of the astonishment she felt couldn't be detected in her voice.

"While you're with him, I'll see to your car door."

Her attention swiveled from the office building back to the mechanic. "Ray," she asked, a little shyly, "would you mind opening the car door on the driver's side for me?"

There was a mocking light to the faded blue eyes, but he did as she asked and moved to her car. He pulled, jerked, and heaved. His fists hammered at the lock, and still the door wouldn't budge. "I'm afraid it's shut solid, miss," he pronounced gravely.

"Just checking." Her eyes shined with a happy light. "Thank you, Ray, thank you very much."

Ray paused and removed his cap to scratch his head, a puzzled look furrowing his brow as Cathy walked toward Grady's office.

Grady was on the phone, his voice low and lazy, when Cathy entered the building. The outer room looked exactly as it had the day of her visit. Newspapers and magazines littered the chairs, the ashtray looked even fuller, the butts balanced carelessly in a large heap. Cathy was standing at the counter, trying to make sense out of one of the charts, when Grady stepped out of his office and came to stand beside her.

His voice was filled with laughter when he took the chart and turned it around. "You're looking at that upside down."

"I knew that," she lied, with the ease of a beguiling child.

"I'm glad you're here. I've been waiting for you," he said, as he took a thick winter coat off a rack.

"I'm not late, am I?" She examined her watch. "It's eleven-fifteen. Two minutes, if that."

Grady's arm was in one sleeve when he hesitated. He looked as if he was going to question her, but lightly shook his head. "Never mind." His smile was full.

His charm might have fazed a lot of women, Cathy decided. Fortunately, she wasn't one of them. "You've been waiting for me? What for?" He hadn't mentioned anything last night.

"I thought you might like to take a short run with me. It's clear enough to get a fantastic view of Mount McKinley."

"A short run?" she questioned. "You don't mean fly, do you?"

He was laughing at her again. "Yes, my sweet schoolmarm, I mean fly. You don't get airsick, do you?"

"How would I know?" she shot back, losing her patience. "I've never flown before. Not ever."

"Never?" he asked, and sounded incredulous.

"Never."

"Then how'd you get to Fairbanks from Kansas?"

She would have thought the answer was obvious. "I drove."

"From Kansas?"

"Yes." He made it sound like an impossible feat. The truth was she'd enjoyed the trip and considered it an adventure.

"There's always a first time. Are you afraid?"

"Darn it, how am I supposed to know? I've never been in a plane. Did you hear what I said?" she asked him, doing her best to disguise the panic in her voice. She rammed both fists inside the thick jacket.

His hand was already on the doorknob. "Do you want to go or don't you?"

Was she afraid? It wasn't that she'd avoided flying—there had never been much opportunity. She'd lived and vacationed in Kansas all her life. But there hadn't been many vacations when she was a child. Her father wouldn't allow the time away from his work. When she'd gotten the job in Alaska it would have been the perfect time to fly, but she'd decided she'd rather drive up, using the excuse it was too expensive to ship her things. In her heart she knew the real reason. If she drove to Fairbanks she could leave home sooner, get away as quickly as possible without raising suspicion.

"Well?" Grady questioned her again.

Grady Jones may have his faults, but Cathy knew he'd be a darn good pilot. When it came down to it, she trusted him. The thought caught her by surprise. She did trust Grady. "All right," she mumbled.

"You don't sound any too sure."

"I'm not," she snapped.

"Here." Grady removed a long red scarf from the coat rack and wrapped it around her neck. "This is my good-luck charm. It'll protect you from harm."

"Wonderful," she murmured sarcastically. "What's going to protect you? You're the pilot." She removed the scarf and handed it back to him. "If it's all the same to you, I think I'd prefer it if you wore the good-luck piece."

Fifteen minutes later they were taxiing onto the runway. Belted into the seat of the Cessna 150 beside Grady, Cathy faced a panel full of gauges and equipment that looked complicated and foreign. Communicating with the air traffic controller, he gave her a reassuring smile and winked as the plane gathered speed. The roar was deafening, but Cathy realized it wasn't the plane's engine making the noise but her heart hammering in her ear. Her stomach lurched wildly as the wheels left the runway and the aircraft began its assent into the blue sky.

A hand squeezed her clenched fist. "That wasn't so bad, was it?"

"Not at all," she lied. The world below became smaller and smaller. Houses and buildings took on an unreal quality that enthralled Cathy. She was silently congratulating herself because she hadn't given way to her fears. Flying wasn't a frightening experience at all, but wonderful and exciting. "This is great," she shouted, to be heard above the noise.

It seemed they were in the air only a few minutes when Grady pointed to Mount McKinley.

Its massive beauty mesmerized her, and Cathy was speechless. The mountain was unlike any other she had seen. She could understand why the native Alaskans had named it Denali, "the Great One." If an artist had painted a picture contrasting the stark white peaks against the blue, blue sky, the painting would have taken on an unreal quality. "It's so big," she said after a while.

"At 20,310 feet, it's the largest mountain in North America. McKinley is three thousand feet higher than its nearest neighbor, extending a distance of one hundred and fifty miles from Rainy Pass to the valley of the Nenana River. Denali National Park, which we're flying over now, has three thousand square miles of subarctic wilderness."

"You sound like a tour guide," Cathy told him, laughing.

His mouth twisted, a fleeting smile touching the sensuous corners. "I've done my share."

"Say, where are we headed? You never did say."

"I didn't?" he teased.

"Come on, fellow, this is no time to announce you're kidnapping me."

"I'll admit it's a tempting thought."

"Grady!" She shifted so she could give him her chilling glare. It never failed to get results with her students. She should have known better than to try it on Grady.

"Don't move," he shouted in warning. "You'll rock the plane."

With a startled gasp, Cathy gripped the seat, her fingers digging into the thick cushion. The blood drained from her face before she noticed the mischievous light glimmering in Grady's deep blue eyes. "You're going to pay for that, you rat."

The humor fled as his eyes grew serious. "That's something I'll look forward to."

The way he was looking at her brought an uncomfortable sensation to the pit of her stomach. She had seen the look in Steve's eyes, the primitive hunger. It was as if he were making love to her in his mind.

"Don't, Grady," she told him, shocked at how incredibly weak she sounded, how affected she was by the look.

His gaze narrowed on her mouth, and Cathy had to fight the temptation to moisten her lips. In an agitated movement she turned her head, pretending to look out the far edge of the window.

The remainder of the flight to Anchorage was accomplished without incident. Grady pointed to interesting sights, but the conversation was stilted and unnatural. He explained that he was picking up a part for a gold-dredging operation that wouldn't be in Anchorage until two-fifteen. They were only going to touch down, get the part, and take off again.

They were back in the air within forty minutes of landing. The sexual tension between them lessened as the kidding resumed on the return flight.

By the time they touched down in Fairbanks, Cathy felt like a seasoned traveler. After Grady had tied down the Cessna, he walked her to her car, which was parked outside his office. A note on the windshield told Cathy the keys were in Grady's office.

A hand resting on her shoulder seemed to burn all the way through her thick coat and sweatshirt. Grady removed it to unlock his office door, and Cathy released an unconscious sigh of relief. She didn't want to feel these things. Not for Grady. Her appreciation for him was growing with every meeting, but she didn't want to become involved with him. Maybe it would be better if she didn't see him again.

"Here are your keys." He handed them to her.

"Thanks, Grady," she answered absently. "I enjoyed the trip. I'm glad I went along."

"I enjoyed the company. We'll do it again sometime."

"Yes, sometime," she responded vaguely. "Good night." She was halfway out the inner office door when a hand at her shoulder turned her around.

His gaze roamed her face, and his smile was gentle but fleeting. His long, masculine fingers curved around the back of her neck, exerting a slight pressure, bringing her toward him. The other hand cupped the side of her face; his thumb ran leisurely over the fullness of her lips before his warm mouth covered hers. As before, the kiss began without passion, a tender meeting of lips. As before, it was pleasant, not an earth-shattering experience. Would she ever feel that again with any man? she wondered. Without conscious thought, Cathy decided she had to know.

Her hands spread over the lean ribs under his coat as she molded herself against him, arching closer as she parted her lips.

Grady moaned, crushing her closer, his mouth slanting over hers, demanding, taking, bruising her lips. He lifted his face from hers and buried it in the side of her neck, his voice muffled as he spoke.

"How was the comparison?"

Three

Cathy could feel Angela Jones's eyes following her as she moved away from the blackboard. The other four children in the basic skills class were busy carefully lettering the sentence Cathy had written on the blackboard. Their small hands tightly clenched their pencils. Timmy Brookes's tongue worked at the side of his mouth as furiously as his fingers worked the lead.

Cathy read over the short paragraph and stepped to Angela's desk. "Is there something wrong?" she whispered, squatting down to watch Angela's expression.

Immediately the small child lowered her eyes, hiding her gaze. Cathy noted the red color that flowered on Angela's cheeks.

"No, Miss Thompson."

"Are you sure?" Cathy asked, and placed a reassuring hand across the child's back.

Angela quickly denied the question with an ardent shake of her head, the long pigtails dancing with the action.

Cathy gave her back a gentle pat before standing. Angela was so shy and withdrawn that it was seldom she said anything more than was required. According to the latest report given her, Cathy knew that Grady's daughter was now being tutored three nights a week after school. The improvement in her work was slow, but nonetheless the child was getting the help she needed.

"Miss Thompson." Cathy heard her name softly whispered. The call cut into her thoughts.

"Yes, Angela." Again she lowered herself so she could bring her attention back to the child.

"Daddy's right. You are real pretty."

The compliment was so unexpected that Cathy could feel her own cheeks fill with color. "Tell your daddy that I think he's real pretty, too."

Angela giggled and placed a cupped hand over her mouth.

Cathy stood and pointed to the blank sheet of paper on the desk. "Now, I think that you should get busy and do your work."

Eagerly, Angela nodded.

Cathy thought about the incident with Angela all day. It was apparent Grady was talking about her in front of the child. Cathy wished he wouldn't. As far as she was concerned, it would be better if she never had anything to do with Grady Jones again. After the kiss at the airfield, Cathy had driven home feeling almost numb. How had he known she was comparing his kisses to another man's? And not just any man, but Steve, the man she had loved more than life. It shocked her that she'd been so readable. Having revealed a part of herself, Cathy wasn't eager to make a repeat performance.

When she arrived home from school that afternoon and sorted through the mail, she discovered a letter from MaryAnne. Her hand was shaking as she examined the envelope.

"It's from MaryAnne," she told Peterkins as she set the letter on the kitchen table. "But you come first." Her tea was already poured as she sat at the table and patted her lap, indicating to her black-haired friend that she was ready for him.

With one leap the dog reached her lap, laying his head on her knees and snuggling his small body into the position he had known since he was a puppy.

Absently, Cathy's fingers ran the length of Peterkins's body, stopping occasionally to scratch his ears. A warmth began to seep into her fingers, and she realized that she was cold, but the chill had nothing to do with the room temperature. It was the same feeling she had every time a letter arrived from home, especially when it was from her sister.

After several minutes, Cathy forced herself to open the envelope. It was a newsy letter, filled with little tidbits of information about old friends, their mother, and Kansas's infamous weather. Casually, at the bottom of the letter, almost as if she'd forgotten to include the information, MaryAnne mentioned that Steve had quit his job.

Cathy felt a wintry feeling wash over her. Steve quit his job? Impossible! He loved his work as a supermarket manager. He had worked at the same store for the same chain from the time he was sixteen. He had been extremely proud of the fact he had worked his way up through the ranks. His goal had been to move from managing the store to working in the corporate offices.

Biting into her trembling bottom lip, Cathy had the desperate feeling that Steve was restless and unhappy. *It's too late!* her mind screamed. *Far too late.*

She stuck the letter in a drawer, delaying the time she would be faced with answering it.

The week passed with surprising quickness. Cathy was looking forward to sleeping in late Saturday morning. Friday she stayed up half the night reading. Unwillingly, she discovered her thoughts drifting to Grady. All week she'd been practicing what she was going to say if he contacted her again. Now it looked as if she needn't have worried. He must have experienced the same doubts she was having. And if she was going to be honest with herself, it was probably best if they didn't continue to see each other. It was too soon, the pain of losing Steve remained too fresh. The day would come when she was ready to meet another man, perhaps even get serious, but not yet. And probably not for a long time.

Peterkins's bark woke her early Saturday morning. "Come on, fella," she groaned, and pounded her pillow. "Give a girl a break. It's Saturday. I don't have to wake up early."

Ignoring her, Peterkins continued to scratch with both paws at the bedroom door.

"All right, all right." She tossed back the thick blankets, grabbed her housecoat from the end of the bed, and paused to stretch, lifting both hands high above her head. She had just finished a giant yawn when the doorbell chimed.

"Someone's at the door? Is that what you're trying to tell me?" Pushing her long reddish-brown hair away from her face, Cathy walked into the living room and tightened the sash to her pink velour housecoat.

Unsuccessfully, she tried to stifle a groan when she glanced through the peephole in the front door. It was Grady. *Go away!* her mind shouted. *Leave me alone! I don't want to see you!* Was she crazy to hope that some form of mental telepathy would transmit her thoughts and make him go?

The doorbell rang again, this time more persistently.

"Come on, Cathy," he called, his tone insistent. "I know you're in there."

So much for sensory communication, Cathy mused angrily.

The security chain intact, she opened the door just enough to make the sound of her voice carry. A rush of cold air scattered gooseflesh up her forearms.

"I'm not dressed yet. Come back later."

At the sensuous sound of his chuckle, Cathy's eyes flashed a stormy gray. "This is a rotten trick to pull early Saturday morning." The sound of her indignation was drowned out by Peterkins's bark. One black paw flew out the crack in the door in a frantic effort to reach the intruder.

"Daddy, look! Miss Thompson has a doggie."

Cathy was pulling Peterkins back from the door by his collar when she heard Angela's excited voice. Grady had brought his daughter with him?

"Are you going to let me in or not?" Grady insisted, his male voice bringing with it the image of the tall, muscular man she could like and distrust within a minute's space.

"Oh, all right," she conceded ungraciously, and closed the door completely to unlatch the chain. Standing far out of view, Cathy pulled open the large front door.

Traitor that he was, Peterkins's short bobbing tail began shaking wildly in greeting.

"She does have a doggie." Angela squealed with delight and fell to her knees the minute she was in the door. Eagerly petting the dog, the child accepted Peterkins's wet tongue as he licked her face and hands. "Oh, Daddy, look, she likes me."

"He," Cathy corrected, crossing her arms ominously in front of her as she cast a frosty glare at Grady.

"What's his name?" Angela wanted to know.

"Peterkins." Cathy's smile was stiff.

"What are you doing here at this unearthly hour?" she demanded in a hissing breath. She hated to display her anger openly in front of Angela. The child was shy, and the least amount of shouting was likely to intimidate her. Grady knew that and was using it against Cathy, which angered her all the more.

"Are you usually this surly in the morning?" His blue gaze lingered briefly on her lips, then lifted.

"Only when I've been rudely awakened. What time is it, anyway?"

"Eight." The lone word came smooth and low.

Charged electric currents vibrated in the air between them. Cathy was uncomfortable enough without adding sexual tension.

"You don't expect to sleep your whole weekend away, do you?" he asked, his eyes doing a lazy inspection of her.

Uncomfortably aware of her housecoat and tousled hair, Cathy lowered her gaze. "Excuse me a minute while I change." No need to add ammunition to the already powerful effect he seemed to have on her.

Cathy leaned against the closed bedroom door, her

composure shattered. Her knees were shaking, and she moved to sit on the edge of the bed. What kind of game was Grady playing? It was almost as if he couldn't decide if he wanted to continue to see her or not. A week had lapsed since the flight to Anchorage. She hadn't heard a word from him. She'd thought she was grateful for that, but was she? Everything was so confused in her mind, she didn't know what she wanted.

Jeans, a pullover sweater, and ankle boots were her normal Saturday attire, and she couldn't see any reason to dress otherwise on Grady's account. A pink ribbon tied back the unruly mass of long hair. After brushing her teeth, she applied a light coat of lip gloss and heaved a giant breath before making her entry.

Peterkins was reveling in Angela's attention. The spaniel had climbed into the little girl's lap while she sat on the living room sofa, as he so often did with Cathy. A bright smile lit up Angela's face as she beamed happily at Cathy.

"It looks like you've made yourself a friend," she told her dog, pausing to scratch his ears.

Peterkins lifted his face but, seeing she didn't expect him to move, was content to stay where he was.

She followed the smell of perking coffee into the kitchen. An open can of ground coffee sat on the countertop while Grady examined the contents of her cupboards.

"Not much into food, are you?"

"You're a fine one to talk," she bit back defensively. "When was the last time you ate a sit-down meal?"

Grady chuckled, infuriating her further. "You are testy in the mornings, aren't you? Here, try this." He handed her a cup of freshly brewed coffee. "This should take the sting out of your tongue."

With ill grace, Cathy accepted the mug, pulled out a kitchen chair, and sat down. Grady joined her, turning the chair around and straddling it. He crossed his forearms over the back of the chair.

"Now, tell me what was so all-fired important that you had to ruin the only day of the week that I can sleep in?" she questioned in one long breath.

"What about tomorrow? You can sleep in Sunday." He asked another question instead of answering hers.

"Church," she informed him politely.

Grady shook his head mockingly. "You are a good girl, aren't you?"

"Will you cut it out?" The hands cupping her mug tightened until the heat of the coffee burned her palms. Slowly she slacked her grip, focusing her attention on the black liquid. "Why are you here? What do you want?"

The hesitation was long enough to cause Cathy to raise her eyes and find him studying her long and hard. The laughter lines had disappeared, and his blue gaze had darkened with purpose. A hand lifted to gently caress her cheek. The rough, callused fingers felt strangely smooth against her face. It was so gentle, so sweet, that Cathy succumbed to the swelling tide of warmth building within her and lowered her lashes. When his mouth touched hers, she breathed in slowly and parted her mouth in welcome.

Peterkins's sharp bark shattered the moment, and Cathy jerked back in surprise. Grady looked no less unsettled as the dog scampered into the kitchen, slipping on the slick linoleum floor and crashing against Grady's leg. Quickly regaining his form, Peterkins's bark was repeated again and again, piercing the quiet.

"Peterkins!" Cathy shouted. "Stop it! Stop it immediately!"

He did as she bid with a defiant air, quickly lowering his rump to the floor, and positioned himself at her feet.

"I didn't know you had a protector." Amusement coated Grady's words.

Cathy couldn't prevent a disbelieving stare that darted from her dog back to Grady. "I didn't, either. I'm as shocked as you." It stood to reason. Steve had been the only man Peterkins had ever seen kissing her. The dog, in his own way, was laying claim to what he considered to be his other master's property. The realization knotted a hard lump in Cathy's stomach.

"What's wrong?" Angela's small voice broke into her thoughts.

"Peterkins didn't like me kissing Cathy," Grady supplied the answer, a laughing glint to his eyes.

"I didn't know teachers kissed." Angela's attention quickly turned from the black-haired spaniel.

"Thanks," Cathy mumbled under her breath to Grady. "I can hear it all over the school grounds Monday."

"Some teachers are so special you can't help kissing them," Grady said, playfully tugging one long pigtail. "Now, why don't you tell Cathy what we have planned for today?" He looped one arm over the thin shoulders, bringing his daughter close to his side.

"Oh, Miss Thompson, it's so special. Daddy said he'd take us for a long drive through Denali National Park. He said we might see bear and moose and deer and rabbits and maybe a wolf. Won't you please, please come? Daddy and I have already packed a picnic. Can Peterkins come, too?" A pleading note entered the young voice. Cathy couldn't remember hearing Angela say so much all at once.

Indecision swelled within her. The trip sounded wonderful. Ever since moving to Fairbanks she had wanted an opportunity to visit the park. To refuse now would burst Angela's happy bubble. But to accept would be giving encouragement to an uncertain relationship.

"Please," Angela repeated.

Cathy nodded and laughed, the sound unnatural, almost forced. "All right."

"And Peterkins?"

Cathy caught the humorous sparkle in Grady's eyes. "Oh, definitely Peterkins."

"You feel the need for protection, do you?" he whispered tauntingly. A hand reached out and captured hers, carrying her fingers to his mouth. Immediately alert, Peterkins growled, baring his white teeth.

Unaccustomed to such behavior from her friendly mutt, Cathy again issued a stern warning.

After a quick breakfast of orange juice and toast, Cathy gathered her coat and the leash for Peterkins. Accepting Angela's hand, Cathy was led to the waiting car. The air was crisp and clear, the vast, cloudless blue sky beckoning. Cathy didn't think there could be a more perfect day for the outing.

Dog and child were relegated to the backseat, leaning as far forward into the front as possible until Grady instructed everyone to secure their seat belts.

Happy for the excuse to do something with her hands, Cathy snapped one section of the cold metal clasp into the other, then primly folded her hands on her lap.

Grady's roguish glance flickered over her, and he

smiled. That was the problem with Grady, Cathy decided. He was too darn handsome for his own good. He expected a woman to be so taken with his male charm that she would fall into his scheme of events. Well, not with her.

"I've got a penny."

"For what?" she said quickly, turning her attention to the road.

"Your thoughts?"

She laughed lightly, almost disliking him for the way he could read her so easily. "They're worth a lot more than that."

"I'm sure they are." Lines crinkled at the corners of his eyes.

"I can't figure you out, Grady Jones."

He looked puzzled. "What's there to figure?"

"Plenty," she murmured, and paused to expel a deep breath, trying not to show how easily he could irritate her. She shifted her position. "I was just beginning to believe that I wouldn't hear from you again."

"I've been busy." The response was clipped, and the muscles of his jaw worked convulsively.

Cathy arched both brows upward in surprise. Grady didn't like to account for his time to anyone. It was probably one of the reasons he owned his own business. Probably one of the reasons he claimed his marriage was in trouble before his wife died.

"Don't get shook," she challenged. "I wasn't exactly sure I *wanted* to see you again."

His laugh was as rich and full as it was unexpected. "There was never any doubt in my mind," he concluded.

"You'll be seeing a lot more of me before this winter is over, so you might as well get accustomed to it now."

"Is that so?" A cold chill ran down her spine. What was it Grady wanted from her? He wasn't the type of man to idly waste his time on anyone or anything. When he wanted something, he went after it. But what did she have to offer him? Cathy supposed she should feel complimented that Grady was interested in her. Instead, his acknowledgment filled her with a sense of quiet desperation.

"Have you taken pictures of the pipeline yet?" The question came out of nowhere, slicing into Cathy's thoughts.

"No, as a matter of fact, I haven't."

"Good, I brought my camera along. We'll stop, and I'll take a few photographs. You can mail some back to Kansas if you like. I imagine your family has never seen anything like this."

Several times Cathy had paused to view the huge twisting, curving cylinder that passed a few miles outside of Fairbanks. It was tall and so much larger than what she had expected.

Grady pulled onto a dirt road that ran alongside the pipeline.

"Wow!" Cathy shook her head in amazement. Standing on the tips of her toes, she was just able to touch the bottom of its round belly. "I've seen it from a distance before, but never this close. I didn't realize it was this huge."

"Huge and expensive," Grady told her as he lifted Angela above his shoulders so she could touch the silver belly. "Eight billion dollars for the seven hundred and ninety-nine miles that stretch from Prudhoe Bay in the

Arctic Ocean to Valdez in the Gulf of Alaska. I believe it works out to something like ten million dollars a mile."

"Ten million dollars?" Cathy repeated with a sense of astonished disbelief. "That can't be right."

"But it is," Grady insisted. "Of course, a lot went into protecting the environment. Those heat exchangers on top of the pillars supporting the pipe serve a dual purpose. First, they protect the permafrost. The heat the oil flowing through the line generates would ruin the permafrost below. If the ground thawed, then the pylons supporting the cylinder would sink and ruin the pipeline."

The wind whipped color into her cheeks, and Cathy couldn't prevent the shiver that raced over her body.

"Need your coat?" Grady questioned.

"No. I think I've seen about everything I want to see." One last time, she stood on her toes in an attempt to touch the underbelly.

"Want me to lift you, too?" Grady's whispered question was meant for her ears alone.

"Hardly."

His gaze ran over her, blue and glinting, and Cathy chose to ignore him, primly turning her back and returning to the car.

"Wait a minute," Grady stopped her. "I want to take your picture."

The wind whipped her hair about her face, and while one hand was lifted to her face to pull back the errant strand, Grady snapped the picture.

"Where are we going now?" Angela questioned from the backseat.

"Denali," Grady answered.

"Goodie." Happiness sounded in the young voice. "When do we get to see the lions and tigers and bears?"

"Keep your eyes peeled because there might be some around here." The words were whispered in such a way as to make her believe something unknown might lurk behind a supporting pylon.

Cathy turned around and smiled softly when she saw Peterkins was resting contentedly on the seat beside Angela. One paw and his chin were propped across her leg, as if to state she shouldn't dare move because he was comfortable.

"I don't think we need fear lions and tigers and bears as much as one wolf." Heavy emphasis was placed on the word *wolf* so that Grady couldn't doubt that she was referring to him.

"A wolf?" Grady repeated the word as if it was distasteful. "I'm sure you must mean fox." He paused and leaned closer to Cathy. "I've often been called a fox."

"Not by me." It was important that she set the record straight.

"Give my obvious charm a while. I'm sure you'll change your mind."

Cathy lifted her chin, doing her best to keep from laughing. "Have you got a year?" she teased.

"Oh, I've got time. As far as you're concerned, there's all the time in the world."

Cathy felt the color flow out of her face as an uncomfortable sensation assaulted her. Grady was doing it again. For a crazy second she wanted to scream at him to stop, leave her alone, give her time to heal after Steve. He was going too fast for her, far too fast.

A bounty of fall colors was in vast display as they traveled into the park.

"Are we there, Daddy?" Angela questioned from the backseat.

"Start looking now," Grady said. "Any minute you're likely to see some wildlife."

Cathy turned to see the child peering out the side window; her brow, so like her father's, was narrowed in concentration. Peterkins, two paws against the front seat cushion, was looking out just as intently.

"During the summer months we wouldn't be able to make this drive," Grady said, and motioned to the far left-hand side of the road. "Look," he said, "there's a moose."

"Where?" Cathy asked excitedly, her eyes frantically searching for the huge mammal.

"I see it!" Angela cried. "I see it!"

Peterkins barked with excitement as Angela bounced around in the backseat.

"Where?" Cathy repeated.

Grady slipped one arm over her, letting it settle on her shoulder as he drew her close. The other hand was used to direct her gaze in the proper direction. Within seconds Cathy caught sight of the moose, his huge antlers and body blending in beautifully with his surroundings. But it wasn't the sight of the magnificent beast that had Cathy's blood pounding in her veins. Being this close to Grady was physically and emotionally exhausting. The temptation was so strong to nestle her face in the curve of his neck that for a moment she closed her eyes.

"Beautiful, isn't he?" Grady said, his mouth moving against her hair.

Cathy nodded, because speaking had suddenly become impossible. A soothing warmth began to spread its way down her arm, and she gently pulled herself from his embrace.

"Yes . . . yes, they are." The words sounded weak, even to herself. "What was it you were saying about not being able to do this during the summer?"

"That's right."

Uncertain, Cathy glanced at Grady. His voice sounded unnatural, as if his mind wasn't on her question. "Visitors are bused through the park during the summer months."

"Why?"

Grady's attention was diverted to the road. "As you've probably noticed, this isn't exactly the best road in Alaska. It's narrow and difficult to maneuver. In several places, turning a camper or car around would be almost impossible. It's simpler to drive tourists through instead of allowing thousands of vehicles in."

"Sounds that way," she said, more for something to say than any sign of agreement.

A couple hours later Angela spotted a brown bear. "Miss Thompson, look," she exclaimed, pointing wildly out the window. "It's Yogi Bear."

"Or a reasonable facsimile," Grady added with a chuckle.

"I thought bears would be hibernating by this time. It's mid-October," Cathy whispered, as if she were afraid the sound of her voice would frighten the creature away. "And speaking of bears, you don't expect me to share my lunch with that fellow, do you?"

Grady's responding laugh was filled with humor. "One question at a time, sweet Dorothy from Kansas."

"The name's Cathy," she reminded him in a chilly tone. The last thing she wanted to be thought of as was a sweet sixteen-year-old desperately seeking a way back home. Her home was Alaska now. The sooner she and everyone around her accepted the fact, the easier it would be.

"Okay, Cathy." Her name was issued softly. "Bears hibernate in the winter, not autumn. The one we saw today is fattening herself up for the months ahead. Second, we don't picnic outside. That would be inviting the attention of our fur-covered friends, and I for one am opposed to sharing my lunch."

"I for two," Angela added.

"Fine, but if we don't eat out-of-doors, just where do we picnic?"

"In the car," Angela said, as if it was the most natural thing in the world.

Unable to resist, Cathy smiled. "Of course."

As promised, Grady provided the lunch an hour later. The fried chicken, biscuits, small dish of coleslaw, and ice-cold pop couldn't have tasted better. It was all so simple that Cathy marveled that her family hadn't done something like this themselves. Picnics were always a formal affair for which her mother spent whole days preparing.

Wiping their fingers with the pre-moistened towelettes enclosed with the chicken, Cathy paused, feeling Grady's gaze, her fingers clenching and unclenching as her eggshell composure began to feel the strain of his appraisal.

"You like Alaska, don't you?"

"Surprisingly, yes. I wasn't prepared for the beauty or

vastness. I don't know that anyone really is. From Kansas it sounded like the ends of the earth, which it is, in a manner of speaking."

"Why'd you come?"

She'd been expecting the question for some time. Giving the impression it was of no importance, she shrugged. "It's a job. If you hadn't noticed, there aren't many of those around these days."

"I have." Grady's tone was faintly dry.

"Anyway, the position was offered, and I jumped at the chance."

"We'll see how much you love it after the first winter."

"I'll make it."

"I'm sure you will." One dark eyebrow flicked upward. "You, my sweet Cathy, are a survivor."

"That I am," she murmured stiffly, suddenly uneasy with the way the conversation was headed. "And what about you? Are you an implant like me?"

"Nope, born and raised here all my life. Tried going to school in the lower forty-eight, but I hated it and came back to where the air is clean and land unspoiled."

"I was born in Fairbanks," Angela added, apparently feeling left out of the conversation.

"At midnight on the coldest night of the year," Grady added. The creases along the sides of his mouth deepened into a familiar smile. "I darn near brought that girl into the world myself."

"I don't suppose her mother should be given any credit?" The words were issued in a teasing undertone.

"As a matter of fact," Grady said, low and cynically, for her alone, "Pam handled her part as best she could." He straightened and turned the ignition key. The engine purred to life as he checked the rearview mirror. "I think it's time for us to head back if we're going to arrive before dark. Anyone for singing?"

Pulling onto the road, they'd advanced only a few feet when Cathy heard a bang and hissing sound. "What was that?"

She witnessed Grady's eyes close in frustration before he turned toward her, presenting a calm façade. "That, my two helpless females, is a flat tire."

Four

❧⸻❦⸻❧

"Would you care to give me a hand?" Grady asked, as he released the jack, lowering the car to the ground.

"Sure, anything," Cathy said, and breathed in relief. "What do you need me to do?"

Wiping his greasy hands with his white handkerchief, Grady glanced upward, a roguish glint to the deep blue eyes. "I was hoping you'd applaud."

Both Cathy and Angela were clapping wildly and laughing when the creases around his mouth suddenly hardened and a wary light was reflected in his gaze.

"Get inside the car." The order was given with a frightening undertone.

Without question, Cathy helped Angela into the backseat and securely shut the door before jerking open her own. A second later, Grady joined her in the front seat.

"What's the matter?" Cathy whispered, her heart hammering at the coiled alertness she felt coming from Grady.

"There's a brown bear about thirty yards ahead, moving toward us. I think the time has come for us to make our exit."

"Peterkins!" Cathy looked around her frantically. Her hand flew to the door handle. "We can't leave without

Peterkins." Her voice was high-pitched and filled with anxiety.

Grady stopped her before she could open the door. "It would be crazy to go out there now. You'd only be attracting trouble."

"I don't care," she insisted, jerking herself free.

The harsh grip of his hand bit into her shoulder. "No," he said, and shoved her against the seat. "If anyone gets him, it'll be me."

Angela began whimpering, the sound of her cries muffled as she covered her face with both hands. "I don't want a bear to eat Peterkins," she wailed.

"Grady, please," Cathy pleaded, lifting her gaze to his. "He won't come to you. It's got to be me."

Indecision flickered over the hard face. "Okay." He gradually released his hold on her. "I'll distract the bear, and you get that damn dog of yours into the car. And for heaven's sake be quick about it."

Grady climbed out first, after instructing Angela not to leave the car for any reason. Cathy took in several deep breaths in an effort to calm herself. The wild beast would sense her fear, and she struggled to breathe evenly and appear calm.

The bear was advancing toward the vehicle, standing on its hind legs, looming eight to ten feet above them. Nothing had ever looked so large or so terrifying.

To her horror, Cathy saw that Peterkins was running toward the animal, barking for all his worth.

Grady moved around to the front of the car, hands dangling at his sides. It took Cathy several moments to realize he was speaking in soothing, low tones, moving slowly toward the huge mammal.

Her heart in her throat, Cathy cupped her mouth with both hands and called her dog.

Peterkins hesitated, stopping to turn around, and glanced at her.

The bear was so close Cathy thought she could smell him, then realized it was the taste of fear that was magnifying her senses. Grady was far closer to the bear than she was. Her own fear was quickly forgotten as she realized the danger Grady was placing himself in for the sake of her dog. She wanted to cry out for Grady to move back. Instead, she concentrated on gaining Peterkins's attention.

Frantically, she called the spaniel, her voice sharp and demanding. This time Peterkins didn't pause, turning around abruptly and running as fast as his short legs would carry him. She squatted down so that he could leap into her arms. Moving as quickly as possible, she hurried back to the relative safety of the car.

Cathy was inside and breathing so hard she was panting. Still, Grady remained outside, slowly retreating until he backed into the front bumper of the car. As if he was in no more danger than he would be attending a Sunday school picnic, he turned and climbed into the front seat, starting the engine and pulling onto the road.

Cathy looked back to note that the bear had turned and reentered the woods. It had probably been the smell of their picnic that had attracted his attention.

Relief washed over her, and for a moment Cathy had to struggle to hold back the tears. "Bad dog." She enunciated each word, her manner and voice stern. "How can you have been so naughty?"

Apparently, Peterkins knew he had done wrong. Dejectedly, he hung his head, and the long ears drooped forward.

"You okay?" Grady asked as an aloof mask came over him.

"I'm fine." She studied him for a minute. The dark bushy brows, the unrelenting set of jaw; his profile appeared almost hawklike. The eyes were a clear shade of deep blue, but sharp and intelligent. The dark hair, although trimmed short, was curly and framed his forehead.

"You sure? You look awfully pale for someone safe and secure." His look flickered over her.

The responding smile was weak. "I'm sure." She lowered her gaze. She liked Grady. That was the problem. If anything had happened to him, she would have felt more than guilt or remorse. The realization was so new she hadn't had time to properly analyze exactly what she was feeling.

"How could you act so calm?" she queried. "Anything could have happened."

"Calm?" he snorted. "Listen, I've been ten thousand feet in the air, lost both engines, and felt less nervous than facing that bear."

Laughter sighed through her as she tipped her head back to rest against the seat. "I don't think I've been more frightened in my life," she admitted.

"Can Peterkins come and sit with me now?" Angela asked, the small voice barely audible.

"Sure." Cathy helped move the dog from the front to the back, then scooted across the cushioned seat to sit closer to Grady. She stopped when their shoulders touched.

His glance was filled with surprise. "To what do I owe this honor?"

Cathy couldn't answer him. She didn't know why she felt the need to be near him. It had been an unconscious movement made without reason. "I'm cold." The excuse was a feeble one, but Grady seemed to accept it, looping an arm over her shoulder and bringing her within the comfort of his embrace.

"Warmer?" he asked a few minutes later.

Cathy nodded.

"Daddy, can I be a Girl Scout?" Angela's head appeared between Grady's and Cathy's.

"Why the sudden interest in Girl Scouts?" Grady questioned, his gaze not leaving the road.

"Melissa Sue's gonna be one, and I thought I should do it, too."

"I think she means Brownie," Cathy inserted. "The school handed out information sheets last week."

"I want to roast marshmallows and eat s'mores and sing songs around a fire."

"That's the picture on the front of the information sheet," Cathy explained.

"There were some marshmallows in your cupboard, weren't there, Cathy?"

Grady's gaze had scanned the contents of her kitchen that morning while she was dressing. "Yes, I think there are."

"Fine. When we get back, Cathy can invite us inside, and while I build a fire in her fireplace, you two ladies can make some hot cocoa and find something to roast marshmallows with."

"Goodie." Angela bounded against the backseat, and

Cathy could hear her telling Peterkins all about the wonderful time they were going to have.

"Now, that was sneaky," Cathy murmured, resting her head against the curve of his shoulder.

"No, just quick thinking," he murmured. His eyes glanced toward her mouth, and the look was so suggestive that Cathy had the desire to blush and look away. The last streaks of light were fading from the darkening sky when they rolled past the Fairbanks city limits.

"I'll drop you two off at the house."

"Three," Angela corrected. "Don't forget Peterkins."

Grady chuckled. "After this afternoon, it's not likely."

"Where are you going?" Cathy asked.

"I've got some paperwork to catch up with. It'll only be an hour or so. You don't mind, do you?"

For a second she wanted to complain and tell him that yes, she did mind. This was the way it had always been with her own father. Not a single day of his life was he able to sever himself from job-related obligations. Memories of Christmas Day were filled with presents and laughter and arranging the big meal around the time her father would return from the office. Cathy should have realized that a whole day was more than Grady could give her, Angela, or anyone else in his life.

"No, I don't mind," she lied. "It'll give Angela and me time to unwind." Barely concealed resentment caused her voice to tremble slightly.

Grady gave her a puzzled look. "If it's going to bother you, say so and I won't go."

The temptation was to take him up on the offer and see just how long he would be able to endure the torture of staying away from his business. Mentally, Cathy gave herself a shake. She was being unreasonable, allowing the childhood memories of an overly work-obsessed father to cloud her perception now.

"No, it's fine, really. Angela and I will have a good time, won't we?" She directed her question to the little girl.

"If I take a bath at your house, can Peterkins come in the tub with me?"

"No."

"Yes," Grady insisted.

Playfully digging the point of her elbow into his stomach, Cathy laughed. "You're a great help, fella. Any more suggestions and Angela and I will come to the office to help you with the paperwork."

Grady parked the car in front of Cathy's house. She half expected him to drop them off and drive away. But he came inside and brought in firewood, stacking it by the fireplace. As he was working, Cathy brewed coffee.

Grady accepted a cup, blowing into the steaming liquid before taking the first sip. His legs were crossed as he leaned against the kitchen counter.

Physically, she was growing more aware of his presence every minute. Something was definitely the matter with her. Only last week she had rated his kiss as interesting. Now she longed for the taste of his mouth over hers. Not because she was falling in love with him, but to compare her reaction one week from the next.

Finishing her coffee, Cathy placed the mug in the kitchen sink. As she moved away from the counter, he placed his hand along the slope of her neck, stopping her. Cathy quit breathing. When his mouth settled over her parted lips, she slipped her arms around his neck. His hand at the small of her back arched her closer.

Passively, she accepted the kiss, neither giving nor taking. If she had stopped to analyze her feelings, she would have realized Grady's kiss had gone from interesting to pleasant. Decidedly pleasant. But it lacked the spark, the urgency, the emotion she'd once shared with Steve.

Grady broke the contact, dragging his mouth from hers. He seemed to know what she was thinking. Cathy could sense it, could feel his hesitation, or was that disappointment? She couldn't tell. Slowly he took control of himself.

His hands cupped her shoulders as he lifted his face, his eyes dark, unreadable.

"Grady," she whispered, feeling confused, wanting to explain, knowing she couldn't. Lowering her eyes, she released a long sigh. "I'm—"

"Don't," he interrupted, and raked a vicious hand through his curly hair. "Don't apologize, understand?"

"Okay."

Without a backward glance, without another word, he left the kitchen. Cathy winced when she heard the front door close.

Now she was upset, not with Grady but with herself. She couldn't help but wonder how long it would take for her broken heart to heal. Another question was exactly how long Steve would continue to dominate her life. Would she ever be able to love, truly love, anyone else?

Sometime later she fixed Angela a sandwich and poured the little girl a glass of milk. Nothing sounded appetizing, and she chose not to eat. Skipping meals was becoming a repeated pattern, and one that must stop.

Grady returned a couple hours later, carrying a brown paper sack and two wine goblets turned upside down between two fingers.

Smiling to herself, Cathy hung up his coat. "Wine and marshmallows. Sounds wonderful," she teased.

His lips brushed her cheek. "The wine is for later," he murmured, for her ears only.

Immediately, Peterkins growled, again taking exception to having another man kiss her.

Cathy cast the spaniel a warning glance. "Where were you when I needed you?" she questioned him. After Grady had left the house, Cathy had discovered Angela playing house with the dog, placing him in the bed and pulling the covers over his head. If he'd been free, the scene in the kitchen would have never been allowed to go as far as it did.

A look of impatience flickered over Grady's expression. "I refuse to be deterred by a mutt," he declared, taking out a huge bone from the bottom of the sack. "If you want to play protector, do it with this." He held up the bone, and Peterkins leaped into the air in a futile attempt to reach the goodie. Grady stooped down to pet the dog. "Later, buddy, later."

Flickering flames leaped out between pieces of wood as Grady, Angela, and Cathy sat on the carpet, their backs supported by the front of the sofa. Shadows danced across the room, forming mime figures on the opposite wall. An empty bag of marshmallows was carelessly tossed onto the coffee table while the last song softly faded.

Angela yawned and crawled onto the couch, tucking her hands and knees into a tight ball. "I'm sleepy, Daddy and Cathy," she said, on another long, drawn-out yawn. "This is almost like being a real family, isn't it?"

Grady's arm rested across Cathy's shoulder. "Yes, it is," he whispered.

Together they sat before the fire. There didn't seem to be a need for words. Her neck rested against his arm, and for the first time in recent memory, Cathy felt utterly content.

In a series of agile movements, Grady placed another log on the fire, moved into the kitchen, and returned with an open bottle of wine and the wineglasses. Peterkins was nowhere to be seen. "Maybe Angela would rest better in a bed. Mind if I put her in your room?" he asked softly, as if afraid he would wake the sleeping child.

"Sure, go ahead," she agreed lazily.

He left her momentarily and smiled when he returned. He lowered himself onto the carpeting beside her. Filling the wineglass, he handed it to Cathy. When his own glass was ready, he paused, holding it up. "To what shall we drink?"

Laying her head against the sofa cushion, Cathy closed her eyes. "To the personals?"

Grady chuckled and gently tapped her glass with his. "To the personals."

They both sipped the wine. "To the Red Baron," she offered next.

"And Snoopy." Grady touched the rim of the glasses again before taking a sip.

The sauvignon blanc was marvelous, light, and refreshing.

"This is good," Cathy murmured, after her second glass. "Very good."

"So is this." He took the stemmed glass out of her hand and placed it on the coffee table.

I should stop him, Cathy thought, lifting a strand of hair away from her face. *It's going to happen all over again. Grady's going to kiss me and I won't be able to respond.* The reasoning was there, but the desire to put a halt to his intentions wasn't.

Grady stared at her for a long minute, his eyes darkening to an intense blue as his hands framed her face. Slowly, as if waiting for her to stop him, he lowered his mouth to hers.

Cathy parted her lips, but whether in protest or welcome she didn't know. Her arms circled his neck as the pressure of his mouth hardened over hers. Where once there had been a feeling of dread, a warmth, an acceptance, began to flow, spreading throughout her until she moaned softly.

Grady broke the contact, his mouth hovering inches above hers until their breaths merged. Gently, lovingly, his hands caressed the sides of her neck, slowly descending over her shoulders while he spread tender kisses on her temples and face.

The gentle quality of his touch brought the first trace of tears to her eyes. *It's the wine,* she told herself. Crying was a ridiculous response to being kissed. This was beautiful, lovely. She should never have drunk the wine.

One tear slid down her flushed cheek. When Grady's lips encountered the wetness, he paused and kissed it away. His mouth met each tear as it escaped, and soon his lips were investigating every inch of her face. Her cheek, her forehead, her chin. When he moved to explore her parted lips, Cathy could taste the saltiness of her own tears in the kiss.

Grady lifted his head and pulled her into his arms. "Are you okay?" The question was breathed against her hair.

For a moment, answering him was impossible. "Just hold me, okay?"

She was pressed so close against his chest that her breasts were flattened, but she didn't care. For the first time in months, she was beginning to feel. A healing balm, a warmth, began to spread its way through her. Cathy didn't know how long Grady held her. Time had lost importance. The only sensation that registered was the soothing, gentle stroke of his hand.

The pressure of his body edged her backward. The carpet felt smooth and comforting against her back. Positioned above her, Grady again studied her, lowering his mouth to kiss her nose and smiling gently into her wary, unsure eyes. The tender touch of his lips produced a languor, a state of dreaminess.

Her fingers spread over his back, but the desire to feel the rippling hard muscles of his shoulders was so very tempting. Her hands slid under his sweater, reveling in the feel of his bare skin.

Grady's kiss devoured her lips until she was breathless and panting. His touch felt right and good. Putting an end to the delicious feeling was what would be wrong, not the intimate caress.

When he moaned and dragged his mouth from hers, burying it in the curve of her neck, Cathy rolled her head to the side to encourage the exploration.

His tongue found the sensitive lobe of her ear, and

dancing shivers skidded over her skin. A soft, muted moan trembled from her. Cathy could feel his mouth form a smile against her hair. Gradually his hold loosened, and he eased himself into a sitting position, helping her up.

"More wine?" His voice was slightly husky and disturbed.

Disoriented, Cathy resumed her former position and nodded. *Don't stop!* she wanted to scream. *The pain is almost gone when you hold me.* Her heart had been more than bruised, it'd been shattered. For so long she'd believed it would take more than one miracle to repair the damage, if at all.

When she didn't answer, Grady handed her a replenished glass. Her fingers were shaking as she accepted the wine. Gently, he kissed her temple and placed an arm across her shoulders, pulling her close to his side.

"Who did this to you?" He whispered the question. "Who hurt you so badly?"

A chill ran down her spine. Cathy began to quiver, faint tremors shaking her shoulders. Heat invaded her body, creeping up from her neck, spreading its crimson color to her ears and face.

"No one." She straightened, crossing her legs. "It's hot in here, isn't it. Should I turn down the heat?"

Grady didn't comment, but he leaned forward and brushed his mouth over her temple. "You're running away again."

"I'm not running from anything." She bounded to her feet. "Have you had dinner? I didn't, and suddenly I'm starved. Do you want anything?" A quick step carried her into the kitchen. Peterkins was scratching at the bedroom door, where he'd cuddled up with Angela. A gnawed bone was in front of the door, his interest having waned.

"Come in, boy," she said, welcoming him inside.

"Do you feel the need for your protector?" Grady moved behind her, placing one hand on her shoulder.

"Will you stop?" she said, shrugging off his touch and forcing herself to sound carefree. "I don't need a protector. I'm perfectly capable of taking care of myself." She raised her hands in karate fashion. "I'll have you know these hands are registered weapons with the FBI." Afraid her eyes would tell him more than she was willing to reveal, she opened the refrigerator and took out a carton of eggs.

Leaning lazily against the counter, Grady's hands gripped the edge of the tile. His look was deceptively aloof, but he couldn't disguise his interest. "If that's the case, do you always cry when a man kisses you?"

"Of course not," she snapped. "It was all that wine you forced me to drink. Now, do you want an omelet or not?"

"If you don't want to talk about it, just say so." A smile crinkled the lines about his eyes, and for a moment Cathy could almost hate him. She couldn't help being curious about what he found so amusing.

Hands positioned challengingly on her hips, she spun around. "All right, I don't want to talk about it. Are you happy?"

"Pleased. I appreciate the honesty."

"Wonderful," she murmured. Taking a mixing bowl from the cupboard, she cracked the eggs against the edge with brutal force, emptying them into the bowl. She didn't know how she was going to force herself to eat. The thought of food was enough to make her sick. "I don't ask you personal questions. I . . . I wouldn't dream of inquiring about your marriage or your relationship with your wife." She waved her hands in the air dramatically, then gripped the fork and furiously whipped the eggs.

Grady watched her movements for a minute. "Those eggs are going to turn into cream if you don't stop whipping them to death."

"It's clear you don't know a thing about cooking, otherwise you'd realize you're supposed to whip the eggs." She took a deep breath. "Besides, how would you feel if I started prying into your life?"

Grady shrugged and then gestured with the open palm of his hand. "My life's an open book."

"Fine," she snapped. "How's your love life? How many times a week did you and your wife make love?" She threw the questions at him in rapid succession, not pausing to breathe between.

"Rotten," he shot right back at her. "And in the end Pam and I didn't."

"Aha!" She pointed an accusing finger at him. "The truth comes out. And just why weren't you and Pam acting like husband and wife?" There was a sense of satisfaction seeing the way his mouth tensed and the way his jaw worked. His eyes narrowed into deep, dark sapphires that were as cold as Arctic ice.

Wiping her fingers with a hand towel, she smiled at him sweetly. "As the saying goes, if it's too hot in the kitchen . . ."

"Pam and I didn't make love because she was no longer interested in lovemaking—or me, for that matter."

Cathy flinched. She hadn't expected him to reveal so

much of his life. In all actuality, she and Grady were two of a kind. "Is that when you began running?" The minute the words were out, Cathy knew she had made another mistake.

"Listen, Cathy." Grady rammed his fists into his pockets. "I don't know where you come off. I've never run from anything or anyone."

"Then why do you work twenty-hour days and spend so little time at home that your daughter hardly knows you?" Now that she'd started, Cathy couldn't make herself stop. Why wouldn't she quit? She couldn't imagine what made her delve into the intimate details of his life as if it was her right to know. She found herself digging at him unmercifully. She had no right to throw stones at him when she was just as vulnerable.

"All right. You want answers, I'll give you answers." His breath came out roughly.

"Grady, no." The words were ripped from her throat. "I'm sorry, I have no right. Can't we agree to leave the past buried? It's obvious we've both been hurt. It won't do either of us any good to dredge up all that pain."

He sighed heavily.

Cathy walked across the kitchen, slipped her arms around his middle, and softly laid her head on his chest. His arms circled her and held her close and tight, pressing her to him while he buried his face in her hair. They stood with their arms around each other in the middle of the kitchen floor until Cathy felt a faint shudder rake through him.

"Did you say something about dinner?" he asked, then firmly kissed the top of her head, breaking the embrace.

Cathy smiled gently to herself. "I did," she said. Not

that she really was interested in cooking—or eating, for that matter. But she put her culinary efforts into creating one of her specialties, a cheese-and-mushroom omelet.

When everything was ready, she carried the two plates to the table. Grady had surprised her by getting the silverware and folding paper napkins.

Cathy was still eating when he pushed the empty plate aside. "You're a good cook."

"Thank you."

"Pam was a good cook."

Cathy lowered her fork to her plate. She wanted to tell him to stop, she didn't want to be compared to another woman.

"In some ways, the two of you are alike."

Cathy shifted uneasily. "Don't."

Grady looked up, surprised. "Don't? Don't what?"

"Compare me with someone else."

He leaned back, lifting the front two chair legs off the ground. "I'm doing a poor job of this." His gaze was full of impatience, but she sensed it was directed more at himself than at her. "What I'm trying to say is that my marriage was over a long time before Pam died. She hated Alaska Cargo. There wasn't a time I flew out on assignment that she didn't believe I was flying to meet another woman."

"Was she always so insecure?"

"No." He shook his head. "It was only after I started the company. In the beginning she was pleased to be a part of it, but after Angela was born she became depressed, lonely, and unhappy."

"Undoubtedly, having her husband around more often would have helped." Her sympathy lay with Grady's wife.

She'd grown up witnessing her mother's loneliness. For all the time her own father spent with her during her growing-up years, Cathy may as well have been fatherless.

Grady chose to ignore the comment. "It was more than insecurity. Several times I recommended she see a professional who could help her deal with these emotions, but she never would." The front chair legs hit the linoleum with a thud.

"Some women are like that." She attempted to sound sympathetic. Her mother was the Rock of Gibraltar, but there were memories of lying in bed pretending to be asleep while listening to her mother cry. Her father had offered so many promises, ones he never had any intention of keeping.

"Pam would regularly pack her bags and threaten to leave me. She seemed to think that would bring me to my senses."

"Did you stop her?"

"No. Why should I?"

"Why should you?" Cathy flared. "We're talking about your wife, the mother of your child. Pam didn't want to leave. What she wanted was for you to tell her you loved her, you needed her. Clearly the poor woman was desperate for some form of affirmation."

Anger shot into Grady's eyes, and he crossed his arms in front of his chest. "Leaving me, or rather threatening to, was all part of Pam's games, of which you know nothing."

"Oh, brother." Cathy stood abruptly and stalked to the other side of the room. "Here it comes, the I-don't-play-games game."

Grady rose and leaned both hands on the table as he glared at her. "You don't know the facts."

"You're right, I don't," she countered. "By your own admission you let your wife pack her suitcase and were so darn proud you couldn't tell her you loved her." She lifted her hand to her face and just as quickly let it drop to her side. "It isn't any wonder Angela is a lost, lonely child."

"Leave my daughter out of this."

"How can you expect a child to feel loved and wanted when her father can't—"

Grady slammed his fist on the table, causing the plates to jump and clatter on the top. "I've had enough of this conversation."

Lifting a hand to remove a strand of hair from her face, Cathy noted that her fingers were shaking and quickly clenched them at her side. "So have I." The words were breathless. Even now she wasn't sure why she'd let this conversation escalate to this point. Grady was right. What went on between him and his wife was none of her affair.

Without another word, Grady left the kitchen, stalked into her bedroom, and returned with a sleeping Angela cradled in his arms.

"I'd like to say the evening has been a pleasant one, but it hasn't," he said, his voice tight and terse. Without so much as glancing backward, he carried the sleeping child with him out the door.

Her sense of righteousness was quick to dissipate. Cathy bit into her bottom lip, regretting her thoughtless words. Lashing out at Grady had ruined a promising relationship. She would never see him again.

Five

Linda Ericson sauntered into the teachers' lounge and sat beside Cathy. "Morning." The greeting was cheerful, followed by a wide smile.

"It's Monday, the first day for parent-teacher conferences. You're not supposed to be so bright and chipper. The least you can do is have a sour look like everyone else," Cathy chastised with a sigh.

Her friend's eager hand covered Cathy's. "I'm too excited to worry about what day of the week it is, or conferences, for that matter."

The sparkle in her friend's eyes captured Cathy's attention immediately.

"I'm late," Linda whispered.

Cathy didn't move. The dark, gray eyes studied Linda's, afraid she was reading more into the words than her friend intended. "You think you might be pregnant?"

Linda laughed, the sound of her happiness filling the room. "That's what it usually means, doesn't it? Dan says we shouldn't get our hopes up until I see the doctor. I've got an appointment this morning; I wanted to take one of those pregnancy tests. I know they're generally reliable, but I prefer to have a doctor to confirm before I say anything to family."

Linda wanted children so badly that Cathy couldn't help but share in her happiness. "Linda, this is great news. You'll be a wonderful mother."

"The doctor appointment's at ten. I'll be back in the office about eleven. All you need to do is stick your head in the door. The expression on my face should be enough to tell you."

Cathy carried her coffee cup into the classroom with her a few minutes later. Linda's hopeful news had boosted her spirits. Since her last meeting with Grady two weeks ago, her disposition had been badly in need of an uplift. Darn Grady Jones, anyway, she thought spitefully, placing the mug on her desk. The coffee sloshed over the rim, and with an impatient sigh she took a tissue and mopped up the liquid. What was it about that man that continued to haunt her? For the last two weeks she'd gone about with a feeling of expectancy. Deep down she hoped he would contact her again. He hadn't, and she didn't blame him. She was the one who owed him an apology for delving into his personal affairs. Besides, if Grady's pride had prevented him from giving his wife the security she needed, he wasn't likely to reach out to her.

Surprisingly, Cathy discovered she missed him. In the short time they'd been seeing each other she had come to like Grady. Realistically, the break was probably inevitable, and the sooner it came in the budding relationship, the better. They were far too different. Her only regret was that they didn't part as friends.

Angela had come up to Cathy's desk the Monday following their argument.

"Yes, Angela." Cathy had smiled gently at the young girl.

Angela's eyes were sad, and for a moment Cathy was tempted to pull her into her arms and hug her.

Angela glanced away shyly. "Daddy says I should call you Miss Thompson from now on."

"I think that would be best in the classroom," Cathy agreed. "But outside of school you can call me Cathy if you like."

The child brightened for a moment, then regretfully shook her head. "I don't think I better," she said, and returned to her desk, her gaze downcast.

Although Angela had always called Cathy by her formal name, the child began coming into the basic skills classroom for a few minutes after school. Together, they would go over her papers. Angela was such a precious child, and it was easy for Cathy to give her the attention and affection the child craved. That shy, toothless grin was enough to endear her to anyone. But even in those few minutes they shared alone, Cathy had always called her Miss Thompson.

Between classes that morning, Cathy hurried to the school office and stuck her head in the door. Linda had her back to her.

"Well?" she questioned expectantly.

Linda turned, her mouth pinched with bitter disappointment. Tears filled the round eyes, and she hurriedly tilted her head upward. "The doctor ran another test . . . I'm not pregnant," she whispered, and held an index finger under each eye, "and this crying has got to stop." She laughed weakly.

"Oh, Linda, I'm so sorry."

"I know." She sniffled. "The doctor explained that because I want a baby so much my mind is working to convince my body that it's pregnant. Sounds crazy, doesn't it?"

"Not at all." Cathy yearned for the words that would ease her friend's disappointment, but could find none.

"Don't you have a class?" Linda asked smoothly.

"Yes." Her head made a jerking action, reinforcing the fact. "Are you going to be all right?"

Linda nibbled briefly at her bottom lip. "I'll be fine. After all these years I should know better than to hope. It's my own stupid fault. Both Dan and I have reached the place where we're forced to accept that we'll probably never have children. That was plan A. The time has come to consider plan B."

"Adoption?"

Linda nodded. "Now, scoot before I have seven first- and second-graders in here looking for their teacher."

Crisp, purpose-filled steps carried Cathy to her classroom.

School was dismissed two hours early the week of parent-teacher conferences. Cathy's part in these meetings was limited. As a basic skills teacher, she usually forwarded the papers and information to the child's regular teacher unless there was a specific problem she needed to discuss with the parent.

Before school that morning, she had delivered the information to each of the teachers who had a conference scheduled with one of her students. She noted that Angela Jones's conference had been assigned for that afternoon. After all the times she had failed to get Grady to

come to the school to discuss Angela and her learning difficulties, Cathy doubted another teacher's success.

She decided to spend the free time changing bulletin
boards. Busy pinning the Thanksgiving figures into the
cork material, Cathy didn't hear Grady walk into the
room.

"Am I interrupting something?" His low-pitched voice
seemed to reach out and grab her.

Cathy gasped audibly and stuck her finger with a
sharp tack. "Darn." She jumped off the chair and placed
her index finger in her mouth, sucking at the blood.

"Sorry, I didn't mean to frighten you." Contrary to
what he said, he didn't sound the least bit contrite.

"Grady Jones." She breathed his name in surprise.

"I'd like to discuss Angela's progress." His smoldering
dark eyes rested on her mouth.

Her heart continued to beat like a jungle drum. "You'll
need to see Angela's teacher. I've given my portion of the
report to her."

He shook his head. "Mrs. Bondi sent me to you." He
stepped into the room and handed her Angela's papers.

"All right." She pulled the chair to her desk and sat
down. Grady brought another from across the room and
set the chair disturbingly close to her own. "What do you
want to know?" she questioned.

"Is the tutor helping?"

Cathy had to bite her tongue to keep from saying Angela's regular teacher could have answered the question
just as well. "Yes, she's doing great."

"Not according to these papers." He flipped page after
page, revealing backward letters and improper figures
and consistently bad grades.

Cathy sighed, her gaze connected with Grady's. "You must accept that Angela's improvement will be slow. This work is extremely difficult for her. But she tries very hard, and I can't help but believe that, given time, there will be a vast difference in the quality of her work." The urge to fight for Angela was almost overpowering. "You will continue having her work with the tutor, won't you?"

The mask he wore faded. "If you believe this extra help will help her."

"I do, Grady." She hadn't meant to use his name. To continue in an impersonal discussion would be impossible if she removed the barriers.

"Angela likes you. I've never seen her take to anyone the way she has to you." His voice was low, almost reluctant.

Cathy looked away, fearing what her eyes would tell him. "I like Angela very much, too."

"And her father?"

"Angela's father is one of the most interesting men I've ever known." She kept her gaze lowered.

"Interesting." He spat the word out contemptuously. "What about handsome, suave, and several other fitting adjectives that freely come to mind?"

An involuntary smile cracked her lips. "I was thinking more along the lines of arrogant, conceited, and high-handed."

"But he's a good kisser," Grady insisted.

Cathy couldn't deny the tenderness she had experienced in his arms the evening they'd returned from Denali. "Yes," she said and sighed, "he's all that and more."

Grady exhaled as though relieved. "How's Peterkins?" Before she could answer, he stood, placing his hands in his pockets, and walked to the window, seemingly interested in the darkening afternoon sky.

"Fine. He's still gnawing on the bone you gave him."

Grady turned around, capturing her gaze. He looked at her hard and long. He was waiting, it seemed, waiting for her to bridge the differences between them. His eyes told her he'd made the effort, done his part, and now it was her turn.

"You want me to apologize for the other night, don't you?" she whispered, and by all that was right, she should. She owed him an apology.

"Not really."

She didn't understand her reluctance. She had no right to speak to him the way she had. Standing, Cathy returned to the desk that contained the colored paper letters she'd been pinning on the bulletin board.

"A plain 'I've missed you' would do nicely."

She lifted an orange letter. "All right, I've missed you." That was an understatement. She whirled and tacked the letter onto the bulletin board.

"Come flying with me."

The blood drummed through her veins with a long list of excuses why she should refuse. Instead, she asked, "When?" She remained facing the wall, unwilling to turn around.

"Now. I've got a short run to do this afternoon, two hours' airtime. I'll take you to dinner afterward."

Cathy squeezed her eyes closed. She'd be crazy to go, she told herself.

"Well?" he questioned smoothly, as if he was sure of her response, as if he realized how exhilarating the first flight had been for her.

Her heart was beating with a wild tempo against her rib cage. "I'd like to," she said, and turned.

A look of satisfaction glinted from Grady's eyes. "Grab your coat," he instructed briskly. "I'm already fifteen minutes late for takeoff."

"But I have to finish—" She stopped in midsentence, letting the rest of her words fade as Grady grabbed her hand and nearly pulled her off balance.

Laughing, Cathy was able to restrain him long enough for her to retrieve her coat and purse. Together they ran down the school hallway. Linda met her coming out of the office, a shocked look drawing open her mouth.

"What in the world?"

"I'll explain later." Cathy waved, and Grady placed an arm around her waist, helping her steps to meet his faster-paced ones.

Before Cathy knew it, she was strapped in the passenger side of the cockpit as Grady reviewed the preflight checklist.

Soon they were taxiing on the runway, waiting for confirmation from the air traffic controller. The okay came in a muffled voice Cathy couldn't hope to decipher.

In response, Grady moved the throttle forward. Cathy closed her eyes at the sudden surge of power. The engines whirled, and within minutes the airplane was ascending into the dark, cloud-filled sky.

Her hand clutched the cushion while gusts of wind buffeted the small aircraft.

Grady's hand touched her forearm. "You can open your eyes now."

Relief eased its way through her. She released a long breath and relaxed. They were climbing rapidly through a layer of thick clouds. Below, the world was obliterated by what looked like a mass of marshmallow topping, and above, a thin layer of gray clouds.

"How are you supposed to see to fly this thing?"

"I don't," Grady said, with a mischievous grin.

"This isn't the time to tease, Grady Jones. If you wish to see a perfectly sane woman panic at ten thousand feet, just continue."

"Seventeen thousand," he corrected.

Her fingers gripped both sides of the safety strap, but she decided not to give him the satisfaction of unsettling her. "It looks like it might snow." She changed the subject deliberately, looking at the sky around her.

"Say a prayer it doesn't."

"Grady." She snarled his name. "If you don't stop, I'll never fly with you again."

The roguish smile was directed at her. Cathy was powerless to resist the force of his masculinity. When his hand moved to cover hers, she turned and smiled back at him.

"Your eyes are about the same color as these clouds." He lifted her fingers to his mouth and lightly brushed his lips over her knuckles. "And when you're angry. Watch out! I swear they harden into the color of burnt silver."

No one had ever spoken to her like that, and Cathy found herself struggling for a witty comeback. "Oh."

"For two weeks I've been flying in a sky that seemed to be filled with you watching every move."

"Oh." She looked away, slightly abashed.

"Is that all you can say?"

"Well, for heaven's sake, what do you want me to say?"

He sighed. "Well, for starters you can say that you've dreamed of me every night."

"I did," she inserted. "But they were nightmares."

Unexpectedly, the plane took a sudden plunge downward. Grady gripped the control, and Cathy's heart leapt wildly to her throat.

"I lied," she whispered through the fear. "They were wonderful dreams, just don't do that again."

Grady's laughter was rich and full. "I didn't do anything. We hit an air pocket, that's all."

"Oh."

"Are we back to those again?"

Two and a half hours later they landed at Fairbanks Airport. Ray was in the hangar, waiting for them. Rubbing her bare hands together to keep her fingers from stiffening with the cold, Cathy hurried into Grady's office. Ray followed her in and handed her a cup of coffee.

Cathy nearly choked on the bitter-tasting fluid. She put the cup down on the desk.

Watching her expression, Grady looped an arm across her shoulders. "One of these days, you're going to kill someone with that stuff you pass off as coffee."

Ray mumbled something unintelligible under his breath. "There are a couple of phone messages on your desk."

"Thanks, Ray." Cathy smiled and caught his returning wink.

Grady's hand was linked with Cathy's. He sharply closed the door with his foot. The minute the door shut, he backed her against the wooden frame.

"I've been waiting two weeks for this." The whisper was a husky caress as his hands framed her face. Slowly, almost as if he was waiting for her to protest, he lowered his mouth to hers. When their lips finally met, the kiss was devastating. Untamed fire shot through her blood, her bones seemed to liquefy, and she eased her arms around his neck, molding herself against him.

Grady dragged his mouth from hers, burying it in her neck, spreading tiny kisses at the delicate hollow of her throat. The door was pressing into her back, offering reality to a world that suddenly seemed to have taken a tailspin. Unexpectedly, Cathy felt the tears well in her eyes and the need to cry again. This kiss was completely unlike that of the night in front of her fireplace. The wine and his gentleness had produced those tears. Now it was the realization that Grady could make her body respond to him, but not her heart.

Grady seemed to sense her withdrawal. He raised his head, his compelling eyes holding hers. A thumb wiped a lone tear from her cheek. Tenderly, he kissed the spot where the moisture had appeared.

"Someday," he whispered, "I'll be able to kiss you and you won't need to cry." His mouth lowered to hers again, his lips, his hands arousing her to an exquisite need, playing havoc with her senses.

After dinner, Grady drove her to the school to pick up her car, then followed her to the house. Parking her Honda inside the garage, Cathy lowered the door, closing it from the outside. Grady had parked at the curb. She sauntered over to his car and opened the passenger door.

"Do you want to come in for coffee?"

Grady looked over to her and smiled, his look absent, preoccupied. "All right."

"Remember, Peterkins is my protector," she said in a teasing tone.

It didn't take long to heat water in the copper kettle. Grady sat at the kitchen table, his eyes following her movements around the compact kitchen. After barking and racing around the house at the sight of his mistress, Peterkins was sleeping on the throw rug in front of the refrigerator.

"I still find it unbelievable that you put an ad in the personal column," she commented as she set the steaming cups on the table. If a woman could have guessed that someone as good-looking and compelling as Grady would place an ad in the paper, every woman in Fairbanks would be answering the personals.

"It seemed the quickest way," Grady said, and blew into the black liquid before taking the first sip.

"The quickest way to do what?" she asked curiously.

"To find a wife."

Her cup made a sharp clang against the saucer. "A what?" she gasped.

"A wife for me, a mother for Angela," he replied calmly. "I just don't have the time for the singles scene. An ad in the paper seemed the most direct route."

"Oh." She gulped on a swallow.

"We're back to those, are we?" Laughter fanned out lines about his eyes. "Don't look so shocked. Why else does someone advertise in the personals?"

Cathy waved her hand, slicing the air. "Companion-ship, seeking new friends, adventure. I don't know."

"Now that it's out, will you?"

"Will I what?"

"Marry me?"

"Grady!" She was so shocked she could barely breathe. "I hardly know you."

"Go ahead, ask me anything you want to know."

"What size shoe do you wear?"

"Ten and a half."

Standing, she walked across the room. "I can't believe we're having this conversation."

"I also eat cornflakes every night about midnight and leave my dirty clothes lying on the bathroom floor."

"Stop!" The whole thing was so ludicrous she couldn't help giggling. "You're crazy."

"I'm serious."

"Grady, please, be reasonable."

"I am. My housekeeper is retiring, Angela is in desperate need of a mother's influence. I've had three housekeepers in three years. The kid needs someone who isn't going to move in and out of her life every few months."

"What about love? I don't love you, and you certainly don't love me."

Grady exhaled a heavy breath and pushed the hair off his forehead. "I knew this was going to come up sooner or later. You're looking for the magic words?"

"No," she answered honestly. "I'd be shocked if I heard them. It just seems to me that a marriage between a man and a woman should be built on something stronger than a little girl's need for a mother."

"I find you desirable, Cathy. We'd have a good life."

"A marriage needs more than mutual attraction," she said, and breathed in deeply.

"I agree."

She flattened a hand against her breast. "Why me?" Grady was handsome enough to attract any woman.

"Several reasons." His voice suggested that it was all academic, that feelings, emotions, didn't really have a part in this kind of logical decision. "The first and most important one is that Angela thinks you're wonderful."

"Don't forget Peterkins. She's pretty crazy about him, too."

"Oh yes, let's not forget the dog. But more than that, you're a sensible woman. Neither one of us is a teenager lost in the throes of passion. You've been hurt, I've been hurt and am looking to build a new life. I like you, I like you very much."

"I like you, too. But marriage?" She shook her head, rejecting the idea.

"I don't expect an answer tonight."

"That's encouraging," she said, on a dry note.

"Think it over and give me a call next week sometime. You have my number, don't you?"

Arms cradling her waist, Cathy nodded. She watched as Grady emptied his cup. He looked tired. Lines of fatigue were penciled about his mouth and his eyes. He stood and placed the cup in the sink. Peterkins raised his head, watching his movements.

"You're exhausted."

"I must be." He ran a weary hand over his face. "I decided I'd rather do without a kiss than fight that mutt."

Cathy smiled. "Peterkins is no mutt." Lifting her fingertip to her mouth, she blew him a kiss. "That'll have to hold you."

He lifted his gaze, his eyes seeking hers. "I'll be waiting."

She let him out, locking the door and leaning against it for support after he'd left. "The man's crazy," she told

Peterkins. "And I'd be even crazier to consider marrying him."

The dog followed her into the bedroom, jumping on the bed and snuggling into a tight ball at the foot of the mattress while she undressed, removed her makeup, and brushed her hair. "It's a stupid idea for everyone concerned."

Peterkins lifted his head, cocking it at an inquiring angle. Cathy stretched out an arm, pointing a finger toward the front door. "You wouldn't believe what he just suggested." Slipping the long flannel gown over her head, she threw back the covers and climbed between the sheets. After reading for a while, she turned out the light. But it was a long time before she went to sleep.

Linda was waiting for Cathy at school the next morning. "When did you start seeing Grady Jones?" she asked, the minute Cathy sat down in the teacher's lounge.

"A while ago," she answered cryptically. "How'd you know that was Grady?"

"Someone told me he was the best-looking man in Fairbanks. One look yesterday and I knew it had to be him. You've been holding out on me, Cathy Thompson."

"No, I haven't," she denied untruthfully. "And don't you dare tell him he's so good-looking, his head's too big as it is." Cathy pushed the coffee aside, its taste bitter and unsatisfying. She hadn't slept well last night. She didn't need until next week to make her decision. It was made. It would be crazy to marry Grady, particularly for the reasons he gave. The proposal had to be the most unromantic thing she'd ever heard.

"How can you go out with someone that handsome and keep from drooling?" Linda questioned.

Rising impatiently to her feet, Cathy rubbed her arms as a sudden chill came over her. "In Grady's case, it's easy."

Linda's hand stopped her. "Before you go to class I want to tell you something." She lowered her gaze. "Dan and I are contacting an adoption agency this week. After yesterday's disappointment, we've decided we can't go on like this."

Cathy witnessed a renewed glow of excitement sparkle in her friend's eyes. "Is this what you want?"

"Oh yes," Linda breathed. "I've wanted to do this all year. It's been Dan who's been dragging his feet."

Squeezing Linda's hand, Cathy offered an encouraging smile. "Put me down as a reference if it'll help."

During her lunch hour, Cathy tried to phone Grady. No need to keep him waiting since she'd made up her mind. As her finger dialed the number she couldn't help smiling. There wasn't anyone more arrogant in the world than Grady Jones to believe a woman would accept a marriage proposal on his terms.

"Alaska Cargo." A gruff, impatient voice came over the line.

"Good afternoon, Ray. This is Cathy Thompson. Can I talk to Grady?"

The gruff voice softened perceptibly. "He's in the air, miss, flying some hunters to camp. Be back this evening. Want me to tell him you called?"

"Please." Replacing the receiver, she released a slow breath. The sooner this whole business was over, the better she'd feel. Grady would be out of her life forever. At least she wasn't naïve enough to believe he would waste any more time on her. Once he'd received her answer, he'd move on to the next most likely candidate. Poor girl.

Because she hadn't gotten her mail the day before, Cathy swung by the post office on her way home from school. An accumulation of bills greeted her, and she threw them on the seat beside her as she drove home. Not until she was inside the house did she notice the letter.

One look at the handwriting told her the letter was from Steve. For a moment, it was as if someone had slammed a fist into her stomach. She couldn't breathe, she couldn't swallow—even standing became impossible. A hand reached out and gripped the back of the kitchen chair as the letter fell from her hand onto the tabletop.

Peterkins barked expectantly, demanding attention, and still Cathy couldn't move.

"It's from Steve," she said, her voice soft, almost choking. "You remember Steve, don't you, Peterkins?"

The spaniel gave her a funny look, jumping up on his hind paws, seeking the affection she usually offered when she walked in the door.

Acting out of habit, she leaned down and ruffled his long black ears. Straightening, she blindly hung her coat in the bedroom and slipped off her shoes, replacing them with fuzzy slippers.

The letter seemed to radiate heat, drawing her back into the kitchen. Like a moth drawn irresistibly to a flame, she was attracted to the letter. Ten months had passed since their argument, seven since the wedding. What did he want now? Now, when she was just beginning to build a new life for herself. Now, when she was beginning to feel again.

The phone rang, jolting her into reality. Her attention

swiveled to the kitchen wall, and she mentally shook herself before lifting the receiver.

"Hello."

"Cathy, is that you? This is MaryAnne."

"MaryAnne," she repeated, stunned. "Is everything all right?"

Her sister's laugh echoed over a line that linked several thousand miles. "Everything's wonderful. I've got some fantastic news," she said, and took a deep breath. "News so good, I couldn't wait for a letter. Mom and I decided to phone. Guess what. No"—she laughed again—"don't guess. You're going to be an aunt. Steve and I are going to have a baby."

"A baby." All these months Cathy had dreaded the thought that her sister would become pregnant. Steve and her sister's child. The pain was suddenly so sharp she could barely breathe.

"I haven't even told Steve yet. Mom went to the doctor with me this morning, and we decided to phone you. I'm at Mom's now."

"Congratulations." Somehow the word made it past the huge lump forming in her throat.

A short silence followed. "Are you all right, Sis? You don't sound right."

"I have a cold," she lied. "A rotten cold. Let me talk to Mom."

By some miracle she made it through the remainder of the conversation. Her mother was ecstatic with the news of her first grandchild, but her voice carried a note of warning. If Cathy hadn't been so upset, she might have been able to decipher the silent message.

Frozen by the impact of the phone call, Cathy stood

for several minutes, unable to turn around and face the letter waiting for her on the table.

Peterkins jumped into her lap when she sat at the table. Long minutes passed before she lifted the letter and gently tore open the envelope.

At the salutation, Cathy squeezed her eyes shut. The letter began, *"My Darling."*

A huge sob broke from her, heaving her shoulders. How could she be *his* darling when he was married to her sister? Cathy forced herself to continue reading. Ten months, almost a year. It had taken him that long to admit he had been wrong. He admitted he married MaryAnne out of spite. Like Cathy, he had been caught in the whirlpool, unable to free himself. A thousand times before the wedding he had thought she would put a stop to everything. When she didn't, he believed she must not truly love him. Now he knew differently. She had to love him, because he loved her so desperately.

Cathy could barely see to read further. Tears were blurring her vision, streaming down her face, as sobs racked her shoulders.

It wasn't too late, he said. He couldn't continue to live with MaryAnne when he loved Cathy. If she wouldn't come to him, he would fly to Alaska and get her. Somehow he'd make things right with MaryAnne.

A bitter anger built deep within her. How could she possibly feel anything but contempt for a man like Steve? Had she loved him so long she didn't know what it was not to care about him?

She took the letter, crumpled it in a tight ball, and hurled it across the room. The force of the action seemed to drain her of energy, and she slumped forward and buried her face in her hands. She cried until there were no more tears. She should hate Steve, he was contemptible. Yet without question, she realized she didn't.

The phone rang a second time, and Cathy blew her nose before answering.

"Hello."

"It's Grady." He sounded stiff, almost formal. "I take it you've made a decision."

"Yes." The one word trembled from parted lips. "I've decided to accept your proposal."

Six

What had she done? Cathy stared at the phone in a dreamlike trance. This couldn't be happening to her. This horrible, stomach-wrenching knot was the same feeling she'd experienced during Steve and MaryAnne's wedding. Now she had agreed to marry Grady. A man already married to his company. A man who openly admitted he didn't love her but needed a mother for his child.

The choice had been made for her. No matter what Steve had done, she couldn't stop loving him. If he were to come to Alaska as he claimed, she wouldn't be able to resist him. Not when her whole being was crying out to be his.

She closed her eyes to block the pain as the tears ran hot and scalding down a face that was ashen. The enormity of her decision was only beginning to hit her. With a sense of urgency, she took a long bath, scrubbing her skin with unnecessary harshness, as if to remove every trace of Steve from her life.

Later she took Steve's letter and placed it in the fireplace, setting it aflame with a match, desperately hoping the action would forever burn him from her life.

Grady came to her house late that night. He had showered, shaved, and changed clothes. From beneath his heavy overcoat he produced a bottle of champagne.

Cathy greeted him with a weak smile; her mouth trembled with the effort. If Grady noticed the puffy, red eyes or the deathlike expression, he said nothing.

"First things first." He set the bottle aside, pulled her into his arms, and kissed her soundly.

Cathy felt like a rag doll with no will, with no desire to accept or refuse Grady's advance. Her arms hung lifelessly at her sides.

When Peterkins growled and nipped at Grady's pant leg, Cathy felt Grady pull away and bury his face in her neck. Simultaneously, he brushed off the dog.

Raising his face, Grady drew in a ragged breath. Cathy could feel his lips move against the top of her head as he issued a half-smothered oath. "We're going to have to do something with this mutt. Sooner or later he's going to have to accept that I'm going to touch you, and as often as I like."

Cathy nodded and broke the embrace. A hand on the spaniel's collar, she placed him in her bedroom and closed the door.

"I'm not sure that was the wisest place to put him," Grady said with a chuckle. "Now, if you want to make yourself useful, bring out two glasses. I'll light a fire and we can enjoy the champagne in here."

Cathy hesitated. She could see no reason to celebrate, not when her life, her hope of ever finding happiness, was forever gone. The corners of her mouth drooped as she struggled within herself. Grady deserved better. At least he had been honest with her. Entering the kitchen, she took down two goblets and brought them in to Grady.

Forcing herself to smile, she settled beside him on the carpet. Peterkins was scratching against the bedroom door, wanting out, but Cathy ignored his repeated pleas.

With their backs supported by the sofa, knees raised, Grady opened the champagne. The plastic top made an exploding noise as the foaming liquid escaped from the spout of the long green bottle. Laughing, Grady poured the sparkling drink into the glasses, handing Cathy the first glass.

The laughter drained from his eyes as his look met hers. He held up his glass to propose a toast. "To many happy years." His voice was low and serious.

Cathy touched her glass to his. "To many years." Purposely, she deleted one word. How could she ever be happy again?

Together they took the first sip. The liquid felt cool and soothing against a parched, raw throat, and Cathy eagerly returned the glass to her lips.

Grady removed the champagne from her hand, setting it aside. An instant later his mouth covered hers. Cathy was better able to respond, placing both hands against his chest. Grady's heartbeat felt strong and loud against her palms.

The moment was broken when the fire crackled. She jerked at the unexpected interruption. His hands tangled in her hair, pressing her face into his sweater. The warmth, the comfort of his embrace was so potent that she slowly lowered her thick eyelashes. Grady would never replace Steve, but he was gentle. She could count on him being tender. Never had there been a time when she needed it more.

After a second glass of champagne, Cathy's smile was

less stiff, her response more relaxed. Grady's kisses were sweet and tender, but he seemed to be restraining himself from deepening his desire.

"Shall we set the date?" he asked her, his arm cocked beneath his head as he stretched out on the carpet.

"Any time you say." She took another large gulp of her drink, needing the fortification.

"Thanksgiving weekend?"

So soon! her mind screamed in alarm. "Sure." She threw her head back, ruffling the mass of long brown curls. "Why not?" Immediately, her mind tossed out several logical reasons why not. Cathy chose to ignore them.

Grady looked pleased. "The wedding will have to be small. You don't mind, do you?"

"No." She preferred a minimal amount of fuss. "Linda Ericson can be my witness, and Angela the flower girl."

Grady shifted his position, sitting upright. "I don't know that I'll be able to take the time for a honeymoon." His eyes seemed to bore into hers.

"I have to go back to school on Monday, anyway." Shrugging her shoulders, she looked away. *Get used to it now,* she told herself. Every important family function, Christmas, Angela's birthday, their anniversary, would all come second behind Alaska Cargo. In the long run, it might even work out better that way.

They emptied the bottle, and Cathy suddenly giggled. "Did I tell you the good news?" Not waiting for his answer, she let the words rush out on a hiccupping sob. "I'm going to be an aunt. My sister . . . my little sister is going to have a baby." The whole living room began to sway, and she reached out to brace herself.

Kissing the tip of her nose, Grady placed a hand on

each of her soft shoulders. "You're drunk, Cathy Thompson."

"I'm not, either," she denied hotly. "But I will be soon."

Her head was throbbing when she woke the next morning. Sitting up, she glanced around and pressed massaging fingers to her temples. The events of the past night were cloudy and unclear.

School. She was supposed to be at school. In an attempt to untangle herself from the sheet and blankets, her head pounded all the harder. Finally, she gave up the effort and fell back against the pillows.

What had happened last night? She couldn't remember undressing. When had Grady left? Dear Lord, he hadn't spent the night, had he? Fearfully, she bolted up again; her eyes flew around her, searching for evidence. Thank goodness, no.

Without making excuses, she phoned the school and reported that she wouldn't be coming in. Later, Linda called to check on her and see if there was anything she could do. Cathy assured her there was nothing. There was nothing anyone could do anymore. Her fate had been cast.

Aspirin dulled the throbbing pain in her head, yet she remained in her housecoat, sitting with Peterkins on her lap in a cold living room. There were no paths her thoughts could travel that hadn't been maneuvered before. She felt numb, lifeless.

The doorbell chimed before noon.

"Who is it?" she asked, surprised at how weak her voice sounded. She didn't open the door.

"Grady," the male voice boomed, and Cathy pressed her fingers to her temples at the rush of pain.

"Let me in."

Releasing a long sigh, Cathy turned the lock and pulled open the door.

"You okay?" His brow was furrowed with concern as he moved into the house. He was dressed in his work clothes. "You look terrible. I called the school and they said you phoned in sick today. I knew I shouldn't have left you last night."

"I'm fine." She ran long fingers through limp, uncombed hair.

"Am I supposed to ignore the large birds circling your house?" he demanded.

Cathy winced at the sound of his raised voice. "The what?"

Impatiently, Grady shook his head. "Never mind. You should be in bed." A rough, male hand cupped her elbow, directing her none too gently toward the bedroom.

"Grady," she hissed. "Let go of me. I'm fine. No thanks to you. I've got a hangover, that's all." Placing the blame on him sounded so logical at that moment.

For a second he looked stunned. "My fault! You're the one who emptied her glass and mine and then insisted we open another bottle. I knew this was going to happen. I should have put an end to it long before I did."

Embarrassed, she looked away. "And . . . and just how did it end?"

Grady's laugh was filled with indulgent amusement as

he brought her into his embrace. "Wouldn't you like to know?"

Bracing her hands against his shoulders, she struggled for release. "You're impossible."

"And you're very beautiful, especially with your clothes off."

Immediately her cheeks flamed crimson. "You're no gentleman, Grady Jones."

"I'm more of a gentleman than you realize," he said and laughed. "Now get dressed. If you aren't feeling all that bad, let's go get the blood tests taken care of."

"How can you act so calm?" Linda questioned.

Cathy looked across the dining room table, complete with Thanksgiving turkey and all the trimmings. "What do you mean?" she answered with a question.

Linda pushed herself away from the table. "The wedding's in two days, your mother's flying in tomorrow night, and you're as cool as a cucumber."

"It'll probably hit her all at once," Grady said, briefly flickering a look to Linda.

"More than likely at the altar," Cathy added, noting not for the first time the way Linda was watching her.

The subject came up again while they were doing the dishes. "I may be an old married lady," Linda began, "but it seems you and Grady are both acting extraordinarily calm. You both appear to look upon this wedding more like a dinner party than a lifetime commitment."

"Oh, honestly, Linda," she said, and rubbed the pan she was drying with more energy than needed. "Both of us are beyond the age when we stare breathlessly into each other's eyes and sigh with deep longing." She placed a hand over her heart and breathed in a giant mocking breath.

Rubbing off the sudsy water, Linda's hand sliced the air with the motion. "It's not only that. No one buys a wedding dress the way you did."

Again Cathy negated her friend's concern with a shake of her head. "I just happen to know what I like, that's all," she replied, somewhat defensively.

"I shopped for weeks for my wedding dress. You walked into one store, picked a suit off the rack, tried it on, and bought it."

"As I said, I know what I like."

Linda tilted her head at a disbelieving angle. "Whatever you say." She paused, taking in a breath before changing the subject. "I'm pleased that Dan and Grady get along so well."

Linda's gaze followed hers into the family room, where Grady and Dan were both intent over a game of chess. Angela was sitting on the carpet in front of the television, watching a Thanksgiving cartoon special. She noted the way Linda's gaze studied the child.

"Have you heard anything from the adoption agency?"

Immediately, a warmth glowed in her friend's expression. "Yes. Both Dan and I are surprised at how fast everything is progressing. We went into the idea of adopting thinking we'd spend several years on a waiting list."

"Won't you?" Everything Cathy had heard about adopting indicated as much.

"Only if we're interested in a Caucasian newborn. The agency has plenty of children needing a family now. Dan and I decided we were willing to make a home for any child. There's even a possibility of our having a preschooler after the first of the year."

"Oh, Linda, that's wonderful news." Again, Cathy's gaze drifted to Angela. She almost had to bite her tongue from telling her friend that she was marrying Grady for almost the identical reason. To give Angela a real home. Her eyes became tender as she studied the little girl. Angela was well named, her look trusting, almost angelic. More and more, she was opening up around Cathy, bouncing into her classroom after school, beaming her a smile as she slipped her hand into Cathy's.

Linda asked her something, and Cathy turned. As she did, her gaze skidded across the diamond engagement ring Grady had given her. Cathy had gasped when he unceremoniously slipped it on her finger. It was a magnificent piece of jewelry, with interweaving gold and diamonds. At first it had weighted her hand, but now she was accustomed to the feel of it, often toying with it, especially when she was nervous. Like when they visited the pastor for a counseling session before the wedding. Cathy could have sworn he knew this was no love match. Both she and Grady had answered his questions as honestly as humanly possible. For a moment she had been half afraid Pastor Wilkens would refuse to marry them.

"Did you want pumpkin or pecan?" Linda repeated the question, gently touching Cathy's sleeve.

"Oh, sorry." She looked up, startled. "Pumpkin, I guess. Want me to check with the men?"

"Go ahead. We've finished these dishes. It's time to dirty more."

Grady's face was knit in concentration as he studied the chessboard. Cathy sat on the arm of the chair, placing a hand across his back, waiting until he had made his move before speaking.

"Do you want pie?"

He looked up at her, the features on his powerful face softening as their eyes met. "No," he said, and glanced abruptly at his watch. "In fact, I think it's about time we left."

A protest rose automatically to her lips, but she nodded her agreement. She was lucky to have spent this much of the holiday with Grady. She knew there were several things he needed to do before the wedding.

They made their farewells, Cathy promising to have Dan and Linda over for a meal right after she and Grady were married. The minute the words were out, Cathy realized she'd said the wrong thing. Newlyweds were supposed to want privacy.

Angela fell asleep in the car on the way home.

"Grady," Cathy braved the unpleasant subject a few minutes later. "I know this is difficult, but we're going to have to look like we're more in love."

"What?" Grady choked, his eyes momentarily leaving the road.

Embarrassed, Cathy looked away. "Well, we're going to be married in a couple days. My mother is going to take one look at us and—"

"And what?" Grady demanded, the edges of his mouth turned upward slightly.

Crossing her arms defiantly, Cathy cast him a fiery glare. "You're not making this any easier."

"I'll behave." His hand squeezed hers, and their fingers locked.

Cathy smiled. She did enjoy Grady. He could be warm

and teasing and a lot of fun. "I don't want my mother to worry about me once she returns to Wichita."

"I'll fawn on your every word," Grady promised, his lips brushing her gloves as he chuckled.

Cathy couldn't prevent a smile. She couldn't imagine Grady being any different from what he was. Sometimes she was curious about his relationship with his first wife, but the questions remained unasked. The curiosity centered more on what Grady would be like when he deeply cared for something other than Alaska Cargo. "Be natural about it, for heaven's sake," she pleaded.

"I will, don't worry."

Grady twisted the cigarette into the ashtray with unnecessary vigor.

"Relax, will you?" Cathy's hand reached for his. The airport was bustling with activity. The Thanksgiving rush of travelers filled the small airport.

Grady's mouth twitched in a series of expressions, curling his lips. "What are you doing?" she asked, with an exaggerated breath.

"I'm practicing looking like I'm in love."

Laughter burst from Cathy, shaking her shoulders. "You're hopeless, you know that?"

His eyes smiled into hers. "This isn't easy, meeting your mother and all. Mothers-in-law and I don't have a fantastic track record."

It was the first time Grady had mentioned Pam's mother. "You don't need to worry," she attempted to assure him, "you'll like my mother. We're a lot alike." More than Grady knew. They both had chosen the same kind of men to marry.

Seeing a plane approach from the runway below, Cathy stood. "That's Mom's flight, right on time." Her heart beat excitedly as she placed her hand in the crook of Grady's arm.

Grady straightened, brushing imaginary lint from his jacket. "How do I look?"

"A little rough around the edges, but you'll do."

"I better," he murmured, in a low growl.

Watching her mother descend from the airplane steps, Cathy had to fight the urge to wave. Her mother was unlikely to see her from outside the building; nonetheless, she stood on tiptoes, raising her hand in greeting.

Her mother paused, looking over her shoulder. Cathy felt the blood rush out of her face, and for a crazy moment she thought she might faint. Following Paula Thompson out of the plane were Steve and MaryAnne.

Seven

⚜

"Cathy." Paula Thompson hugged her daughter tightly, patting her back. "You look marvelous."

MaryAnne's arms circled her sister next, holding her as if it had been years instead of months since Cathy had moved to Alaska. Patting her flat stomach, she asked with a good-natured laugh, "Can you tell I'm pregnant?"

"Of course." By some miracle, Cathy managed to keep her voice level.

Steve moved forward, expecting the same greeting she had given her mother and sister. Removing herself from his reach, she turned and looped an arm into Grady's. "Mom, MaryAnne, Steve, this is Grady Jones, my soon-to-be husband." She managed to avoid eye contact with Steve, but a feeling of cold dread raced through her. Why was he here? What did he hope to accomplish?

Formal greetings were exchanged between her family and Grady. Although her mother's expression was friendly, Cathy was quick to note the worry in her slightly narrowed blue eyes. Her mother knew her best of all, and it would take more than reassuring words to fool this woman.

"I understand you own your own business?" Paula Thompson asked Grady.

Undoubtedly her mother had been mulling over the question ever since Cathy had phoned and told her about the wedding. Like any mother, Cathy realized, hers didn't want to have a daughter repeat the mistakes she had made.

"Listen," Cathy interrupted, "let's go to the house and have coffee. I know Angela is anxious to meet everyone." The remainder of her things had been moved into Grady's house that morning. With the wedding scheduled for noon the next day, it made more sense to spend the night in a hotel with her mother than to pay rent on an empty house.

"You should have brought Angela with you," her mother admonished gently. "I think I'm fortunate to receive a built-in granddaughter," she added.

"She's a bit shy," Cathy explained, looking to Grady. "We both felt she'd be more comfortable meeting you in familiar surroundings."

Cathy gave her mother's waist a tiny squeeze, silently expressing her appreciation for her easy acceptance of the little girl.

As they headed down the terminal to retrieve the luggage, Grady leaned over and whispered, "You can let go of my arm now. I think the circulation's been cut off."

"Oh, sorry," she murmured, and relaxed her hold.

"Is everything okay?" he questioned, his voice laced with concern. "You look pale all of a sudden. You're not getting those pre-wedding jitters, are you?"

"Of course." She tried to laugh it off. "Every woman does." A husky defensiveness remained in her voice, and she felt Grady's piercing gaze study her.

———

The minute Steve walked in the door, Peterkins went wild. Barking excitedly, he raced around the room in several wide loops, leaping from the couch to the chair and back down to the carpet before vaulting into Steve's waiting arms.

Crouched to the floor, Steve gave the spaniel his full attention. "You remember me, do you, boy?" Ruffling the long, black ears, he accepted as his due Peterkins's adoration.

Uncomfortably aware of Grady's eyes following her, Cathy ignored the unspoken questions he seemed to be hurling at her.

"I get quite a different reception from Cathy's dog," Grady commented after Peterkins had calmed down. Cathy wasn't fooled by the veiled interest.

"Peterkins and I go way back, don't we, boy?" Steve directed his attention to the dog before he turned and smiled boldly at Cathy.

Her legs turned to Jell-O, and she sat with her mother, Angela positioned between them. She wanted to shout at Steve to leave her alone. Couldn't he see how difficult this situation was for her? Had he always been so selfish, so uncaring? Cathy had wondered how she'd react to Steve when she saw him again. Now that he was here, in the same room, and they were separated by only a few feet, she felt embarrassed, uneasy.

Her peripheral vision caught a glimpse of a muscle that jerked in Grady's harsh features as he stood and sauntered to the fireplace. He placed another log on the already roaring fire.

"I gave Cathy the dog," Steve explained.

"That was a long time ago," she qualified hurriedly.

"Not that long ago," Steve contradicted. He was toying with her, in a cat-and-mouse game. She wanted to scream at him to stop. It was almost as if Steve wanted to make her as uncomfortable as possible, punish her for marrying Grady, hurt her further.

Her mother was busy making friends with Angela. She sat beside the little girl, an arm draped over her thin shoulders, and told her bits and pieces of information about Kansas. MaryAnne, feeling tired, had gone to rest in the spare bedroom for a few minutes.

Apart from a few whispers coming from Angela and Paula Thompson, the room seemed to crackle with an electric tension.

Grady came to stand behind Cathy, and he placed his hands on her shoulders, staking claim to his ownership. Cathy bit into a quivering lip, praying Steve would accept the unspoken message.

In that instant, he caught her eyes. A lazy, knowing grin deepened the creased lines at the sides of his mouth. Steve knew. He knew how confused she was and planned to use it against her.

Cathy closed her eyes to the rush of bitterness and sucked in a stabbing breath. With a determined effort she forced herself to lift a hand and place it on top of Grady's. Her eyes were imploring Steve to accept her decision. But one glance at the narrowed anger flashing at her and Cathy realized he would ignore her entreaty now. Just as he'd done the day of his wedding.

Making an excuse to check on MaryAnne, Cathy stood and moved slowly down the hallway to the bedroom. As quietly as possible, she cracked the door, not wanting to disturb her sister unnecessarily.

"Is that you, Steve?" The weak voice came from across the room.

"No, it's Cathy. You go ahead and rest." Just as quietly, she moved to close the door.

"Don't go." MaryAnne sat up in bed and motioned for Cathy to join her. Raising her arms high above her head, she stretched and released a wide yawn. "It's crazy how tired I get." She placed a protective hand on her abdomen, gently caressing the slight roundness there. "This little one seems to think I should spend my life sleeping. Mom said it was the same with her."

Cathy sat on the end of the bed. "You're happy about this baby, aren't you?"

"Oh yes," she said, and breathed in fervently. Tears shimmered in her deep gray eyes, and a delicate finger wiped them away. "Look at me," she said, with a shaky laugh. "I cry so easy. Just wait until you're pregnant, Cath. I'm so emotional lately. I don't know how Steve puts up with me."

"Has he been understanding?"

MaryAnne nodded eagerly. "I can't tell you how great he's been about everything. Are you and Grady planning on a family?"

The question took Cathy by surprise. She didn't know; they'd never discussed it. "Not right away." Her fingers nervously traced the flower pattern of the bedspread. "We'll wait awhile."

"Don't wait too long," MaryAnne advised solemnly. "I don't think a man can love you any more than when you're carrying his child."

A searing pain shot through Cathy, and she bit her tongue to keep from crying out at the intensity of its force. Did Steve love her sister? Truly love her? Had his feelings changed once he realized MaryAnne was pregnant? He hadn't known about the baby when he wrote the letter. The letter. A hundred times she'd regretted burning it. She would never have Steve, but she could have had the confirmation of his love for her. In her agony, she had destroyed that.

Silently, he entered the room behind her, and for a second Cathy thought her mind had conjured up his image. Gently she shook her head to force herself into reality. Desperately she wanted to hate the virile man that walked to his wife's side. Instead, she felt only a deep, undying love. Before she betrayed herself, Cathy made an excuse and left.

Paula Thompson met her outside the bedroom door. "I'm going to freshen up a bit. Grady said something about our all leaving for dinner, and I want to redo my makeup."

"I'll see if Angela needs anything," Cathy said, avoiding looking directly at her mother.

"Cathy." A hand on her sleeve stopped her. "I like Grady, but I don't mind telling you I've been very worried about you."

Cathy's pulse rate soared to double time. Had her mother guessed her true feelings for Grady? "Why?" She strived to sound incredulous as she walked into the bathroom with her mother and sat on the toilet seat as Paula Thompson washed her face.

"You've been in Alaska such a short time. Are you sure of your feelings for Grady?"

"Honestly, Mom." She laughed lightly, handing her a fresh towel. "Of course I am." The words slipped out without thought. Naturally, she knew how she felt about Grady. But it wasn't love.

"Stepping into a ready-made family has me concerned."

"But I love Angela."

"I can understand why. She's a precious child."

A smile parted Cathy's soft mouth. Her mother was like this. Even when Cathy was a teenager, their most serious discussions were often done in the most unlikely places or under the silliest conditions. Once they had a terrible argument in the aisle of a grocery store about a boy Cathy was dating. Cathy guessed that her mother was uneasy bringing up the discussion and tried to do so in the most natural way possible.

"Probably the one thing that worries me the most is Grady's business. I don't want you married to a man like your father." She didn't need to elaborate.

Now it wasn't easy to disguise her feelings. "Just because a man owns his own company doesn't make him a workaholic." Cathy stiffened and stood, easing her way around her mother in the small bathroom. "I know the signs."

"Don't make the mistakes I did." Paula's voice was soft in warning.

"I won't." Cathy prayed she sounded convincing as she left the room, silently closing the door.

Grady's narrowed look sliced her as she entered the living room. She wasn't fooled by the easygoing façade he had assumed in front of her family. He was angry. Cathy knew him well enough to take warning from the hard set of his jaw.

"You're the one who looks pale all of a sudden." The gaiety sounded forced. "Don't tell me you're getting pre-wedding jitters." She tossed his own words back at him.

"No." The word was clipped, impatient. The slant of his mouth didn't suggest humor or a smile.

"Is something the matter?" A frown flickered across her face, drawing her delicate brows together.

"You tell me."

Cathy hesitated, fighting the growing panic. Grady knew. With all the innuendos Steve had been hurling at him, it would be a miracle if he didn't know. Dear Lord, how was she ever going to make it through the wedding? "I'm not up to playing guessing games with you. If you want to clear the air, that's up to you," she said in wary anger.

Grady rammed a hand through his thick, curly hair and walked to the fireplace, bracing a foot against the hearth. He turned, his eyes fiery, but the anger was quickly disguised.

Hands clenched in front of her, Cathy watched the transformation in Grady's features and followed his gaze.

"Can I give Cathy the present now, Daddy?" Angela requested softly. "Remember, you said I could be the one to give it to her."

He answered his daughter with a curt nod.

Angela skipped down the hall and returned a minute later with a brightly wrapped box. "Daddy said that it's trad—" She stumbled over the word.

"Tradition." Grady helped her out.

Angela shook her head, the soft curls bobbing with the

action. "Daddy said it was tradition for the bribe to get a wedding gift from the groom."

"Bride," Grady corrected.

"This is yours. Daddy and I bought it together." Proudly, she handed Cathy the small package.

Cathy's eyes met his across the room. She hadn't gotten him a gift. She wanted to apologize, make an excuse, but nothing seemed to make it past the lump of surprise growing in her throat.

"Go ahead, open it," Angela encouraged. "I wanted to buy you a real pretty tea set, but Daddy said you needed this more."

Slowly Cathy lowered herself to a sitting position, and almost immediately Angela joined her. It was obvious the child had wrapped the gift. It looked as if a whole roll of cellophane tape had been used. The bow was glued on top and the paper was twice the size needed.

"Do you want me to help you?" Angela volunteered, eagerly ripping away the pink bow.

The paper revealed a jeweler's box. Cathy paused, glancing up at Grady.

"Go ahead, open it," Angela urged. "Daddy said you needed one of these real bad."

Returning her attention to the oblong velvet case, she gently lifted the lid. An expensive gold watch and intricate watchband stared back at her. A rush of pleasure and surprise shot her gaze to Grady. "It's beautiful." Silly tears filled her eyes, blurring the tall male figure across the room. "Thank you."

"Daddy said you'd like it." Angela sounded so proud. Cathy reached for her, hugging her close as a tear weaved a crooked path down her face. So many times over the past weeks Grady had teased her about her watch and her timekeeping methods. No gift could have been more perfect. No gift could have touched her more.

Suddenly, Grady was there, kneeling at her side. He took the case from her hand. "Let me help you put it on."

Placing a hand on either side of his face, she turned his head toward her. Only a few inches of space separated them, but from the hard look in his eyes it could have been several miles.

"Thank you," she repeated softly, and gently laid a tearstained cheek over his.

Grady emitted a low groan as he tilted his head slightly and unerringly located her mouth. The kiss was hard and deep, pressing his mouth against her teeth, grinding her lips. Cathy didn't fight him, but remained passive under the brutal possession. There was pleasure with the pain, almost as if the pain were necessary for her to experience the pleasure.

"Do you still want to thank me?" He breathed the question against her throat.

"Yes." Her response was so low Cathy barely heard herself speak.

"Is that the way people kiss all the time?" Angela queried.

Cathy had forgotten the little girl's presence, as she was sure Grady had.

"Not always," Grady murmured, his voice faintly husky. He broke the contact, and Cathy marveled at his control. Outwardly, he appeared unmoved by their exchange, while she was left breathless and uncertain. He paused and unemotionally removed the watch from the black velvet case and placed it on her wrist.

"Throw the other one out," he said in a jeering demand and stood and stalked to the other side of the room.

Cathy understood what he was asking. He wanted her to throw away the past, to begin again. On shaking legs she stood, walked to his side at the fireplace, opened the screen, and carelessly tossed the old watch inside.

Grady's arm circled her waist, bringing her close to his side. Cathy felt his harshly released breath against her hair.

Paula Thompson left the hotel room, kissing Cathy on the cheek and promising to meet her at the church. A tear sparkled in her mother's eyes as the door closed with a soft clinking sound.

Dressed and ready, Cathy wore a close-fitting white wool suit. She had purchased it just as Linda suggested, without thought or concern, but now she realized that the outfit couldn't have been more perfect.

Hauntingly beautiful was the term her mother had used. *Haunting* was the word Cathy would agree upon. *Beautiful* she wasn't sure. She didn't feel beautiful. Scared, tense, nervous, wanting to get this whole thing over as quickly as possible were the sensations that came to her. This should be the happiest day of her life, and she felt much as she had at her father's funeral. With a deep sense of loss and fear of what the future would hold.

Someone knocked at the hotel room door. Cathy glanced at the new gold watch, thinking Linda and Dan were early. Not that it mattered. She was ready. Arrangements had been made for them to take her to the church.

Only it wasn't Linda and Dan.

"Steve." She breathed his name with a sense of unreality.

His look was haggard as he pushed his way past her into the room.

Her hand still on the doorknob, Cathy closed her eyes. Looking at him, seeing the torment in his eyes, knowing her own doubts were there for him to see, was almost more than she could bear. "Where's MaryAnne?" Desperately, she hoped her sister's name would be enough to bring him to his senses.

A hand on each shoulder pinned her against the wall as his mouth greedily sought hers.

Cathy fought him as long as she could. Frantically, she shifted her face from side to side in an effort to free her lips. Palms pushing against his chest, she tore her mouth from his. From the moment Steve had walked off the plane she had worried something like this would happen. Desperately, she was afraid that once he touched her she wouldn't have the will to resist him. She was wrong. His kiss didn't ignite any spark of desire. She felt nothing. Nothing.

"Stop," she insisted. "Stop."

Steve reached for her again, but with renewed strength, she braced her hands against him and shoved him back.

Steve took one step toward her and paused. "Tell me you don't love me and I'll leave."

Did she love him? The pain of his betrayal had been so sharp and so intense she had assumed her love for him was as strong today as it was the day he married her sister. But was it?

He must have recognized the indecision on her face. Steve extended a hand to her, palm up, imploring. "I love you." The admission came on a husky whisper. "I've loved you forever. I was wrong to ever let you go. To have married MaryAnne."

Now it wasn't only her legs that were trembling, but her whole body. "She's my sister!" Cathy shouted, because it was the only way she knew to fight him. "Mary-Anne is going to have your baby."

Steve ran a weary hand over his face. "I should never have married her."

"But you did," she reminded him forcefully.

His gaze was riveted to her face. "You don't love Grady. Why are you doing this? Why are you marrying him when you love me?"

Cathy swallowed at the lump of painful hoarseness in her throat. "Why did you marry my sister when you didn't love her?" Her only defense was to keep reminding herself that it was MaryAnne, her pregnant sister, who was involved in this. The younger sister she'd loved and protected all her life.

"Come with me," Steve begged. "Now, before it's too late. We can fly out of here before anyone knows we're gone."

"What a touching scene."

Shock came crashing in on Cathy as she saw Grady poised in the open door. His mouth, his eyes, his jaw, every feature stamped with undisguised contempt.

Steve recovered first. "She doesn't love you." He triumphantly hurled the words at Grady. "It's me she cares about."

Grady shrugged, as if her feelings were of no significance to him. He walked into the room and closed the door. "You two are so in love with each other, it doesn't matter whose life you ruin, is that it?"

"Cathy loves me and I love her." Steve came to stand protectively at her side. "No one can stop us now. Not even you, Jones. I'll kill you rather than let you take Cathy now."

Grady flicked a hair from the shoulder of his suit coat, again giving the impression of lazy indulgence. "I welcome the opportunity for you to try," he said in a low drawl. "But there's no need for us to fight when Cathy can make her own decision."

"Tell him you love me and are coming with me," Steve implored, his fingers biting into her shoulders.

Cathy stared blankly from one man to the other in shocked dismay. Her head was screaming one thing and her heart pleading another.

When she hesitated, Steve paled visibly. "Darling, I was wrong to marry MaryAnne. You'd only be worsening the situation to marry Grady. Don't ruin the rest of our lives."

"Well?" Grady questioned, his eyes as hard as stone.

Paralysis gripped her throat.

"Two wrongs don't make a right," Steve said, a desperate ring to his voice.

Why did Steve make sense? Was it her heart? The memory of her sister's expression as she placed a loving hand over her abdomen flashed through Cathy's mind. She looked to Grady. He stood proud and tall. He wouldn't tell her he loved her, he wouldn't issue a single word of inducement. Not that he needed her, not that he wanted her. Nothing.

The heart that had only begun to mend shattered

again as she walked to Grady's side and placed her hand on his arm. Out of the corner of her eye she saw Steve slump to the bed and defeatedly bury his face in his hands.

Everyone was waiting at the church when Grady and Cathy arrived. With time to compose herself, Cathy freshened her makeup and offered her sister and Linda a feeble smile.

"You look as nervous as I did the day Steve and I were married," MaryAnne said with a laugh. "And speaking of Steve, he phoned the church a few minutes ago. He's feeling sick. I think it may be something he ate yesterday. You don't mind if I slip away after the ceremony, do you? I want to make sure he's okay."

"Of course," Cathy assured her.

Standing in the church foyer, Linda pinned the pink rosebud corsage onto Paula Thompson's dress before handing Cathy a small bouquet of the same color flowers.

"That Grady." Linda laughed, retying the sash to Angela's pink satin dress. "I told him he wasn't supposed to see the bride before the wedding, but he insisted he do the honors instead of Dan and me. I imagine you were shocked when you opened the hotel room and discovered your husband-to-be."

"Yes, I was." More than anyone would ever know.

Heaving a long sigh, Linda stepped back and inspected everyone. "Perfect." She smiled. "Just perfect."

Together the small party moved up to the altar and were joined by Pastor Wilkens. Cathy's only thought was how she was ever going to find the proper gift to thank

Linda for everything she'd done to make this wedding run smoothly.

The next thing Cathy remembered was the pastor telling Grady he could kiss the bride. Instinctively, she lowered her eyelids as Grady's mouth moved over hers. The contact was brief and could hardly be considered a kiss. Not that it mattered.

As she warned she would, MaryAnne slipped out of the church to return to the hotel as soon as the ceremony was finished. A room had been reserved in a restaurant for a wedding meal. A cake decorated with dainty pink rosebuds was waiting on a table surrounded by gifts.

With Grady's hand pressing into the small of her back, he led her through the remainder of the formalities. The meal tasted like cotton, but she managed to choke down a few bites. Somehow she was able to cut the cake and feed Grady a bite. Camera flashes seemed to come at her from every direction as Dan and Linda thought it important to record every detail of the day. Cathy couldn't understand it, but she submitted weakly to the ordeal, accepting it as just another irritation.

Finally, they could escape. Ray tossed the suitcases into the back of the plane and helped Cathy climb aboard. A faint smile touched her lips as she noted Ray had painted JUST MARRIED on the side of the plane below ALASKA CARGO. If she had been in a decent mood she would have laughed at the sight of Ray standing on the runway on a bitter cold November afternoon dressed in his warmest gear and hurling rice at them.

Cathy hardly paid attention as they taxied onto the runway, waiting for instructions from the air traffic controller. With a burst of power, they took off. It wasn't until they were unable to see the Fairbanks city lights that Cathy spoke.

"Where are we going?" Only now that they were in the air did it interest her.

"For our honeymoon."

Her sharply inhaled breath became a soundless gasp. "I . . . I thought you said we didn't have time for a honeymoon. The school is expecting me back Monday morning."

"You'll be there," he said shortly.

Grady seemed disinclined to talk as they flew through an ebony night. The drone of the engine lured Cathy into a restless slumber.

She woke when Grady began his approach to another airfield. Rubbing a hand over her eyes, she looked to this man who was now her husband. His expression was tight, unyielding.

"Where are we?" she asked, in a quiet voice.

He didn't look at her. "Does it matter?"

"No." Sadly, she shook her head. Absently, she toyed with the wedding band so recently placed on her finger. Grady shot her an irritated look, and she stopped, knotting her fingers.

They landed and taxied into a hangar, and Grady helped her step out of the plane.

Without a word, he lifted their suitcases, and with long, purpose-filled strides, he walked away.

Stunned, Cathy watched him go. He hadn't spoken a word to her. At the gate, he paused and turned. "Are you coming or not?" he snapped.

For an instant, Cathy was tempted to stomp her foot and scream "Not!" Instead she inhaled a slow breath, swung her purse strap over her shoulder, and followed him out of the hangar.

The air was warmer, the cold less brittle. The stars were out in a brilliant display of God's handiwork, like rare jewels laid upon rippling folds of black satin. Funny, she hadn't noticed how beautiful the night was when they were in the air.

Grady was several feet ahead of her, and she was forced to half run, half walk to keep up with him. Still, she didn't know where they were. Grady paused in front of a sedan and placed the suitcases on the concrete while he produced a key from the car's undercarriage.

He unlocked the driver's side, climbed inside, leaned across, and unlocked her door. Cathy opened the passenger side herself.

The silence grew and grew until she was sure she'd scream if he didn't say something soon. Again, her fingers unconsciously toyed with the wedding band.

"Will you stop?" he demanded in a gruff, angry voice.

"Stop what?"

"Playing with that ring." His foot forcefully hit the car brakes. If it hadn't been for the restraining seat belt, Cathy would have been jerked forward. His cold gaze flickered over her briefly before he focused his attention on the road again. "Get this and get it straight," he ground out through clenched teeth. "That ring is on your finger to stay."

"Yes," she murmured in a tight whisper. "I understand."

By the time they arrived at the hotel, Cathy had guessed they were in Anchorage. She glanced around the expensively decorated lobby as Grady registered. Muted musical sounds drifted from the cocktail lounge.

"This way." Grady touched her shoulder to gain her attention, then just as quickly removed his hand.

She followed him into the elevator, watching the heavy metal doors glide closed. Her attention centered on the orange light indicating the floor number. The elevator made a swishing sound as it came to a halt on the ninth floor. Grady preceded her into the long, narrow hallway, leaving her to follow.

Unlocking the door, he pushed it inward and placed the suitcases just inside. Unexpectedly, he swung Cathy into his arms.

She gave a startled gasp, her arms looping automatically around his neck as he carried her over the threshold. His foot closed the door. Blue eyes seemed to burn into gray, scorching her with the heat of his impatient desire.

"This is going to be a real marriage. You understand that, don't you, Cathy?"

She had expected nothing less. Slowly, she nodded.

Her feet were lowered to the plush carpeting and he sat her on the bed.

His hand loosened the tie around his neck before he unbuttoned the pale blue shirt.

Cathy watched him with a sense of wonder.

Seeing him undress, she stood to unfasten the tiny buttons of the wool jacket. Hanging it in the closet, she slipped off her pumps, flexing her toes into the carpet. With her back to Grady, she unzipped the skirt and hung it beside the jacket.

A hand at her shoulder turned her around. Her hand was at her throat, prepared to undo the collar of the pink silk blouse. Grady removed her hand, untying the sash himself.

She looked at him as he slowly unfastened each button of her blouse. The silken material slid off her shoulders and fell to the floor.

A hand at her back unhooked the lace bra as it too, fell unheeded to the floor. Her heart was pounding so loud it was difficult to breathe. A hand cupped each breast, and the action sent out sensual ripples that spread radiating warmth over every part of her. His mouth spread tiny kisses over her throat, and Cathy angled her head to grant him easier access.

When he released her, she blinked in confusion as a shaft of cold air raced over her.

Again their eyes met as his hands slid over her ribs, pulling her close so that her front nestled against the black curly hairs of his chest.

"Why do you have to be so damned beautiful?" Grady questioned before his mouth captured hers.

Eight

The alarm buzzed, and Cathy rolled over and blindly fumbled for the clock on the nightstand. Urgent fingers groped for the button that would put an end to the irritating noise. Success. The bleeping stopped, and she sighed unevenly. Five a.m., and it was pitch-dark in their bedroom. With his back to her, Grady continued to sleep soundly.

Rousing her husband, Cathy slipped a hand over his lean, muscular ribs and gently shook him. "Grady, wake up."

Her words were followed by a low, protesting moan.

He rolled toward her, and instantly Cathy scooted to her side of the bed. No need to throw temptation his way. Although they'd been married three months, she still was amazed at how much he desired her. Always gentle and encouraging, he was a wonderful lover. Meekly, she submitted to him. She was, after all, his wife. She gave of herself what she could, knowing it wasn't enough to satisfy either of them.

Unexpectedly, she was happy, as happy as she could ever be without Steve. And content with her life. Grady had been right when he'd told her Angela needed a mother. The child had blossomed under Cathy's love and

attention. Sometimes it was difficult to believe this bub-
bly, happy little girl was the same child she had met last
September.

Grady reached across the mattress and scooted her to
his side. Instinctively, she stiffened as his lips kissed the
nape of her neck.

"Don't go all wintry on me," he whispered. "I just
want to hold you a few minutes."

He did that some mornings, when he was reluctant to
get out of a warm bed. Her head was cradled in the crook
of his arm, and she could feel the even rise and fall of his
chest beneath her palm. His breath stirred the hairs at the
top of her head as his hand gently stroked the curve of
her hip. The moment was serene and tranquil.

"Where are you flying today?" She whispered the question, not wanting the sound of her voice to shatter the
quiet.

"Deadhorse."

Cathy released a ragged sigh. She didn't often ask him
what time he would be home or if she should hold dinner
for him. He resented her questions and had snapped at
her more than once when she had innocently inquired.

Cathy didn't know why she'd asked this morning. A
bush pilot from another company in Fairbanks had lost a
man the week before flying supplies into Nome for an oil
company. The plane had engine trouble and was forced to
make a crash landing. Grady had joined the search party.
They found the plane and the man two days later. He had
frozen to death. For several days afterward, her stomach
had tightened every morning when Grady left for the airfield. Not that she didn't respect his talent or his abilities,
but the other man had been an excellent pilot, too.

His hand brushed the hair from her temple, and he kissed her lightly before throwing back the blankets and climbing out of bed.

Instantly a chill ran over her, and she sat up and reached for her housecoat lying across the foot of the mattress. Peterkins had slept there from the time he was a puppy, but not anymore. The dog spent his nights with Angela now; Grady didn't want him in their bedroom. Cathy had struggled not to argue with him, but in the end she silently conceded it was probably for the best.

Snuggling her bare feet into thick, fuzzy slippers, she knotted the sash and started for the kitchen. The coffee was perking, and she poured Grady a cup when he joined her. His lunch was packed and his thermos filled when he gave her a kiss goodbye. Watching his headlights disappear down the deserted street from the living room window, Cathy felt like an ordinary, everyday wife. Only her heart reminded her she wasn't.

Scraping oatmeal-raisin cookies off the cookie sheet, Cathy nervously bit into her bottom lip. Eight-thirty, and Grady wasn't home. In the past, if he was going to be later than seven or so, he phoned, or had Ray do it for him. The thoughtfulness had surprised her. But there had been no phone call tonight.

"Time for bed," she reminded Angela, who was watching television in the living room.

"Can I have a cookie?"

"Okay, but get your pajamas on first."

The little girl nodded eagerly, racing into her bedroom. Peterkins followed in hot pursuit. Fifteen minutes later,

Cathy prayed with the child, kissed her tenderly on the cheek, and tucked the blankets around her securely.

She had just closed the bedroom door when the phone rang. Her heart leaped to her throat as she hurried into the kitchen. *Dear God,* she prayed, *let Grady be all right.*

"Hello." Her voice sounded slightly breathless, as if she'd been running.

"Cathy?"

It was Linda Ericson, an excited, happy Linda Ericson.

"Is that you, Cathy?" her friend questioned.

Cathy tried to keep the disappointment out of her voice. "Yes, hello, Linda."

"Oh, Cathy, guess what? I'm going to be a mother."

"You're pregnant?" Cathy breathed in disbelief.

"Well, sort of." She laughed easily, her happiness bubbling over. "Dan and I just finished talking with the adoption agency, and we're getting a little girl about the same age as Angela. We're so excited. I really can't talk now—there are about thirty-five relatives I've got to phone. I'll explain everything in the morning. I've got so much to do. Dan and I are picking her up in two weeks."

They spoke for a few minutes longer, and Cathy offered her heartfelt enthusiasm. A smile trembled on her lips as she thought about having a baby; then, sadly, she shook her head. No, it was too soon yet, for both of them.

By nine-fifteen, Cathy was more than worried, she was near frantic, pacing the floor. Certainly Ray would know what was happening.

Lifting the telephone receiver, she paused for an instant, unsure. She'd never phoned Grady at work since they'd been married. Clenching her fist, she released a rough breath. Grady would hate it if he found out. She dialed anyway.

"Yes," the impatient male voice answered.

A rush of pleasure raced over her, and, weak with relief, she lowered herself into a kitchen chair. Without a word, she replaced the receiver. Grady need never know it was she who had phoned.

Less than a half-hour later he stormed in the back door. Cathy was reading in the living room, and she started at the violent sound of the kitchen door slamming. She laid the book aside and stood.

"Grady, what's wrong?"

His mouth was thinned into a tight line of suppressed anger. "That was you on the phone, wasn't it?"

The thought came to deny the whole thing, but the habit of being honest was deeply ingrained. "Yes," she answered without blinking, her shoulders squared.

"Why didn't you say something?" His voice was harsh, impatient.

"I . . . I was worried. You've always phoned when you were going to be late."

"Why didn't you say something?" he demanded a second time.

"Because." She stamped her foot, angry with herself, angry with him. "I knew you'd be mad as hell, and I was right."

Hands rested challengingly on his hips, his eyes narrowed with a menacing look. "Don't ever do that again. Understand?"

"Yes, your worshipfulness," she returned in mock servitude.

Grady ran a hand over his face. He looked tired, emotionally and physically weary. "Pam used to do that," he murmured in a tight voice.

This wasn't the first time Grady had compared her to his first wife, and she didn't like it any better now than she did before. "Listen, Grady," she said forcefully, punctuating her words with an accusing finger. "I'm not Pam."

"Then don't act like her," he returned calmly.

Anger simmered in the depth of her deep gray eyes. "If you were so miserable with your first wife, then why didn't you divorce her? Why do you hurl accusations at me that have to do with her? You're being unfair, Grady Jones."

He reached for a cigarette from inside his shirt pocket. "I couldn't leave her," he said calmly. "She was sick." He pivoted sharply and left the room.

Cathy followed him into their bedroom. "Did you walk away every time Pam and you had an argument? No wonder she packed her bags. It was a desperate attempt to get some reaction out of you."

Grady swiveled. She had never seen a man look angrier. He didn't say another word for the rest of the evening.

If there had been a wintry feeling in their bed before, that night it was an Arctic blast. Ramrod stiff, Cathy lay on her back, staring sightlessly at the dark ceiling. She couldn't sleep, not with this terrible tension hanging between them.

It's your own fault, she told herself. It was a childish prank to hang up the phone without speaking. *But it's his fault, too,* she continued to reason. He could have phoned. Why not tonight when he had in the past? Not that it mattered who or what had caused the argument. Grady would never apologize.

"Grady," she asked quietly, "are you asleep?" She knew he wasn't.

"No." Even his whisper sounded gruff and impatient, as if he didn't want to have anything to do with her.

She held her breath, reaching down inside herself. Apologizing wasn't going to be easy. "I don't want to fight with you," she began. "I'll never phone you like that again."

He was silent for so long Cathy wondered if he had heard her. "Grady?" she repeated his name.

"I heard." He scooted across the short distance and pulled her into his arms, holding her the same way he had that morning.

Her dark hair fanned out across his shoulder. Was Grady Jones capable of admitting he was in the wrong? Pride, determination, arrogance were so much a part of this man that she wondered if anything or anyone was capable of bringing him to his knees. "Why didn't you phone and let me know you were going to be late?" she questioned weakly.

"I thought Ray had," came his response, in a low voice. He paused before adding, "I shouldn't have compared you to Pam."

It was the closest she was going to get to an apology, as minute as it was, and Cathy couldn't help feeling encouraged. "There's something you should know about Pam." Grady breathed in deeply, and the sound seemed to echo around the bedroom. "Pam was mentally ill. I did everything I could to help her, but she didn't want help. She hated me; she hated Angela. In the end, she hated herself. Angela was less than two when Pam committed suicide."

Cathy was speechless. From all the bits and pieces of information Grady had given her, she should have guessed that the desperate ploys for attention Pam had used pointed to a deeper problem.

"I'm sorry," she whispered. Her hand caressed his jaw and felt the muscles work convulsively beneath her fingers. Slowly she lowered her lashes, knowing what it had cost him to tell her about Angela's mother.

Fiercely, his arms closed around her, holding her so close that for a moment she was afraid he might crush her. His breathing was labored, as if revealing this part of himself and his first marriage had physically drained him.

Her heart cried out to this man who was her husband. The guilt he must have endured, the helplessness, the frustration. Tenderly, she weaved her fingers through his hair, holding his head to her breast. A longing rose within her to assure him, to console him, but Grady didn't need the words. He needed her.

An exploring hand sought her breast, and the warmth of his fingers seemed to burn through the thin nylon gown. She didn't resist when he shifted positions and removed the offending material, slipping it over her head. His mouth rocked over hers as he gently laid her back against the mattress.

Long fingernails dug into the muscled strength of his bare back as his mouth sought the places he knew would excite her beyond reason.

When she was weak with her need for him, Grady

paused and lifted his face. "Don't fight me tonight," he muttered thickly. "I need you."

How could she give him more than she was already? He wasn't referring to a physical struggle but a mental one. He wanted all of her, her heart as well as her soul. So much more than what she could offer him. Her arms curved around him as a bitter sob erupted from her throat.

Grady paused, and Cathy felt the regret run through his body. Gently he gathered her in his arms and kissed away a tear that had slipped through her lashes. A rough, callused hand caressed her cheek. "Don't cry," he whispered. "I understand."

In a crazy way, she was sure he did.

"I'll be back before eight," Cathy explained, and leaned down to kiss Grady on the cheek. The gaily wrapped gift was clenched in one hand.

"Mite stingy, aren't you?" he said, with a stern look, before tossing the newspaper to the carpet. He grabbed her by the waist and pulled her into his lap.

Angela giggled with delight. "Are you going to kiss her, Daddy?"

"You bet your boots I am," he told his daughter, and proceeded to do just that. The kiss was cajoling, a sensuous attack that spoke more of passion than farewell. Her senses reeling, Cathy made a weak effort to fight him off. He had been like this since the night of their first argument. The night he had told her about Pam. They hadn't made love since, but he was more loving than she had dreamed possible. Making excuses to touch her, bringing her small gifts, almost as if he were courting her.

"Grady," she whispered, struggling to maintain an even breath, "I've got to go or I'll be late."

He chuckled and helped her up, escorting her to the back door. "Drive carefully."

"I will." The shower was for Linda Ericson. The adoption had gone through, and Dan and Linda were going to pick up six-year-old Katy that weekend. Cathy, with the other teachers from school, had decided to throw a surprise shower for her.

"I want a kiss goodbye, too," Angela insisted, running into the kitchen.

"Honestly." Cathy feigned her dismay. "You'd think I was going to be gone a year instead of a few hours. What about you, Peterkins, do you want me to kiss you goodbye, too?"

The spaniel barked, and she stooped to rub his floppy, black ears.

When Cathy returned two hours later, she sensed almost immediately that something was wrong. Even before she walked in the back door, a strange, eerie feeling came over her. She paused just inside the back porch as a chill raced down her spine.

Soft sobs could be heard coming from the living room. Grady was holding his daughter on his lap, gently rocking her, comforting her. He didn't seem to know Cathy was home. Setting her purse on the table, she walked into the room.

"What's wrong?"

Angela took one look at Cathy and burst into giant sobs. "I'm so sorry," she pleaded, her young shoulders shaking pitifully.

Puzzled, Cathy knelt on the carpet in front of the pair. Even Grady looked unnaturally pale. "Sweetheart, there's nothing you could have done to make you cry like this. Now tell me what's made you so sad," she whispered reassuringly, and gently soothed the hair from the child's forehead.

Angela buried her face in her father's shoulder.

Grady's eyes burned into hers. "Peterkins is dead," he said without preamble.

Shock rippled over her. Cathy felt as if the world had suddenly come to a screeching halt. Her eyes pleaded with Grady to tell her it wasn't true.

"What happened?" Somehow the words made it through the expanding lump of disbelief and pain that filled her throat. She knew she'd gone deathly pale.

"Peterkins wanted to go outside, and Angela let him out the back door. When he didn't immediately want to come back in, she forgot about him for a minute or two. When she checked, he was lying at the back door. He'd been attacked by an animal; he died before I got to the vet. Dr. McFeeney said it was probably a wild dog."

As Grady recounted the details, Cathy had the feeling that this wasn't happening. It was a dream, it couldn't be real. She nodded, not knowing how she could be so calm. "Angela," she whispered soothingly, "it's not your fault. Any one of us could have let him out."

Gentle cries racked the small shoulders as Angela climbed out of Grady's lap and placed her arms around Cathy's neck.

Tears blurred her eyes as Cathy wrapped the child in her embrace.

An hour passed before Angela had cried herself into a state of exhaustion. She fell asleep in Cathy's arms. Grady carried her into her bedroom and paused until Cathy pulled back the bed covers. She lingered in the room, stroking the hair from Angela's face until she was confident the little girl would sleep.

Grady was waiting for her in the living room and handed her a glass. "Drink this," he instructed.

Without question, she did as he asked. The liquid burned all the way down her throat, but immediately a warmth began to seep into her bones.

"I did everything I could." Apparently, Grady felt the need to assure her he wouldn't have wished any harm on the dog.

"I know." Deliberately, she took another sip from the glass. "Where is he?"

"Cathy." Grady's voice was gentle.

"I want to see him one last time, please, Grady."

He stood and came to kneel beside her, taking both her hands in his. "You can't. The vet has disposed of the body."

She nodded, lowering her lashes. It was too late; she would never see her little spaniel again.

Grady held her for a long time that night. He fell asleep with her pressed close to his side. For several hours, Cathy lay listening to the rhythmic flow of his breathing while happy scenes with Peterkins continued to play in her mind. When the tears came, they slipped from the corners of her eyes and onto the pillow. Not wishing to wake Grady, she carefully scooted out of the bed, put on her housecoat and slippers, and wandered into the living room. The hurt flowed freely once she was alone.

Knees drawn up beneath her chin, she gently rocked back and forth. Steve had given her Peterkins. Now there was nothing of him or their relationship in her life. Everything was gone. Peterkins was the only good thing Steve had ever given her. Everything he'd done had been a source of pain. Perhaps she should feel a sense of freedom. But she didn't, only an aching emptiness for the dog she would never see again. She felt nothing for Steve. Had felt nothing for him in a long time.

Cathy stopped the rocking motion, shocked at her thoughts. She felt nothing for Steve. She didn't love him, she realized that now. The day his letter had arrived, she had known. It hadn't been the shock of him wanting her badly enough to destroy her sister; it hadn't been the letter. That day was when she realized she couldn't possibly love a man like Steve. Her reaction to Grady's proposal wasn't out of fear that she would go to Steve. It was in response to the knowledge of exactly what kind of man she had once loved so deeply.

What was the real reason she had married Grady? Had she loved him? As soon as she asked the question, Cathy recognized the truth. It had happened so gradually she'd been unaware of her true feelings.

Silvery moonlight filled the room as fresh tears made wet tracks down her cheeks. Cathy heard Grady's movements behind her before she saw him. She yearned for the comfort of his embrace; she wanted to tell him the truth she had discovered. But the words wouldn't come, not now, in her grief.

As if he understood her need for gentleness, Grady sat on the sofa beside her. Tenderly, he gathered her in his arms, brushing the damp curls off her cheek and kissing away each tear. Linking her hands behind his neck, she lifted her soft, moist lips to Grady. With an eagerness she would have been unable to explain, she willingly met each kiss with an abandon he had never known from her. She felt the surprise wash over Grady.

He paused, taking in a ragged breath, his eyes studying her. He stood, lifting her effortlessly. She looped her arms around his neck and released a long sigh as she rested her head on his shoulder.

He laid her on the mattress of their bed and leaned forward to cover her parted lips with his mouth. Again and again his mouth sought hers until the world was reeling with her need. Her lips parted in protest when he broke the contact. He groaned his own dissatisfaction and caressed her face with his shaven cheek. Brushing her ear with his lips, he questioned, "Cathy, are you sure?"

She nodded eagerly, her mouth finding the thick column of his throat, as her fingers pressed him close.

Cathy woke before dawn. The room was filled with golden streaks from the shifting moon. A sadness seemed to be pressing against her heart, and she remembered the loss of her dog. She turned to Grady, gliding her hand over his chest and laying her head on his shoulder. Their lovemaking the night before had been gentle and sweet.

The memory of his tenderness was enough to bring a tear to her eye. How blind she had been, how stupid, not to realize how deeply she loved this man. Pressed close, their legs entwined, Cathy fell back to sleep.

"Okay, Cathy, you can come look!" Excitedly, Angela ran into the kitchen and grabbed Cathy's hand. All morning, Grady and his daughter had been acting strange, sharing some deep, dark secret.

Wiping her hands on a terry-cloth dish towel, Cathy allowed Angela to drag her into the living room. A large box with a bright red bow sat in the middle of the carpet.

"Go ahead," Angela urged. "Open it."

Cathy glanced to Grady, who regarded her with an amused expression. "Go ahead," he added his encouragement. His voice was gentle, almost caressing. He'd been that way with her from the time Peterkins had died two weeks before. There had never been a time in her life that she had felt closer to anyone than she had to Grady these past weeks. He was often home early now, spending high-quality time with Angela in the evenings, as if he suddenly realized what it meant to be a father. If this was the honeymoon, Cathy decided, she never wanted it to end.

A whimpering sound came from the box, and Cathy's eyes rounded. Perplexed, she lifted the lid to discover a small puppy huddled in the corner. Quickly, she stifled a cry of dismay. She didn't want another dog. No one would ever replace Peterkins. She felt Grady's eyes on her, narrowing with impatience.

As if acting in slow motion, she reached inside the cardboard box and lifted out the tiny basset hound.

"Isn't he gorgeous?" Angela cried. "Daddy let me pick him out." Cathy looked at the big brown eyes, the white nose and black ears. She didn't think he was gorgeous. Without thought, she handed the puppy to Angela, tears blurring her vision as she ran into the bedroom and closed the door.

Grady followed her. "What's wrong?" he demanded. The uncompromising set of his jaw told her how angry he was.

Lifting her hand, she pointed to the living room. "I don't want that dog. Why . . . why didn't you ask me?" Her voice shook treacherously. "A puppy isn't going to take Peterkins's place."

"I didn't expect he would." Grady jerked his fingers through his hair. When he lifted his head, she noted that much of the anger was gone. "This dog is more for Angela than you. No matter how much we assure her, she still carries some guilt over the loss of Peterkins. She loved him almost as much as you did, and now there's a void in her life. For her sake, will you take the dog?"

Standing quietly beside the bed, Cathy nodded, not knowing of any way she could refuse.

Angela eyed them warily when they came out of the bedroom. "Did you have an argument?" she questioned softly. "Melissa Sue said her parents have arguments all the time. She said her mother goes to the bedroom and closes the door, and that's what you did, Cathy."

"No," Grady answered for her. "Cathy and I were discussing something, that's all."

"You don't like the puppy, do you?"

Cathy knew better than to disguise her feelings from the child. She sat and pulled Angela to her side. "Sometimes when you love someone so much, it takes a long time to heal the hurt of having them gone. Right now I miss Peterkins too much to think about another dog. But that doesn't mean I'll always feel that way. So for right now, can we make the puppy your special friend?"

Angela regarded her quizzically. "You mean you want me to feed him and take care of him and train him and do all those things?"

"Yes, for right now," Cathy confirmed.

The tiny face showed no qualms. "Does that mean I can name him, too?"

"I think that would only be fair," Cathy said with a gentle smile. "What would you like to call him?"

"Arnie," Angela replied without hesitating. "There's a boy in my class named Arnie and he has a silly smile and when I saw the puppy I thought of Arnie and his smile."

"Then Arnie it is."

Grady was quiet most of the day. He spent part of the afternoon at the office, something he hadn't done on a weekend for a long time. Later, when musing over the events of the day, Cathy wondered if Grady thought she was referring to Steve when she was explaining to Angela about how it sometimes takes a long time to get over loving someone. She decided to make certain that night that there be no misunderstanding.

A roast was baking in the oven as Angela and Cathy peeled apples for a pie when Grady came in the back door. Immediately, Cathy set everything aside and slipped her hands over his shoulders and kissed him hard and long.

"What was that for?" he asked, his breathing irregular as his hands cupped her hips. Abruptly, he dropped his arms and turned away.

"Can't a wife kiss her husband if she wants?" she

asked saucily. Something sharp bit into her pant leg, and she jerked her foot back. "Ouch!"

Arnie's teeth were caught in the denim fabric of her jeans, and he was tossing his head back and forth in a frenzied effort to gain release.

"Arnie," Angela snapped.

Cathy bent down to free herself, lifting the puppy from the floor and cradling him in her arms. "I don't know how anyone can call you gorgeous," she teased, referring to Angela's remark. "You're an ugly looking mutt to me."

"Ugly Arnie," Angela repeated, with a happy smile that revealed two newly formed front teeth. "That's a good name."

"It's a horrible name," Grady said, in a sharp, cutting tone. "In fact, the whole idea of another dog was a rotten one."

The smile disappeared from Angela's face as the hurt shivered over her. Moisture filled her eyes.

"That's not true," Cathy replied in confusion. "I . . . I thought we agreed—" She stopped midsentence as Grady stalked from the room.

Cathy watched him go, stunned and disbelieving. Something was wrong, something was very wrong. Grady hadn't spoken to her in this harsh tone since their wedding day. Just a few hours before, his look had been filled with tenderness. Now the deep, smoky blue eyes were hard and unreadable.

"I'm sure your father didn't mean that," Cathy tried to reassure Angela before following Grady into their bedroom. She stood in the doorway, watching him open and close dresser drawers, carelessly dumping clothes in a duffel bag. "Are you going somewhere?" she questioned in a shaky, unsure voice.

"Isn't it obvious?" His jaw was clenched, all expression hidden from her.

"Where?"

He straightened and cast her an irritated glance. "Did you suddenly join the FBI?"

"No." She stepped inside the room and leaned against the door, shutting it. With her back pressed against the wood, she watched his hurried movements. "What's wrong? You're angry about something, and I want to know what it is."

Grady's mouth compressed into a taut line. "Things aren't going well at the field. I've got to fly into Nome tonight on an emergency run. I probably won't be back until Sunday afternoon." He relayed the information reluctantly, as if he resented having to make explanations.

"Maybe Angela and I could fly up with you; it'd only take us a minute to pack our things."

"No." He didn't even pause to consider her suggestion.

"I'll miss you, Grady," she admitted, and her voice wavered slightly.

His sigh was heavy before he swung the bag over his shoulder. On the way out the door, he paused to caress her cheek, then his hand lowered to the nape of her neck, urging her mouth to his.

Cathy didn't need encouragement. She turned, slipping her arms around his waist and answering the hungry demand of his kisses. Cathy experienced a sense of triumph when she heard the duffel bag drop to the floor. His arms grasped her waist, lifting her from the floor. Eagerly, she spread kisses over his face, teasing him with small, biting nips that promised but didn't deliver. Finally he groaned, moving his hand to the back of her head, forcing her mouth to his. Twisting, tasting, teasing, his open mouth sought hers with a greed she had become accustomed to from Grady. Her body flooded with a warm excitement, and when he lifted his head, his breathing was more ragged than her own.

The honeymoon wasn't over.

Nine

~~~~~~~~~~~~~~~~~~~~

"Is Daddy home yet?" Angela asked, placing a hand over her mouth to hide a wide yawn.

"Not yet, sweetheart." Cathy pulled the pajama-clad child into her lap. "What woke you, a bad dream?"

Snuggling in Cathy's arms, Angela nodded. "I had a dream you went away like Louise and Mrs. Rafferty and Miss Bittle."

Carefully smoothing the hair away from Angela's sleepy face, Cathy kissed her troubled brow. "I'm not going away. Don't you know how much I love you and your father? I could never leave you."

"Are you going to have babies?" Angela lifted her head so she could watch Cathy's expression, as if this information was important to her.

"Would you like a little brother or sister?" Cathy could well understand Angela's hesitancy. She had been an only child for seven years. It wasn't until recently that Grady had given the little girl the attention and love she needed. It wouldn't be unreasonable for her to be jealous, or wish to remain the focus of their attention.

Eagerly, the young head bobbed up and down. "Melissa Sue's mother is preg—going to have a baby. She's going to be a big sister. I want you to have a baby, too."

Hugging her all the closer, Cathy gently swayed in the wooden rocker. "Then I think we'll discuss the subject with your dad very soon."

With the small head pressed gently against her breast, Cathy continued to rock until Angela's even breathing convinced her the little girl was asleep.

She sat in the rocker for a long time, staring at the clock over the fireplace. Midnight. Grady hadn't been home before eleven in almost a week, not since he returned from Nome. Ray telephoned regularly every night to tell her Grady would be late. For the first couple of times she waited up for him, but he'd adamantly insisted he'd rather she didn't. From then on she'd been in bed pretending to be asleep. Grady knew that. She was sure of it. Although he played his own game of creeping around, undressing in the dark and crawling into bed, staying as far as possible on his side of the mattress. At first Cathy assumed he was simply too tired to make love, but after a week she was beginning to wonder. Other than a fleeting caress or a perfunctory kiss, he hadn't touched her since flying to Nome. The sensation that something was wrong persisted. But what? And why wouldn't Grady say anything if there were? Unwilling to read something more into his actions, she had remained perplexed. Things had been so beautiful in the past that she didn't wish to start an unnecessary argument.

But tonight she was awake and would remain so until Grady was home. Whatever was wrong needed to be set right. Gradually, she fell asleep in the rocking chair with Angela in her arms. Ugly Arnie's bark from the back porch roused her at about one, and she heard Grady stop to pet the pooch and quietly enter the house through the kitchen.

He paused when he saw her, stopping just inside the room. "I thought I told you not to wait up for me."

"Shh-shh," Cathy responded, placing a finger over her lips. Instead of words, she extended her hand in silent entreaty.

His gaze holding hers, Grady walked across the floor, stopping just in front of the rocking chair. "Is Angela sick?" Lines of concern knitted his brow.

Unable to break the spell of tenderness that suddenly seemed to exist between them, Cathy shook her head. "No, it was a bad dream," she whispered. "She thought I was going away."

Grady's mouth tightened into a grim line. "Are you?"

The question shocked her. "Of course not. How can you even think such a thing?" She spoke louder than she intended to, and Angela stirred, sitting upright.

"Daddy," she said, rubbing her eyes. "You're home."

Grady lifted his daughter into his arms. "Well, sleepyhead, are you ready to go to bed?"

"You know what Cathy said?" More alert now, Angela looped her arms around her father's neck, joining her fingers, and she leaned back so she could look at him. "Cathy said you and her might have babies. She said that I'd be a big sister someday, just like Melissa Sue."

The room suddenly seemed to go still. Grady flickered an irritated gaze at Cathy before carrying Angela into her bedroom.

She heard him talking softly to the child but couldn't make out what he was saying. Sitting on the top of their bed, she waited until he had showered and changed.

Grady looked surprised that she was still up when he entered the bedroom.

"Can we talk a minute?" Her senses were clamoring, desperately wanting things to be right between them.

He sat on the edge of the mattress, his back facing her. "Not tonight," he responded curtly. "I'm tired." Pulling back the covers, he climbed into the bed and leaned to turn off the bedside lamp.

The room was instantly dark, and not knowing what else she could do, Cathy followed, crawling beneath the covers and scooting to Grady's side, placing a hand over his ribs and cuddling close.

"You're not pregnant, are you?" The question was low, almost angry.

"No," she replied, a sudden chill coming over her at the displeasure in his voice.

"Good." The word was clipped and disturbing.

No more than a minute later, Grady was asleep. Cathy listened to the even flow of his breathing for hours.

The pattern was repeated the next week. Grady worked long hours, and the time he spent at home became less and less. Cathy seldom waited up for him, and when she did, he was abrupt and irritable. But every night in his sleep he would gather her in his arms and hold her so tight that she never doubted his need for her.

Determined to clear the air and talk to her husband, Cathy purposely lay awake. April had arrived, and the days were growing longer. Spring was beginning to color the earth, and she would have survived her first winter. Even Ugly Arnie had claimed a spot in her heart, and the pain of losing Peterkins grew less and less every day.

The only problem that continued to tax her was

Grady's behavior. Had he guessed how much she loved him? Had the depth of her feelings frightened him? Grady had gone into this marriage openly admitting he didn't love her. Now that her feelings were in the open, did he find it an embarrassment? Doubts and questions seemed to grope at her from every direction.

A sound filtered through the confusion, and Cathy realized he was home. Lying perfectly still, she waited as he fussed in the kitchen. Usually she kept a dinner plate ready for him so he could eat when he got home. The movements were hushed, as if he would do anything not to wake her.

A few minutes later the shower ran, and when Grady appeared, the drops of beaded moisture that clung to his hair were shining in the moonlight.

"Grady." She whispered his name.

He sat on the edge of the mattress and leaned forward, bracing a hand on either side of her head. "Sh-hh," he mouthed soothingly, "go back to sleep. I'm sorry I woke you."

Seeing him there in the moonlight, the blue eyes so intense, his face barely inches above her own, she said again, "Grady," his name a husky caress on her lips. Of their own volition, her arms circled his neck and urged his mouth to hers. The resistance was only momentary, and with a muted groan his mouth closed over hers, parting her lips. The kiss lingered and lingered, as if he couldn't get enough of her. His arms closed around her so fiercely that she was half lifted from the bed.

Within the rapturous circle of his arms, she eagerly met each kiss until they were both breathless and reeling from the effects.

"Cathy."

Never had she heard her name sound so beautiful. Within one word she recognized his need, his longing, and sighed heavily, knowing her needs, her longings were equal to his. His thumb traced her lips in a featherlight caress and was followed by hungry, almost desperate kisses. Her mouth was warm and trembling when he laid her back against the pillow and joined her in the bed.

The next afternoon, Cathy sat at the kitchen table, helping Angela with her schoolwork. The girl had made giant strides over the past months. She no longer saw the tutor, as Cathy had worked with her from the time she and Grady were married. Teasingly, she claimed she was a bargain wife because of all the money she saved him. Grady had laughed and assured her she was worth far more to him than a tutor. But that had been before. Before he worked sixteen-hour days, before he accepted assignments that would keep him away from home as long as possible. Before he flew both night and day.

Unconsciously, Cathy expelled her breath in a lingering sigh. Last night everything had been so perfect, so beautiful. They hadn't spoken, not a word. Their lovemaking had been urgent, fierce. He held her close afterward and asked if he'd hurt her. When she assured him he hadn't, Grady kissed her gently and fell into a deep sleep.

The phone rang, startling her. Angela popped off the chair and raced across the kitchen.

"Hello, this is the Jones residence, Angela speaking." The words were polite and eager. "Oh, hi, Ray. Yes, she's here." Angela handed the phone to Cathy.

"Yes," she said, and breathed in irritation. Not tonight, not again. She knew even before Ray said anything that Grady would be late again.

"Grady wanted me to phone and let you know he'll be late tonight."

Disappointment shivered over her until she thought she could cry with it. "Thanks for calling," she replied stiffly.

Ray seemed reluctant to hang up. "Things okay with you, Missus Jones?" he questioned after a long minute.

Cathy wanted to scream no, something was terribly wrong but she didn't know what. "I'm fine, thank you, Ray. And you?"

"Working hard," he grumbled, "but not half as hard as that husband of yours. If Grady pushes himself much further, he's going to end up sick, or worse."

Cathy shuddered at the thought and didn't doubt the truth of the statement. "Why is he staying again tonight—did he say?"

"Nope, Grady don't say much to anyone anymore."

"He's not flying, is he?"

"Not that I know of, but as I said, Grady doesn't confide much to me." The voice was husky and did little to disguise the concern in Ray's voice.

Cathy thought about the call for a long time afterward. Her mother's warning played back in her mind. *Don't make the same mistakes I did*. Was there something her mother could have done in the beginning of her marriage that would have changed the way her father had been?

"Daddy won't be home until late, will he?" Sad eyes the identical color of Grady's filled with tears the child couldn't restrain. "It's just like it was before you and Daddy got married. He never used to have dinner at home then, either."

"Tonight I think we're going to surprise your father." Cathy stood, scooting the kitchen chair to the table.

Wiping the tear from her cheek, Angela was instantly at her side. "What are we going to do?"

"If Grady can't come home for dinner, we'll take dinner to him."

"A picnic?" The tiny voice was immediately filled with excitement. "Can Ugly Arnie come, too?"

"I don't see why not. If Mohammed won't go to the mountain, then—" Cathy stopped, because Angela was giving her funny looks. Tugging a long braid, Cathy laughed. "Never mind."

Cathy made a big deal of packing the picnic basket. Somehow in one small wicker container they were able to squeeze chicken, potato salad, wine, cheese, bread, fruit, cookies, and a doggie biscuit. Singing a song Angela had learned at school, they drove to the airfield, Ugly Arnie barking and howling from Angela's arms.

Ray met them, wiping his greasy hands on an equally greasy pink cloth as a smile lit up tired old eyes. His face was a huge network of wrinkles that extended from his forehead to his round chin, a smile creating giant grooves in the sides of his mouth.

Angela bounded from the front seat and ran to meet the older man. "Hello, Ray. We brought Daddy a surprise."

"Well, if it isn't Miss Angela Jones herself," Ray said with a crooked grin. "Could hardly tell it was Grady's girl, you've grown so much. Pretty as a picture, too, just like Cathy."

Angela glowed with pleasure. "Do you still keep chocolate in your pocket? You used to when I was a little kid."

Ray edged back his hat with the tip of his index finger. "Can't say that I do. Guess I have to check my toolbox." He tossed Cathy a wink. "You go ahead and see Grady. I'll take care of the young'un."

Cathy nodded, her eyes silently thanking him. As she headed toward the office, she heard Ray ask Angela about Ugly Arnie, his question followed by a boisterous laugh.

The door to Grady's office was closed, and she knocked tentatively.

"It's open," came his harsh response.

She entered the room and watched as a look of shock came over his face.

"What are you doing here?" he demanded as he stood.

Setting the picnic basket on the floor, she offered him a feeble smile. "Angela and I decided we were tired of eating alone, so we brought dinner to you."

"How touching."

Blinking back the incredible rush of hurt, she didn't move. He didn't want her here, didn't want to have her connected in any way with his company. It was as if she were a separate part of his life that could be tucked away and brought out when it was convenient. She had been fooling herself with the belief she would ever come to mean more to him than Alaska Cargo. "I . . . I take it that it's . . . inconvenient for us to intrude on you." Her lungs hurt with the effort to hold the tears in check. After last night she had expected things to be different.

"Yes." His narrow gaze seemed capable of cutting

through granite rock. "I thought I made it clear a long time ago that I didn't want you calling here or coming here."

"You didn't mention anything about my coming to—"

"Honestly, Cathy," he interrupted, "you're being obtuse."

She bit into a trembling bottom lip, angry at herself for the open display of emotion. An aching loneliness swept over her, and she lowered her gaze, studying the intricate pattern of the floor. "I don't mind you working so hard or so late, but it's hurting Angela. I wish you'd make an effort to be home for her sake."

"Not yours?" The question was tossed at her jeeringly.

She swallowed at the huge lump forming in her throat. "No," she lied, "not mine."

The silence hung like a stormy, gray cloud between them.

"Is that all?" Grady questioned angrily.

"Yes." She nodded, her eyes avoiding his. "I won't trouble you again."

"Good."

Tears welled in her eyes, and she angrily walked to the door. "After all, I know exactly why you married me. As a live-in babysitter, my place isn't here or sharing your life."

Her accusations seemed to anger him all the more, and he slammed his fist against the top of his desk. "My reasons or lack of reasons for marrying you have nothing to do with this."

"Then what does?"

A weary look stole over him, and he rubbed a hand over his face and eyes. "Nothing. I'll try and be home for dinner for Angela, but I won't promise anything."

"I suppose I should thank you for that, but somehow it's not in me." The parting words were issued in a contemptuous tone.

To his credit, Grady made a genuine effort to be home for dinner. Afterward, he spent time with Angela, but when the little girl was in bed he often made an excuse to return to the office. Within a week he was back to the late nights, although he'd speak to Angela over the phone if he was going to miss dinner.

This whole craziness with Grady had been going on for almost a month, and Cathy had yet to learn what was troubling him. He hardly spoke to her unless it was necessary. Only when he was asleep did he hold her close or display any affection.

"Daddy's birthday is tomorrow," Angela announced at the breakfast table Monday morning.

Cathy continued to stir her coffee. The black liquid formed a whirlpool that swirled long after she removed her spoon.

"Can I bake him a cake all by myself?" Angela questioned between bites of hot cereal. "And Ugly Arnie and me could put up a sign and have a surprise party and make hats and decorate the table and—"

Laughing, Cathy waved her hand to stop the child. "I get the idea."

"Oh, Cathy, can I please, can I, all by myself for Dad?" Round blue eyes studied her imploringly.

"Sure." She attempted a smile. "It'll be fun." Nothing was fun anymore. After a while, even Linda had noted something was wrong. Cathy had been able to disguise most of her unhappiness because Linda was preoccupied with Katy. When she questioned her, Cathy had done her best to brush off Linda's concern, but her crushed spirit was impossible to hide, and when asked, Cathy had burst into tears. How could she tell Linda what was wrong when she didn't know herself?

"I can bake the cake all by myself?" Angela questioned again. "And the frosting?"

"Only if you let me lick the beaters," Cathy teased.

Cathy rose with Grady the next morning, packing his lunch and filling the thermos with coffee.

"What time will you be home tonight?" Her back was to him. She didn't need to turn around to feel Grady's resentment. He hated accounting for his time to her or anyone. She wouldn't have asked him now except that Angela had worked so hard planning a surprise party.

"I'll be home when I get here," he responded tightly. "Don't push me, Cathy."

She whirled around, her eyes flashing angry sparks. "Don't push you?" she hurled back. "Blast it, Grady Jones, either you be on time for dinner or . . . or . . ." She couldn't think of anything that would put a chink in the steel-hard wall he had erected, blocking her out of his life.

"Or what?" he taunted, his voice grating as if he found her sudden display of temper amusing.

Defeated, she avoided his eyes. "Please, Grady, just be home."

He didn't answer her. Instead, he grabbed his lunch and stalked out the back door.

———

"Cathy, come look," Angela called from the living room. "Everything's ready." The decorated cake sat in the middle of the dining room table surrounded by several small gifts. Across the doorway hung Angela's banner, made of bold colored letters spelling out HAPPIE BIRTHDAY, LOVE ANGELA. Beside the name she had drawn a paw print. From the time Angela walked in the door that afternoon, she had spent every minute working on getting ready for the party. Proudly, she had baked the cake and frosted it. Thirty-four candles were tilted on a lopsided surface.

For her party, Cathy had baked Grady's favorite salmon casserole and tossed a fresh spinach salad.

"Perfect." She surveyed the room with a proud glint shining from her eyes. Silently, she was pleading for Grady to be on time, just this once. Surely he must have known she had asked him for a reason.

Everything was prepared and waiting at six-thirty. The table was set with their best dishes. The chilled bottle of wine was ready to open. Angela changed into the pink satin dress she had worn for the wedding, and Cathy was amazed to note that the child had shot up a good inch in the five months since she'd married Grady.

"Wear something fancy, too," Angela insisted, and proceeded to go through Cathy's closet, choosing a dress.

Cathy smiled weakly at the sleek evening gown Angela brought out. The dress was the only really fancy one she owned. She had worn it to a Christmas party two years ago with Steve. Even as she'd placed it in the suitcase when packing for Alaska, she had asked herself why she was bringing it. The temptation had been so strong to hold on to any part of the relationship that she kept it. It had been childish, stupid. She realized that now. Her love for Grady had opened her eyes to several things she'd refused to recognize in the past.

"No." Cathy struggled to keep her voice even. "I don't think I should wear that dress, it's too fancy. Let's pick out something else."

With a disappointed sigh, Angela did as she was asked. Finally, Cathy agreed to wear the white wool suit she had worn on her wedding day.

Next Angela insisted they wait in the living room. The minute they heard Grady the plan was to hide, then scream "Surprise!" when he walked into the room. Eager and fidgeting, Angela waited until almost seven-thirty.

"This is ridiculous," Cathy complained, and stormed into the kitchen to telephone his office. The phone rang several times before there was an answer.

"Yeah."

Ray. Cathy swallowed and turned her back to Angela, who was anxiously watching her. "Ray, is Grady there?"

"No," the gruff voice returned. "He left about an hour ago. Anything wrong, Missus Jones?"

She wanted to scream that everything was wrong. Grady couldn't disappoint Angela this way, it would break the child's heart after she had worked so hard. "Do you happen to know where he went?" She hated to pry and pressed her mouth closed so tight that her teeth hurt.

Ray hesitated. "Can't say that I do, but as I explained not long ago, Grady don't say much to me anymore."

With shaking hands, she switched the telephone from one ear to the other. "It's Grady's birthday and Angela had everything ready for a party and—"

"Don't tell him," Angela cried, tugging furiously on Cathy's wool jacket. "It's supposed to be a surprise." Huge tears welled in the child's eyes.

"If you happen to see Grady . . ." She let the rest of what she was going to say fade. If Ray had heard Angela in the background, there wasn't any need to continue.

"I'll see what I can do." The sound of his voice was stern and impatient. Cathy realized that for the first time in her acquaintance with Ray, the older man was angry, really angry.

By the time she replaced the receiver, Angela was crying in earnest. Huge sobs shook her small frame, and Cathy cradled the child in her arms, fighting back her own disappointment.

Before nine Angela fell asleep on the sofa. Cathy left her where she was and covered her with a blanket. Nothing could convince the child to eat. Angela insisted she'd have dinner when her father came home.

After changing her clothes, Cathy took the casserole out of the oven and set it on top of the range. Having warmed for so many hours, the casserole was overdone and crisp, pulled away from the edges of the dish. Her lower lip was quivering, and Cathy couldn't remember a time when she was more angry. Grady had done this on purpose. He had stayed away because she had asked him to come home. If he was looking for a way to punish and hurt her, he had succeeded. All her life, Cathy had believed marriage was forever. Divorce was unheard of in her family. Five months was all it'd taken to destroy her marriage, and the craziest part was that she didn't even know the reason. Moisture brimmed in her eyes, and she furiously wiped the tears from her cheek.

With a burst of energy, she brought out the sewing machine. A few weeks ago she'd cut out a skirt pattern for Angela. Maybe if she kept busy she'd forget how much her heart ached.

She'd been sewing for about an hour when she heard the back door open. Stiffening her back, she concentrated on her task and ran the material through the machine at fifty miles an hour.

"What a domestic scene," Grady mocked, as he strolled into the room. His arms were crossed in front of his chest as he stepped in front of the kitchen table.

Jabbing a pin into the cushion, Cathy ignored him.

"I bet you wish that was me you were poking." His mouth curled into a snarl as he harshly ground out the words.

Cathy ignored him completely, tucking the material together before carefully lowering the metal pressure foot and needle. She could feel Grady's gaze raking her.

"I understand you sent Ray out looking for me."

The taste of blood filled her mouth as she bit into her lip to keep from changing her expression. Again she chose to ignore him, knowing if she said anything she would regret it later. For now, it was utterly important to sew.

Placing his palms on the tabletop, he leaned forward. Cathy could smell beer on his breath and closed her eyes to the thought of him drinking in some tavern to avoid coming home simply because she'd asked it of him. More and more, the evidence pointed to exactly that.

"All right, Cathy, what are you so mad about?"

His face was so close to hers that all she had to do was turn her head to look him in the eye. Without a word, she continued to stick pins into the cotton material.

"Dear Lord, the silent treatment. I should have known I'd get it from you sooner or later." He exhaled slowly, his breath ragged and uneven. "You must have taken lessons from Pam. That was one of her tricks."

Remaining outwardly stoic, her nails cut into the palms of her hands. "I asked you before not to compare me with Pam," she said in an even, controlled voice that was barely above a whisper.

"If you don't want to be compared to her, then maybe you shouldn't be as unreasonable as she was," he sneered.

"Unreasonable." She hurled the material onto the table and stood abruptly, knocking the kitchen chair to the floor. Jamming an index finger into his chest, she stood to the full extent of her nearly five feet eleven inches and punctuated her speech with several more vicious pokes. "I told you once before, Grady Jones, I'm not Pam. And what was between the two of you is separate from me. Is that understood?"

Grady looked taken aback for a moment, but he was quick to recover. His laugh was cruel. "All women are alike."

Cathy recoiled as if his words had physically struck her. Could this be the same man she'd married? The same man she had come to love? Struggling within herself, she closed her eyes and heaved a sigh, swallowing back bitter words.

"I'll admit you're a much better bed partner." The savagery in his voice did little to disguise his own hurt. "What do you do, pretend I'm Steve?"

Their eyes clashed, and Cathy could barely see the blurry figure that swam before her. Inhaling a sharp breath, she hurried out of the kitchen. Somehow she made it to their bedroom and threw open the closet door. Dumping clothes over her arm, she carried them across the hall to the guest bedroom, making trip after trip until all her things had been transported to the spare room.

Grady stood outside the room in the narrow hallway, watching her. "I expected some kind of reaction to that remark." He laughed, but the sound contained no amusement. "The truth always gets a reaction."

"The truth?" Wave after wave of excruciating pain rippled over her. "You wouldn't know the truth if it hit you in the face."

A cold mask came over his expression, his gaze so hard and piercing that the tears froze in Cathy's eyes.

"Daddy, Daddy."

The child's voice diverted his attention from her, and he turned as Angela hurled herself into his arms. "Happy birthday, Daddy. Did you find my surprise? Did you see the cake I baked for you? Cathy let me do it all by myself. We planned a party for you, but you were late. Come and open your gifts now, okay? Ugly Arnie got you one, too, but really it's from Cathy."

"Yes, Grady," she whispered, her voice trembling, "happy birthday."

Ten

As Cathy tucked Angela into bed an hour later, the little girl beamed a contented smile. "We really surprised Daddy, didn't we?"

"Yes, we did," Cathy confirmed.

"He liked all his presents, too, didn't he?" Angela whispered the question.

"I'm sure he did," Cathy said. The flesh at the back of her neck began to tingle, and she was aware that Grady had come into Angela's room. "Now it's way past your bedtime, so go to sleep, okay?"

"Okay," Angela agreed.

Tenderly, Cathy kissed the child's brow and stood. She stepped around Grady as she left the room and walked into the kitchen. She was placing the cover on the sewing machine when Grady found her a few minutes later.

An electricity hung in the air like an invisible curtain between them.

"I'll do that." Grady took the portable sewing machine cover, snapped it in place, and returned it to the heated back porch, where she kept it stored. Ugly Arnie, seeing the golden opportunity to get into the house, shot between Grady's legs and scampered into the kitchen.

"Hey, fellow, you know better," Cathy admonished

gently, scooping him into her arms. "You belong on the porch at night. Angela will let you in tomorrow morning."

"Here, I'll take him," Grady offered, extending his arms. His eyes avoided meeting Cathy's.

Before handing Grady the pup, she gave the dog an affectionate squeeze and kissed the top of his head. Ugly Arnie would never claim the part of her affection that belonged to Peterkins. But more and more she recognized the wisdom Grady had shown by getting her another dog.

"You like the puppy now, don't you?" Grady questioned softly, giving her a sideways glance as he lowered Ugly Arnie to the floor and cautiously closed the back door.

"Yes, I'm grateful that we have him. You were right, there would have been a void in all our lives with Peterkins gone." She drew in a deep breath and turned toward the stove. "Did you eat?"

"No."

Cathy reached into the cupboard to take down a plate.

"Don't fix me anything. I'm not hungry." He took a cigarette from his pocket.

Cathy was surprised at the suppressed violence with which he lit it. He placed the filter between his lips, inhaled deeply, then blew out the smoke with a vengeance.

"You can't live on cigarettes and coffee." Grady was losing weight, she noticed, not for the first time. His clothes were beginning to hang on him. But then so had she. Why were they doing this to each other?

"Don't forget the beer. I expect you to throw that at me any minute."

She felt her fists clench involuntarily. "Don't put words

in my mouth, Grady. If you drink or smoke or work twenty-four hours a day it has nothing to do with me. You've made my position in your life clear."

"Oh, and how's that?" He leaned indolently against the kitchen counter, crossing his arms as he regarded her steadily.

Tears sprang into her eyes, and she averted her gaze. What good would it do to accuse each other? Not tonight, not when she was hurt and angry. "Grady, I'm tired." She made the excuse. "I don't want to talk about it now. All I want is a good night's sleep. Maybe you can get by on three and four hours' rest, but I can't."

He jammed the cigarette into the ashtray with unnecessary force. "I suppose you're waiting for some humble apology—"

"No," she interrupted him abruptly. "I'm not. There's very little I expect from you anymore."

A faint shadow of regret and uncertainty was revealed in his expression as he followed her out of the kitchen.

She paused in the hallway outside their bedroom. Her things had been haphazardly thrown across the mattress in the guest bedroom. In the room she shared with Grady, the dresser drawers were left open and dangling, a testimony to their argument a few hours before. Where should she sleep? Should she make a pretense of going into the other room and waiting for Grady to stop her? Would he? Should she cling to the last vestige of her pride and march into the other guest bedroom?

As if he understood her dilemma, Grady stopped a few feet behind her and said, "Maybe it would be better for all concerned if you slept in the other room."

Cathy swallowed the horrible pain that blocked her throat. Even breathing became difficult.

"That was what you wanted, wasn't it?" The question came at her harshly. "You're the one who wanted out."

Pride directed her actions. "Yes, I did," she murmured sadly, and entered the room, softly closing the door. She stood there for several moments, fighting the urge to throw away her pride, rush to Grady, and demand to know what had happened—what had gone wrong with them. Instead, she strode to the bed and began making neat piles of clothes on the floor so she would have a place to sleep.

Sleep. Her lip curled up in a self-derisive movement. What chance was there with Grady across the hall? He may well have been on the other side of the world for all the good it did her. She rolled over, hoping to find a more comfortable position on the lumpy mattress. If she lay still, she could hear Grady's movements from the room opposite hers. Was he even half as miserable as she was? Did he long for her the way she yearned for the comfort of his arms? Did he care about this marriage? How much longer could they continue with this tension between them? Questions seemed to come at her from all sides. But Cathy found no answers.

"You look awful."

Linda's observation flustered Cathy as she poured herself a cup of coffee in the teachers' lounge early the next morning. "I'm okay." She brushed off her friend's concern and added a teaspoon of sugar to the coffee, hoping something sweet would give her the fortitude to make it through the first class.

"Things aren't right with you and Grady, are they?"

Linda never had been one to skirt around a subject. If she had something on her mind, she said it.

"No, they're not," Cathy replied truthfully, and set her mug on the circular table.

"Why?"

Cathy rested her hand over the top of her mug; the steam generated heat that burned her palm. "I don't know." Tears just beneath the surface welled in the dark depth of her gray eyes. "I just don't know." She hung her head, unwilling for Linda to see the ever-ready flow of emotion.

"Then find out." Linda made everything sound so simple, so basic.

"Don't you think I've tried?" The sound of Cathy's voice fluctuated drastically. "I'd give anything to know what's wrong between us. Grady's pulling away from me more and more every day. I hardly see him anymore and . . . and we aren't even sleeping together. The crazy thing is"—she stopped and took in a quivering breath—"I haven't the foggiest idea why."

"Talk to him, for heaven's sake," Linda suggested, as if it was the most logical thing to do. "You can't go on like this, Cath. You're so pale now, your face is ashen, and you've lost weight."

"It isn't that easy," Cathy snapped in a waspish tone, then immediately regretted the small display of temper. Linda was only trying to help. There had never been a time in Cathy's life when she felt she needed a friend more.

"I'm sure it isn't," Linda agreed in a sober voice. "But nothing worthwhile ever is. What you need is some time together alone."

"But there's Angela." Several times in the past weeks the opportunity had come to confront Grady, but Angela had always been present. Although she dearly loved the child, Cathy didn't feel she should air their differences in front of her.

"I'll take Angela," Linda offered.

Cathy looked up, surprised.

"No, I mean it. I've been wanting Katy and Angela to see more of each other, I'd like for the girls to become good friends. I'll pick her up after school, and that way when Grady gets home you two will be alone and can talk this thing out without an audience."

"Oh, Linda, would you?"

"What are friends for?" she asked with a warm smile.

Cathy's spirits lifted immediately. This was what she and Grady needed. Whatever had happened, whatever she'd done, the air would finally be cleared.

Not until that afternoon when Cathy was sitting at her desk contemplating the confrontation with Grady did she consider that the change in his personality might not be because of their relationship. Maybe something was wrong with Alaska Cargo. Certainly something as traumatic as his business would account for the personality switch. More than that, Grady was unlikely to confide in her if he was experiencing troubles with his company.

Linda picked up Angela at the house a few minutes before five, and Cathy stood in the driveway, waving, as the car pulled onto the street. Two brown heads bobbed up and down from the backseat, and Cathy smiled at her friend's eagerness to be indoctrinated into the delights of motherhood.

Releasing a sigh, Cathy looked around her. The sun was shining and the sky was that fantastic blue, blue she had marveled at when first moving to Alaska. The day held promise, more promise than she had felt in a long time.

Ugly Arnie tangled with her feet as she came in the door, and she stooped to pet his short fur. "How is it a handsome fellow like you got stuck with a name like Ugly Arnie?" She giggled and stopped midstep, aghast at the sound. She had laughed! Cathy couldn't remember how long ago it had been since she had found something amusing.

Glancing at her watch, she noted that it could be long hours before Grady arrived home. He was flying into Anchorage for supplies. She'd overheard him telling Angela as much that morning. If there was something wrong with the business, there was only one person she knew who would tell her. Ray.

Without questioning the wisdom of her actions, she drove to the field. Ray walked out of the hangar, a look of surprise furrowing his brow as he advanced toward her.

"Howdy, Ray." Her voice was carried with the wind. It whipped at her hair, tossing the long tendrils across her face. She pulled the strands free from her cheek with an index finger. "Grady's not around, is he?"

Ray shook his head, wiping his hands on the ever-present rag that hung from his back hip pocket. "Nope, he's in the air."

"Good." She laughed at Ray's expression. "It's you I want to talk to."

"Me?" The older man looked ever more astonished.

"Don't suppose you have any of that stuff you call coffee around?"

"Put a fresh pot on only yesterday," he teased, with a roguish grin. "Let's go in the office; we're not as likely to be disturbed there."

Cathy followed him, and Ray stepped aside in a gentlemanly gesture, allowing her to precede him into the office. Glancing around her, a smile touched the edges of her mouth. The room never seemed to change. The same newspapers littered the worn chairs, the ashtray was just as full, and the counter just as crowded.

"Here." Ray handed her a white foam cup filled with steaming coffee.

Cathy blew into the liquid before taking a tentative sip, then grimaced at the bitter taste. Grady claimed all the hair on his chest was due to Ray's coffee. One sip and she didn't doubt the statement.

Ray pulled out a chair for her to sit down as he leaned against the counter, his hand cupping the mug.

"I want to talk to you about Grady," Cathy said, her eyes nervously avoiding his.

"To be truthful," Ray replied, "I'd like to ask you a few things, too."

"You would?" Her head shot up.

"Grady ain't been himself lately."

"I know," Cathy said with a sigh. "Ray, I'm worried. I thought it might be something at the office."

The mechanic's mouth twisted in a wry smile. "I assumed it was something at home."

"You mean you don't know what's wrong, either?" Her voice was filled with disappointment.

The thin shoulders lifted with a shrug. "After you were first married, Grady seemed more content than I can remember him being in a long time. He even hired a couple extra men to take on some of the flying he used to do so that he could spend more time at home. Several days he'd come into work whistling, happy as I've ever seen him. Then suddenly"—he paused and snapped his fingers—"everything changed."

"But what?" she cried out softly.

Sadly, Ray shook his head. "I don't know. I just don't know. But I don't mind telling you, I'm plenty concerned. He's going to kill himself if he doesn't let up soon."

A feeling of utter helplessness washed over her.

"You love him, don't you?" The question was more a statement of fact.

"Oh yes," she said, and breathed, "very much."

Satisfied, Ray nodded. "Then things will work out, don't you fret."

Later, as Cathy pulled into the driveway, she felt reassured by Ray's attitude. Ugly Arnie scampered to the front door and jumped against her pant legs in greeting. "Come on, boy," she instructed, not bothering to remove her coat. She strode into the spare room and immediately returned her things to the master bedroom where they belonged. It took far longer to cart her things back than it had to remove them the night before. Hands resting on her hips, she surveyed the room once everything had been transported. With a satisfied smile, she released a small breath.

The phone rang, and she hurried into the kitchen.

"Hello."

"Hi." It was Linda. "I hope I'm not interrupting anything."

"No, Grady's not home yet. Is something wrong?"

"Not really, but Angela forgot her suitcase and she was wondering if you would bring it over. I've assured her several times that she can wear Katy's pajamas tonight, but apparently the suitcase contains some irreplaceable treasures."

Cathy smiled. "I'll bring it right away." They spoke for a few minutes longer before Cathy replaced the receiver.

The suitcase was on top of Angela's bed, and Cathy couldn't contain the amusement that softly edged up her mouth. It looked as if Angela had packed everything she owned. Opening the clasp, she viewed enough clothes for a three-week vacation, plus several stuffed animals and the child's favorite books.

Hauling the suitcase into the living room, Cathy turned at the unexpected sound. Grady stood poised in the kitchen doorway.

Her gray eyes blinked at the tall, dejected figure. He looked more defeated than she had ever seen him, his shoulders hunched as if he was carrying the heaviest of burdens.

Held motionless by the agony in his eyes, Cathy inhaled a sharp breath, watching the color drain out of his face. What was wrong? She followed his gaze, which rested on the suitcase in her hand, then stared back into his bloodless features. *He thinks I'm leaving him,* she thought miserably.

A half-sob broke through the paralysis that gripped her throat. *He thinks I'm running away.* An eternity passed, and still she couldn't pull her eyes from him.

Tears clouded her vision, and for the first time Cathy realized how useless the situation was between them. Things had gone too far, and there was nothing she could do to save this marriage.

Every step was agony as she turned around and walked across the room.

"Don't go."

Cathy stopped, her face incredulous. "What did you say?" she asked in a hushed whisper.

Eleven

Grady continued to stare at her, his eyes dark and haunted. He ran a weary hand over his face and looked away. "Don't leave me."

Did he think she was playing games with him the way Pam had done, packing her things, threatening to leave?

"Why?" The question was bitter.

"I need you." He sounded gruff, almost defensive. "I know how much you love Steve, but—"

"Steve!" she cried, dropping the suitcase. "How can you think I want Steve when I'm in love with you?"

The dark, tortured eyes deepened, followed by a short, bitter laugh. "Cathy, don't lie to me," he murmured, in a hoarse whisper.

"Lie?" The muscles of her throat were constricting so tightly that she could barely swallow. "I love you so much that if you push me out of your life any further, I think I'll die."

Disbelief drove creases into his brow. "But I love you." The words were issued in an aching whisper as he advanced a step into the room.

Cathy didn't need any encouragement to meet him halfway. She walked into his arms, knowing how much the words had cost him. Grady's arm closed around her so fiercely that she couldn't breathe. Not that it mattered when he told her of his love.

His breathing was ragged and uneven as he buried his face in her hair, and she felt him shudder against her. For a long, breathless moment he did nothing more than hold her. Never had Cathy felt such peace, such contentment.

His kiss was filled with so much need that the single meeting of their lips was enough to erase all the pain and uncertainty of the past month.

"I need you," he breathed into her hair. "I didn't mean to fall in love with you. I thought we could marry and I'd remain detached from any emotional commitment."

Her hands reached to his face, gently caressing the proud line of his jaw. "I love you so much, how could you have doubted?"

Grady broke the embrace and took several short steps before pivoting back to her. "We'd only seen each other a couple of times before I guessed that you'd been deeply hurt by another man. It didn't take much longer to realize you were still in love with him." He paused and ran his fingers through the curly hair at the side of his head. "I think I almost preferred it that way. You had a relationship you were trying to forget, and so did I."

"But the past is over," she whispered. "I confess I thought I was in love with Steve when we married. But I wasn't. Not until the night Peterkins died did I realize that I couldn't love Steve when I was in love with you."

She saw the look of surprise that flashed over his features, and moved to his side, lifting her lips to his lean jaw.

He cupped her face with his hands, his thumb tracing her lips, his mouth following.

With her arm wrapped around his waist, Cathy laid

her head on his chest and heard the rapid, staccato beat of his heart.

"That was the first night you initiated our lovemaking," he whispered against her hair.

"There'll be more times," she promised, with a contented smile. "You were so tender, so gentle that night, almost as if my pain were your own."

"It was." His breath stirred the hairs at the crown of her head. "I knew how much you cared about Peterkins. I also knew that Steve had given you the dog. Getting a puppy so soon afterward wasn't a brilliant idea, but when I saw the way you looked at Arnie . . ."

"Ugly Arnie," she corrected.

"Ugly Arnie," he repeated, a smile evident in his voice. "I realized then that you would probably never get over loving Steve."

"But you're wrong," she said, almost desperately. "Peterkins was separate from Steve. I was so afraid you would misconstrue that. You left for the office that day, and I knew my reaction to Ugly Arnie had hurt you. I was angry with myself when later I realized it was at that point that you drew away from me."

"That wasn't it." His hold on her relaxed, and she heard the deep, uneven breath he expelled. "When I got to the office that day, a letter from Steve was waiting for me."

Shock jerked her head back as she stared at Grady. "A letter from Steve? Why?"

Gently, he kissed her forehead. "He reminded me that you were in love with him. It seemed so logical, especially after the scene that morning with the puppy and you telling Angela that when a person loves someone it takes a long time to forget that person."

"But, Grady," she said in a determined tone, "I was referring to the dog, not Steve."

Tight-lipped, he nodded. "But at the time I didn't doubt the truth of his statement. Steve said that if I had any deep feelings for you, then I would see the truth and would set you free."

"No," she gasped, and tightened her arms around his middle.

"Steve told me what had happened and how he'd gotten caught in a chain of events that led to the wedding with your sister. He explained how things got so involved and tangled to the point that he couldn't back out of the marriage. He said it was the same thing that had happened with us."

"But, Grady, that's not true. You know it," she whispered emphatically. "You were there at the hotel room; you gave me the choice."

"But I knew when you came to me you loved Steve. The letter made so much sense. The man admitted what a terrible mistake he made in marrying MaryAnne. But he realized what he'd done and loved and needed you. He begged me, Cathy, he begged me to set you free. A man doesn't do that kind of thing lightly. He loves you."

"No, he doesn't," she contradicted forcefully. "If Steve had really cared for me he would never have married my sister."

Grady's look was hard, resolute. "I didn't expect to love you. After the letter arrived I knew I should probably do the noble thing and send you to Steve. I guess these past weeks I was attempting to drive you away. Then today one look at you with that suitcase and I knew if you left a part of me would die. I love you more than I thought it was possible to love another human being. You've brought happiness and joy into my life and Angela's."

"But, Grady." Both hands cupped his jaw, and she turned his face so she could look into the intense blue eyes. "I wasn't leaving."

A disbelieving look came over him. "But the suitcase—"

"Is for Angela, she's spending the night with Linda, Dan, and Katy." She laughed softly, her heart overflowing with an unrestrained happiness. "Angela's staying with them so you and I could talk. I couldn't bear to have things as they were between us. I had to find out what was bothering you."

Grady's look was tender and searching. "For a month I've lived with a terrible guilt, knowing I should set you free and holding on to you. For a time I tried to convince myself that I couldn't let you go for Angela's sake. But I was only trying to fool myself. I love you, Cathy Thompson Jones. You are my wife and will remain so all our lives." He spoke in a tone that was almost reverent.

"And you, Grady Jones, are my husband, the man I want to share my life with, to father my children. You must promise me never, ever to hide anything like that from me again. To never doubt me or my love."

"I promise." The words were emitted on a husky breath just before his lips sealed the vow.

Contentedly, Cathy lay in her husband's arms. Slowly her eyelids lowered as she suppressed a yawn. Grady's arm curved around her possessively, and she nestled into the crook of his arm.

"Are you happy?" he questioned, and brushed his lips over her temple.

"Blessedly so." One long fingernail drew tantalizing circles over his bare chest, tangling the curly hairs that grew in abundance there.

Grady lackadaisically ran his fingers through the long silken strands of her hair and gradually down the fragile hollow of her throat. His lips were pressed against her hair as if he couldn't yet believe she was here with him in their bed.

"Don't ever send me to the guest bedroom again," she said with a sigh, turning her face so her tongue could provocatively explore his neck and throat. She paused in her examination. "The mattress is lumpy."

Grady laughed quietly. "Never again."

"Did you notice I moved my things back in here this afternoon?"

"No." He raised himself up on one elbow, his gaze doing a sweeping inspection of the room.

"I wasn't about to give up on us, Grady. Not when I love you so much."

"I don't think I've ever noticed how talkative you are," he murmured, smoothing the hair away from the sides of her face. A moan of anticipation came deep from within him as he lowered his mouth to hers, crushing her body with his.

Immediately, Cathy was aware of his need and answered with her own, wrapping her arms around him. A long time passed before either of them spoke again.

"Grady," she whispered, loving the feel of his hands as they cupped her breasts. "I'm going to have a baby."

The room became instantly silent; even Grady's breathing seemed to have stopped.

"A baby," he repeated incredulously.

The silence grew and grew.

"How?"

"How?" She laughed and pressed her lips to the pulse hammering wildly at the base of his neck. "Would you like me to show you . . . how?"

"You know what I mean."

"I do?" she teased.

"A baby," he murmured huskily. "Why didn't you say something before? You should never have kept this from me." He took in a huge, wondrous breath. "I guessed as much when Angela said something about being a big sister not long ago; I even asked you. But you denied it."

"Grady," Cathy attempted to explain, but his arms closed around her fiercely, and she asked, "Are you pleased?"

"Oh yes, very pleased. When are you due?"

Laughter bubbled from her throat. "In about nine months, give or take a week."

"Nine months?" he shot back with a chuckle. "Should we start now?"

The sharp trill of the phone broke into the conversation. Instantly, Cathy sat up in the bed, pulling the sheet over her naked breasts. "Angela," she said in alarm. "I didn't take her the suitcase."

A half-hour later, Grady and Cathy had dressed and were on their way out the back door. Grady carried the large suitcase in one hand and slipped the other arm around his wife's waist, pulling her close to his side.

"I've been thinking I'd like you to teach me to fly," she said, a tremulous smile lighting up her face.

Grady's look was tender as his gaze rested on her. "Want to learn to soar to unknown heights, is that it?"

Cathy laughed, leaning against the quiet strength of this man she loved. "When I'm with you, Grady Jones, who needs a plane?"

Thanksgiving Prayer

One

The radiant blue heavens drew Claudia Masters's eyes as she boarded the jet for Nome, Alaska. Her heart rate accelerated with excitement. In less than two hours she would be with Seth—manly, self-assured, masterful Seth. She made herself comfortable and secured the seat belt, anticipating the rumble of the engines that would thrust the plane into the air.

She had felt some uncertainty when she boarded the plane that morning in Seattle. But she'd hastily placed a phone call during her layover in Anchorage and been assured by Seth's assistant that yes, he had received her message, and yes, he would meet her at the airport. Confident now, Claudia relaxed and idly flipped through a magazine.

A warmth, a feeling of contentment, filled her. Cooper's doubts and last-ditch effort to change her mind were behind her now, and she was free to make her life with Seth.

Cooper had been furious with her decision to leave medical school. But he was only her uncle. He hadn't understood her love for her Alaskan oilman, just as he couldn't understand her faith in the Lord.

A smile briefly curved her soft mouth upward. Cooper

had shown more emotion in that brief twenty-minute visit to his office than she'd seen in all her twenty-five years.

"Quitting med school is the dumbest idea I've ever heard," he'd growled, his keen brown eyes challenging the serene blue of hers.

"Sometimes loving someone calls for unusual behavior," she had countered, knowing anything impractical was foreign to her uncle.

For a moment all Cooper could do was stare at her. She could sense the anger drain from him as he lowered himself into the desk chair.

"Contrary to what you may believe, I have your best interests at heart. I see you throwing away years of study for some ignorant lumberjack. Can you blame me for doubting your sanity?"

"Seth's an oilman, not a lumberjack. There aren't any native trees in Nome." It was easier to correct Cooper than to answer the questions that had plagued her, filling her with doubts. The choice hadn't been easy; indecision had tormented her for months. Now that she'd decided to marry Seth and share his life in the Alaskan wilderness, a sense of joy and release had come over her.

"It's taken me two miserable months to realize that my future isn't in any hospital," she continued. "I'd be a rotten doctor if I couldn't be a woman first. I love Seth. Someday I'll finish medical school, but if a decision has to be made, I'll choose Seth Lessinger every time."

But Cooper had never been easily won over. The tense atmosphere became suddenly quiet as he digested the thought. He expelled his breath, but it was several seconds before he spoke. "I'm not thinking of myself, Claudia. I want you to be absolutely sure you know what you're doing."

"I am," she replied with complete confidence.

Now, flying high above the lonely, barren Alaska tundra, Claudia continued to be confident she was doing the right thing. God had confirmed the decision. Seth had known from the beginning, but it had taken her much longer to realize the truth.

Gazing out the plane window, she viewed miles upon miles of the frozen, snow-covered ground. It was just as Seth had described: a treeless plain of crystalline purity. There would be a summer, he'd promised, days that ran into each other when the sun never set. Flowers would blossom, and for a short time the tundra would explode into a grassy pasture. Seth had explained many things about life in the North. At first she'd resented his letters, full of enticements to lure her to Nome. If he really loved her, she felt, he should be willing to relocate in Seattle until she'd completed her studies. It wasn't so much to ask. But as she came to know and love Seth, it became evident that Nome was more than the location of his business. It was a way of life, Seth's life. Crowded cities, traffic jams, and shopping malls would suffocate him.

She should have known that the minute she pushed the cleaning cart into the motel room. Her being a housekeeper at the Wilderness Motel had been something of a miracle in itself.

Leaning back, Claudia slowly lowered her lashes as the memories washed over her.

———

Ashley Robbins, her lifetime friend and roommate, had been ill—far too sick to spend the day cleaning rooms. By the time Ashley admitted as much, it was too late to call the motel and tell them she wouldn't be coming to work, so Claudia had volunteered to go in her place.

Claudia had known from the moment she slid the pass key into the lock that there was something different, something special, about this room.

Her hands rested on her slender hips as she looked around. A single man slept here. She smiled as she realized how accurate she was becoming at describing the occupants of each room, and after just one day. She was having fun speculating. Whoever was staying in here had slept uneasily. The sheet and blankets were pulled free of the mattress and rumpled haphazardly at the foot of the king-size bed.

As she put on the clean sheets, she couldn't help wondering what Cooper would think if he could see her now. He would be aghast to know she was doing what he would call "menial work."

As she lifted the corner of the mattress to tuck in the blanket, she noticed an open Bible on the nightstand, followed by the sudden feeling that she wasn't alone. As she turned around, a smile lit up her sky-blue eyes. But her welcome died: no one was there.

After finishing the bed, she plugged in the vacuum. With the flip of the switch the motor roared to life. A minute later she had that same sensation of being watched, and she turned off the machine. But when she turned, she once again discovered she was alone.

Pausing, she studied the room. There was something about this place: not the room itself, but the occupant.

She could sense it, feel it: a sadness that seemed to reach out and touch her, wrapping itself around her. She wondered why she was receiving these strange sensations. Nothing like this had ever happened to her before.

A prayer came to her lips as she silently petitioned God on behalf of whoever occupied this room. When she finished she released a soft sigh. Once, a long time ago, she remembered reading that no one could come to the Lord unless someone prayed for them first. She wasn't sure how scriptural that was, but the thought had stuck with her. Often she found herself offering silent prayers for virtual strangers.

After cleaning the bathroom and placing fresh towels on the rack, she began to wheel the cleaning cart into the hallway. Again she paused, brushing wisps of copper-colored hair from her forehead as she examined the room. She hadn't forgotten anything, had she? Everything looked right. But again that terrible sadness seemed to reach out to her.

Leaving the cart, she moved to the desk and took out a postcard and a pen from the drawer. In large, bold letters she printed one of her favorite verses from Psalms. It read: "May the Lord give you the desire of your heart and make all your plans succeed." Psalm 20:4. She didn't question why that particular verse had come to mind. It didn't offer solace, even though she had felt unhappiness here. Perplexed and a little unsure, she tucked the card into the corner of the dresser mirror.

Back in the hall, she checked to be sure the door had locked automatically. Her back ached. Ashley hadn't been kidding when she said this was hard work. It was that and more. She was so glad that had been her final room for the day. A thin sheen of perspiration covered Claudia's brow, and she pushed her thick, naturally curly hair from her face. Her attention was still focused on the door when she began wheeling the cart toward the elevator. She hadn't gone more than a few feet when she struck something. A quick glance upward told her that she'd run into a man.

"I'm so sorry," she apologized immediately. "I wasn't watching where I was going." Her first impression was that this was the largest, most imposing man she'd ever seen. He loomed above her, easily a foot taller than her five-foot-five frame. His shoulders were wide, his waist and hips lean, and he was so muscular that the material of his shirt was pulled taut across his broad chest. He was handsome in a reckless-looking way, his hair magnificently dark. His well-trimmed beard was a shade lighter.

"No problem." The stranger smiled, his mouth sensuous and appealing, his eyes warm.

Claudia liked that. He might be big, but one look told her he was a gentle giant.

Not until she was in her car did she realize she hadn't watched to see if the giant had entered the room where she'd gotten such a strange feeling.

By the time Claudia got back to the apartment, Ashley looked better. She was propped against the arm of the sofa, her back cushioned by several pillows. A hand-knit afghan covered her, and a box of tissues sat on the coffee table, the crumpled ones littering the polished surface.

"How'd it go?" she asked, her voice scratchy and unnatural. "Were you able to figure out one end of the vacuum from the other?"

"Of course." Claudia laughed. "I had fun playing house, but next time warn me—I broke my longest nail."

"That's the price you pay for being so stubborn," Ashley scolded as she grabbed a tissue, anticipating a sneeze. "I told you it was a crazy idea. Did old Burns say anything?"

"No, she was too grateful. Finding a replacement this late in the day would have been difficult."

Fall classes at the University of Washington had resumed that Monday, and Ashley had been working at the motel for only a couple of weeks, one of the two part-time jobs she had taken to earn enough to stay in school.

Claudia knew Ashley had been worried about losing the job, so she'd been happy to step in and help. Her own tuition and expenses were paid by a trust fund her father had established before his death. She had offered to lend Ashley money on numerous occasions, but her friend had stubbornly refused. Ashley believed that if God wanted her to have a degree in education, then He would provide the necessary money. Apparently He did want that for her, because the funds were always there when she needed them.

Ashley's unshakable faith had taught Claudia valuable lessons. She had been blessed with material wealth, while Ashley struggled from one month to the next. But of the two of them, Claudia considered Ashley the richer.

Claudia often marveled at her friend's faith. Everything had been taken care of in her own life. Decisions had been made for her. As for her career, she'd known from the time she was in grade school that she would be a doctor, a dream shared by her father. The last Christmas before his death he'd given her a stethoscope. Later she realized that he must have known he wouldn't be alive to see their dream fulfilled. Now there was only Cooper, her pompous, dignified uncle.

"How are you feeling?"

Ashley sneezed into a tissue, which did little to muffle the sound. "Better," she murmured, her eyes red and watery. "I should be fine by tomorrow. I don't want you to have to fill in for me again."

"We'll see," Claudia said, hands on her hips. Ashley was so stubborn, she mused—she seemed to be surrounded by strong-willed people.

Later that night she lay in bed, unable to sleep. She hadn't told Ashley about what had happened in the last room she'd cleaned. She didn't know how she could explain it to anyone. Now she wished she'd waited to see if the stranger outside had been the one occupying that room. The day had been unusual in more ways than one. With a yawn, she rolled over and forced herself to relax and go to sleep.

The clouds were gray and thick the next morning. Claudia was up and reading over some material from one of her classes when Ashley strolled into the living room, looking just as miserable as she had the day before.

"Don't you ever let up?" she complained with a long yawn. "I swear, all you do is study. Take a break. You've got all quarter to hit the books."

With deliberate slowness Claudia closed the textbook. "Do you always wake up so cheerful?"

"Yes," Ashley snapped. "Especially when I feel I could be dying. You're going to be a doctor—do something!"

Claudia brandished the thick book, which happened to be on psychology. "All right," she said. "Take two aspirin, drink lots of liquids, and stay in bed. I'll check on you later."

"Wonderful," Ashley murmured sarcastically as she stumbled back into her bedroom. "And for this she goes to medical school."

A half hour later Claudia tapped lightly before letting herself into Ashley's bedroom. "Feel any better?"

"A little." Ashley spoke in a tight voice. She was curled into a ball as if every bone ached.

"You probably have a touch of the flu to go along with that rotten cold."

"This isn't a touch," Ashley insisted vehemently. "This is a full-scale beating. Why did this have to happen to me now?"

"Don't ask me," Claudia said, as she set a tray of tea and toast on the nightstand. "But have you ever stopped to think that maybe your body has decided it needs a rest? You're going to kill yourself working at the motel and the bookstore, plus doing all your coursework. Something's got to give, and in this instance it's your health. I think you should take warning."

"Uh-oh, here it comes." Ashley groaned and rolled over, placing the back of her hand to her forehead. "I wondered how long it would take to pull your corny doctor routine on me."

"It's not corny." Claudia's blue eyes flashed. "Don't you recognize good advice when you hear it?"

Ashley gestured weakly with her hand. "That's the problem, I guess. I don't."

"Well, trust me. This advice is good," Claudia said and fluffed up a pillow so Ashley could sit up comfortably.

"I'm better, honest," Ashley said and coughed. "Good enough to work. I hate the thought of you breaking another fingernail."

"Sure you do, Ash, sure you do."

Claudia wheeled the cleaning cart from one room to the next without incident. The small of her back ached, and she paused to rub it. She hadn't exactly done much housecleaning in her life.

Her fingers trembled when she inserted the pass key into the final room—the same one she had finished with yesterday. Would she feel the same sensations as before? Or had it all been her imagination? The room looked almost identical to the way it had yesterday. The sheets and blankets were rumpled at the foot of the bed, as if the man had once again slept restlessly.

Her attention flew to the mirror, and she was pleased to note that the card was gone. Slowly she walked around the room, waiting to feel the sensations she'd had yesterday, but whatever she had felt then was gone. Maybe she had conjured up the whole thing in her mind. The brain could do things like that. She should know. She'd studied enough about the human mind these past couple of years.

She was placing the fresh white towels in the bathroom when a clicking noise was followed by the sound of the door opening.

She stiffened, her fingers nervously toying with the towel as she pretended to straighten it.

"Hello." The male voice came from behind her, rich and deep.

"Hello," she mumbled and managed a smile as she turned. The man she had bumped into yesterday was framed in the doorway. Somehow she had known this was his room. "I'll be out of your way in a minute."

"No," he insisted. "Don't go. I want to talk to you."

Turning away from him, she moistened her suddenly parched lips.

"Do I frighten you?" he asked.

Claudia realized that his size probably intimidated a lot of people. "No," she answered honestly. This man could probably lift a refrigerator by himself, yet he wouldn't hurt an ant. She wasn't sure how she knew that, but she did.

"Are you the one who left this?" He pulled the card she'd placed in the mirror from his shirt pocket.

Numbly she nodded. She didn't know anything about motel policy. What if she'd gotten Ashley into trouble?

His thick brows lifted, as if he'd expected more than a simple movement of her head. "Why?" The single word seemed to be hurled at her.

"I . . . I don't really know," she began weakly, surprised at how feeble her voice sounded. "If it offended you, then please accept my apology."

"I wasn't displeased," he assured her. "But I was a little curious about your reasons." He released her gaze as he put the card back into his shirt pocket. "Do you do this often?"

Claudia looked away uneasily. "No. Never before."

His dark eyes narrowed on her. "Do you think we

could have a cup of coffee somewhere when you're through? I really would like to talk to you."

"I . . ." She looked down at the uniform skirt the motel had provided and noticed a couple of smudges.

"You look fine."

No doubt he assumed she did this full-time, which made his invitation into an interesting opportunity. So many times she had wished she could meet someone without the fear of intimidating him with her brains and financial situation. Although she wasn't an heir to millions, she would receive a large sum of cash at age thirty or the day she married—whichever came first.

"I'd like that." Obviously this stranger needed to speak to someone. The open Bible on his nightstand had convinced her that he was a Christian. Was it because he was lonely that she had felt that terrible sadness in the room? No, she was sure it was more than loneliness— a lot more.

"Can we meet someplace?" he suggested. "There's a coffee shop around the corner."

"Fine," she said, and nodded, knowing Cooper would have a fit if he knew what she was doing. "I can be ready in about twenty minutes."

"I'll see you there." He stepped aside, and she could feel him studying her as she moved back toward her cart. What was the matter with her? She had never done anything as impulsive as agreeing to meet a stranger for coffee.

Finished for the day, Claudia returned the cart to Mrs. Burns, who thanked her for helping out again. Next she made a stop in the ladies' room. One glance in the mirror made her groan at her reflection. Her hair was an unruly auburn mass. She took the brush from her purse and ran it through her long curls until they practically sparked with electricity. Her thick, naturally curly hair had always been a problem. For several years now she had kept it long and tied away from her face with a ribbon at the base of her neck. When she first applied and was accepted into medical school, she'd been determined to play down her femininity. Women weren't the rarity they once were, but she didn't want her gender, combined with her money, to prejudice any of her classmates against her. There had been some tension her first year, but she had long since proved herself.

The coffee shop was crowded, but her searching gaze instantly located the stranger, who towered head and shoulders above everyone else. Even when he was sitting down, his large, imposing build couldn't be disguised. Weaving her way between chairs, she sauntered toward him.

The welcome in his smile warmed her. He stood and pulled out a chair for her. She noticed that he chose the one beside him, as if he wanted her as close as possible. The thought didn't disturb her, but her reaction to him did. She wanted to be close to him.

"I suddenly realized I don't know your name," she said after sitting down.

"Seth Lessinger." He lifted a thick eyebrow in silent inquiry. "And yours?"

"Claudia Masters."

"I'm surprised they don't call you Red with that hair."

In any other family she might well have been tagged with the nickname, but not in hers. "No, no one ever has." Her voice sounded strangely husky. To hide her discomfort, she lifted the menu and began studying it, although she didn't want anything more than coffee.

The waitress arrived, and Claudia placed her order, adding an English muffin at Seth's urging. He asked for a club sandwich.

"What brings you to Seattle?" Claudia asked once the waitress was gone. She found herself absently smoothing a wrinkle from the skirt.

"A conference."

"Are you enjoying the Emerald City?" She was making small talk to cover up her nervousness. Maybe meeting a strange man like this wasn't such a good idea after all.

"Very much. It's my first visit to the Northwest, and I'll admit, it's nicer than I expected. Big cities tend to intimidate me. I never have understood how anyone can live like this, surrounded by so many people."

Claudia didn't mean to smile, but amusement played at the edges of her mouth. "Where are you from? Alaska?" She'd meant it as a joke and was surprised when he nodded in confirmation.

"Nome," he supplied. "Where the air is pure and the skies are blue."

"You make it sound lovely."

"It's not," he told her with a half-smile. "It can be dingy and gray and miserable, but it's home."

Her coffee arrived, and she cupped the mug, grateful to have something to do with her hands.

He seemed to be studying her, and when their gazes clashed, a lazy smile flickered from the dark depths of his eyes.

"What do you do in Nome?" she asked to distract herself from the fact that his look was disturbingly like a gentle caress. Not that it made her uncomfortable; the effect was quite the opposite. He touched a softness in her, a longing to be the woman she had denied for so long.

"I'm a commissioning agent for a major oil company."

"That sounds interesting." She knew the words came out stiff and stilted.

"It's definitely the right job for me. What about you?"

"Student at the University of Washington." She didn't elaborate.

A frown creased the wide brow. "You look older than a college student."

She ignored that and focused her gaze on the black coffee. "How long will you be in Seattle?"

If he noticed she was disinclined to talk about herself, he didn't say anything. "I'll be flying back in a few days. I'd like to be home by the end of the week."

A few days, her mind echoed. She would remember to pray for him. She believed that God brought everyone into her life for a specific reason. The purpose of her meeting Seth might be for her to remember to pray for him. He certainly had made an impression on her.

"How long have you been a Christian?" he inquired.

"Five years." That was another thing Cooper had never understood. He found this "religious interest" of hers amusing. "And you?" Again she directed the conversation away from herself.

"Six months. I'm still an infant in the Lord, although my size disputes that!" He smiled, and Claudia felt mesmerized by the warmth in his eyes.

She returned his smile, suddenly aware that he was as defensive about his size as she was about her money and her brains.

"So why *did* you leave that Bible verse on the mirror?"

This was the crux of his wanting to talk to her. How could she explain? "Listen, I've already apologized for that. I realize it's probably against the motel policy."

A hand twice the size of her own reached over the table and trapped hers. "Claudia." The sound of her name was low-pitched and reassuring. "Don't apologize. Your message meant more to me than you can possibly realize. My intention is to thank you for it."

His dark, mysterious eyes studied hers. Again Claudia sensed more than saw a sadness, a loneliness, in him. She made a show of glancing at her watch. "I . . . I really should be going."

"Can I see you again? Tomorrow?"

She'd been afraid he was going to ask her that. And also afraid that he wouldn't.

"I was planning on doing some grocery shopping at the Pike Place Market tomorrow," she said without accepting or refusing.

"We could meet somewhere." His tone held a faint challenge. At the same time, he sounded almost unsure.

Claudia had the impression there wasn't much that unsettled this man. She wondered what it was about her that made him uncertain.

"All right," she found herself agreeing. "But I feel I'd better warn you, if you find large cities stifling, downtown Seattle at that time of the day may be an experience you'd rather avoid."

"Not this time," he said with a chuckle.

They set a time and place as Seth walked her back to the motel lot, where she'd left her car. She drove a silver compact, even though Cooper had generously given her a fancy sports car when she was accepted into medical school. She'd never driven it around campus and kept it in one of Cooper's garages. Not that she didn't appreciate the gift. The car was beautiful, and a dream to drive, but she already had her compact and couldn't see the need for two cars. Not when one of them would make her stand out and draw unnecessary and unwanted attention. Never had she been more grateful for the decision she'd made than she was now, though. At least she wouldn't have to explain to Seth why a hotel housekeeper was driving a car that cost as much as she made in a year.

"Hi," Claudia said later as she floated into the apartment, a Cheshire Cat grin on her face.

"Wow!" Ashley exclaimed from the sofa. "You look like you've just met Prince Charming."

"I have." Claudia dropped her purse on the end table and sat on the sofa arm opposite the end where Ashley was resting. "He's about this tall." She held her hand high above her head. "With shoulders this wide." She held her hands out ridiculously wide to demonstrate. "And he has the most incredible dark eyes."

"Oh, honestly, Claudia, that's not Prince Charming. That's the Incredible Hulk," Ashley admonished.

Claudia tilted her head to one side, a slow smile spreading over her mouth. "'Incredible' is the word, all right."

———

Not until the following morning, when Claudia dressed in her best designer jeans and cashmere sweater, with knee-high leather boots, did Ashley take her seriously.

"You really did meet someone yesterday, didn't you?"

Claudia nodded, pouring steaming cocoa into a mug. "Want some?"

"Sure," Ashley said, then hesitated. "When did you have the chance? The only place you've been is school and"—she paused, her blue eyes widening—"the Wilderness and back. Claudia," she gasped, "it isn't someone from the motel, is it?"

Two pieces of toast blasted from the toaster with the force of a skyrocket. Deftly Claudia caught them in the air. "Yup."

For the first time in recent history, Ashley was speechless. "But, Claudia, you can't . . . I mean . . . all kinds of people stay there. He could be *anyone* . . ."

"Seth isn't just anyone. He *is* a big guy, but he's gentle and kind. And I like him."

"I can tell," Ashley murmured with a worried look pinching her face.

"Don't look so shocked. Women have met men in stranger ways. I'm seeing him this afternoon. I told him I have some grocery shopping to do." When she saw the glare Ashley was giving her, Claudia felt obliged to add, "Well, I do. I wanted to pick up some fresh vegetables. I was just reading an article on the importance of fiber in the diet."

"We bought a whole month's worth of food last Saturday," Ashley mumbled under her breath.

"True." Claudia shrugged, then picked up a light

jacket. "But I think we could use some fresh produce. I'll be sure and pick up some prunes for you."

Seth was standing on the library steps waiting when Claudia arrived. Again she noted his compelling male virility. She waited at the bottom of the stairs for him to join her. The balmy September breeze coming off Puget Sound teased her hair, blowing auburn curls across her cheek. He paused, standing in front of her, his eyes smiling deeply into hers.

The mesmerizing quality of his gaze held her motionless. Her hand was halfway to her face to remove the lock of maverick hair, but it, too, was frozen by the warmth in his look, which seemed to reach out and caress her. She had neither the will nor the desire to glance away.

The rough feel of his callused hand removing the hair brought her out of the trance. "Hello, Claudia."

"Seth."

"You're beautiful." The words appeared to come involuntarily.

"So are you," she joked. The musky scent of his aftershave drifted pleasantly toward her, and an unwilling sigh broke from between her slightly parted lips.

Someone on the busy sidewalk bumped into Claudia, throwing her off balance. Immediately Seth reached out protectively and pulled her close. The iron band of his arm continued to hold her against him far longer than necessary. His touch warmed her through the thin jacket. No man had ever been able to awaken this kind of feeling in her. This was uncanny, unreal.

Two

"Are you ready to call it quits?" Claudia asked. Seth had placed a guiding hand on her shoulder, and she wondered how long his touch would continue to produce the warm, glowing sensation spreading down her spine.

"More than ready," he confirmed.

The Pike Place Market in the heart of downtown Seattle had always been a hub of activity as tourists and everyday shoppers vied for the attention of the vendors displaying their wares. The two of them had strolled through the market, their hands entwined. Vegetables that had been hand-picked that morning were displayed on long tables, while the farmers shouted their virtues, enticing customers to their booths. The odd but pleasant smell of tangy spices and fresh fish had drifted agreeably around them.

"I did warn you," she said with a small laugh. "What's the life expectancy of someone from Nome, Alaska, in a crowd like this?"

Seth glanced at his watch. "About two hours," he said. "And we've been at it nearly that. Let's take a break."

"I agree."

"Lunch?"

Claudia nodded. She hadn't eaten after her last class,

hurrying instead to meet Seth. Now she realized she was hungry. "Sounds good."

"Chinese okay?"

For once it was a pleasure to have someone take her out and not try to impress her with the best restaurant in town, or how much money he could spend. "Yes, that's fine."

He paused. "You sure?"

She squeezed his hand. "Very sure. And I know just the place."

They rode the city bus to Seattle's International District and stepped off into another world. Seth looked around in surprise. "I didn't know Seattle had a Chinatown."

"Chinatown, Little Italy, Mexico, all within a few blocks. Interesting, isn't it?"

"Very."

They lingered over their tea, delaying as long as possible their return to the hectic pace of the world outside.

"Why do you have a beard?" Claudia asked curiously. She didn't mean to be abrupt, but his beard fascinated her—it looked so soft—and the question slipped out before she could stop herself.

Seth looked surprised by the question, rubbing the dark hair in question with one hand as he spoke. "Does it bother you? I can always shave it off."

"Oh, no," she protested instantly. "I like it. Very much. But I've always been curious why some men choose to grow their beards."

"I can't speak for anyone else, but my beard offers

some protection to my face during the long winter months," he explained.

His quick offer to shave it off had shocked Claudia with the implication that he would do it for her. She couldn't understand his eagerness.

"I've about finished my shopping. What about you?" She hated to torture him further.

The tiny teacup was dwarfed by his massive hands. "I was finished a long time ago."

"Want to take a walk along the waterfront and ride the trolley?" she suggested, looking for reasons to prolong their time together.

"I'd like that."

While Seth paid for their meal she excused herself to reapply her lipstick and comb her hair. Then, hand in hand, they walked the short distance back to the heart of downtown Seattle. They paused in front of a department store to study a window display in autumn colors.

Her eyes were laughing into his when he placed a possessive hand around her waist, drawing her close to his side. Then they stepped away from the window and started down the street toward the waterfront.

It was then that Claudia spotted Cooper walking on the opposite side of the street. Even from this distance she could see his disapproving scowl, and she felt the blood drain from her face. The differences between these two men were so striking that to make a comparison struck her as ludicrous.

"I'll get us a taxi," Seth suggested, his eyes showing concern. "I've been walking your legs off." Apparently he thought her pale face was the result of the brisk pace he'd set.

"No, I'd rather walk," she insisted, and reached for his hand. "If we hurry, we can make this light."

Their hands were still linked when she began to run toward the corner. There had never been any chance of their reaching the crosswalk before the light changed, but even so, she hurried between the busy shoppers.

"Claudia." Seth stopped, placing his arm over her shoulders, his wide brow creased with concern. "What's the matter?"

"Nothing," she said hesitantly, looking around. She was certain Cooper had seen them, and she didn't want him to ruin things. "Really, let's go." Her voice was raised and anxious.

"Claudia."

Cooper's voice coming from behind her stopped her heart.

"Introduce me to your friend," he said in a crisp, businesslike tone.

Frustration washed over her. Cooper would take one look at Seth and condemn him as one of the fortune hunters he was always warning her about.

"Cooper Masters, this is Seth Lessinger." She made the introduction grudgingly.

The two men eyed each other shrewdly while exchanging handshakes.

"Masters," Seth repeated. "Are you related to Claudia?"

Cooper ignored the question, instead turning toward Claudia. "I'll pick you up for dinner Sunday at about two. If that's convenient?"

"It was fine last week and the week before, so why should it be any different this week?"

Her uncle flashed her an impatient glance.

"Who is this man?" Seth asked, the look in his eyes almost frightening. Anger darkened his face. He dropped his hand to his side, and she noted how his fist was clenched until his knuckles turned white.

Claudia watched, stunned. *He thinks I'm Cooper's wife.* Placing a hand on his forearm, she implored, "Seth, let me explain."

He shook his arm free. "You don't need to say anything more. I understand. Do you do this kind of thing often? Is this how you get your thrills?"

For a moment she was speechless, the muscles of her throat paralyzed with anger. "You don't understand. Cooper's my uncle."

"And I believe in Santa Claus," Seth returned sarcastically.

"I've warned you about men like this," Cooper said at the same time.

"Will you please be quiet!" she shouted at him.

"There's no excuse for you to talk to me in such a tone," Cooper countered in a huff.

People were beginning to stare, but she didn't care. "He really is my uncle." Desperately her eyes pleaded with Seth, asking for understanding and the chance to explain. *His* eyes were dark, clouded and unreasonable.

"You don't want to hear, do you?" she asked him.

"We definitely need to have a discussion, Claudia," Cooper interrupted again.

"You're right, I don't." Seth took a step away from her.

Claudia breathed in sharply, the rush of oxygen making her lungs hurt. She bit her lip as Seth turned and walked away. His stride was filled with purpose, as if he couldn't get away from her fast enough.

"You've really done it this time," she flared at her uncle.

"Really, Claudia," he said with a relieved look. "That type of man is most undesirable."

"That man"—she pointed at Seth's retreating figure — "is one of the most desirable men I've ever known." Without waiting for his response, she turned and stalked away.

An hour later, Claudia was banging pans around in the kitchen. Ashley came through the front door and paused, watching her for a moment. "What's wrong?"

"Nothing," Claudia responded tersely.

"Oh, come on. I always know when you're upset, because you bake something."

"That's so I can eat it."

Ashley scanned the ingredients that lined the counter. "Chocolate chip cookies," she murmured. "This must really be bad. I'm guessing you had another run-in with Cooper?"

"Right again," Claudia snapped.

"You don't want to talk about it?"

"That's a brilliant deduction." With unnecessary force, she cracked two eggs against the mixing bowl.

"You want me to quit interrogating you, huh?"

Claudia paused, closing her eyes as the waves of impatience rippled over her. "Yes, please."

"All right, all right. I'm leaving."

Soon the aroma of freshly baked cookies filled the apartment, though Claudia didn't notice. Almost automatically she lifted the cookies from the baking sheet and placed them on a wire rack to cool.

"I can't stand it anymore." Ashley stumbled into the kitchen dramatically. "If you don't want to talk, fine, but at least let me have a cookie."

Claudia sighed, placed four on a plate and set it on the kitchen table.

Ashley poured herself a tall glass of milk and sat down, her eyes following Claudia's movements. "Feel like talking now?" she asked several minutes later. There was a sympathetic tone in her voice that came from many years of friendship.

Ashley had been Claudia's only friend as a child. Ashley's mother had been Claude Masters's cook and housekeeper, and she had brought her daughter with her to keep the lonely Claudia company. The two of them had been best friends ever since.

"It's Seth," Claudia admitted and sighed, taking a chair opposite Ashley.

"Seth? Oh, the guy you met at the motel. What happened?"

"We ran into Cooper, and he had a fit of righteous indignation over seeing me with someone who wasn't wearing a business suit and a silk tie. To complicate matters, Seth apparently thought Cooper and I were married, or at least used to be. He didn't wait for an explanation."

Ashley's look was thoughtful. "You really like him, don't you?"

Claudia worried the soft flesh of her bottom lip. "Yes," she said simply. "I like him very much."

"If he's so arrogant that he wouldn't wait for you to

explain, then I'd say it was his loss," Ashley said, attempting to comfort her.

"No." Claudia shook her head and lowered her gaze to the tabletop. "In this case, I think I'm the one who lost."

"I don't think I've ever heard you talk this way about a man. What makes him so special?"

Claudia's brow furrowed in concentration. "I'm not really sure. He's more attractive than any man I can remember, but it's not his looks. Or not only his looks, anyway." She smiled. "He's a rare man." She paused to formulate her thoughts. "Strong and intelligent."

"You know all this and you've only seen him twice?" Ashley sounded shocked.

"No." Claudia hung her head, and her long auburn curls fell forward to hide her expression. "I sensed more than I saw, and even then, I'm only skimming the surface. This man is deep."

"If he's so willing to jump to conclusions, I'd say it's his own fault—"

"Ashley, please," Claudia interrupted. "Don't. I know you're trying to make me feel better, but I'd appreciate it if you didn't."

"All right." Ashley was quiet for a long time. After a while she took a chocolate chip cookie and handed it to Claudia.

With a weak smile, Claudia accepted the cookie. "Now, that's what I need."

They talked for a while, but it wasn't until they headed into the living room that Claudia noticed Ashley's suitcase in front of the door.

"You're going away?"

"Oh, I almost forgot. I talked to Mom this morning, and she wants me home for a few days. Jeff and John have the flu, and she needs someone there so she can go to work. I shouldn't be any more than a couple of days, and luckily I'm not on the schedule to work until the weekend. You don't mind, do you?"

"Not at all," Claudia said with a smile. Although Ashley's family lived in the nearby suburb of Kent, Ashley shared the apartment with Claudia because it was easier for her to commute to school. But she occasionally moved back home for a few days when her family needed her.

"You're sure you'll be all right?"

"Are you kidding?" Claudia joked. "The kitchen's full of cookies!"

Ashley laughed, but her large blue eyes contained a knowing look. "Don't be too hard on Cooper," she said, and gave Claudia a small hug before she left.

What good would it do to be angry with her uncle? Claudia thought. He had reacted the only way he knew how. Anger wouldn't help the situation.

The apartment felt large and lonely with Ashley gone. Claudia turned on the television and flipped through the channels, hoping to find something interesting, feeling guilty because she was ignoring her schoolwork. Nothing interesting on. Good, she decided, and forced herself to hit the books. This quarter wasn't going to be easy, and the sooner she sharpened her study habits, the better.

Two hours later she took a leisurely bath, dressed in a long purple velour robe, curled up on the sofa and lost herself in a good book. Long ago she'd recognized that reading was her escape. When things were really bothering her, she would plow through one mystery after another, not really caring about the characters or the plot so long as the book was complicated enough to distract her from her troubles.

The alarm rang at six, and she stumbled out of bed, then stepped into the shower. As she stood under the hot spray, her thoughts drifted to Seth Lessinger. She felt definitely regretful at the way things had ended. She would have liked to get to know him better. On Sunday she would definitely have a talk with Cooper. She was old enough to choose who she wanted to date without his interference. It was bad enough being forced to endure a stilted dinner with him every Sunday afternoon.

She dressed in jeans, a long-sleeved blouse, and a red sweater vest. As she poured herself a cup of coffee, she wondered how long she would have to force thoughts of Seth from her mind. The mystery novel had diverted her attention last night, but she couldn't live her life with her nose in a book. Today and tomorrow she would be busy with school, but this was Thursday, and she wasn't looking forward to spending the evenings and weekend alone. She decided to ask a friend in her psych class if she wanted to go to a movie tonight.

She sat sipping from her mug at the kitchen table, her feet propped on the opposite chair, and read the morning paper. A quick look at her watch and she placed the cup in the sink and hurried out the door for school.

Claudia pulled into the apartment parking lot early that afternoon. It seemed everyone had already made plans for this evening, so she was on her own. Several of her friends were attending the Seahawks game. She loved football, and decided to microwave popcorn and watch the game on television. She had no sooner let herself into the apartment and hung up her jacket when the doorbell rang.

The peephole in the door showed an empty hall. Odd, but it could be her neighbor's son collecting for the jogathon. Claudia had sponsored the ten-year-old, who was trying to earn enough money for a soccer uniform. Todd had probably seen her pull into the parking lot. She opened the door and looked out into the hallway.

"Claudia?" There was surprise in his tone as he stepped away from the wall he'd been leaning on.

"Seth." Her heart tripped over itself.

"What are you doing here?" they both asked at the same time.

Claudia smiled. It was so good to see him, it didn't matter what had brought him here.

"I was looking for Ashley Robbins, the motel maid," he told her.

"Ashley?" Her curiosity was evident in her voice. "Come in," she said, then closed the door after him. "Ashley's gone home for a few days to help out her parents. Do you know her?"

"No." He stroked the side of his beard. "But I was hoping she could tell me how to find you."

"We're roommates," she explained, no doubt unnecessarily. "So . . . you were looking for me? Why?"

He looked slightly ill at ease. "I wanted to apologize for yesterday. I could at least have stayed and listened to your explanation."

"Cooper really is my uncle."

"I should have known you wouldn't lie. It wasn't until later that I realized I'd behaved like an idiot," he said, his face tight and drawn. "If I hadn't reacted like a jealous fool, I would have realized you would never lead anyone on like that."

"I know what you thought." She paused and glanced away. "And I know how it looked—how Cooper wanted it to look."

Seth ran a hand over his face. "Your uncle." He chuckled. Wrapping his arms around her, he lifted her off the ground and swung her around. Hands resting on the hard muscles of his shoulders, she threw back her head and laughed.

Soon the amusement died as their gazes met and held. Slowly he released her until her feet had securely settled on the carpet. With infinite gentleness, his hand brushed her face, caressing her smooth skin. It was so beautiful, so sweet, that she closed her eyes to the sensuous assault. Her fingers clung to his arms as he drew her into his embrace, and her lips trembled, anticipating his kiss.

Seth didn't disappoint either of them as his mouth settled firmly over hers. His hand slid down her back, molding her against him, arching her upward to meet the demand of his kiss.

Claudia felt her limbs grow weak as she surrendered to the sensations swirling inside her. Her hands spread over his chest, feeling she belonged there in his arms.

When he freed her mouth, his lips caressed the sensitive cord along the side of her neck.

"Does this mean you'll give me another chance?" he murmured, his voice faintly husky from the effects of the kiss.

"I'd say the prognosis is excellent," she replied, her breathing still affected. "But I'd like to explain a few things."

She led the way into the kitchen, poured mugs of coffee and added sugar to his the way she'd seen him do.

When she set his cup on the table, Seth reached for her hand and kissed her fingers. "Your family has money?" he asked.

"Yes, but I don't," she explained. "At least not yet. Cooper controls the purse strings for a little while longer. My father was Claude Masters. You may or may not have heard of him. He established a business supply corporation that has branch offices in five states. Dad died when I was in high school. Cooper is president of the company now, and my legal guardian." Her soft mouth quirked to one side. "He takes his responsibility seriously. I apologize if he offended you yesterday."

Humor glinted briefly in his expression. "The only thing that could possibly offend me is if you were married." He laughed, and she stared at him curiously. "I'll never wear five-hundred-dollar business suits. You understand that?"

Nodding, she smiled. "I can't imagine you in a suit at all."

"Oh, I've been known to wear one, but I hate it."

Again she smiled.

"Do you hate having money?" He was regarding her steadily, his wide brow creased.

"No," she replied honestly. "I like having money when I need it. What I hate is being different from others, like Ashley and you. I have a hard time trusting people. I'm never really sure whether they like *me*. I find myself looking at any relationship with a jaundiced eye, wondering what the other person is expecting to receive from my friendship." She lowered her gaze, her fingers circling the top of the mug. "My father was the same way, and it made him close himself off from the world. I was brought up in a protected environment. I fought tooth and nail to convince Cooper I should attend the University of Washington. He wanted to send me to study at a private university in Switzerland."

"I'm glad you're here."

Claudia watched as Seth clenched and unclenched his hands.

"Do you think the reason I came back is because I figured out you have money?" he finally asked.

Something in his voice conveyed the seriousness of the question. "No, I don't think you're the type of person to be impressed by wealth. Just knowing you this little while, I believe if you wanted money, you'd have it. You're that type of man." Having stated her feelings, she fell silent.

"God gives the very best." The throaty whisper was barely discernible, and she glanced up, her blue eyes questioning.

"Pardon?"

Seth took her hand and carried it to his lips. The coarse hairs of his beard prickled her fingertips. "Nothing," he murmured. "I'll explain it to you later."

"I skipped lunch and I'm hungry, so I was going to fix myself a sandwich. Would you like one?" she offered.

"I would. In fact, you don't even need to ask. I'm always hungry. Let me help," he volunteered. "Believe it or not, I'm a darn good cook."

"You can slice the cheese if you like." She flashed him a happy smile.

"I hope you don't have any plans for the evening," he said, easing a knife through the slab of cheese. "I've got tickets for the game. The Seahawks are playing tonight, and I . . ." He paused, his look brooding, disconcerted.

"What's wrong?"

He sighed, walked to the other side of the small kitchen and stuck his huge hands inside his pants pockets. "Football isn't much of a woman's sport, is it?"

"What makes you say that?"

"I mean . . ." He looked around uneasily. "You don't have to go. It's not that important. I know that someone like you isn't—"

She didn't give him the chance to finish. "Someone like me," she repeated, "would love going to that game." Her eyes were smiling into his.

Amusement dominated his face as he slid his arms around her waist. One hand toyed with a strand of her hair. "We'll eat a sandwich now, then grab something for dinner after the game. All right, Red?" He said the name as if it were an endearment. "You don't mind if I call you that, do you?"

"Only you," she murmured just before his mouth claimed hers. "Only you."

The day was wonderful. They spent two hours talking almost nonstop. Claudia, who normally didn't drink more than a cup or two of coffee, shared two pots with Seth. She told him things she had never shared with anyone: her feelings during her father's short illness and after his death; the ache, the void in her life, afterward; and how the loss and the sadness had led her to Christ. She told him about her lifelong friendship with Ashley, the mother she had never known, medical school and her struggle for acceptance. There didn't seem to be anything she couldn't discuss with him.

In return he talked about his oil business, life in Nome, and his own faith.

Before they knew it, it was time to get going. Claudia hurried to freshen up, but took the time to spray a light perfume at her pulse points. After running a comb through the unruly curls that framed her face, she tied them back at the base of her neck with a silk scarf. Seth was waiting for her in the living room. Checking her appearance one last time, she noted the happy sparkle in her eyes and paused to murmur a special thank-you that God had sent Seth back into her life.

Seth helped her into her jacket. Then he lovingly ran a rough hand up and down her arm as he brought her even closer to his side.

"I don't know when I've enjoyed an afternoon more," he told her. "Thank you."

"I should be the one to thank you, Seth." She avoided eye contact, afraid how much her look would reveal.

"I knew the minute I saw you that you were someone very special. I didn't realize until today how right my hunch was." He looked down at her gently. "It wasn't so long ago that I believed Christians were a bunch of do-gooders. Not long ago that I thought religion was for the weak-minded. But I didn't know people like you. Now I wonder how I managed to live my life without Christ."

Claudia tugged at Seth's hand as she excitedly walked

up the concrete ramp of the Kingdome. "The game's about to start." They'd parked on the street, then walked the few blocks to the stadium, hurrying up First Avenue. The traffic was so heavy that they were a few minutes later than planned.

"I love football," she said, her voice high with enthusiasm.

"Look at all these people." Seth stopped and looked around in amazement.

"Seth," she groaned. "I don't want to miss the kickoff."

Because the game was being televised nationwide, the kickoff was slated for five o'clock Pacific time. More than sixty thousand fans filled the Kingdome to capacity. Seahawk fever ran high, and the entire stadium was on its feet for the kickoff. In the beginning she only applauded politely so she wouldn't embarrass Seth with her enthusiasm. But when it came to her favorite sport, no one could accuse her of being unemotional. Within minutes she was totally involved with the action on the field. She cheered wildly when the Seahawks made a good play, then shouted at the officials in protest of any call she thought was unfair.

Seth's behavior was much more subdued, and several times when she complained to him about a call, she found that he seemed to be watching her more closely than the game.

There was something about football that allowed her to be herself, something that broke down her natural reserve. With her class schedule, she couldn't often afford the time to attend a game. But if at all possible she watched on TV, jumping on the furniture in exaltation, pounding the couch cushions in despair. Most of her classmates wouldn't have believed it was her. At school she was serious, all about the work, since she still felt the need to prove herself to her classmates. Although she had won respect from most of the other students, a few still believed her name and money were the only reasons she had been accepted.

"Touchdown!" Her arms flew into the air, and she leaped to her feet.

For the first time since the game had started, Seth showed as much emotion as she did. Lifting her high, he held her tight against him. Her hands framed his face, and it seemed the most natural thing in the world, as she stared into his dark, hungry eyes, to press her lips to his. Immediately he deepened the kiss, wrapping his arms around her, lifting her higher off the ground.

The cheering died to an excited chatter before either of them was aware of the crowd.

"We have an audience," he murmured huskily in her ear.

"It's just as well, don't you think?" Her face was flushed lightly. She had known almost from the beginning that the attraction between them was stronger than anything she had experienced with another man. Seth seemed to have recognized that, as well. The effect they had on each other was strong and disturbing. He had kissed her only three times, and already they were aware of how easy it would be to let their attraction rage out of control. It was exciting, but it was also frightening.

———

After the game—which the Seahawks won—they stopped for hamburgers. When Seth had finished his meal, he returned to the counter and bought them each an ice cream sundae.

"When you come to Alaska, I'll have my Inuit friends make you some of their ice cream," he said. His eyes flashed her a look of amusement.

Claudia's stomach tightened. *When* she came to Alaska? She hadn't stopped to think about visiting America's last frontier. From the beginning she had known that Seth would be in Seattle for only a few days. She had known and accepted that as best she could.

Deciding it was best to ignore the comment, she cocked her head to one side. "Okay, I'll play your little game. What's Inuit ice cream?"

"Berries, snow, and rancid seal oil."

"Well, at least it's organic."

Seth chuckled. "It's that, all right."

Claudia twisted the red plastic spoon, making circles in the soft ice cream. She avoided Seth's gaze, just as she had been eluding facing the inevitable.

Gathering her resolve, hoping maybe his plans had changed, she raised her face, her eyes meeting his. "When will you be returning to Nome?"

He pushed his dessert aside, his hand reaching for hers. "My flight's booked for tomorrow afternoon."

Three

The muscles of Claudia's throat constricted. "Tomorrow," she repeated, knowing she sounded like a parrot. Lowering her gaze, she continued, "That doesn't leave us much time, does it?" She'd thought she was prepared. After all, she reminded herself yet again, she'd known from the beginning that Seth would only be in Seattle for a few days.

Lifting her eyes to his watchful gaze, she offered Seth a weak smile. "I know this sounds selfish, but I don't want you to go."

"Then I won't," he announced casually.

Her head shot up. "What do you mean?"

The full force of his magnetic gaze was resting on her. "I mean I'll stay a few more days."

Her heart seemed to burst into song. "Over the weekend?" Eyes as blue as the Caribbean implored him. "My only obligation is dinner Sunday with Cooper, but you could come. In fact, I'd like it if you did. My uncle will probably bore you to tears, but I'd like you to get to know each other. Will you stay that long?" She tilted her head questioningly, hopefully.

Seth chuckled. She loved his laugh. The loud, robust sound seemed to roll from deep within his chest. She'd watched him during the football game and couldn't help laughing with him.

"Will you?" she repeated.

"I have the feeling your uncle isn't going to welcome me with open arms."

"No." She smiled beguilingly. "But I will."

The restaurant seemed to go still. Seth's gaze was penetrating, his voice slightly husky. "Then I'll stay, but no longer than Monday."

"Okay." She was more than glad, she was jubilant. There hadn't been time to question this magnetic attraction that had captured them, and deep down she didn't want to investigate her feelings, even though she knew this was all happening too fast.

Seth slipped his arm around her waist as they walked to the car. He held open the door for her and waited until she was seated. Unconsciously she smoothed the leather seat cushion, the texture smooth against the tips of her fingers. The vehicle had surprised her. Seth didn't fit the luxury-car image, but she hadn't mentioned it earlier, before the game.

"This thing *is* a bit much, isn't it?" His gaze briefly scanned the interior. The high-end sedan was fitted with every convenience, from the automatic sunroof to a satellite sound system to built-in Bluetooth technology.

"So why did you rent it?" she felt obliged to ask.

"Why did I—heavens, no! This is all part of the sisters' efforts to get me to sign the contract."

"The sisters?"

"That's a slang expression for the major oil conglomerates. They seem to feel the need to impress me. They originally had me staying at one of those big downtown hotels, in a suite that was over seven hundred dollars a night. I didn't feel comfortable with that and found my own place. But I couldn't refuse the car without offending some important people."

"We all get caught in that trap sometimes."

Seth agreed with a short, preoccupied nod. Although the game had finished over an hour earlier, the downtown traffic was at a standstill. Cautiously he eased the car into the heavy flow of bumper-to-bumper traffic.

While they were caught in the snarl of impatient drivers, Claudia studied his strong profile. Several times his mouth tightened, and he shook his head in disgust.

"I'm sorry, Seth," she said solemnly, and smiled lamely when he glanced at her.

He arched his thick brows. "You're sorry? Why?"

"The traffic. I should have known to wait another hour, until things had thinned out a bit more."

"It's not your fault." His enormous hand squeezed hers reassuringly.

"Don't you have traffic jams in Nome?" she asked, partly to keep the conversation flowing, and partly to counteract the crazy reaction her heart seemed to have every time he touched her.

"Traffic jams in Nome?" He smiled. "Red, Nome's population is under four thousand. Some days my car is the only one on the road."

Her eyes narrowed suspiciously. "You're teasing? I thought Nome was a major city."

He laughed as he returned both hands to the wheel, and her heartbeat relaxed. "The population of the entire state is only 700,000, a fraction of Washington's nearly seven million." A smile softened his rugged features. "Anchorage is the largest city in Alaska, with under 300,000 residents."

An impatient motorist honked, and Seth pulled forward onto the freeway entrance ramp. The traffic remained heavy but finally it was at least moving at a steady pace.

"I couldn't live like this," he said and expelled his breath forcefully. "Too many people, too many buildings, and," he added with a wry grin, "too many cars."

"Don't worry. You won't have to put up with it much longer," she countered with a smile that she hoped didn't look as forced as it felt.

Seth scowled thoughtfully and didn't reply.

He parked the car in the lot outside her apartment building and refused her invitation to come in for coffee. "I have a meeting in the morning, but it shouldn't go any longer than noon. Can I see you then?"

She nodded, pleased. "Of course." She would treasure every minute she had left with him. "Shall I phone Cooper and tell him you're coming for dinner Sunday?"

"He won't mind?"

"Oh, I'm sure he will, but if he objects too strongly, we'll have our own dinner."

He reached out to caress the delicate curve of her cheek and entwined his fingers with the auburn curls along the nape of her neck. "Would it be considered bad manners to hope he objects strenuously?" he asked.

"Cooper's not so bad." She felt as if she should at least make the effort to explain her uncle. "I don't think he means to come off so pompous, he just doesn't know how else to act. What he needs is a woman to love." She smiled inwardly. "I can just hear him cough and sputter if I were to tell him that."

"*I* need a woman to love," Seth whispered as his mouth found hers. The kiss was deep and intense, as if to convince her of the truth of his words.

Claudia wound her arms around his neck, surrendering to the mastery of his kiss. *He's serious*, her mind repeated. *Dead serious*. The whole world seemed right when he was holding her like this. He covered her neck and the hollow of her throat with light, tiny kisses. She tilted her head to give him better access, reveling in the warm feel of his lips against the creamy smoothness of her skin. A shudder of desire ran through her, and she bit into her bottom lip to conceal the effect he had on her senses.

Taking a deep breath, he straightened. "Let's get you inside before this gets out of hand." His voice sounded raw and slightly uneven.

He kissed her again outside her apartment door, but this kiss lacked the ardor of a few minutes earlier. "I'll see you about noon tomorrow."

With a trembling smile she nodded.

"Don't look at me like that," he groaned. His strong hands stroked the length of her arms as he edged her body closer. "It's difficult enough to say good night."

Standing on tiptoe, she lightly brushed her mouth over his.

"Claudia," he growled in warning.

She placed her fingertips over her moist lips, then over his, to share the mock kiss with him.

He closed his eyes as if waging some deep inner battle, then covered her fingers with his own.

"Good night," she whispered, glorying in the way he reacted to her.

"I'll see you tomorrow."

"Tomorrow," she repeated dreamily.

Dressed in her pajamas and bathrobe, Claudia sat on top of her bed an hour later, reading her Bible. Her concentration drifted to the events of the past week and all the foreign emotions she had encountered. This thing with Seth was happening too fast, far too fast. No man had ever evoked such an intensity of emotion within her. No man had made her feel the things he did. Love, real love, didn't happen like this. The timing was all wrong. She couldn't fall in love—not now. Not with a man who was only going to be in Seattle for a few more days. But why had God sent Seth into her life when it would be so easy to fall in love with him? Was it a test? A lesson in faith? She was going to be a doctor. The Lord had led her to that decision, and there wasn't anything in her life she was more sure of. Falling in love with Seth Lessinger could ruin that. Still troubled, she turned off the light and attempted to sleep.

Claudia was ready at noon, but for what she wasn't sure. Dressed casually in jeans and a sweater, she thought she might suggest a drive to Snoqualmie Falls. And if Seth felt ambitious, maybe a hike around Mount Si. She didn't have the time to do much hiking herself, but she enjoyed the outdoors whenever possible. The mental picture of idly strolling with Seth, appreciating the beautiful world

God had provided, was an appealing one. Of course, doing anything with Seth was appealing.

When he hadn't shown up or called by one, she started to get worried. Every minute seemed interminable, and she glanced at her watch repeatedly. When the phone rang at one-thirty, she grabbed the receiver before it had a chance to ring again.

"Hello?" she said anxiously.

"Red?" Seth asked.

"Yes, it's me." He didn't sound right; he seemed tired, impatient.

"I've been held up here. There's not much chance of my getting out of this meeting until late afternoon."

"Oh." She tried to hide the disappointment in her voice.

"I know, honey, I feel the same way." The depth of his tone relayed his own frustration. "I'll make it up to you tonight. Can you be ready around seven for dinner? Wear something fancy."

"Sure." She forced a cheerful note into her voice. "I'll see you then. Take care."

"I've got to get back inside. If you happen to think of me, say a prayer. I want this business over so we can enjoy what's left of our time."

If she thought of him? She nearly laughed out loud. "I will," she promised, knowing it was a promise she would have no trouble keeping.

Cooper phoned about ten minutes later. "You left a message for me to call?" he began.

Claudia half suspected that he expected her to apologize for the little scene downtown with Seth. "Yes," she replied evenly. "I'm inviting a guest for dinner Sunday."

"Who?" he asked, and she could almost picture him bracing himself because he knew the answer.

"Seth Lessinger. You already met him once this week."

The line seemed to crackle with a lengthy silence. "As you wish," he said tightly.

A mental picture formed of Cooper writing down Seth's name. Undoubtedly, before Sunday, her uncle would know everything there was to know about Seth, from his birth weight to his high school grade point average.

"We'll see you then."

"Claudia," Cooper said, then hesitated. Her uncle didn't often hesitate. Usually he knew his mind and wasn't afraid to speak it. "You're not serious about this"—he searched for the right word—"man, are you?"

"Why?" It felt good to turn the tables, answering her cagey uncle with a question of her own. Why should he be so concerned? She was old enough to do anything she pleased.

He allowed an unprecedented second pause. "No reason. I'll see you Sunday."

Thoughtfully she replaced the receiver and released her breath in a slow sigh. Cooper had sounded different, on edge, not like his normal self at all. Her mouth quivered with a suppressed smile. He was worried; she'd heard it in his voice. For the first time since he'd been appointed her guardian, he had showed some actual feelings toward her. The smile grew. Maybe he wasn't such a bad guy after all.

Scanning the contents of her closet later that afternoon, Claudia chose a black lace dress she had bought on impulse the winter before. It wasn't the type of dress she would wear to church, although it wasn't low-cut or revealing. It was made of Cluny lace and had a three-tiered skirt. She had seen it displayed in an exclusive boutique and hadn't been able to resist, though she was angry with herself afterward for buying something so extravagant. She was unlikely to find a reason to wear such an elegant dress, but she loved it anyway. Even Ashley had been surprised when Claudia had showed it to her. No one could deny that it was a beautiful, romantic dress.

She arranged her auburn curls into a loose chignon at the top of her head, with tiny ringlets falling at the sides of her face. The diamond earrings she popped in had been her mother's, and Claudia had worn them only a couple of times. Seth had said fancy, though, so he was going to get fancy!

He arrived promptly at seven. One look at her and his eyes showed surprise, then something else she couldn't decipher.

Slowly his gaze traveled over her face and figure, openly admiring the curves of her hips and her slender legs.

"Wow."

"Wow yourself," she returned, equally impressed. She'd seen him as a virile and intriguing man even without the rich dark wool suit. But now he was compelling, so attractive she could hardly take her eyes off him.

"Turn around. I want to look at you," he requested, his attention centered on her. His voice sounded ragged, as if seeing her had stolen away his breath.

Claudia did as he asked, slowly twirling around. "Now you."

"Me?" He looked stunned.

"You." She laughed, her hands directing his movements. Self-consciously he turned, his movements abrupt and awkward. "Where are we going?" she asked while she admired.

"The Space Needle." He took her coat out of her hands and held it open for her. She turned and slid her arms into the satin-lined sleeves. He guided it over her shoulders, and his hands lingered there as he brought her back against him. She heard him inhale sharply before kissing the gentle slope of her neck.

"Let's go," he murmured, "while I'm still able to resist other temptations."

Seth parked outside the Seattle Center, and they walked hand in hand toward the city's most famous landmark.

"Next summer we'll go to the Food Circus," she mentioned casually. If he could say things about her visiting Alaska, she could talk the same way to him.

Seth didn't miss a step, but his hand tightened over hers. "Why next summer? Why not now?"

"Because you've promised me dinner on top of the city, and I'm not about to let you out of that. But no one visiting Seattle should miss the Food Circus. I don't even know how many booths there are, all serving exotic dishes from all over the world. The worst part is having to make a decision. When Ashley and I go there, we each buy something different and divide it. That way we each get to taste more new things." She stopped talking and smiled. "I'm chattering, aren't I?"

"A little." She could hear the amusement in his voice.

The outside elevators whisked them up the Space Needle to the observation deck six-hundred-and-seven feet above the ground. The night was glorious, and brilliant lights illuminated the world below. Seth stood behind her, his arms looped over her shoulders, pulling her close.

"I think my favorite time to see this view is at night," she said. "I love watching all the lights. I've never stopped to wonder why the night lights enthrall me the way they do. But I think it's probably because Jesus told us we were the light of the world, and from up here I can see how much even one tiny light can illuminate."

"I hadn't thought of it like that," he murmured close to her ear. "But you have to remember I'm a new Christian. There are a lot of things I haven't discovered yet."

"That's wonderful, too."

"How do you mean?"

She shrugged lightly. "God doesn't throw all this knowledge and insight at us at once. He lets us digest it little by little, as we're able."

"Just as any loving father would do," Seth said quietly.

They stood for several minutes until a chill ran over Claudia's arms.

"Cold?" he questioned.

"Only a little. It's so lovely out here, I don't want to leave."

"It's beautiful, all right, but it's more the woman I'm with than the scenery."

"Thank you," she murmured, pleased by his words.

"You're blushing," he said as he turned her around to face him. "I don't believe it—you're blushing."

Embarrassed, she looked away. "Men don't usually say such romantic things to me."

"Why not? You're a beautiful woman. By now you must have heard those words a thousand times over."

"Not really." The color was creeping up her neck. "That's the floating bridge over there." She pointed into the distance, attempting to change the subject. "It's the largest concrete pontoon bridge in the world. It connects Mercer Island and Seattle."

"Claudia," Seth murmured, his voice dipping slightly, "you are a delight. If we weren't out here with the whole city looking on, I'd take you in my arms and kiss you senseless."

"Promises, promises," she teased and hurried inside before he could make good on his words.

They ate a leisurely meal and talked over coffee for so long that she looked around guiltily. Friday night was one of the busiest nights for the restaurant business, and they were taking up a table another couple could be using.

"I'll make us another cup at my place," she volunteered.

Seth didn't argue.

The aroma of fresh-brewed coffee filled the apartment. Claudia poured two cups and carried them into the living room.

Seth was sitting on the long green couch, flipping through the pages of one of the medical journals she had stacked on the end table.

"Are you planning on specializing?"

She nodded. "Yes, pediatrics."

His dark brown eyes became intent. "Do you enjoy children that much, Red?"

"Oh, yes," she said fervently. "Maybe it's because I was an only child and never had enough other kids around. I can remember lining up my dolls and playing house."

"I thought every little girl did that?"

"At sixteen?" she teased, then laughed at the expression on his face. "The last two summers I've worked part-time in a day care center, and the experience convinced me to go into pediatrics. But that's a long way down the road. I'm only a second-year med student."

When they'd finished their coffee, she carried the cups to the kitchen sink. He followed her, slipping his hands around her waist. All her senses reacted to his touch.

"Can I see you in the morning?" he asked.

She nodded, afraid her voice would tremble if she spoke. His finger traced the line of her cheek, and she held her breath, bracing herself as his touch trailed over her soft lips. Instinctively she reached for him, her hands gliding up his chest and over the corded muscles of his shoulders, which flexed beneath her exploring fingers.

He rasped out her name before his mouth hungrily descended on hers. A heady excitement engulfed her. Never had there been a time in her life when she was more gloriously happy. The kiss was searing, turbulent, wrenching her heart and touching her soul.

"Red?" His hold relaxed, and with infinite care he studied her soft, yielding eyes, filled with the depth of her emotions. "Oh, Red." He inhaled several sharp breaths and pressed his forehead to hers. "Don't tempt me like this." The words were a plea that seemed to come deep from within him.

"You're doing the same thing to me," she whispered softly, having trouble with her own breathing.

"We should stop now."

"I know," she agreed, but neither of them pulled away.

How could she think reasonable thoughts when he was so close? A violent eruption of Mount St. Helens couldn't compare with the ferocity of her emotions.

Slowly she pulled back, easing herself from his arms.

He dropped his hands to his sides. "We have to be careful, Red. My desire for you is strong, but I want us to be good. I don't think I could ever forgive myself if I were to lead us into temptation."

"Oh, Seth," she whispered, her blue eyes shimmering with tears. "It's not all you. I'm feeling these things just as strongly. Maybe it's not such a good idea for us to be alone anymore."

"No." His husky voice rumbled with turmoil. A tortured silence followed. He paced the floor, raking his fingers through his thick brown hair. "It's selfish, I know, but there's so little time left. We'll be careful and help one another. It won't be much longer that we'll be able . . ." He let the rest of the sentence fade.

Not much longer, her mind repeated.

He picked up the jacket he'd discarded over the back of a chair and held out a hand to her. "Walk me to the door."

Linking her fingers with his, she did as he asked. He paused at the door, his hand on the knob. "Good night."

"Good night," she responded with a weak smile.

He bent downward and gently brushed her lips. Although the contact was light, almost teasing, Claudia's response was immediate. She yearned for the feel of his arms again, and felt painfully empty when he turned away and closed the door behind him.

They spent almost every minute of Saturday together. In the morning Seth drove them to Snoqualmie Falls, where they ate a picnic lunch, then took a leisurely stroll along the trails leading to the water. Later in the day they visited the Seattle Aquarium on the waterfront, and ate a dinner of fresh fish and crusty, deep-fried potatoes.

When she got home that night, there was a message from Cooper. When she called back, he said he just wanted to tell her that he was looking forward to getting to know Seth over Sunday dinner, a gesture that surprised her.

"He's a good man," her uncle announced. "I've been hearing quite a few impressive things about your friend. I'll apologize to him for my behavior the other day," he continued.

"I'm sure Seth understands," she assured him.

She hadn't known Seth for even a week, and yet it felt like a lifetime. Her feelings for him were clear now. She had never experienced the deep womanly yearnings Seth aroused within her. The attraction was sometimes so strong that it shocked her—and she could tell that it shocked him, too. Aware of their vulnerability, they'd carefully avoided situations that would tempt them. Even though Seth touched her often and made excuses to caress her, he was cautious, and their kisses were never allowed to deepen into the passion they'd shared the night they dined at the Space Needle.

On Sunday morning Claudia woke early, with an eagerness that reminded her of her childhood. The past week had been her happiest since before her father's death.

She and Seth attended the early morning church service together, and she introduced him to her Christian family. Her heart filled with emotion as he sat beside her in the wooden pew. There was nothing more she would ask of a man than a deep, committed faith in the Lord.

Afterward they went back to her apartment. The table was set with her best dishes and linen. Now she set out fresh-squeezed orange juice and delicate butter croissants on china plates. A single candle and dried-flower centerpiece decorated the table.

She had chosen a pink dress and piled her hair high on her head again, with tiny curls falling free to frame her face. Although Seth would be leaving tomorrow, she didn't want to deal with that now, and she quickly dismissed the thought. Today was special, their last day together, and she refused to let the reality of a long separation trouble her.

"I hope you're up to my cooking," she said to him as she took her special egg casserole from the oven.

He stood framed in the doorway, handsome and vital. He still wore his dark wool suit, but he held his tie in one hand as if he didn't want that silken noose around his neck any longer than absolutely necessary.

Just having him this close made all her senses pulsate with happiness, and a warm glow stole over her.

"You don't need to worry. My stomach can handle just out anything," he teased gently. He studied her for a ment. "I can't call you Red in a dress like that." He came to her and kissed her lightly. Claudia sighed at the sweetness of his caress.

"I hope I don't have to wait much longer. I'm starved."

"You really *are* always hungry," she teased. "But how can you think about food when I'm here to tempt you?"

"It's more difficult than you know," he said with a smile. "Can I do anything?"

Claudia answered him with a short shake of her head.

"Then are you going to feed me or not?" His roguish smile only highlighted his irresistible masculinity.

The special baked egg recipe was one Ashley's mother had given her. Claudia was pleased when Seth asked for seconds.

When he finished eating, he took a small package from his coat pocket. "This thing has been burning a hole in my pocket all morning. Open it now."

Claudia took the package and shook it, holding it close to her ear. "For me?" she asked, her eyes sparkling with excitement.

"I brought it with me from Nome."

From Nome? That was certainly intriguing. Carefully she untied the bow and removed the red foil paper, revealing a black velvet jeweler's box.

"Before you open it, I want to explain something." He leaned forward, resting his elbows on the table. "For a long time I've been married to my job, building my company. It wasn't until . . ." He hesitated. "I won't go into the reason, but I decided I wanted a wife. Whenever I needed anything in the past, I simply went out and bought it, but I knew finding a good woman wouldn't work like that. She had to be someone special, someone I could love and respect, someone who shared my faith. The more I thought about the complexities of finding that special woman, the more I realized how difficult it would be to find her."

"Seth—"

"No, let me explain," he continued, reaching for her hand. He gripped it hard, his eyes studying her intently. "I was reading my Bible one night and came across the story of Abraham sending a servant to find a wife for Isaac. Do you remember the story?"

She nodded, color draining from her features. "Seth, please—"

"There's more. Bear with me." He raised her hand to his lips and very gently kissed her fingers. "If you remember, the servant did as Abraham bade and traveled to the land of his master's family. But he was uncertain. The weight of his responsibility bore heavily upon him. So the servant prayed, asking God to give him a sign. God answered that prayer and showed the servant that Rebekah was the right woman for Isaac. Scripture says how much Isaac loved his wife, and how she comforted him after the death of his mother, Sarah."

"Seth, please, I know what you're going to say—"

"Be patient, my love," he interrupted her again. "After reading that account, I decided to trust the Lord to give me a wife. I was also traveling to the land of my family. Both my mother and father originally came from Washington State. I prayed about it. I also purchased the engagement ring before I left Nome. And like Abraham's servant, I, too, asked God for a sign. I was beginning to lose hope. I'd already been here several days before you placed that card with the verse in the mirror. You can't imagine how excited I was when I found it."

Claudia swallowed tightly, recalling his telling her that the message had meant more to him than she would ever know. She wanted to stop him, but the lump in her throat had grown so large that speaking was impossible.

"I want you to come back to Nome with me tomorrow, Red. We can be married in a few days."

Four

Claudia's eyes widened with incredulous disbelief. "Married in a few days?" she repeated. "But, Seth, we've only been together less than a week! We can't—"

"Sure we can," he countered, his eyes serious. "I knew even before I found the Bible verse in the mirror that it was you. Do you remember how you bumped into me that first day in the outside corridor?" Although he asked the question, he didn't wait for the answer. "I was stunned. Didn't you notice how my eyes followed you? Something came over me right then. I had to force myself not to run and stop you. At the time I assumed I was simply physically reacting to a beautiful woman. But once I found the Bible verse on the mirror, I knew."

"What about school?" Somehow the words made it past the large knot constricting her throat.

A troubled look tightened his mouth. "I've done a lot of thinking about that. It's weighed heavily on me. I know how much becoming a doctor means to you." He caught her hand and gently kissed the palm. "Someday, Red, we'll be able to move to Anchorage and you can finish med school. I promise you that."

Taking her hand from his, Claudia closed the jeweler's box. The clicking sound seemed to be magnified a thousand times, a cacophony of sound echoing around the room.

"Seth, we've only known each other a short time. So much more goes into building the foundation for a relationship that will support a marriage. It takes more than a few days."

"Rebekah didn't even meet Isaac. She responded in faith, going with the servant to a faraway land to join a man she had never seen. Yet she went," he argued.

"You're being unfair," she said as she stood and walked to the other side of the room. Her heart was pounding so hard she could feel the blood pulsating through her veins. "We live in the twentieth century, not biblical times. How do we know what Rebekah was feeling? Her father was probably the one who said she would go. More than likely, Rebekah didn't have any choice in the matter."

"You don't know that," he said.

"You don't, either," she shot back. "We hardly know each other."

"You keep saying that! What more do you need to know?"

She gestured weakly with her hands. "Everything."

"Come on, Red. You're overreacting. You know more about me than any other woman ever has. We've done nothing but talk every day. I'm thirty-six, own and operate the Arctic Barge Company, wear size thirteen shoes, like ketchup on my fried eggs and peanut butter on my pancakes. My tastes are simple, my needs few. I tend to be impatient, but God and I are working on that. Usually I don't anger quickly, but when I do, stay clear. After we're married, there will undoubtedly be things we'll need to discuss, but nothing we shouldn't be able to settle."

"Seth, I—"

"Let me see," he continued undaunted. "Did I leave anything out?" He paused again. "Oh yes. The most important part is that I love you, Claudia Masters."

The sincerity with which he said the words trapped the oxygen in her lungs, leaving her speechless.

"This is the point where you're supposed to say, 'And I love you, Seth.'" He rose, coming to stand directly in front of her. His hands cupped her shoulders as his gaze fell lovingly upon her. "Now, repeat after me: *I . . . love . . . you.*"

Claudia couldn't. She tried to say something, but nothing would come. "I can't." She had to choke out the words. "It's unfair to ask me to give up everything I've worked so hard for. I'm sorry, Seth, really sorry."

"Claudia!" His mouth was strained and tight; there was no disguising the bitter disappointment in his voice. "Don't say no, not yet. Think about it. I'm not leaving until tomorrow morning."

"Tomorrow morning." She closed her eyes. "I'm supposed to know by then?"

"You should know now," he whispered.

"But I don't," she snapped. "You say that God gave you a sign that I was to be the wife He had chosen for you. Don't you find it the least bit suspicious that God would say something to you and *nothing* to me?"

"Rebekah didn't receive a sign," he explained rationally. "Abraham's servant did. She followed in faith."

"You're comparing two entirely different times and situations."

"What about the verse you stuck in the mirror? Haven't

you ever wondered about that? You told me you'd never done anything like that before."

"But . . ."

"You have no argument, Red."

"I most certainly do."

"Can you honestly say you don't feel the electricity between us?"

How could she? "I can't deny it, but it doesn't change anything."

Seth smoothed a coppery curl from her forehead, his touch gentle, his eyes imploring. "Of course it does. I think that once you come to Nome you'll understand."

"I'm not going to Nome," she reiterated forcefully. "If you want to marry me, then you'll have to move to Seattle. I won't give up my dreams because of a six-day courtship and your feeling that you received a sign from God."

Seth looked shocked for a moment but recovered quickly. "I can't move to Seattle. My business, my home and my whole life are in Nome."

"But don't you understand? That's exactly what you're asking *me* to do. My education, my home, and my friends are all here in Seattle."

Seth glanced uncomfortably around the room, then directed his gaze back to her. His dark eyes were filled with such deep emotion that it nearly took Claudia's breath away. Tears shimmered in her eyes, and his tall, masculine figure blurred as the moisture welled.

Gently Seth took her in his arms, holding her head to his shoulder. His jacket felt smooth and comforting against her cheek.

Tenderly he caressed her neck, and she could feel his breath against her hair. "Red, I'm sorry," he whispered with such love that fresh tears followed a crooked course down her wan cheeks. "I've known all this from the first day. It's unfair to spring it on you at the last minute. I know it must sound crazy to you now. But think about what I've said. And remember that I love you. Nothing's going to change that. Now dry your eyes and we'll visit your uncle. I promise not to mention this again today." He kissed the top of her head and gently pulled away.

"Here." She handed him the jeweler's box.

"No." He shook his head. "I want you to keep the ring. You may not feel like you want it now, but you will soon. I have to believe that, Red."

Her face twisted with pain. "I don't know that I should."

"Yes, you should." Brief anger flared in his eyes. "Please."

Because she couldn't refuse without hurting him even more, Claudia agreed with an abrupt nod.

Since she certainly couldn't wear the ring, she placed the velvet box in a drawer. Her hand trembled when she pushed the drawer back into place, but she put on a brave smile when she turned toward Seth.

To her dismay, his returning smile was just as sad as hers.

Cooper knew something was wrong almost immediately. That surprised Claudia, who had never found her uncle to be sensitive to her moods. But when he asked what was troubling her, she quickly denied that anything was. She couldn't expect him to understand what was happening.

The two men eyed each other like wary dogs that had

crossed paths unexpectedly. Cooper, for his part, was welcoming, but Seth was brooding and distant.

When they sat down to dinner, Seth smiled ruefully.

"What's wrong?" Claudia asked.

"Nothing," he said, shaking his head. "It's just this is the first time I've needed three spoons to eat one meal."

Cooper arched his thick brows expressively, as if to say he didn't know how anyone could possibly do without three spoons for anything.

Claudia looked from one man to the other, noting the differences. They came from separate worlds. Although she found Cooper's attitudes and demeanor boring and confining, she was, after all, his own flesh and blood. If she were to marry Seth, give up everything that was important to her, and move to Alaska, could she adjust to his way of life?

During the remainder of the afternoon she often found her gaze drawn to Seth. He and Cooper played a quiet game of chess in the den, while she sat nearby, studying them.

In the few days they had spent together, she had been witness to the underlying thread of tenderness that ran through Seth's heart. At the same time, he was self-assured, and although she had never seen the ruthless side of his nature, she didn't doubt that it existed. He was the kind of man to thrive on challenges; he wasn't afraid of hardships. But would she?

Resting her head against the back of the velvet swivel rocker, she slowly lowered her gaze. The problem was that she also knew Seth was the type of man who loved intensely. His love hadn't been offered lightly; he wanted her forever. But most of all, he wanted her now—today.

At thirty-six he had waited a long time to find a wife. His commitment was complete. He had looked almost disbelieving when she hadn't felt the same way.

Or did she? She couldn't deny that the attraction between them was powerful, almost overwhelming. But that was physical, and there was so much more to love than the physical aspect. Spiritually they shared the same faith. To Claudia, that was vital; she wouldn't share her life with a man who didn't believe as she did. But mentally they were miles apart. Each of them had goals and dreams that the other would never share. Seth seemed almost to believe medical school was a pastime, a hobby, for her. He had no comprehension of the years of hard work and study that had gotten her this far. The dream had been ingrained in her too long for her to relinquish it on the basis of a six-day courtship. And it wasn't only her dream, but one her beloved father had shared.

Seth hadn't understood any of that. Otherwise he wouldn't have asked her to give it all up without a question or thought. He believed that God had shown him that she was to be his wife, and that was all that mattered. If only life were that simple! Seth was a new Christian, eager, enthusiastic, but also unseasoned—not that she was a tower of wisdom and discernment. But she would never have prayed for anything so crazy. She was too down to earth—like Cooper. She hated to compare herself to her uncle, but in this instance it was justified.

Cooper's smile turned faintly smug, and Claudia realized he was close to putting Seth in check, if not checkmate. She didn't need to be told that Seth's mind was preoccupied with their conversation this morning and not on the game. Several times in the last hour he had lifted his gaze to hers. One look could reveal so much, although until that day she had never been aware just how *much* his eyes could say. He wanted her so much, more than he would ever tell her. Guiltily her lashes fluttered downward; watching him was hurting them both too much.

Not long afterward he kissed her good night outside her apartment, thanking her for the day. The lump that had become her constant companion blocked her throat, keeping her from thanking him for the beautiful solitaire diamond she would probably never wear.

"My flight's due to take off at seven-thirty," he said without looking at her.

"I'll be there," she whispered.

He held her then, so tightly that for a moment she found it impossible to breathe. She felt him shudder, and tears prickled her eyes as he whispered, "I love you, Red."

She couldn't say it, couldn't repeat the words he desperately longed to hear. She bit her tongue to keep from sobbing. She longed to tell him how she felt, but the words wouldn't come. They stuck in her throat until it constricted painfully and felt raw. Why had God given her a man who could love her so completely when she was so wary?

Claudia set the alarm for five. If Seth's flight took off at seven-thirty, then she should meet him at the airport at six. That early, he would be able to clear security quickly. On the ride back from Cooper's she'd volunteered to drive him, but he'd declined the invitation and said he would take a taxi.

Sleep didn't come easily, and when it did, her dreams were filled with questions. Although she searched everywhere, she couldn't find the answers.

———

Claudia's blue eyes looked haunted and slightly red when she woke up, though she tried to camouflage the effects of her restless night with cosmetics.

The morning was dark and drizzly as she climbed inside her car and started the engine. The heater soon took the bite out of early morning, and she pulled onto the street. With every mile her heart grew heavier. A prayer came automatically to her lips. She desperately wanted to do the right thing: right for Seth, right for her. She prayed that if her heavenly Father wanted her to marry Seth, then He would make the signs as clear for her as He'd apparently done for Seth. Did she lack faith? Was that the problem.

"No," she answered her own question aloud. But her heart seemed to respond with a distant "yes" that echoed through her mind.

She parked in the garage, pulled her purse strap over her shoulder and hurried along the concourse. *I'm doing the right thing*, she mentally repeated with each step. Her heels clicked against the marble floor, seeming to pound out the message—right thing, right thing, right thing.

She paused when she saw Seth waiting for her, as promised, in the coffee shop. The only word for the way he looked was "dejected." She whispered a prayer, seeking strength and wisdom.

"Morning, Seth," she greeted him, forcing herself to smile.

His expression remained blank as he purposely looked away from her.

This was going to be more difficult than she'd imagined. The atmosphere was so tense and strained, she could hardly tolerate it. "You're angry, aren't you?"

"No," he responded dryly. "I've gone beyond the anger stage. Disillusioned, perhaps. You must think I'm a crazy man, showing up with an engagement ring and the belief that God had given me this wonderful message that we were to marry."

"Seth, no." She placed a hand on his arm.

He looked down at it and moved his arm, breaking her light hold. It was almost as if he couldn't tolerate her touch.

"The funny thing is," he continued, his expression stoic, "until this minute I didn't accept that I'd be returning to Alaska alone. Even when I woke up this morning, I believed that something would happen and you'd decide to come with me." He took a deep breath, his gaze avoiding hers. "I've behaved like a fool."

"Don't say that," she pleaded.

He glanced at her then, with regret, doubt and a deep sadness crossing his face. "We would have had beautiful children, Red." He lightly caressed her cheek.

"Will you stop talking like that?" she demanded, becoming angry. "You're being unfair."

He tilted his head and shrugged his massive shoulders. "I know. You love me, Red. You haven't admitted it to yourself yet. The time will come when you can, but I doubt that even then it will make much difference. Because, although you love me, you don't love me enough to leave the luxury of your life behind."

She wanted to argue with him, but she couldn't. Unbidden tears welled in the blue depths of her eyes, and she lowered her head, blinking frantically to still their fall.

She held her head high and glared at him with all her anguish in her eyes for him to see. "I'm going to forgive you for that, because I know you don't mean it. You're hurting, and because of that you want me to suffer, too." Tugging the leather purse strap over her shoulder, she stood and took a step back. "I can't see that my being here is doing either of us any good. I wish you well, and I thank you for six of the most wonderful days of my life. God bless you, Seth." She turned and stalked away down the corridor. For several moments she was lost in a painful void. Somehow she managed to make it to a ladies' room.

Avoiding the curious stares of others, she wiped the tears from her face and blew her nose. Seth had been cold and cruel, offering neither comfort nor understanding. Earlier she had recognized that his capacity for ruthlessness was as strong as his capability for tenderness, but she'd never been exposed to the former. Now she had. How sad that they had to part like this. There had been so much she'd longed to say, but maybe it was better left unsaid.

When she felt composed enough to face the outside world, she moved with quick, purposeful steps toward the parking garage.

She had gone only a few feet when a hand gripped her shoulder and whirled her around. Her cry of alarm was muffled as she was dragged against Seth's muscular chest.

"I thought you'd gone," he whispered into her hair, a desperate edge to his voice. "I'm sorry, Red. You're right. I didn't mean that—not any of it."

He squeezed her so tightly that her ribs ached. Then he raised his head and looked around at the attention they were receiving. He quickly pulled her into a secluded nook behind a pillar. The minute he was assured they were alone, his mouth sought hers, fusing them together with a fiery kiss filled with such emotion that she was left weak and light-headed.

"I need you," he whispered hoarsely against the delicate hollow of her throat. He lifted his face and smoothed a curl from her forehead, his eyes pleading with her.

Claudia was deluged with fresh pain. She needed him, too, but here in Seattle. She couldn't leave everything behind, not now, when she was so close to making her dream come true.

"No, don't say it." He placed a finger over her mouth to prevent the words of regret from spilling out. "I understand, Red. Or at least I'm trying to understand." He sighed heavily and gently kissed her again. "I have to go or I'll never make it through security in time."

He sounded so final, as if everything between them was over. She blinked away the tears that were burning her eyes. No sound came from her parched throat as he gently eased her out of his embrace. Her heart hammered furiously as she walked with him to the security line.

A feeling of panic overcame her when she heard the announcement that Seth's plane was already being boarded. The time was fast approaching when he would be gone.

Once again he gently caressed her face, his dark eyes burning into hers. "Goodbye, Red." His lips covered hers very gently.

In the next instant, Seth Lessinger turned and strolled out of her world.

Part of her screamed silently in tortured protest as she watched him go and longed to race after him. The other part, the more level-headed, sensible part, recognized that there was nothing she could do to change his leaving. But every part of her was suffering. Her brain told her that she'd done the right thing, but her heart found very little solace in her decision.

The days passed slowly and painfully. Claudia knew Ashley had grown worried over her loss of appetite and the dark shadows beneath her eyes. She spent as much time as she could in her room alone, blocking out the world, but closing the door on reality didn't keep the memories of Seth at bay. He was in her thoughts continually, haunting her dreams, obsessing her during the days, preying on her mind.

She threw herself into her studies with a ferocity that surprised even Ashley, and that helped her handle the days, but nothing could help the nights. Often she lay awake for hours, wide-eyed and frustrated, afraid that once she did sleep her dreams would be haunted by Seth. She prayed every minute, it seemed—prayed harder than she had about anything in her life. But no answer came. No flash of lightning, no writing on the wall, not even a Bible verse stuck to a mirror. Nothing. Wasn't God listening? Didn't He know that this situation was tormenting her?

Two weeks after Seth's departure she still hadn't heard from him. She was hollow-eyed, and her cheeks were beginning to look gaunt. She saw Ashley glance at her with concern more than once, but she put on a weak smile and dismissed her friend's worries. *No*, she insisted, *she was fine. Really.*

The next Saturday Ashley was getting ready to go to work at the University Book Store near the U. W. campus when one of the girls she worked with, Sandy Hoover, waltzed into the apartment.

"Look." She proudly beamed and held out her hand, displaying a small diamond.

"You're engaged!" Ashley squealed with delight.

"Jon asked me last night," Sandy burst out. "I was so excited I could hardly talk. First, like an idiot, I started to cry, and Jon didn't know what to think. But I was so happy, I couldn't help it, and then I wasn't even able to talk, and Jon finally asked me if I wanted to marry him or not and all I could do was nod."

"Oh, Sandy, I'm so happy for you." Ashley threw her arms around her friend and hugged her. "You've been in love with Jon for so long."

Sandy's happy smile lit her eyes. "I didn't ever think he'd ask me to marry him. I've known so much longer than Jon how I felt, and it was so hard to wait for him to feel the same way." She sighed, and a dreamy look stole over the pert face. "I love him so much it almost frightens me. He's with me even when he isn't with me." She giggled. "I know that sounds crazy."

It didn't sound so crazy to Claudia. Seth was thousands of miles away, but in some ways he had never left. If anything was crazy, it was the way she could close her eyes and feel the taste of his mouth over hers. It was the memory of that last gentle caress and the sweet kiss that was supposed to say goodbye.

She was so caught up in her thoughts she didn't even notice that Sandy had left until Ashley's voice broke into her reverie.

"I wish you could see yourself," Ashley said impatiently, her expression thoughtful. "You look so miserable that I'm beginning to think you should see a doctor."

"A doctor isn't going to be able to help me," Claudia mumbled.

"You've got to do something. You can't just sit around here moping like this. It isn't like you. Either you settle whatever's wrong between you and Seth or I'll contact him myself."

"You wouldn't," Claudia insisted.

"Don't count on it. Cooper's as worried about you as I am. If I don't do something, *he* might."

"It isn't going to do any good." Claudia tucked her chin into her neck. "I simply can't do what Seth wants. Not now."

"And what *does* he want? Don't you think it's time you told me? I'm your best friend, after all."

"He wants me to marry him and move to Nome," Claudia whispered weakly. "But I can't give up my dream of a medical degree and move to some no-man's-land. And he just as adamantly refuses to move to Seattle. As far as I can see, there's no solution."

"You idiot!" Ashley flared incredulously. "The pair of you! You're both behaving like spoiled children, each wanting your own way. For heaven's sake, does it have to be so intense? You've only known each other a few days. It would be absurd to make such a drastic change in your life on such a short acquaintance. And the same thing goes for Seth. The first thing to do is be sure of your feelings—both of you. Get to know each other better and establish a friendship, then you'll know what you want."

"Good idea. But Seth's three thousand miles away, in

case you'd forgotten, and forming a relationship when we're thousands of miles apart isn't going to be easy."

"How did you ever make the dean's list, girl?" Ashley asked in a scathing tone. "Ever hear of letters? And I'm not talking e-mail, either. I mean the real thing, pen on paper, to prove you put a little time and thought into what you're saying. Some people have been known to faithfully deliver those white envelopes as they fill their appointed rounds—through snow, through rain—"

"I get the picture," Claudia interrupted.

She had thought about writing to Seth, but she didn't have his address and, more importantly, didn't know what she could say. One thing was certain, the next move would have to come from her. Seth was a proud man. He had made his position clear. It was up to her now.

Ashley left for work a few minutes later, and Claudia once again mentally toyed with the idea of writing to Seth. She didn't need to say anything about his proposal. As usual, her level-headed friend had put things into perspective. Ashley was right. She couldn't make such a major decision without more of a basis for their relationship than six days. They could write, phone, and even visit each other until she was sure of her feelings. Because, she realized, she couldn't go on living like this.

The letter wasn't easy. Crumpled pieces of paper littered the living room floor. When it got to the point that the carpet had all but disappeared under her discarded efforts, she paused and decided it would go better if she ate something. She stood, stretched, and was making herself a sandwich when she realized that, for the first time since Seth had left, she was actually hungry. A pleased smile spread slowly across her face.

Once she'd eaten, the letter flowed smoothly. She wrote about the weather and her classes, a couple of idiosyncrasies of her professors. She asked him questions about Nome and his business. Finally she had two sheets of neat, orderly handwriting, and she signed the letter simply "Claudia." Reading it over, she realized she'd left so much unsaid. Chewing on the end of her pen, she scribbled a postscript that said she missed him. Would he understand?

She had the letter almost memorized by the time she dropped it into a mailbox an hour later. She'd walked it there as soon as she'd finished writing it, afraid she would change her mind if she let it lie around all weekend. She hadn't even tried to find his address, even though she was sure she could track him down on the internet. She simply wrote his name and Nome, Alaska. If it arrived, then it would be God's doing. This whole relationship was God's doing.

Calculating that the letter would arrive on Wednesday or Thursday, she guessed that, if he wrote back right away, she could have something from him by the following week. Until then, she was determined to let it go and try to think of anything else. That night she crawled into bed and, for the first time in two and a half desolate weeks, slept peacefully.

All day Thursday, Claudia was fidgety. Seth would get her letter today if he hadn't already. How would he react to it? Would he be glad, or had he given up on her completely? How much longer would it be before she knew? How long before she could expect an answer? She smiled as she let herself into the apartment; it was as if she expected something monumental to happen. By ten she'd finished her studies, and, after a leisurely bath she read her Bible and went to bed, unreasonably disappointed.

Nothing happened Friday, either. Steve Kali, another medical student, asked her out for coffee after anatomy lab, and she accepted, pleased by the invitation. Steve was nice. He wasn't Seth, but he was nice.

The phone rang Saturday afternoon. She was bringing in the groceries and dropped a bag of oranges as she rushed across the carpet to answer it.

"Hello." She sounded out of breath.

"Hello, Red," Seth's deep, rich voice returned.

Her hand tightened on the receiver, and her heartbeat accelerated wildly. "You got my letter?" Her voice was still breathless, but this time it had nothing to do with hurrying to answer the phone.

"About time. I didn't know if I'd ever hear from you."

Claudia suddenly felt so weak that she had to sit down. "How are you?"

"Miserable," he admitted. "Your letter sounded so bright and newsy. If you hadn't added that note at the bottom, I don't know what I would have thought."

"Oh, Seth," she breathed into the phone. "I've been wretched. I really do miss you."

"It's about time you admitted as much. I had no idea it would take you this long to realize I was right. Do you want me to fly down there so we can do the blood tests?"

"Blood tests?"

"Yes, silly woman. Alaska requires blood tests for a marriage license."

Five

"Marriage license? I didn't write because I was ready to change my mind," Claudia said, shocked. Did Seth believe this separation was a battle of wills and she'd been the first to surrender? "I'm staying here in Seattle. I thought you understood that."

Her announcement was followed by a lengthy pause. She could practically hear his anger and the effort he made to control his breathing. "Then why did you write the letter?" he asked at last.

"You still don't understand, do you?" She threw the words at him. "Someday, Seth Lessinger, I'm going to be a fabulous doctor. That's been my dream from the time I was a little girl." She forced herself to stop and take a calming breath; she didn't want to argue with him. "Seth, I wrote you because I've been miserable. I've missed you more than I believed possible. I thought it might work if you and I got to know one another better. We can write and—"

"I'm not interested in a pen pal." His laugh was harsh and bitter.

"Neither am I," she returned sharply. "You're being unfair again. Can't we compromise? Do we have to do everything your way? Give me time, that's all I'm asking."

Her words were met with another long silence, and for an apprehensive second she thought he might have hung up on her. "Seth," she whispered, "all I'm asking is for you to give me more time. Is that so unreasonable?"

"All right, Red, we'll do this your way," he conceded. "But I'm not much for letter writing, and this is a busy time of the year for me, so don't expect much."

She let out the breath she hadn't realized she'd been holding and smiled. "I won't." It was a beginning.

Seth's first letter arrived four days later. Home from her classes before Ashley, Claudia stopped to pick up the mail in the vestibule. There was only one letter, the address written in large, bold handwriting. She stared at it with the instant knowledge that it was from Seth. Clutching the envelope tightly, she rushed up the stairs, fumbled with the apartment lock and barged in the front door. She tossed her coat and books haphazardly on the couch before tearing open the letter. Like hers, his was newsy, full of tidbits of information about his job and what this new contract would do for his business, Arctic Barge Company. He talked a little about the city of Nome and what she should expect when she came.

Claudia couldn't prevent the smile that trembled across her lips. When she came, indeed! He also explained that when she packed her things she would have to ship everything she couldn't fit in her suitcases. Arrangements would need to be made to have her belongings transported on a barge headed north. The only way into Nome was either by air or by sea, and access by sea was limited to a few short weeks in the summer before the water froze again. The pressure for her to make her decision soon was subtle. He concluded by saying that he missed her and, just in case she'd forgotten, he loved her. She read the words and closed her eyes to the flood of emotions that swirled through her.

She answered the letter that night and sent off another two days later. A week passed, but finally she received another long response from Seth, with an added postscript that there was a possibility he would be in Seattle toward the end of October for a conference. He didn't know how much unscheduled time he would have, but he was hoping to come a day early. That, he said, would be the time for them to sit down and talk, because letters only made him miss her more. He gave her the dates and promised to contact her when he knew more. Again he told her that he loved her and needed her.

Claudia savored both letters, reading them so many times she knew each one by heart. In some ways, their correspondence was building a more solid relationship than having him in Seattle would have. If he'd been here, she would have been more easily swayed by her physical response to him. This way she could carefully weigh each aspect of her decision, and give Seth and the move to Nome prayerful consideration. And she *did* pray, fervently, every day. But after so many weeks she was beginning to believe God was never going to answer.

One afternoon Ashley saw her reading one of Seth's letters for the tenth time and laughingly tossed a throw pillow at her.

"Hey," Claudia snapped, "what did you do that for?"

"Because I couldn't stand to see you looking so miserable!"

"I'm not miserable," Claudia denied. "I'm happy. Seth wrote about how much he wants me to marry him and . . . and . . ." Her voice cracked, and she swallowed back tears that burned for release. "I . . . didn't know I would cry about it."

"You still don't know what you want, do you?"

Claudia shook her head. "I pray and pray and pray, but God doesn't seem to hear me. He gave Seth a sign, but there's nothing for me. It's unfair!"

"What kind of confirmation are you looking for?" Ashley sat beside Claudia and handed her a tissue.

Claudia sniffled and waved her hand dramatically. "I don't know. Just something—anything! When I made my commitment to Christ, I told Him my life was no longer my own but His. If He wants me digging ditches, then I'll dig ditches. If He wants me to give up medical school and marry Seth, then I'll do it in a minute. Seth seems so positive that it's the right thing, and I'm so unsure."

Ashley pinched her lips together for a moment, then went into her bedroom. She returned a minute later with her Bible. "Do you remember the story of Elijah?"

"Of course. I would never forget the Old Testament prophets."

Ashley nodded as she flipped through the worn pages of her Bible. "Here it is. Elijah was hiding from the wicked Jezebel. God sent the angel of the Lord, who led Elijah into a cave. He told him to stay there and wait, because God was coming to speak to him. Elijah waited and waited. When a strong wind came, he rushed from the cave and cried out, but the wind wasn't God. An earthquake followed, and again Elijah hurried outside, certain this time that the earthquake was God speaking to him.

But it wasn't the earthquake. Next came a fire, and again Elijah was positive that the fire was God speaking to him. But it wasn't. Finally, when everything was quiet, Elijah heard a soft, gentle whisper. That was the Lord." Ashley transferred the open Bible to Claudia's lap. "Here, read the story yourself."

Thoughtfully Claudia read over the chapter before looking up. "You're telling me I should stop looking for that bolt of lightning in the sky that spells out *Marry Seth*?"

"Or the handwriting on the wall," Ashley added with a laugh.

"So God is answering my prayers, and all I need to do is listen?"

"I think so."

"It sounds too simple," Claudia said with a sigh.

"I don't know that it is. But you've got to quit looking for the strong wind, the earthquake, and the fire, and listen instead to your heart."

"I'm not even a hundred percent sure I love him. I don't think I know him well enough yet." The magnetic physical attraction between them was overwhelming, but there was so much more to love and a lifetime commitment.

"You'll know," Ashley assured her confidently. "I don't doubt that for a second. When the time is right, you'll know."

Claudia felt as if a weight had been lifted from her, and she sighed deeply before forcefully expelling her breath. "Hey, do you know what today is?" she asked, then answered before Ashley had the opportunity. "Columbus Day. A day worthy of celebrating with something special." Carefully she tucked Seth's letter back inside the envelope. "Let's bring home Chinese food and drown our doubts in pork fried rice."

"And egg rolls," Ashley added. "Lots of egg rolls."

By the time they returned to the apartment, Claudia and Ashley had collected more than dinner. They had bumped into Steve Kali and a friend of his at the restaurant, and after quick introductions, the four of them realized they could get two extra items for free if they combined their orders. From there it was a quick step to inviting the guys over to eat at their place.

They sat on the floor in a large circle, laughing and eating with chopsticks directly from the white carryout boxes, passing them around so everyone could try everything.

Steve's friend, Dave Kimball, was a law student, and he immediately showed a keen interest in Ashley. Claudia watched with an amused smile as her friend responded with some flirtatious moves of her own.

The chopsticks were soon abandoned in favor of forks, but the laughter continued.

"You know what we're celebrating, don't you?" Ashley asked between bites of ginger-spiced beef and tomato.

"No." Both men shook their heads, glancing from one girl to the other.

"Columbus Day," Claudia supplied.

"As in 'Columbus sailed the ocean blue'?" Steve jumped up and danced around the room singing.

Everyone laughed.

The phone rang, and since Steve was right near it, he

picked up the cordless. "I'll get that for you," he volunteered, then promptly dropped the receiver. "Oops, sorry," he apologized into the receiver.

Claudia couldn't help smiling as she realized she was having a good time. It felt good to laugh again. Ashley was right, this whole thing with Seth was too intense. She needed to relax. Her decision had to be based on the quiet knowledge that marriage to Seth was what God had ordained.

"I'm sorry, would you mind repeating that?" Steve said into the phone. "Claudia? Yeah, she's here." He covered the receiver with the palm of his hand. "Are you here, Claudia?" he asked with a silly grin.

"You nut. Give me that." She stood and took the phone. "Hello." With her luck, it would be Cooper, who would no doubt demand to know what a man was doing in her apartment and answering her phone, no less. "This is Claudia."

"What's going on?"

The color drained from her flushed cheeks. "Seth? Is that you?" she asked incredulously. Breathlessly, she repeated herself. "Seth, it is really you?"

"It's me," he confirmed, his tone brittle. "Who's the guy who answered the phone."

"Oh." She swallowed, and turned her back to the others. "He's a classmate of mine. We have a few friends over," she explained, stretching the truth. She didn't want Seth to get the wrong impression. "We're celebrating Columbus Day . . . you know, Columbus, the man who sailed across the Atlantic looking for India and discovered America instead. Do you celebrate Columbus Day in

Alaska?" she asked, embarrassingly aware that she was babbling.

"I know what day it is. You sound like you've been drinking."

"Not unless the Chinese tea's got something in it I don't know about."

"Does the guy who answered the phone mean anything to you?"

The last thing Claudia wanted to do was make explanations to Seth with everyone listening. On the other hand, carrying the phone into her bedroom so they could talk privately would only invite all kinds of questions she didn't want to answer. "It would be better if we . . . if we talked later," she said, stammering slightly.

"Everyone's there listening, right?" Seth guessed.

"Right," she confirmed with a soft sigh. "Do you mind?"

"No, but before you hang up, answer me one thing. Have you been thinking about how much I love you and want you here with me?"

"Oh, Seth," she murmured miserably. "Yes, I've hardly thought of anything else."

"And you still don't know what you want to do?" he asked, his voice heavy with exasperation.

"Not yet."

"All right, Red. I'll call back in an hour."

In the end it was almost two hours before the phone rang again. Steve and Dave had left an hour earlier, and Ashley had made a flimsy excuse about needing to do some research at the library. Claudia didn't question her and appreciated the privacy.

She answered the phone on the first ring. "Hello."

"Now tell me who that guy was who picked up the phone before," Seth demanded without even a greeting.

Claudia couldn't help it. She laughed. "Seth Lessinger, you sound almost jealous."

"Almost?" he shot back.

"His name's Steve Kali, and we have several classes together, that's all," she explained, pleased at his concern. "I didn't know you were the jealous sort," she said gently.

"I never have been before. And I don't like the way it feels, if that makes you any happier."

"I'd feel the same way," she admitted. "I wish you were here, Seth. Ashley and I walked by a skating rink tonight and stopped to watch some couples skating together. Do you realize that you and I have never skated? If I close my eyes, I can almost feel your arm around me."

Seth sucked in his breath. "Why do you say things like that when we're separated by thousands of miles? Your sense of timing is really off. Besides, we don't need skating as an excuse for me to be near you," he murmured, his voice low. "Listen, honey, I'll be in Seattle a week from Saturday."

"Saturday? Oh, Seth!" She was too happy to express her thoughts coherently. "It'll be so good to see you!"

"My plane arrives early that morning. I couldn't manage the extra day, but I'll phone you as soon as I can review the conference schedule and figure out when I'll be able to see you."

"I won't plan a thing. No," she said, laughing, "I'll

plan everything. Can you stay over through Monday? I'll skip classes and we can have a whole extra day alone."

"I can't." He sounded as disappointed as she felt.

They talked for an hour, and Claudia felt guilty at the thought of his phone bill, but the conversation had been wonderful.

Did she love him? The question kept repeating itself for the next two weeks. If she could truthfully answer that one question, then everything else would take care of itself. Just talking to him over the phone had lifted her spirits dramatically. But could she leave school and everything, everyone, she had ever known and follow him to a place where she knew no one but him and would have no way to follow her dream?

Her last class on the day before he arrived was a disaster. Her attention span was no longer than a four-year-old's. Time and time again she was forced to bring herself back into reality. So many conflicting emotions and milestones seemed to be coming at her. The first big tests of the quarter, Seth's visit. She felt pounded from every side, tormented by her own indecision.

Steve walked out of the building with her.

"Why so glum?" he asked. "If anyone's got complaints, it should be me." They continued down the stairs, and Claudia cast him a sidelong glance.

"What have you got to complain about?"

"Plenty," he began in an irritated tone. "You remember Dave Kimball?"

She nodded, recalling Steve's tall, sandy-haired friend

who had flirted so outrageously with Ashley. "Sure, I remember Dave."

"We got picked up by the police a couple of nights ago."

She glanced apprehensively at him. "What happened?"

"Nothing, really. We'd been out having a good time and decided to walk home after a few beers. About halfway to the dorm, Dave starts with the crazies. He was climbing up the streetlights, jumping on parked cars. I wasn't doing any of that, but we were both brought into the police station for disorderly conduct."

Claudia's blue eyes widened incredulously. Steve was one of the straightest, most clean-cut men she had met. This was so unlike anything she would have expected from him that she didn't know how to react.

"That's not the half of it," he continued. "Once we were at the police station, Dave kept insisting that he was a law student and knew his rights. He demanded his one phone call."

"Well, it's probably a good thing he did know what to do," she said.

"Dave made his one call, all right." Steve inhaled a shaky breath. "And twenty minutes later the desk sergeant came in to ask which one of us had ordered the pizza."

Claudia couldn't stop herself from bursting into giggles, and it wasn't long before Steve joined her. He placed a friendly arm around her shoulders as their laughter faded. Together they strolled toward the parking lot.

"I do feel bad about the police thing . . ." she said. Before she could complete her thought, she caught sight of a broad-shouldered man walking toward her with crisp strides. She knew immediately it was Seth.

His look of contempt was aimed directly at her, his rough features darkened by a fierce frown. Even across the narrowing distance she recognized the tight set of his mouth as he glared at her.

Steve's arm resting lightly across her shoulders felt as if it weighed a thousand pounds.

Six

Claudia's mouth was dry as she quickened her pace and rushed forward to meet Seth. If his look hadn't been so angry and forbidding, she would have walked directly into his arms. "When—how did you get here? I thought you couldn't come until tomorrow?" Only now was she recovering from the shock of seeing him.

An unwilling smile broke his stern expression as he pulled her to him and crushed her in his embrace.

Half lifted from the sidewalk, Claudia linked her hands behind his neck and felt his warm breath in her hair. "Oh, Seth," she mumbled, close to tears. "You idiot, why didn't you say something?"

So many emotions were filling her at once. She felt crushed yet protected, jubilant yet tearful, excited but afraid. Ignoring the negatives, she began spreading eager kisses over his face.

Slowly he released her, and the two men eyed each other skeptically.

Seth extended his hand. "I'm Seth Lessinger, Claudia's fiancé."

She had to bite her lip to keep from correcting him, but she wouldn't say anything that could destroy the happiness of seeing him again.

Steve's eyes were surprised, but he managed to mumble a greeting and exchange handshakes. Then he made some excuse about catching a ride and was gone.

"Who was that?"

"Steve," she replied, too happy to see him to question the way he had introduced himself to her friend. "He answered the phone the other night when you called. He's just a friend, don't worry."

"Then why did he have his arm around you?" Seth demanded with growing impatience.

Claudia ignored the question, instead standing on the tips of her toes and lightly brushing her mouth over his. His whiskers tickled her face, and she lifted both hands to his dark beard, framing his lips so she could kiss him soundly.

His response was immediate as he pulled her into his arms. "I've missed you. I won't be able to wait much longer. Who would believe such a little slip of nothing could bring this giant to his knees? Literally," he added. "Because I'll propose again right here on the sidewalk if you think it will make a difference."

Claudia's eyes widened with feigned offense. "Little slip of nothing? Come on, you make me sound like some anorexic supermodel."

He laughed, the robust, deep laugh that she loved. "Compared to me, you're pint-size." Looping his arm around her waist, he walked beside her. She felt protected and loved beyond anything she had ever known. She smiled up at him, and his eyes drank deeply from hers as a slow grin spread over his face, crinkling tiny lines at his eyes. "You may be small, but you hold a power over me I don't think I'll ever understand."

Leaning her head against his arm, Claudia relaxed. "Why didn't you say anything about coming today?"

"I didn't know that I was going to make the flight until the last minute. As it was, I hired a pilot out of Nome to make the connection in Fairbanks."

"You could have called when you landed."

"I tried, but no one answered at the apartment and your cell went straight to voicemail."

She pulled the phone out of her purse and checked. "Oops. I turned it off during class, and I guess I forgot to turn it on again." She remedied that as she asked, "So how'd you know where to find me?"

"I went to your apartment to wait for you and ran into Ashley just getting home. She drew me a map of the campus and told me where you'd be. You don't mind?"

"Of course not," she assured him with a smile and a shake of her head. "I just wish I'd known. I could have ducked out of class and met you at the airport."

By then they had reached her car. Seth asked to drive, so she gave him her keys. It wasn't until they were stuck in heavy afternoon traffic that she noticed Seth was heading in the opposite direction from her apartment.

"Where are we going?" She looked down at her jeans and Irish cable-knit sweater. She wasn't dressed for anything but a casual outing.

"My hotel," he answered without looking at her, focusing his attention on the freeway. "I wanted to talk to you privately, and from the look of things at your place, Ashley is going to be around for a while."

Claudia knew just what he was talking about. Ashley was deep into a project that she'd been working on for two nights. Magazines, newspapers, and pages of scribbled notes were scattered over the living room floor.

"I know what you mean about the apartment." She laughed softly in understanding.

He slowed the car as he pulled off the freeway and onto Mercer Avenue. "She's a nice girl. I like her. Those blue eyes of hers are almost as enchanting as yours."

Something twitched in Claudia's stomach. Jealousy? Over Ashley? She was her best friend! Quickly she tossed the thought aside.

Seth reached for her hand. Linking their fingers, he carried her hand to his mouth and gently kissed her knuckles. Shivers tingled up her arm, and she smiled contentedly.

The hotel lobby was bristling with activity. In contrast, Seth's room in the conference hotel was quiet and serene. Situated high above the city, it offered a sweeping view of Puget Sound and the landmarks Seattle was famous for: the Pacific Science Center, the Space Needle, and the Kingdome.

The king-size bed was bordered on each side by oak nightstands with white ceramic lamps. Two easy chairs were set obliquely in front of a hi-def television and state-of-the-art gaming system. Claudia glanced over the room, feeling slightly uneasy.

The door had no sooner closed than Seth placed a hand on her shoulder and turned her around to face him. Their eyes met, hers uncertain and a little afraid, his warm and reassuring. When he slipped his arms around her, she went willingly, fitting herself against the hard contours of his solid body. Relaxing, she savored the fiery warmth of his kiss. She slipped her hands behind his neck and yielded with the knowledge that she wanted him to kiss her, needed his kisses. Nothing on earth came so close to heaven as being cradled in his arms.

Arms of corded steel locked around her, held her close. Yet he was gentle, as if she were the most precious thing in the world. With a muted groan, he dragged his mouth from hers and showered the side of her neck with urgent kisses.

"I shouldn't be doing this," he moaned hoarsely. "Not when I don't know if I have the will to stop." One hand continued down her back, arching her upward while the fingers of the other hand played havoc with her hair.

Claudia's mind was caught in a whirl of desire and need. This shouldn't be happening, but it felt so right. For a moment she wanted to stop him, tell him they should wait until they were married—*if* they married. But she couldn't speak.

Seth pulled away and paused, his eyes searching hers. His breath came in uneven gasps.

She knew this was the time to stop, to back away, but she couldn't. The long weeks of separation, the doubts, the uncertainties that had plagued her night and day, the restless dreams, all exploded in her mind as she lifted her arms to him. It had been like this between them almost from the beginning, this magnetic, overpowering attraction.

Slowly Seth lowered his mouth to hers until their breaths merged, and the kiss that followed sent her world into a crazy spin.

"I can't do it," he whispered hoarsely into her ear, the bitter words barely distinct. "I can't," he repeated, and broke the embrace.

His voice filtered through her consciousness, and she forced her eyes open. Seth was standing away from her. He wasn't smiling now, and his troubled, almost tormented, expression puzzled her.

"Seth," she asked softly, "what is it?"

"I'm sorry." He crossed his arms and turned his back, as if offering her the chance to escape.

Her arms felt as if they'd been weighed down with lead, and her heart felt numb, as if she'd been exposed to the Arctic cold without the proper protective gear.

"Forgive me, Red." Seth covered his eyes with a weary hand and walked across the room to stand by the window. "I brought you here with the worst of intentions," he began. "I thought if we were to make love, then all your doubts would be gone." He paused to take in a labored breath. "I knew you'd marry me then without question."

Understanding burned like a laser beam searing through her mind, and she half moaned, half cried. Her arms cradled her stomach as the pain washed over her. Color blazed in her cheeks at how close she had come to letting their passion rage out of control. It had been a trick, a trap, in order for him to exert his will over her.

Several long moments passed in silence. Claudia turned to Seth, whose profile was outlined by the dim light of dusk. He seemed to be struggling for control of his emotions.

"I wouldn't blame you if you hated me after this," he said at last.

"I . . . I don't hate you." Her voice was unsteady, soft and trembling.

"You don't love me, either, do you?" He hurled the words at her accusingly and turned to face her.

The muscles in her throat constricted painfully. "I don't know. I just don't know."

"Will you ever be completely sure?" he asked with obvious impatience.

Claudia buried her face in her hands, defeated and miserable.

"Red, please don't cry. I'm sorry." The anger was gone, and he spoke softly, reassuringly.

She shivered with reaction. "If . . . if we did get married, could I stay here until I finished med school?"

"No," he returned adamantly. "I want a wife and children. Look at me, Red. I'm thirty-six. I can't wait another five or six years for a family. And I work too hard to divide my life between Nome and Seattle."

Wasn't there any compromise? Did everything have to be his way? "You're asking for so much," she cried.

"But I'm offering even more," he countered.

"You don't understand," she told him. "If I quit med school now, I'll probably never be able to finish. Especially if I won't be able to come back for several years."

"There isn't any compromise," he said with a note of finality. "If God wants you to be a doctor, He'll provide the way later. We both have to trust Him for that."

"I can't give up my entire life. It's not that easy," she whispered.

"Then there's nothing left to say, is there?" Dark shadows clouded his face, and he turned sharply and resumed his position in front of the window.

There didn't seem to be anything left to do but to leave quietly. She forced herself to open the door, but she knew she couldn't let it end like this. She let the door click softly shut.

At the sound Seth slammed his fist against the window ledge. Claudia gave a small cry of alarm, and he spun to face her. His rugged features were contorted with anger as he stared at her. But one look told her that the anger was directed at himself and not her.

"I thought you'd gone." His gaze held hers.

"I couldn't," she whispered.

He stared deeply into her liquid blue eyes and paused as if he wanted to say something, but finally he just shook his head in defeat and turned his back to her again.

Her eyes were haunted as she covered the distance between them. She slid her hands around his waist, hugging him while she rested a tearstained cheek against his back.

"We have something very special, Red, but it's not going to work." The dejected tone of his voice stabbed at her heart.

"It *will* work. I know it will. But I want to be sure, very sure, before I make such a drastic change in my life. Give me time, that's all I'm asking."

"You've had almost six weeks."

"It's not enough."

He tried to remove her hands, but she squeezed tighter. "We're both hurt and angry tonight, but that doesn't mean things between us won't work."

"I could almost believe you," he murmured and turned, wrapping her securely in his arms.

She met his penetrating gaze and answered in a soft, throbbing voice, "Believe me, Seth. Please believe me."

His gaze slid to her lips before his mouth claimed hers in a fierce and flaming kiss that was almost savage, as if to punish her for the torment she had caused him. But it didn't matter how he kissed her as long as she hadn't lost him.

They had dinner at the hotel but didn't return to Seth's room. They discussed his conference schedule, which would take up pretty much all of Saturday. His plane left Sunday afternoon. They made plans to attend the Sunday morning church service together, and for her to drive him to the airport afterward.

Her heart was heavy all the next day. Several times she wished she could talk to him and clear away the ghosts of yesterday. For those long, miserable weeks she had missed him so much that she could hardly function. Then, at the first chance to see each other again, they had ended up fighting. Why didn't she know what to do? Was this torment her heart was suffering proof of love?

The question remained unanswered as they sat together in church Sunday morning. It felt so right to have him by her side. Claudia closed her eyes to pray, fervently asking God to guide her. She paused, recalling the verses she had found in the Gospel of Matthew just the other night, verses all about asking, seeking, knocking. God had promised that anyone who asked would receive, and anyone who sought would find. It had all sounded so simple and straightforward when she read it, but it wasn't—not for her.

When she finished her prayer and opened her eyes, she felt Seth's gaze burn over her, searching her face. She longed to reassure him but could find no words. Gently she reached for his hand and squeezed it.

They rode to the airport in an uneasy silence. Their

time had been bittersweet for the most part. What she had hoped would be a time to settle doubts had only raised more.

"You don't need to come inside with me," he said as they neared the airport. His words sliced into her troubled thoughts.

"What?" she asked, confused and hurt. "But I'd like to be with you as long as possible."

He didn't look pleased with her decision. "Fine, if that's what you want."

The set of his mouth was angry and impatient, but she didn't know why. "You don't want me there, do you?" She tried to hide the hurt in her voice.

His cool eyes met her look of defiance. "Oh, for goodness' sake, settle down, Red. I take it all back. Come in if you want. I didn't mean to make a federal case out of this."

Claudia didn't want to argue again, not during this last chance to spend time together. Seth continued to look withdrawn as they parked in the concrete garage and walked into the main terminal.

She reached out tentatively and rested her hand on his arm. "Friends?" she asked and offered him a smile.

He returned the gesture and tenderly squeezed her delicate hand. "Friends."

The tension between them eased, and she waited while Seth hit the check-in kiosk. He returned with a wry grin. "My flight's been delayed an hour. How about some lunch?"

She couldn't prevent the smile that softly curved her mouth. Her eyes reflected her pleasure at the unexpected time together.

Claudia noted that Seth barely touched his meal. Her appetite wasn't up to par, either. Another separation loomed before them.

"How long will it be before you'll be back?" she asked as they walked toward the security line.

There was a moment of grim hesitation before Seth answered. "I don't know. Months, probably. This conference wasn't necessary. If it hadn't been for you, I wouldn't have attended, but I can't afford to keep taking time away from my business like this."

Claudia swallowed past the lump forming in her throat. "Thanksgiving break is coming soon. Maybe I could fly up and visit you. I'd like to see the beauty of Alaska for myself. You've told me so much about it already." Just for a moment, for a fleeting second, she was tempted to drop everything and leave with him now. Quickly she buried the impulsive thought and clenched her fists inside the pockets of her wool coat.

Seth didn't respond either way to her suggestion.

"What do you think?" she prompted.

He inclined his head and nodded faintly. "If that's what you'd like."

Claudia had the feeling he didn't really understand any of what she'd been trying to explain about her dreams and what it would mean to her to move, or how big a step it was for her to offer to visit.

When he couldn't delay any longer and had to get in line to pass through the security screening process, her façade of composure began to slip. It was difficult not to cry, and she blinked several times, not wanting Seth to remember her with tears shimmering in her eyes. With a proud lift of her chin, she offered him a brave smile.

He studied her unhappy face. "Goodbye, Red." His eyes continued to hold hers.

Her hesitation before her answer only emphasized her inner turmoil. "Goodbye, Seth," she whispered softly, a slight catch in her voice.

He cupped her face with the palm of his hand, and his thumb gently wiped away the single tear that was weaving a slow course down her pale cheek. Claudia buried her chin in his hand and gently kissed his callused palm.

Gathering her into his embrace, Seth wrapped his arms around her as he buried his face in her neck and breathed deeply. When his mouth found hers, the kiss was gentle and sweet, and so full of love that fresh tears misted her eyes.

His hold relaxed, and he began to pull away, but she wouldn't let him. "Seth." She murmured his name urgently. She had meant to let him go, relinquish him without a word, but somehow she couldn't.

He scooped her in his arms again, crushing her against him with a fierceness that stole her breath away. "I'm a man," he bit out in an impatient tone, "and I can't take much more of this." He released her far enough to study her face. His dark eyes clearly revealed his needs. "I'm asking you again, Claudia. Marry me and come to Nome. I promise you a good life. I need you."

Claudia felt raw. The soft, womanly core of her cried out a resounding yes, but she couldn't let herself base such a life-changing decision on the emotion of the moment. She didn't want to decide something so important to both of them on the basis of feelings. Indecision and uncertainty raced through her mind, and she could neither reject nor accept his offer. Unable to formulate words, she found a low, protesting groan slipping from her throat. Her brimming blue eyes pleaded with him for understanding.

Seth's gaze sliced into her as a hardness stole over his features, narrowing his mouth. Forcefully he turned and, with quick, impatient steps, joined the line of passengers waiting to pass security and head to their gates.

Unable to do anything more, she watched him until he was out of sight, and then she turned and headed dejectedly back to the garage. At least she'd canceled her regular Sunday dinner with Cooper, so she wouldn't have to put on a happy face for him, and could just go home and give in to her depression.

The following week was wretched. At times Claudia thought it would have been easier not to have seen Seth again than endure the misery of another parting. To complicate her life further, it was the week of midterm exams. Never had she felt less like studying. Each night she wrote Seth long, flowing letters. School had always come first, but suddenly writing to him was more important. When she did study, her concentration waned and her mind wandered to the hurt look on Seth's face when they'd said goodbye. That look haunted her.

She did poorly on the first test, so, determined to do better on the next, she forced herself to study. With her textbooks lying open on top of the kitchen table, she propped her chin on both hands as she stared into space. Despite her best intentions, her thoughts weren't on school but on Seth. The illogical meanderings of her mind continued to torment her with the burning question of her future. Was being a pediatrician so important if it meant losing Seth?

"You look miserable," Ashley commented as she strolled into the kitchen to pour herself a glass of milk.

"That's because I feel miserable," Claudia returned, trying—and failing—to smile.

"There's been something different about you since Seth went back to Alaska again."

"No there hasn't," Claudia denied. "It's just the stress of midterms." Why did she feel the need to make excuses? She'd always been able to talk to Ashley about anything.

Her roommate gave her a funny look but didn't say anything as she turned and went back to the living room.

Angry with herself and the world, Claudia studied half the night, finally staggering into her bedroom at about three. That was another thing. She hadn't been sleeping well since Seth had gone.

Ashley was cooking dinner when Claudia got home the next afternoon. After her exam, she'd gone to the library to study, hoping a change of scenery would help keep her mind off Seth and let her concentrate on her studies.

"You had company," Ashley announced casually, but she looked a bit flushed and slightly uneasy.

Claudia's heart stopped. Seth. He had come back for her. She needed so desperately to see him again, to talk to him.

"Seth?" she asked breathlessly.

"No, Cooper. I didn't know what time you were going to get home, so instead of waiting here, he decided to run an errand and come back later," Ashley explained.

"Oh." Claudia didn't even try to disguise the disappointment in her voice. "I can do without another unpleasant confrontation with my uncle. I wonder how he found out about how badly I did on that test already."

"Why do you always assume the worst with Cooper?" Ashley demanded with a sharp edge of impatience. "I, for one, happen to think he's nice. I don't think I've ever seen him treat anyone unfairly. It seems to me that you're the one who—" She stopped abruptly and turned back toward the stove, stirring the browning hamburger with unnecessary vigor. "I hope spaghetti sounds good."

"Sure," Claudia responded. "Anything."

Cooper didn't return until they had eaten and were clearing off the table. Claudia made a pot of coffee and brought him a cup in the living room. She could feel him studying her.

"You don't look very good," he commented, taking the cup and saucer out of her hand. Most men would have preferred a mug, but not Cooper.

"So Ashley keeps telling me." She sat opposite him. "Don't do the dishes, Ash," she called into the kitchen. "Wait until later and I'll help."

"No need." Ashley stuck her head around the kitchen door. "You go ahead and visit. Shout if you need anything."

"No, Ashley," Cooper stood as he spoke. "I think that it might be beneficial if you were here, too."

Ashley looked from one of them to the other, dried her hands on a towel and came into the room.

"I don't mean to embarrass you, Ashley, but in all fairness I think Claudia should know that you were the one to contact me."

Claudia's gaze shot accusingly across the room to her friend. "What does he mean?"

Ashley shrugged. "I've been so worried about you lately. You're hardly yourself anymore. I thought if you talked to Cooper, it might help you make up your mind. You can't go on like this, Claudia." Her voice was gentle and stern all at the same time.

"What do you mean?" Claudia vaulted to her feet. "This is unfair, both of you against me."

"Against you?" Cooper echoed. "Come on now, Claudia, you seem to have misjudged everything."

"No I haven't." Tears welled in her eyes, burning for release.

"I think it would probably be best if I left the two of you alone." Ashley stood and excused herself, returning to the kitchen.

Claudia shot her an angry glare as she stepped past. Some friend!

"I hope you'll talk honestly with me, Claudia," Cooper began. "I'd like to know what's got you so upset that you're a stranger to your own best friend."

"Nothing," she denied adamantly, but her voice cracked and the first tears began spilling down her cheeks.

She was sure Cooper had never seen her cry. He looked at a loss as he stood and searched hurriedly through his suit jacket for a handkerchief. Just watching him made her want to laugh, and she hiccupped in an attempt to restrain both tears and laughter.

"Here." He handed her a white linen square, crisply pressed. Claudia didn't care; she wiped her eyes and blew her nose. "I'm fine, really," she declared in a wavering voice.

"It's about Seth, isn't it?" her uncle prompted.

She nodded, blowing her nose again. "He wants me to marry him and move to Alaska."

The room suddenly became still as he digested the information. "Are you going to do it?" he asked in a quiet voice she had long ago learned to recognize as a warning.

"If I knew that, I wouldn't be here blubbering like an idiot," she returned defensively.

"I can't help but believe it would be a mistake," he continued. "Lessinger's a good man, don't misunderstand me, but I don't think you'd be happy in Alaska. Where did you say he was from again?" he asked.

"Nome."

"I don't suppose there's a med school in Nome where you could continue your studies?"

"No." The word was clipped, impatient.

Cooper nodded. "You were meant to be a doctor," he said confidently as he rose to his feet. "You'll get over Seth. There's a fine young man out there somewhere who will make you very happy when you finally meet."

"Sure," she agreed without enthusiasm.

Cooper left a few minutes later, and at the sound of the door closing, Ashley stepped out of the kitchen. "You aren't mad, are you?"

At first Claudia had been, but not anymore. Ashley had only been thinking of her welfare, after all. And thanks to her friend's interference, now she knew where Cooper stood on the subject and what she would face if she did decide to marry Seth.

———

"Oh, Seth," she whispered that night, sitting up in bed. He hadn't contacted her since his return to Nome, not even answering her long letters, though she had eagerly checked the mail every day. Once again, she understood that the next move would have to be from her. Her Bible rested on her knees, and she opened it for her devotional reading in Hebrews. She read Chapter 11 twice, the famous chapter on faith. Had Rebekah acted in faith when the servant had come to her family, claiming God had given him a sign? Flipping through the pages of her Bible, she turned to Genesis to reread the story Seth had quoted when he had given her the engagement ring and they had argued. She had said that Rebekah probably didn't have any choice in the matter, but reading the story now, she realized that the Bible said she had. Rebekah's family had asked her if she was willing to go with Abraham's servant, and she'd replied that she would.

Rebekah had gone willingly!

Claudia reread the verses as a sense of release came over her. Her hands trembled with excitement as she closed the Bible and stopped to pray. The prayer was so familiar. She asked God's guidance and stated her willingness to do as He wished. But there was a difference this time. This time the peace she had so desperately sought was there, and she knew that at last she could answer Seth in faith, and that her answer would be yes.

Slipping out of the sheets, she opened the drawer that contained the jeweler's box holding the engagement ring. With a happy sigh she hugged it to her breast. The temptation to slip the ring on her finger now was strong, but she would wait until Seth could do it.

Claudia slept peacefully that night for the first time

since Seth had left. And the next morning she stayed in her pajamas, with no intention of going to school.

Ashley, who was dressed and ready to go out the door, looked at her in surprise. "Did you oversleep? I'm sorry I didn't wake you, but I thought I heard you moving around in your room."

"You did," Claudia answered cheerfully, but her eyes grew serious as her gaze met Ashley's. "I've decided what to do," she announced solemnly. "I love Seth. I'm going to him as soon as I can make the arrangements."

Ashley's blue eyes widened with joy as she laughed and hugged her friend. "It's about time! I knew all along that the two of you belonged together. I'm so happy for you."

Once the decision was made, there seemed to be a hundred things to be dealt with all at once. Claudia searched the internet for the number she needed, then phoned Seth's company, her fingers trembling, and reached his assistant, who told her that he had flown to Kotzebue on an emergency. She didn't know when he would be returning, but she would give him the message as soon as he walked in the door. Releasing a sigh of disappointment, Claudia replaced the headset in the charger.

Undaunted by the uncertainties of the situation, she drove to the university and officially withdrew from school. Next she purchased the clothes she would be needing to face an Arctic winter, along with a beautiful wedding dress. Finally, focusing on her luck in finding an available dress that was a perfect fit and not on the difficult conversation to come, she drove to Cooper's office.

He rose and smiled broadly when she entered. "You

look in better spirits today," he said. "I knew our little talk would help."

"You'd better sit down, Cooper," she said, smiling back at him. "I've made my decision. I love Seth. I've withdrawn from school, and I've made arrangements for my things to be shipped north as soon as possible. I'm marrying Seth Lessinger."

Cooper stiffened, his eyes raking over her. "That's what you think."

Seven

It was dark and stormy when the plane made a jerky landing on the Nome runway, jolting her back to the present, away from the memories of the difficult emotional journey that had brought her to this point. Claudia shifted to relieve her muscles, tired and stiff from the uncomfortable trip. The aircraft had hit turbulent weather shortly after takeoff from Anchorage, and the remainder of the flight had been far too much like a roller-coaster ride for her taste. More than once she had felt the pricklings of fear, but none of the other passengers had shown any concern, so she had accepted the jarring ride as a normal part of flying in Alaska.

Her blue eyes glinted with excitement as she stood and gathered the small bag stored in the compartment above the seat. There wasn't a jetway to usher her into a dry, warm airport. When she stepped from the cozy interior of the plane, she was greeted by a solid blast of Arctic wind. The bitter iciness stole her breath, and she groped for the handrail to maintain her balance. Halfway down the stairs, she was nearly knocked over by a fresh gust of wind. Her hair flew into her face, blinding her. Momentarily unable to move either up or down, she stood stationary until the force of the wind decreased.

Unexpectedly the small bag was wrenched from her numb fingers and she was pulled protectively against a solid male form.

Her rescuer shouted something at her, but the wind carried his voice into the night and there was no distinguishing the message.

She tried to speak but soon realized the uselessness of talking. She was half carried, half dragged the rest of the way down. Once on solid ground, they both struggled against the ferocity of the wind as it whipped and lashed against them. If he hadn't taken the brunt of its force, Claudia had a feeling she might not have made it inside.

As they neared the terminal, the door was opened by someone who'd been standing by, watching. The welcoming warmth immediately stirred life into her frozen body. Nothing could have prepared her for the intensity of the Arctic cold. Before she could turn and thank her rescuer, she was pulled into his arms and crushed in a smothering embrace.

"Seth?" Her arms slid around his waist as she returned the urgency of his hug.

He buried his face in her neck and breathed her name. His hold was almost desperate, and when he spoke, his voice was tight and worried.

"Are you all right?" Gently his hands framed her face, pushing back the strands of hair that had been whipped free by the wind. He searched her features as if looking for any sign of harm.

"I'm fine," she assured him and, wrapping her arms around him a second time, pressed her face into his parka. "I'm so glad to be here."

"I've been sick with worry," he ground out hoarsely.

"The storm hit here several hours ago, and there wasn't any way your flight could avoid the worst of it."

"I'm fine, really." Her voice wobbled, not because she was shaky from the flight but from the effect of being in Seth's arms.

"If anything had happened to you, I don't know . . ." He let the rest fade and tightened his already secure hold.

"I'm glad we won't have to find out," she said and lightly touched her lips to the corner of his mouth.

He released her. The worried look in his eyes had diminished now that he knew she was safe. "Let's get out of here," he said abruptly, and left her standing alone as he secured her luggage. Everything she could possibly get into the three large suitcases—along with whatever she could buy locally—would have to see her through until the freight barge arrived in the spring.

They rode to the hotel she'd booked herself into in his four-wheel-drive SUV. They didn't speak, because Seth needed to give his full attention to maneuvering safely through the storm. Claudia looked out the windshield in awe. The barren land was covered with snow. The buildings were a dingy gray. In her dreams she had conjured up a romantic vision of Seth's life in Nome. Reality shattered the vision as the winds buffeted the large car.

The hotel room was neat and clean—not elegant, but she'd hoped for a certain homey, welcoming appeal. It was not to be. It contained a bed with a plain white bedspread, a small nightstand, a lamp, a phone, a TV, and one chair. Seth followed her in, managing the suitcases.

"You packed enough," he said with a sarcastic undertone. She ignored the comment, and busied herself by removing her coat and hanging it in the bare closet. She gave him a puzzled look. Something was wrong. He had hardly spoken to her since they'd left the airport. At first she'd assumed the tight set of his mouth was a result of the storm, but not now, when she was safe and ready for his love. Her heart ached for him to hold her. Every part of her longed to have him slip the engagement ring onto the fourth finger of her left hand.

"How's everything in Seattle?" Again that strange inflection in his voice.

"Fine."

He remained on the far side of the room, his hands clenched at his sides.

"Let me take your coat," she offered. As she studied him, the gnawing sensation that something wasn't right increased.

He unzipped his thick parka, but he didn't remove it. He sat at the end of the bed, his face tight and drawn. Resting his elbows on his knees, he leaned forward and buried his face in his hands.

"Seth, what's wrong?" she asked calmly, although she was far from feeling self-possessed.

"I've only had eight hours' sleep in the last four days. A tanker caught fire in port at Kotzebue, and I've been there doing what I could for the past week. You certainly couldn't have chosen a worse time for a visit. Isn't it a little early for Thanksgiving break?"

She wanted to scream that this wasn't a visit, that she'd come to stay, to be his wife and share his world. But she remained quiet, guided by the same inner sense that she had to take this carefully.

Quietly Seth stood and stalked to the far side of the small room. She noticed that he seemed to be limping slightly. He paused and glanced over his shoulder, then turned away from her.

Uncertainty clouded her deep blue eyes, and her mind raced with a thousand questions that she didn't get a chance to ask, because he spoke again.

"I'm flying back to Kotzebue as soon as possible. I shouldn't have taken the time away as it is." He turned around, and his eyes burned her with the intensity of his glare. His mouth was drawn, hard and inflexible. "I'll have one of my men drive you back to the airport for the first available flight to Anchorage." There was no apology, no explanation, no regrets.

Claudia stared back at him in shocked disbelief. Even if he had assumed she was here for a short visit, he was treating her as he would unwanted baggage.

Belying the hurt, she smiled lamely. "I can't see why I have to leave. Even if you aren't here, this would be a good opportunity for me to see Nome. I'd like to—"

"Can't you do as I ask just once?" he shouted.

She lowered her gaze to fight the anger building within her. Squaring her shoulders, she prepared for the worst. "There's something I don't know, isn't there?" she asked in quiet challenge. She wanted to hear the truth, even at the risk of being hurt.

Her question was followed by a moment of grim silence. "I don't want you here."

"I believe you've made that obvious." Her fingers trembled, and she willed them to hold still.

"I tried to reach you before you left."

She didn't comment, only continued to stare at him with questioning eyes.

"It's not going to work between us, Claudia," he announced solemnly. "I think I realized as much when you didn't return with me when I gave you the ring. You must think I was a fool to propose to you the way I did."

"You know I didn't. I—"

He interrupted her again. "I want a wife, Claudia, not some virtuous doctor out to heal the world. I need a woman, someone who knows what she wants in life."

White-lipped, she stiffened her back and fought her building rage with forced control. "Do you want me to hate you, Seth?" she asked softly as her fingers picked an imaginary piece of lint from the sleeve of her thick sweater.

He released a bitter sigh. "Yes. It would make things between us a lot easier if you hated me," he replied flatly. He walked as far away as the small room would allow, as if he couldn't bear to see the pain he was causing her. "Even if you were to change your mind and relinquish your lofty dreams to marry me, I doubt that we could make a marriage work. You've been tossing on a wave of indecision for so long, I don't think you'll ever decide what you really want."

She studied the pattern of the worn carpet, biting her tongue to keep from crying out that she knew what she wanted now. What would be the point? He had witnessed her struggle in the sea of uncertainty. He would assume that her decision was as fickle as the turning tide.

"If we married, what's to say you wouldn't regret it later?" he went on. "You've wanted to be a doctor for so many years that, frankly, I don't know if my love could satisfy you. Someday you might have been able to return to medical school—I would have wanted that for you—but my life, my business, everything I need, is here in

Nome. It's where I belong. But not you, Red." The affectionate endearment rolled easily from his lips, seemingly without thought. "We live in two different worlds. And my world will never satisfy you."

"What about everything you told me about the sign from God? You were the one who was so sure. You were the one who claimed to feel a deep, undying love." She hurled the words at him bitterly, intent on hurting him as much as he was hurting her.

"I was wrong. I don't know how I could have been so stupid."

She had to restrain herself from crying out that it had never been absurd, it was wonderful. The Bible verse in the mirror had meant so much to them both. But she refused to plead, and the dull ache in her heart took on a throbbing intensity.

"That's not all," he added with a cruel twist. "There's someone else now."

Nothing could have shocked her more. "Don't lie to me, Seth. Anything but that!"

"Believe it, because it's true. My situation hasn't changed. I need a wife, someone to share my life. There's"—he hesitated—"someone I was seeing before I met you. I was going to ask her to marry me as soon as I got the engagement ring back from you."

"You're lucky I brought it with me, then!" she shouted as she tore open her purse and dumped the contents out on the bedspread. Carelessly she sorted through her things. It took only a couple of seconds to locate the velvet box, turn around, and viciously hurl it at him.

Instinctively he brought his hands up and caught it.

Their eyes met for a moment; then, without another word, he tucked it in his pocket.

A searing pain burned through her heart.

Seth seemed to hesitate. He hovered for a moment by the door. "I didn't mean to hurt you." Slowly he lowered his gaze to meet hers.

She avoided his look. Nothing would be worse than to have him offer her sympathy. "I'm sure you didn't," she whispered on a bitter note, and her voice cracked. "Please leave," she requested urgently.

Without another word, he opened the door and walked away.

Numb with shock, Claudia couldn't cry, couldn't move. Holding up her head became an impossible task. A low, protesting cry came from deep within her throat, and she covered her mouth with the palm of one hand. Somehow she made it to the bed, collapsing on the mattress.

When Claudia woke the next morning the familiar lump of pain formed in her throat at the memory of her encounter with Seth. For a while she tried to force herself to return to the black cloud of mindless sleep, but to no avail.

She dressed and stared miserably out the window. The winds were blustery, but nothing compared to yesterday's gales. Seth would have returned to Kotzebue. Her world had died, but Nome lived. The city appeared calm; people were walking, laughing, and talking. She wondered if she would ever laugh again. What had gone wrong? Hadn't she trusted God, trusted in Seth's love? How could her world dissolve like this? The tightness in her throat grew and grew.

The small room became her prison. She waited an impatient hour, wondering what she should do, until further lingering became intolerable. Since she was here, she might as well explore the city Seth loved.

The people were friendly, everyone offering an easy smile and a cheery good morning as she passed. There weren't any large stores, nothing to compare with Seattle. She strolled down the sidewalk, not caring where her feet took her. Suddenly she saw a sign proclaiming ARCTIC BARGE COMPANY—Seth's business. A wave of fresh pain swamped her, destroying her fragile composure, and she turned and briskly walked in the opposite direction. Ahead, she spotted a picturesque white church with a bell in its steeple. She was hopeful that she would find peace inside.

The interior was dark as she slipped quietly into the back pew. Thanksgiving would be here at the end of the month—a time for sharing God's goodness with family and friends. She was trapped in Nome with neither. When she'd left Seattle, her heart had nearly burst with praise for God. Now it was ready to burst with the pain of Seth's rejection.

She didn't mean to cry, but there was something so peaceful and restful about the quiet church. A tear slipped from the corner of her eye, and she wiped it aside. She'd left Seattle so sure of Seth's love, filled with the joy of her newfound discovery that she loved him, too, and was ready to be his wife. She'd come in faith. And this was where faith had led her. To an empty church, with a heart burdened by bitter memories.

She'd painted herself into a dark corner. She'd lost her apartment. In the few days between her decision and her flight, Ashley had already found herself a cheaper place and a new roommate. If she did return to school, she would be forced to repeat the courses she'd already taken—not that there was any guarantee she would even be admitted back into the program. Every possession she owned that wasn't in her suitcases had been carefully packed and loaded onto a barge that wouldn't arrive in Nome for months.

She poured out her feelings in silent prayer. She still couldn't believe that she had come here following what she thought was God's plan, and now it seemed she had made a terrible mistake. Lifting the Bible from the pew, she sat and read, desperately seeking guidance, until she caught a movement from the corner of her eye. A stocky middle-aged man was approaching.

"Can I help you?" he asked her softly.

She looked up blankly.

He must have read the confusion in her eyes. "I'm Paul Reeder, the pastor," he said, and sat beside her.

She held out her hand and smiled weakly. "Claudia Masters."

"Your first visit to Nome?" His voice was gentle and inquiring.

"Yes, how'd you know?" she couldn't help but wonder aloud.

He grinned, and his brown eyes sparkled. "Easy. I know everyone in town, so either you're a visitor or I've fallen down in my duties."

She nodded and hung her head at the thought of why she had come to Nome.

"Is there something I can do for you, child?" he asked kindly.

"I don't think there's much anyone can do for me anymore." Her voice shook slightly, and she lowered her lashes in an effort to conceal the desperation in her eyes.

"Things are rarely as difficult as they seem. Remember, God doesn't close a door without opening a window."

She attempted a smile. "I guess I need someone to point to the window."

"Would you feel better if you confided in someone?" he urged gently.

She didn't feel up to explanations but knew she should say something. "I quit school and moved to Alaska expecting . . . a job." The pastor was sure to know Seth, and she didn't want to involve this caring man in the mess of her relationship. "I . . . I assumed wrong . . . and now . . ."

"You need a job and place to live," he concluded for her. A light gleamed in the clear depths of his eyes. "There's an apartment for rent near here. Since it belongs to the church, the rent is reasonable. As for your other problem . . ." He paused thoughtfully. "Do you have any specific skills?"

"No, not really." Her tone was despairing. "I'm in medical school, but other than that—"

"My dear girl!" Pastor Reeder beamed in excitement. "You are the answer to our prayers. Nome desperately needs medical assistants. We've advertised for months for another doctor—"

"Oh, no, please understand," Claudia said, "I'm not a doctor. All I have is the book knowledge so far."

Disregarding her objections, Pastor Reeder stood and

anxiously moved into the wide aisle. "There's someone you must meet."

A worried frown marred Claudia's smooth brow. She licked her dry lips and followed the pastor as he pulled on his coat and strode briskly from the church and out to the street.

They stopped a block or two later. "While we're here, I'll show you the apartment." He unlocked the door to a small house, and Claudia stepped inside.

"Tiny" wasn't the word for the apartment. It was the most compact space Claudia had ever seen: living room with a sleeper sofa, miniature kitchen, and a very small bathroom.

"It's perfect," she stated positively. Perfect if she didn't have to return to Seattle and face Cooper. Perfect if she could show Seth she wasn't like a wave tossed to and fro by the sea. She had made her decision and was here to stay, with or without him. She had responded in faith; God was her guide.

"The apartment isn't on the sewer," the pastor added. "I hope that won't inconvenience you."

"Of course not." She smiled. It didn't matter to her if she had a septic tank.

He nodded approvingly. "I'll arrange for water delivery, then."

She didn't understand but let the comment pass as he showed her out and locked the door behind them.

He led her down the street. "I'm taking you to meet a friend of mine, Dr. Jim Coleman. I'm sure Jim will share my enthusiasm when I tell him about your medical background."

"Shouldn't I sign something and make a deposit on the apartment first?"

Pastor Reeder's eyes twinkled. "We'll settle that later. Thanksgiving has arrived early in Nome. I can't see going through the rigmarole of deposits when God Himself has sent you to us." He handed her the key and smiled contentedly.

The doctor's waiting room was crowded with people when Claudia and Pastor Reeder entered. Every chair was taken, and small children played on the floor.

The receptionist greeted them warmly. "Good morning, Pastor. What can I do for you? Not another emergency, I hope."

"Quite the opposite. Tell Jim I'd like to see him, right away, if possible. I promise to take only a few minutes of his time."

They were ushered into a private office and sat down to wait. The large desk was covered with correspondence, magazines, and medical journals. A pair of glasses had been carelessly tossed on top of the pile.

The young doctor who entered the room fifteen minutes later eyed Claudia skeptically, his dark eyes narrowing.

Eagerly Paul Reeder stood and beamed a smile toward Claudia. "Jim, I'd like to introduce you to God's Thanksgiving present to you. This is Claudia Masters."

She stood and extended her hand. The smile on her face died as she noted the frown that flitted across the doctor's face.

His handshake was barely civil. "Listen, Paul, I don't have the time for your matchmaking efforts today. There are fifteen people in my waiting room and the hospital just phoned. Mary Fulton's in labor."

Her eyes snapped with blue sparks at his assumption and his dismissive tone. "Let me assure you, Dr. Coleman, that you are the last man I'd care to be matched with!"

A wild light flashed in Jim's eyes and it looked as if he would have snapped out a reply if Pastor Reeder hadn't scrambled to his feet to intervene.

"I'll not have you insulting the woman the good Lord sent to help you. And you, Claudia"—he turned to her, waving his finger—"don't be offended. Jim made an honest mistake. He's simply overworked and stressed."

Confusion and embarrassment played rapidly over the physician's face. "The Lord sent her?" he repeated. "You're a nurse?"

Sadly Claudia shook her head. "Medical student. Ex-medical student," she corrected. "I don't know if I'll be much help. I don't have much practical experience."

"If you work with me, you'll gain that fast enough." He looked at her as if she had suddenly descended from heaven. "I've been urgently looking for someone to work on an emergency medical team. With your background and a few months of on-the-job training, you can take the paramedic test and easily qualify. What do you say, Claudia? Can we start again?" His boyish grin offered reassurance.

She smiled reluctantly, not knowing what to say. Only minutes before she'd claimed to be following God, responding to faith. Did He always move so quickly? "Why not?" she said with a laugh.

"Can you start tomorrow?"

"Sure," she confirmed, grateful that she would be kept so busy she wouldn't have time to remember that the reason she had come to Nome had nothing to do with paramedic training.

A message was waiting for her when she returned to the hotel. It gave a phone number and name, with information for upcoming flights leaving Nome for Anchorage. Crumpling the paper, Claudia checked out of the hotel.

She spent the rest of the afternoon unpacking and settling into the tiny apartment. If only Cooper could see her now!

Hunger pangs interrupted her work, and she realized she hadn't eaten all day. Just as she was beginning to wonder about dinner, there was a knock on the door. Her immediate thought was that Seth had somehow learned she hadn't returned to Seattle. Though that was unlikely, she realized, since Seth was no doubt back in Kotzebue by now.

Opening the door, she found a petite blonde with warm blue eyes and a friendly smile. "Welcome to Nome! I'm Barbara Reeder," she said, and handed Claudia a warm plate covered with aluminum foil. "Dad's been talking about his miracle ever since I walked in the door this afternoon, and I decided to meet this Joan of Arc myself." Her laugh was free and easy.

Claudia liked her immediately. Barbara's personality was similar to Ashley's, and she soon fell into easy conversation with the pastor's daughter. She let Barbara do most of the talking. She learned that the woman was close to her own age, worked as a legal assistant and was engaged to a man named Teddy. Claudia felt she needed a friend, someone bright and cheerful to lift her spirits from a tangled web of self-pity, and Barbara seemed like the answer to a prayer.

"Barbara, while you're here, would you mind explaining about the bathroom?" She had been shocked to discover the room was missing the most important fixture.

Barbara's eyes widened. "You mean Dad didn't explain that you aren't on the sewer?"

"Yes, but—"

"Only houses on the sewers have flush toilets, plumbing, and the rest. You, my newfound friend, have your very own 'honey bucket.' It's like having an indoor outhouse. When you need to use it, just open the door in the wall, pull it inside and—*voilà*."

Claudia looked up shocked. "Yes, but—"

"You'll need to get yourself a fuzzy cover, because the seat is freezing. When you're through, open the door, push it back outside and it'll freeze almost immediately."

"Yes, but—"

"Oh, and the water is delivered on Monday, Wednesday, and Friday. Garbage is picked up once a week, but be sure and keep it inside the house, because feral dogs will get into it if it's outside."

"Yes, but—"

"And I don't suppose Dad explained about ordering food, either. Don't worry, I'll get you the catalog, and you'll have plenty of time to decide what you need. Grocery prices are sometimes as much as four times higher than Seattle, so we order the nonperishables once a year. The barge from Seattle arrives before winter."

Claudia breathed in deeply. The concepts of honey buckets, no plumbing, and feral dogs were almost too much to grasp in one lump. This lifestyle was primitive compared to the way things were in Seattle. But she would grow stronger from the challenges, grow—or falter and break.

Concern clouded Barbara's countenance. "Have I discouraged you?"

Pride and inner strength shimmered in Claudia's eyes. "No, Nome is where I belong," she stated firmly.

Jim Coleman proved to be an excellent teacher. Her admiration for him grew with every day and every patient. At the end of her first week, Claudia was exhausted. Together they had examined and treated a steady flow of the sick and injured, eating quick lunches when they got a few free minutes between patients. At the end of the ten-to-twelve-hour days, he was sometimes due to report to the hospital. She spent her evenings studying the huge pile of material he had given her to prepare for the paramedic exam that spring. She marveled at how hard he drove himself, but he explained that his work load wasn't by choice. Few medical professionals were willing to set up practice in the frozen North.

Barbara stopped by the apartment during Claudia's second week with an invitation for Thanksgiving dinner. Jim had also been invited, along with Barbara's fiancé and another couple. Claudia thanked her and accepted, but she must have appeared preoccupied, because Barbara left soon afterward.

Claudia closed the door after her, leaning against the wood frame and swallowing back the bitter hurt. When she'd left Seattle, she'd told Ashley that she was hoping the wedding would be around Thanksgiving. Now she would be spending the day with virtual strangers.

"Good morning, Jim," Claudia said cheerfully the next day as she entered the office. "And you, too, Mrs. Lucy."

The receptionist glanced up, grinning sheepishly to herself.

"Something funny?" Jim demanded brusquely.

"Did either of you get a chance to read Pastor Reeder's sign in front of the church this morning?" Mrs. Lucy asked.

Claudia shook her head and waited.

"What did he say this time?" Jim asked, his interest piqued.

"The sign reads 'God Wants Spiritual Fruit, Not Religious Nuts.'"

Jim tipped his head back and chuckled, but his face soon grew serious. "I suggest we get moving," he said. "We've got a full schedule."

He was right. The pace at which he drove himself and his staff left little time for chatting. With so many people in need of medical attention and only two doctors dividing the load, they had to work as efficiently as possible. By six Claudia had barely had time to grab a sandwich. She was bandaging a badly cut hand after Jim had stitched it when he stuck his head around the corner.

"I want you to check the man in the first room. Let me know what you think. I've got a phone call waiting for me. I'll take it in my office and join you in a few minutes."

A stray curl of rich auburn hair fell haphazardly across her face as she stopped outside the exam room a few minutes later, and she paused long enough to tuck it around her ear and straighten her white smock.

Tapping lightly, her smile warm and automatic, she entered the room. "Good afternoon, my name's—"

Stopping short, she felt her stomach pitch wildly. Seth. His eyes were cold and hard, and his mouth tightened ominously as he asked, "What are *you* doing here?"

Eight

"I work here," Claudia returned, outwardly calm, although her heartbeat was racing frantically. She had realized it would be only a matter of time before she ran into Seth, and had in fact been mildly surprised it hadn't happened before now. But nothing could have prepared her for the impact of seeing him again.

His mouth tightened grimly. "Why aren't you in Seattle?" he demanded in a low growl.

"Because I'm here," she countered logically. "Why should you care if I'm in Seattle or Timbuktu? As I recall, you've washed your hands of me."

Her answer didn't please him, and he propelled himself from the examination table in one angry movement. But he couldn't conceal a wince of pain.

Clearly he was really hurting. "Jim asked me to look at you—now get back on the table."

"Jim?" Seth said derisively. "You seem to have arrived at a first-name basis pretty quickly."

Pinching her lips tightly together, she ignored the implication. "I'm going to examine you whether you like it or not," she said with an authority few patients would dare to question.

His dark eyes narrowed mutinously at her demand.

Winning any kind of verbal contest with him had been impossible to date. She wouldn't have been surprised if he'd limped out of the office rather than obey her demand. He might well have done exactly that if Jim Coleman hadn't entered at that precise minute.

"I've been talking to the hospital," he remarked, handing Claudia Seth's medical chart. Sheer reflex prevented the folder from falling as it slipped through her fingers. She caught it and glanced up guiltily.

Jim seemed oblivious to the tense atmosphere in the room. "Have you examined the wound?" he asked her, and motioned for Seth to return to the table.

Seth hesitated for a moment before giving in. With another flick of his hand, Jim directed Seth to lie down. Again he paused before lying back on the red vinyl cushion. He lay with his eyes closed, and Claudia thought her heart would burst. She loved this man, even though he had cast her out of his life, tossing out cruel words in an attempt to make her hate him. He had failed. And surely he had lied, as well. He couldn't possibly have decided to marry someone else so quickly.

Jim lifted the large bandage on Seth's leg, allowing Claudia her first look at the angry wound. Festering with yellow pus, the cut must have been the source of constant, throbbing pain. When Jim gently tested the skin around the infection Seth's face took on a deathly pallor, but he didn't make a sound as he battled to disguise the intense pain. A faint but nonetheless distinct red line extended from the wound, reaching halfway up his thigh.

"Blood poisoning," Claudia murmured gravely. She could almost feel his agony and paled slightly. Anxiously she glanced at Jim.

"Blood poisoning or not, just give me some medicine and let me out of here. I've got a business to run. I can't be held up here all day while you two ooh and ah over a minor cut." He spoke sharply and impatiently as he struggled to sit upright.

"You seem to think you can work with that wound," Jim shot back angrily. "Go ahead, if you don't mind walking on a prosthetic leg for the rest of your life. You need to be in the hospital."

"So *you* say," Seth retorted.

Stiff with concern, Claudia stepped forward when Seth let out a low moan and lay back down.

"Do whatever you have to," he said in a resigned tone.

"I'd like to talk to you in my office for a minute, Claudia," Jim said. "Go ahead and wait for me there."

The request surprised her, but she did as he asked, pacing the small room as she waited for him. He joined her a few minutes later, a frown of concern twisting his features.

"I've already spoken to the hospital," he announced as he slumped defeatedly into his chair. "There aren't any beds available." He ran a hand over his face and looked up at her with unseeing eyes. "It's times like these that make me wonder why I chose to work in Nome. Inadequate facilities, no private nurses, overworked staff . . . I don't know how much more of the stress my health will take."

She hadn't known Jim long, but she had never seen him more frustrated or angry.

"I've contacted the airport to have him flown out by charter plane, but there's a storm coming. Flying for the next twelve hours would be suicidal," he continued. "His leg can't wait that long. Something's got to be done before that infection spreads any farther." He straightened and released a bitter sigh. "I don't have any choice but to send you home with him, Claudia. He's going to need constant care or he could lose that leg. I can't do it myself, and there's no one else I can trust."

She leaned against the door, needing its support as the weight of what he was asking pressed heavily on her shoulders—and her heart. Despite the emotional cost to herself, she couldn't refuse.

Patiently Jim outlined what Seth's treatment would entail. He studied Claudia for any sign of confusion or misunderstanding, then gave her the supplies she would need and reminded her of the seriousness of the infection.

An hour later, with Seth strongly protesting, Claudia managed to get him into his house and into his bed. After propping his leg up with a pillow, she removed the bandage to view the open wound again. She cringed at the sight, thinking of how much pain he had to be in.

Her eyes clouded with worry as she worked gently and efficiently to make him as comfortable as possible. She intentionally avoided his gaze in an attempt to mask her concern.

He appeared somewhat more comfortable as he lay back and rested his head against a pillow. A tight clenching of his jaw was the only sign of pain he allowed to show on his ruggedly carved features. She didn't need to see his agony to know he was in intense pain, though.

"Why are you here?" he asked, his eyes closed as he echoed the question he'd asked when she walked into the exam room.

"I'm taking care of your leg," she replied gently. "Don't talk now, try to sleep if you can." Deftly she opened the bag of supplies and laid them out on the dresser. Then, standing above him, she rested her cool hand against his forehead. She could feel how feverish he was.

At the tender touch of her fingers, he raised his hand and gripped her wrist. "Don't play games with me, Red." He opened his eyes to hold her gaze. "Why are you in Nome?" The words were weak; there wasn't any fight left in him. Protesting Jim's arrangements had depleted him of strength. Now it took all his effort to disguise his pain. "Did you come back just to torment me?"

"I never left," she answered, and touched a finger to his lips to prevent his questions. "Not now," she whispered. "We'll talk later, and I'll explain then."

He nodded almost imperceptibly and rolled his head to the side.

Examining the cut brought a liquid sheen to her eyes. "How could you have let this go so long?" she protested. Jim had explained to her that Seth had fallen against a cargo crate while in Kotzebue. Claudia recalled that he'd had a slight limp the day he picked her up from the airport. Had he let the injury go untreated all that time? Was he crazy?

He didn't respond to her question, only exhaled a sharp breath as she gently began carefully swabbing the wound. She bit into her lip when he winced again, but it was important to clean the cut thoroughly. Jim had given Seth antibiotics and painkillers before leaving the office, but the antibiotics needed time to kick in, and as for the painkillers, their effect had been minor.

When she'd finished, she heated hot water in the kitchen, then steeped strips of cloth in the clean water. After allowing them to cool slightly, she placed them over his thigh, using heat to draw infection from the wound. His body jerked taut and his mouth tightened with the renewed effort to conceal his torment. She repeated the process until the wound was thoroughly cleansed, then returned to the kitchen.

"I'm going to lose this leg," Seth mumbled as she walked into the bedroom.

"Not if I can help it," she said with a determination that produced a weak smile from him.

"I'm glad you're here," he said, his voice fading.

She gently squeezed his hand. "I'm glad I'm here, too." Even if she did eventually return to Seattle, she would always cherish the satisfaction of having been able to help Seth.

He rested fitfully. Some time later, she again heated water, adding the medicine Jim had given her to it as it steamed. A pungent odor filled the room. As quietly as possible, so as not to disturb him, she steeped new strips of fabric. Cautiously she draped them around the swollen leg, securing them with a large plastic bag to keep them moist and warm as long as possible. When the second stage of Jim's instructions had been completed, she slumped wearily into a chair at Seth's bedside.

Two hours later she repeated the process, and again after another two-hour interval. She didn't know what time it was when Jim arrived. But Seth was still asleep, and there didn't seem to be any noticeable improvement in his condition.

"How's the fever?" Jim asked as he checked Seth's pulse.

"High," she replied, unable to conceal her worry.

"Give him time," Jim cautioned. He gave Seth another injection and glanced at his watch. "I'm due at the hospital. I'll see what I can do to find someone to replace you."

"No!" she said abruptly. Too abruptly. "I'll stay."

Jim eyed her curiously, his gaze searching. "You've been at this for hours now. The next few could be crucial, and I don't want you working yourself sick."

"I'm going to see him through this," she said with determination. Avoiding the question in his eyes, she busied herself neatening up the room. She would explain later if she had to, but right now all that mattered was Seth and getting him well.

Jim left a few minutes later, and she paused to fix herself a meal. She would need her strength, but although she tried to force herself to eat, her fears mounted, dispelling her appetite.

The small of her back throbbed as she continued to labor through the night. Again and again she applied the hot cloths to draw out the infection.

Claudia fidgeted anxiously when she took his temperature and discovered that his fever continued to rage, despite her efforts. She gently tested the flesh surrounding the wound and frowned heavily.

Waves of panic mounted again a few minutes later when he stirred restlessly. He rolled his head slowly from side to side as the pain disturbed his sleep.

"Jesus, please help us," Claudia prayed as she grew more dismayed. Nothing she did seemed to be able to control Seth's fever.

She'd repeatedly heard about the importance of remaining calm and clearheaded when treating a patient. But her heart was filled with dread as the hours passed, each one interminable, and still his fever raged. If she couldn't get his fever down, he might lose his leg.

His Bible lay on the nightstand, and she picked it up, holding it in both hands. She brought the leather-bound book to her breast and lifted her eyes to heaven, murmuring a fervent prayer.

Another hour passed, and he began to moan and mumble incoherently as he slipped into a feverish delirium. He tossed his head, and she was forced to hold him down as he struggled, flinging out his arms.

He quieted, and she tenderly stroked his face while whispering soothing words of comfort.

Unexpectedly, with an amazing strength, Seth jerked upright and cried out in anguish, "John . . . watch out . . . no . . . no . . ."

Gently but firmly she laid him back against the pillow, murmuring softly in an effort to calm him. Absently she wondered who John was. She couldn't remember Seth ever mentioning anyone by that name.

He kept mumbling about John. Once he even laughed, the laugh she loved so much. But only seconds later he cried out in anguish again.

Tears that had been lingering so close to the surface quickly welled. Loving someone as she loved Seth meant that his torment became her own. Never had she loved this completely, this strongly.

"Hush, my darling," she murmured softly.

She was afraid to leave him, even for a moment, so she pulled a chair as close as she could to his bedside and sank wearily into it. Exhaustion claimed her mind, wiping it clean of everything but prayer.

Toward daylight Seth seemed to be resting more comfortably, and Claudia slipped into a light sleep.

Someone spoke her name, and Claudia shifted from her uncomfortable position to find Seth, eyes open, regarding her steadily.

"Good morning," he whispered weakly. His forehead and face were beaded with sweat, his shirt damp with perspiration. The fever had broken at last.

A wave of happiness washed through her, and she offered an immediate prayer of thanksgiving.

"Good morning," she returned, her voice light as relief lightened her heart. She beamed with joy as she tested his forehead. It felt moist but cool, and she stood to wipe the sweat from his face with a fresh washcloth.

He reached out and stopped her, closing his hand over her fingers, as if touching her would prove she was real. "I'm not dreaming. It *is* you."

She laughed softly. "The one and only." Suddenly conscious of her disheveled appearance, she ran her fingers through her tangled hair and straightened her blouse.

His gaze was warm as he watched her, and she felt unexpectedly shy.

"You told me you never left Nome?" The inflection in his voice made the statement a question.

"I didn't come here to turn around and go back home," she said and smiled, allowing all the pent-up love to burn in her eyes.

His eyes questioned her as she examined his leg. The

improvement was remarkable. She smiled, remembering her frantic prayers during the night. Only the Great Physician could have worked this quickly.

She helped Seth sit up and removed his damp shirt. They worked together silently as she wiped him down and slipped a fresh shirt over his head. Taking the bowl of dirty water and tucking his shirt under her arm, she smiled at him and walked toward the door.

"Red, don't go," he called urgently.

"I'll be right back," she assured him. "I'm just going to take these into the kitchen and fix you something to eat."

"Not now." He extended his hand to her, his look intense. "We need to talk."

She walked back to the dresser to deposit the bowl before moving to the bed. Their eyes locked as they studied each other. The radiant glow of love seemed to reach out to her from his gaze. She took his hand in her own and, raising it to her face, rested it against her cheek and closed her eyes. She didn't resist as the pressure of his arm pulled her downward. She knelt on the carpet beside the bed and let herself be wrapped in his embrace.

His breathing was heavy and labored as he buried his face in the gentle slope of her neck. This was what she'd needed, what she'd yearned for from the minute she stepped off the plane—Seth and the assurance of his love.

"I've been a fool," he muttered thickly.

"We both have. But I'm here now, and it's going to take a lot more than some angry words to pry me out of your arms." She pulled away slightly, so she would be able to look at him as she spoke. "I need to take some responsibility here," she murmured, and brushed the hair from the sides of his face. He captured her hand and pressed a kiss against her palm. "I'd never once told you I loved you."

His hand tightened around hers punishingly. "You love me?"

"Very much." She confirmed her words with a nod and a smile. "You told me so many times that you needed me, but I discovered I'm the one who needs you."

"Why didn't you tell me when you arrived that you intended to stay?" He met her eyes, and she watched as his filled with regret.

"I'm a little slow sometimes," she said, ignoring his question in favor of explaining how she'd come to realize she loved him. She sat in the chair but continued to hold his hand in hers. "I couldn't seem to understand why God would give you a sign and not say anything to me. I was miserable—the indecision was disrupting my whole life. Then one day I decided to read the passage in Genesis that you'd talked about. I read about Abraham's servant and learned that Rebekah had been given a choice and had made the decision to accompany the servant. I felt as if God was offering me the same decision and asking that I respond in faith. It didn't take me long to recognize how much I loved you. I can't understand why I fought it so long. Once I admitted it to myself, quitting school and leaving Seattle were easy."

"You quit school?"

"Without hesitation." She laughed with sudden amusement. "I'd make a rotten doctor. Haven't you noticed that I become emotionally involved with my patients?"

"What about your uncle?"

"He's accepted my decision. He's not happy about it, but I think he understands more than he lets on."

"We'll make him godfather to our first son," Seth said, and slipped a large hand around her nape, pulling her close so her soft mouth could meet his. The kiss was so gentle that tears misted her eyes. His hands framed the sides of her face as his mouth slanted across hers, the contact deepening until he seemed capable of drawing out her soul.

Jim Coleman stopped by later, but only long enough to quickly check Seth's leg and give him another injection of antibiotic. He was thrilled that the fever had broken, but he spoke frankly with Seth and warned him that it would take weeks to regain the full use of the leg.

He hesitated once, and Claudia was sure he'd noticed the silent communication and emotional connection that flashed between her and Seth. Jim's eyes narrowed, and the corner of his mouth twitched. For a fleeting moment she thought the look held contempt. She dismissed the idea as an illusion based on a long night and an overactive imagination. Jim left shortly afterward, promising to return that evening.

She heated a lunch for the two of them and waited until Seth had eaten. He fell asleep while she washed the dishes. When she checked on him later, her heart swelled with the wonder and joy of their love. How many other married couples had received such a profound confirmation of their commitment as they had? He had spoken of a son, and she realized how much she wanted this man's child.

Smiling, she rested her hands lightly on her flat stomach and started to daydream. They would have tall lean sons with thick dark hair, and perhaps a daughter. A glorious happiness stole through her.

Content that Seth would sleep, she opened the other bedroom door, crawled into the bed and drifted into a deep sleep. Her dreams were happy, confident of the many years she would share with Seth.

When she awoke later she rolled over and glanced at the clock. Seven. She had slept for almost five hours. Sitting up, she stretched, lifting her arms high above her head, then rotated her neck to ease the tired muscles.

The house was quiet as she threw back the covers and walked back to Seth's room. He was awake, his face turned toward the wall. Something prevented her from speaking and drawing attention to herself. His posture said that he was troubled, worried. What she could see of his face was tight. Was he in pain? Was something about his business causing him concern?

As if feeling her regard, he turned his head and their eyes met. His worried look was gone immediately, replaced by a loving glance that sent waves of happiness through her.

"Hello. Have you been awake long?" she asked softly.

"About an hour. What about you?"

"Just a few minutes." She moved deeper into the room. "Is something troubling you, Seth? You had a strange look just now. I don't exactly know how to describe it . . . sadness, maybe?"

His hand reached for hers. "It's nothing, my love."

She felt his forehead, checking for fever, but it was cool, and she smiled contentedly. "I don't know about you, but I'm starved. I think I'll see what I can dig up in the kitchen."

He nodded absently.

As she left the room, she couldn't help glancing over her shoulder. Her instincts told her that something wasn't right. But what?

A freshly baked pie was sitting in the middle of the kitchen table, and she glanced at it curiously. When had that appeared? She shrugged and opened the refrigerator. Maybe Seth had some eggs and she could make an omelette. There weren't any eggs, but a gelatin salad sat prominently on the top shelf. Something was definitely going on here. When she turned around, she noticed that the oven light was on, and a quick look through the glass door showed a casserole dish warming. Someone had been to the house when she'd been asleep and brought an entire meal. How thoughtful.

"You didn't tell me you had company," she said a little while later as she carried a tray into the bedroom for him.

He was sitting on the edge of the mattress, and she could see him clench his teeth as he attempted to stand.

"Seth, don't!" she cried and quickly set the tray down to hurry to his side. "You shouldn't be out of bed."

He sank back onto the mattress and closed his eyes to mask a resurgence of pain. "You know, I think you're right about that."

"Here, let me help you." With an arm around his shoulders, she gently lifted the injured leg and propped it on top of a thick pillow. When she'd finished, she turned to him and smiled. She couldn't hide the soft glow that warmed her eyes as she looked at this man she loved.

Sitting up, his back supported by pillows, he held his

arms out to her and drew her into his embrace. His mouth sought hers, and the kisses spoke more of passion than gentleness. But she didn't care. She returned his kisses, linking her hands around his neck, her fingers exploring the black hair at the base of his head. His hands moved intimately over her back as if he couldn't get enough of her.

"I think your recovery will impress Dr. Coleman, especially if he could see us now," she teased and tried to laugh. But her husky tone betrayed the extent of her arousal. When Seth kissed her again, hard and long, she offered no resistance.

Crushed in his embrace, held immobile by the steel band of his arm encircling her waist, she submitted happily to the mastery of his kisses.

When they took a break to breathe, she smiled happily into his gleaming eyes. "There are only a few more days before Thanksgiving," she murmured, and kissed him. "I have so much to thank God for this year—more happiness than one woman was ever meant to have. I had hoped when I first came that we might be married Thanksgiving week. It seemed fitting somehow." She relaxed as she realized that she truly had no more doubts. She was utterly his.

Although Seth continued to hold her, she felt again the stirring sense of something amiss. When she leaned her head back to glance at him, she saw that his look was distant, preoccupied.

"Seth, is something wrong?" she asked, worried.

A smile of reassurance curved his lips, but she noticed that it didn't reach his eyes. "Everything's fine."

"Are you hungry?"

He nodded and straightened so that she could bring him the tray. "You know me. I'm always hungry."

But he hardly touched his meal.

She brought him a cup of coffee after taking away the dinner tray, then sat in the chair beside the bed, her hands cupping her own hot mug.

"If you don't object, I'd like Pastor Reeder to marry us," she said, and took a sip of coffee.

"You know Paul Reeder?" He looked over at her curiously.

She nodded. "I'm very grateful for his friendship. He's the one who introduced me to Jim Coleman. He also rented me an apartment the church owns—honey bucket and all," she said with a smile. "I'm going to like Nome. There are some wonderful people here, and that very definitely includes Pastor Reeder."

"Paul's the one who talked to me about Christ and salvation. I respect him greatly."

"I suspected as much." She recalled Seth telling her about the pastor who had led him to Christ. From the first day she had suspected it was Pastor Reeder. "Jim needed help with an emergency, so I didn't get to church last Sunday to hear him preach, but I bet he packs a powerful sermon."

"He does," Seth said, and looked away.

Claudia's gaze followed his, and she realized that Jim Coleman had let himself into the house. The two men eyed each other, and an icy stillness seemed to fill the room. She looked from one man to the other and lightly shook her head, sure she was imagining things.

"I think you'll be impressed with how well Seth is

doing," she said, and moved aside so Jim could examine the wound himself.

Neither man spoke, and the tension in the room was so thick that she found herself stiffening. Something was wrong between these two, *very* wrong.

Claudia walked Jim to the front door when he was done with the exam. Again he praised her efforts. "He might have lost that leg if it hadn't been for you."

"I was glad to help," she said, studying him. "But I feel God had more to do with the improvement than I did."

"That could be." He shrugged and expelled a long, tired sigh. "He should be okay by himself tonight if you want to go home and get a good night's sleep."

"I might," she responded noncommittally.

He nodded and turned to leave. She stopped him with a hand on his arm. "Jim, something's going on between you and Seth, isn't it?"

"Did he tell you that?"

"No."

"Then ask *him*," he said, casting a wary glance in the direction of Seth's bedroom.

"I will," she replied, determined to do just that.

Seth's eyes were closed when she returned to his room, but she wasn't fooled. "Don't you like Jim Coleman?" she asked right out.

"He's a fine Christian man. There aren't many doctors as dedicated as he is."

"But you don't like him, do you?"

Seth closed his eyes again and let out a sharp breath. "I don't think it's a question of how I feel. Jim doesn't like me, and at the moment I can't blame him," he responded cryptically.

She didn't know what to say. It was obvious Seth didn't want to talk about it, and she didn't feel she should pry. It hurt a little, though, that he wouldn't confide in her. There wasn't anything she would ever keep from him. But she couldn't and wouldn't force him to talk, not if he wasn't ready. She left him to rest and went into the kitchen to clean up.

An hour later she checked on him and saw that he appeared to be asleep. Leaning down, she kissed his brow. She was undecided about spending another night. A hot shower and a fresh change of clothes sounded tempting.

"Seth," she whispered, and he stirred. "I'm going home for the night. I'll see you early tomorrow morning."

"No." He sat up and winced, apparently having forgotten about his leg in his eagerness to stop her. "Don't go, Red. Stay tonight. You can leave in the morning if you want." He reached for her, holding her so tight she ached.

"Okay, my love," she whispered tenderly. "Just call if you need me."

"I'll need you all my life. Don't ever forget that, Red."

He sounded so worried that she frowned, drawing her delicate brows together. "I won't forget."

Claudia woke before Seth the next morning. She was in the kitchen putting on a pot of coffee when she heard a car pull up outside the kitchen door.

Barbara Reeder slammed the car door closed and waved. Claudia returned the wave and opened the door for her friend.

"You're out bright and early this morning," Claudia said cheerfully. "I just put on coffee."

"Morning." Barbara returned the smile. "How's the patient?"

"Great. It's amazing how much better he is after just two days."

"I was sorry to miss you yesterday." Barbara pulled out a chair and set her purse on the table while she unbuttoned her parka.

"Miss me?" Claudia quizzed.

"Yes, I brought dinner by, but you were in the bedroom sound asleep. From what I understand, you were up all night. You must have been exhausted. I didn't want to wake you, so I just waved at your patient, left the meal and headed out."

"Funny Seth didn't say anything," Claudia said, speaking her thoughts out loud.

Barbara's look showed mild surprise. "Honestly, that man! You'd think it was top secret or something." Happiness gleamed in her eyes, and she held out her left hand so Claudia could admire the sparkling diamond. "Teddy and I are going to be married next month."

Nine

❦

"Teddy?" Claudia repeated. She felt as if someone had kicked her in the stomach. Seth hadn't been lying after all. There really was another woman. Somehow she managed to conceal her shock.

"It's confusing, I know," Barbara responded with a happy laugh. "But Seth has always reminded me of a teddy bear. He's so big and cuddly, it seemed natural to call him Teddy."

Claudia's hand shook as she poured coffee into two mugs. Barbara continued to chat excitedly about her wedding plans, explaining that they hoped to have the wedding before Christmas.

Strangely, after that first shock Claudia felt no emotion. She sipped her coffee, adding little to the conversation.

Barbara didn't seem to notice. "Teddy changed after John's death," she said, and blew on her coffee to cool it.

"John," Claudia repeated. Seth had called out that name several times while his fever was raging.

"John was his younger brother, his partner in Arctic Barge. There was some kind of accident on a barge—I'm not sure I ever got the story straight. Seth was with him when it happened. Something fell on top of him and ruptured his heart. He died in Seth's arms."

Claudia stared into her coffee. From that first day when she'd walked into his room at the Wilderness Motel, she'd known there was a terrible sadness in Seth's life. She'd felt it even then. But he had never shared his grief with her. As much as he professed to love her and want her for his wife, he hadn't shared the deepest part of himself. Knowing this hurt as much as his engagement to Barbara.

"Could I ask a favor of you?" Claudia said and stood, placing her mug in the kitchen sink. "Would you mind dropping me off at my apartment? I don't want to take Seth's car, since I don't know when I'll be back. It should only take a minute."

"Of course. Then I'll come back and surprise Seth with breakfast."

He would be amazed all right, Claudia couldn't help musing.

She managed to maintain a fragile poise until Barbara dropped her off. Waving her thanks, she entered her tiny home. She looked around the room that had so quickly become her own and bit the inside of her cheek. With purposeful strides she opened the lone closet and pulled out her suitcases. She folded each garment with unhurried care and placed it neatly inside the luggage.

Someone knocked at the door, but she obstinately ignored the repeated rapping.

"Open up, Claudia, I know you're in there. I saw Barbara drop you off." It was Jim Coleman.

"Go away!" she called, and her voice cracked. A tear

squeezed free, despite her determination not to cry, and she angrily wiped it away with the back of her hand.

Ignoring her lack of an invitation, Jim pushed open the door and stepped inside the room.

"I like the way people respect my privacy around here," she bit out sarcastically, wondering how she could have been foolish enough to leave her door unlocked. "I don't feel up to company at the moment, Jim. Another time, maybe." She turned away and continued packing.

"I want you to listen to me for a minute." Clearly he was angry.

"No, I won't listen. Not to anyone. Go away, just go away." She pulled a drawer from the dresser and flipped it over, emptying the contents into the last suitcase.

"Will you stop acting like a lunatic and listen? You can't leave now."

She whirled around and placed both hands challengingly on her hips. "Can't leave? You just watch me. I don't care where the next plane's going, I'll be on it," she shot back, then choked on a sob.

He took her in his arms. She struggled at first, but he deflected her hands and held her gently. "Let it out," he whispered soothingly.

Again she tried to jerk away, but, undeterred, he held her fast, murmuring comforting words.

"You knew all along, didn't you?" she asked accusingly, raising hurt, questioning eyes to search his face.

He arched one brow and shrugged his shoulders. "About Barbara and Seth? Of course. But about *you* and Seth? How could I? But then I saw the two of you, and no one could look at you without knowing you're in love. I was on my way to his house this morning when I saw Barbara with you. Something about your expression told me you must have found out the truth. Did you say anything to her?"

Claudia shook her head. "No. I couldn't. But why does it have to be Barbara?" she asked unreasonably. "Why couldn't it be some anonymous woman I could feel free to hate? But she's bright and cheerful, fun to be around. She's my friend. And she's so in love with him. You should have heard her talk about the wedding."

"I have," he stated, and rammed his hands into his pockets. He walked to the other side of the couch that served as her bed.

"I'm not going to burst that bubble of happiness. I don't think Seth knows what he wants. He's confused and unsure. The only thing I can do is leave."

Jim turned and regarded her steadily. "You can't go now. You don't seem to understand what having you in Nome means to me, to all of us. When Pastor Reeder said you were God's Thanksgiving gift to us, he wasn't kidding. I've been praying for someone like you for months." He heaved a sigh, his eyes pleading with her. "For the first time in weeks I've been able to do some of the paperwork that's cluttering my desk. And I was planning to take a day off next week, the first one in three months."

"But you don't know what you're asking."

"I do. Listen, if it will make things easier, I could marry you."

The proposal was issued sincerely, and his gaze didn't waver as he waited for her reaction.

She smiled "Now you're being ridiculous."

His taut features relaxed, and she laughed outright at how relieved he looked.

"Will you stay a bit longer, at least until someone answers our advertisement in the medical journals? Two or three months at the most."

Gesturing weakly with one hand, Claudia nodded. She was in an impossible position. She couldn't stay, and she couldn't leave. And there was still Seth to face.

Jim sighed gratefully. "Thank you. I promise you won't regret it." He glanced at his watch. "I'm going to talk to Seth. Something's got to be done."

She walked him to the door, then asked the question his proposal had raised in her mind. "Why haven't you ever married?"

"Too busy in med school," he explained. "And since I've been here, there hasn't been time to date the woman I wanted." He pulled his car keys from his pocket.

There was something strange about the way he spoke, or maybe it was the look in his eyes. Suddenly it all came together for her. She stopped him by placing a hand on his arm. "You're in love with Barbara, aren't you?" If she hadn't been caught up in her own problems, she would have realized it long ago. Whenever Jim talked about Barbara there was a softness in his voice that spoke volumes.

He began to deny his feelings, then seemed to notice the knowing look in Claudia's blue eyes. "A lot of good it's done me." His shoulders slumped forward in defeat. "I'm nothing more than a family friend to her. Barbara's been in love with Seth for so long, she doesn't even know I'm around. And with the hours I'm forced to work, there hasn't been time to let her know how I feel."

"Does Seth love her?" Pride demanded that she hold her chin high.

"I don't know. But he must feel genuine affection for her or he wouldn't have proposed."

Both of them turned suddenly introspective, unable to find the words to comfort each other. He left a minute later, and she stood at the window watching him go.

She walked over to her suitcases and began to unpack. As she replaced each item in the closet or the drawers, she tried to pray. God had brought her to Nome. She had come believing she would marry Seth. Did He have other plans for her now that she was here? How could she bear to live in the same city as Seth when she loved him so completely? How could she bear seeing him married to another?

No sooner had the last suitcase been tucked away than there was another knock at the door.

Barbara's cheerful smile greeted her as she stuck her head in the front door. "Are you busy?"

Claudia was grateful that she had her back turned as she felt tears come into her eyes. Barbara was the last person she wanted to see. It would almost be preferable to face Seth. Inwardly she groaned as she turned, forcing a smile onto her frozen lips.

"Sure, come in."

Barbara let herself in and held out a large gift-wrapped box. "I know you're probably exhausted and this is a bad time, but I wanted to give this to you, and then I'll get back to Teddy's."

Numbly Claudia took the gift, unable to look higher than the bright pink bow that decorated the box. Words seemed to knot in her throat.

"I'll only stay a minute," Barbara added. "Jim Coleman came by. It looked like he wanted to see Teddy alone for a few minutes, so I thought it was the perfect time to run this over."

"What is it?" The words sounded strange even to herself.

"Just a little something to show my appreciation for all you've done for Teddy. All along, Dad's said that God sent you to us. You've only been here a short time, but already you've affected all our lives. Teddy could have lost his leg if it hadn't been for you. And Dad said your being here will save Jim from exhausting himself with work. All that aside, I see you as a very special sister the Lord sent to me. I can't remember a time when I've felt closer to anyone more quickly." She ended with a shaky laugh. "Look at me," she mumbled, wiping a tear from the corner of her eye. "I'm going to start crying in a minute, and that's all we both need. Now go ahead and open it."

Claudia sat and rested the large box on her knees. Carefully she tore away the ribbon and paper. The ever-growing lump in her throat constricted painfully. Lifting the lid, she discovered a beautiful hand-crocheted afghan in bold autumn colors of gold, orange, yellow, and brown. She couldn't restrain her gasp of pleasure. "Oh, Barbara!" She lifted it from the box and marveled at the weeks of work that had gone into its creation. "I can't accept this—it's too much." She blinked rapidly in an effort to forestall her tears.

"It's hardly enough," Barbara contradicted. "God sent you to Nome as a helper to Jim, a friend to me, and a nurse for my Teddy."

A low moan of protest and guilt escaped Claudia's parched throat. She couldn't refuse the gift, just as she couldn't explain why she'd come to Nome.

"How . . . how long have you been engaged?" she asked in a choked whisper.

"Not very long. In fact, Teddy didn't give me the ring until a few days ago."

Claudia's gaze dropped to rest on the sparkling diamond. She felt a sense of relief that at least it wasn't the same ring he'd offered *her*.

"His proposal had to be about the most unromantic thing you can imagine," she said with a girlish smile. "I didn't need a fortune-teller to realize he's in love with someone else."

Claudia's breathing grew shallow. "Why would you marry someone when he . . . ?" She couldn't finish the sentence and, unable to meet Barbara's gaze, she fingered the afghan on her lap.

"It sounds strange, doesn't it?" Barbara answered with a question. "But I love him. I have for years. We've talked about this other girl. She's someone he met on a business trip. She wasn't willing to leave everything behind for Teddy and Nome. Whoever she is, she's a fool. The affection Teddy has for me will grow, and together we'll build a good marriage. He wants children right away."

With a determined effort Claudia was able to smile. "You'll make him a wonderful wife. And you're right, the other girl *was* a terrible fool." Her mouth ached with the effort of maintaining a smile.

Luckily Barbara seemed to misread the look of strain on Claudia's pale face as fatigue. Standing, she slipped her arms into her thick coat. "I imagine Jim's done by now. I'd better go, but we'll get together soon. And don't forget Thanksgiving dinner. You're our guest of honor."

Claudia felt sick to her stomach and stood unsteadily. The guest of honor? This was too much.

Together they walked to the door.

"Thank you again for the beautiful gift," Claudia murmured in a wavering voice.

"No, Claudia, *I* need to thank *you*. And for so much—you saved the leg and maybe the life of the man I love."

"You should thank God for that, not me."

"Believe me, I do."

Barbara was halfway out the door when Claudia blurted out, "What do you think of Jim Coleman?" She hadn't meant to be so abrupt and quickly averted her face.

To her surprise, Barbara stepped back inside and laughed softly. "I told Dad a romance would soon be brewing between the two of you. It's inevitable, I suppose, working together every day. The attraction between you must be a natural thing. I think Jim's a great guy, though he's a bit too arrogant for my taste. But you two are exactly right for one another. Jim needs someone like you to mellow him." A smile twinkled in her eyes. "We'll talk more about Jim later. I've got to get back. Teddy will be wondering what's going on. He was asleep when Jim arrived, so I haven't had a chance to tell him where I was going."

That afternoon Jim phoned and asked if Claudia could meet him at the office. An outbreak of flu had hit town, and several families had been affected. He needed her help immediately.

Several hours later, she was exhausted. She came home

and cooked a meal, then didn't eat. She washed the already clean dishes and listened to a radio broadcast for
ten minutes before she realized it wasn't in English.

The water in her bathtub was steaming when there
was yet another knock at her door. The temptation to let
it pass and pretend she hadn't heard was strong. She
didn't feel up to another chat with either Barbara or Jim.
Again the knock came, this time more insistent.

Impatiently she stalked across the floor and jerked
open the door. Her irritation died the minute she saw that
it was Seth. He was leaning heavily on a cane, his leg
causing him obvious pain.

"What are you doing here?" she demanded. "You
shouldn't be walking on that leg."

Lines of strain were etched beside his mouth. "Then
invite me inside so I can sit down." He spoke tightly, and
she moved aside, then put a hand on his elbow as she
helped him to the couch.

Relief was evident when he lowered himself onto it.
"We have to talk, Red," he whispered, his eyes seeking
hers.

Fearing the powerful pull of his gaze, she turned away.
The control he had over her senses was frightening. "No,
I think I understand everything."

"You couldn't possibly understand," he countered.

"Talk all you like, but it isn't going to change things."
She moved to the tiny kitchen and poured water into the
kettle to heat. He stood and followed her, unable to hide
a grimace of pain as he moved.

"Where are you going?" he demanded.

"Sit down," she snapped. The evidence of his pain
upset her more than she cared to reveal. "I'm making us

coffee. It looks like we can both use it." She moved across the room and gestured toward the bathroom door. "Now I'm going to get a pair of slippers. I was about to take a bath, and now my feet are cold." She'd taken off her shoes, and the floor was chilly against her bare feet. "Any objections?"

"Plenty, but I doubt they'll do any good."

She was glad for the respite as she found her slippers and slid her feet inside. She felt defenseless and naked, even though she was fully clothed. Seth knew her too well. The bathroom was quiet and still, and she paused to pray. Her mind was crowded with a thousand questions.

"Are you coming out of there, or do I have to knock that door down?" he demanded in a harsh tone.

"I'm coming." A few seconds later she left the bathroom and entered the kitchen to pour their coffee.

"I can't take this. Yell, scream, rant, rave, call me names, but for goodness' sake, don't treat me like this. As if you didn't care, as if you weren't dying on the inside, when I know you must be."

She licked her dry lips and handed him the steaming cup. "I don't need to yell or scream. I admit I might have wanted to this morning, when I talked to Barbara, but not now. I have a fairly good understanding of the situation. I don't blame you. There was no way for you to know I was coming to Nome to stay." She made a point of sitting in the lone chair across the room from him, her composure stilted as she clutched the hot mug.

"Look at me, Red," he ordered softly.

She raised unsure eyes to meet his and time came to a halt. The unquestionable love that glowed in his dark eyes was her undoing. She vaulted to her feet and turned away from him before the anguish of her own eyes became obvious.

"No," she murmured brokenly.

He reached for her, but she easily sidestepped his arm. "Don't touch me, Seth."

"I love you, Claudia Masters." His words were coaxing and low.

"Don't say that!" she burst out in a half-sob.

"Don't look! Don't touch! Don't love!" His voice was sharp "You're mine. I'm not going to let you go."

"I'm *not* yours," she cut in swiftly. "You don't own me. What about Barbara? I won't see you hurt her like this. She loves you, she'll make you a good wife. You were right about me. I don't belong here. I should be in Seattle with my family, back in medical school. I never should have come."

"That's not true and you know it," he said harshly, the blood draining from his face.

"Answer me something, Seth." She paused, and her lips trembled. For a moment she found it difficult to continue. "Why didn't you tell me about your brother?"

If possible, he paled even more. "How do you know about John? Did Barbara tell you?"

Claudia shook her head. "You called out to him that first night when your fever was so high. Then Barbara said something later, and I asked her to explain."

He covered his face with his hands. "I don't like to talk about it, Red. It's something I want to forget. That feeling of utter helplessness, watching the life flow out of John. I would have told you in time. To be frank, it hasn't been a year yet, and I still have trouble talking about it." He straightened and wiped a hand across his face. "John's death has been one of the most influential events of my life. I could find no reason why I should live and my brother should die. It didn't make sense. Other than the business, my life lacked purpose. I was completely focused on personal gain and satisfaction. That was when I talked to Pastor Reeder, seeking answers, and that led to my accepting Jesus Christ. And both John's death and my acceptance of the Lord led to my decision that it was time for me to get married and have a family."

Unable to speak, Claudia nodded. She had been with him the other night as he relived the torment of his brother's death. She had witnessed just a little of the effect it had had on his life.

"I'll be leaving Nome in a couple of months," she said. "Once Jim finds someone to help at the clinic. I want—"

"No," Seth objected strenuously.

"I'm going back to Seattle," she continued. "And someday, with God's help, I'll be one of Washington's finest pediatricians."

"Red, I admit I've made a terrible mess of this thing. When I told you God and I were working on the patience part of me, I wasn't kidding." His voice was low and tense. "But I can't let you go, not when I love you. Not when . . ."

"Not when Barbara's wearing your ring," she finished for him.

"Barbara . . ." he began heatedly, then stopped, defeated. "I have to talk to her. She's a wonderful woman, and I don't want to hurt her."

Claudia laughed softly. "We're both fools, aren't we? I think that at the end of three months we'd be at each other's throats." She marveled at how calm she sounded.

"You're going to marry me." Hard resolve flashed in his eyes.

"No, Seth, I'm not. There's nothing anyone can say that will prevent me from leaving."

He met her look, and for the first time she noticed the red stain on his pant leg. Her composure flew out the window. "Your wound has opened. It was crazy for you to have come here," she said, her voice rising. "I've got to get you home and back into bed."

"You enjoy giving orders, don't you?" he bit out savagely. "Marry Barbara. Go home. Stay in bed." He sounded suddenly weary, as if the effort of trying to talk to her had become too much. "I'll leave, but you can be sure that we're not through discussing the subject."

"As far as I'm concerned, we are." She ripped her coat off the hanger and got her purse.

"What are you doing now?"

"Taking you home and, if necessary, putting you back in bed."

Carefully Seth forced himself off the couch. The pain the movement caused him was clear in his eyes. Standing, he leaned heavily on the cane and dragged his leg as he walked.

"Let me help." She hastened to his side.

"I'm perfectly fine without you," he insisted.

Claudia paused and stepped back. "Isn't that the point I've been making?"

The next days were exhausting. The flu reached epidemic proportions. Both Jim and Claudia were on their feet eighteen hours a day. She traveled from house to house with him, often out to the surrounding villages, because the sick were often too ill to come into the city.

When the alarm sounded early the morning of the fifth day, she rolled over and groaned. Every muscle ached, her head throbbed, and it hurt to breathe. As she stirred from the bed, her stomach twisted into tight cramps. She forced herself to sit up, but her head swam and waves of nausea gripped her. A low moan escaped her parted lips, and she laid her head back on the pillow. She groped for the telephone, which sat on the end table beside the bed, and sluggishly dialed Jim's number to tell him she was the latest flu victim.

He promised to check on her later, but she assured him that she would be fine, that she just needed more sleep.

After struggling into the bathroom and downing some aspirin, she went back to bed and floated naturally into a blissful sleep.

Suddenly she was chilled to the bone and shivering uncontrollably, unconsciously incorporating the iciness into her dreams. She was lost on the tundra in a heavy snowstorm, searching frantically for Seth. He was lost, and now she was, too. Then it was warm, the snowflakes ceased, and the warmest summer sun stole through her until she was comfortable once again.

"Red?" A voice sliced into her consciousness.

Gasping, Claudia opened her eyes, and her gaze flew to the one chair in the room. Seth was sitting there, his leg propped on the coffee table. A worried frown furrowed his brow. As she struggled to a sitting position, she pulled the covers against her breast and flashed him a chilling glare. "How did you get in here?" The words emerged in a hoarse whisper, the lingering tightness in her chest still painful.

"Jim Coleman got a key from Paul Reeder and let me in. He was concerned about you. I thought it was only right that I volunteer to watch over you. I owe you one."

"You don't owe me anything, Seth Lessinger, except the right to leave here when the time comes."

He responded with a gentle smile. "We'll talk about that later. I'm not going to argue with you now, not when you're sick. How are you feeling?"

"Like someone ran over me with a two-ton truck." She leaned against the pillow. The pain in her chest continued, but it hurt a bit less to breathe if she was propped up against something solid. Her stomach felt better, and the desperate fatigue had fled.

"I haven't had a chance to talk to Barbara," he said as his gaze searched her face. "She's been helping Jim and her father the last couple of days. But I'm going to explain things. We're having dinner tonight."

"Seth, please." She looked away. "Barbara loves you, while I . . ."

"You love me, too."

"I'm going back to Seattle. I was wrong to have ever come north."

"Don't say that, Red. Please."

She slid down into the bed and pulled the covers over her shoulders. Closing her eyes, she hoped to convince him she was going back to sleep.

Imitation became reality, and when she opened her eyes again, the room was dark and Seth was gone. A tray had been placed on the table, and she saw that it held a light meal he had apparently fixed for her.

Although she tried to eat, she couldn't force anything down. The world outside her door was dark. There was very little sunlight during the days now, making it almost impossible to predict time accurately. The sun did rise, but only for a few short hours, and it was never any brighter than the light of dusk or dawn.

She was still awake when Seth returned. His limp was less pronounced as he let himself into her apartment.

"What are you doing here?" She was shocked at how weak her voice sounded.

"Barbara's got the flu," he murmured defeatedly. "I only got to see her for a couple of minutes." He sighed heavily as he lowered himself into the chair.

Instantly Claudia was angry. "You beast! You don't have any business being here! You should be with her, not me. She's the one who needs you, not me."

"Barbara's got her father. You've only got me," he countered gently.

"Don't you have any concern for her at all? What if she found out you were here taking care of me? How do you think she'd feel? You can't do this to her." A tight cough convulsed her lungs, and she shook violently with the spasm. The exertion drained her of what little strength she possessed. Wearily she slumped back and closed her eyes, trying to ignore the throbbing pain in her chest.

Cool fingers rested on her forehead. "Would you like something to drink?"

She looked up and nodded, though the effort was almost more than she could manage. The feeble attempt brought a light of concern to Seth's eyes.

The tea he offered hurt to swallow, and she shook her head after the first few sips.

"I'm phoning Jim. You've got something more than the flu." A scowl darkened his face.

"Don't," she whispered. "I'm all right, and Jim's so busy. He said he'd stop by later. Don't bother him. He's overworked enough as it is." Her heavy eyelids drooped, and she fell into a fitful slumber.

Again the rays of the sun appeared in her dream, but this time with an uncomfortably fiery intensity. She thrashed, kicking away the blankets, fighting off imaginary foes who wanted to take her captive.

Faintly she could hear Jim's voice, as if he were speaking from a great distance.

"I'm glad you phoned." His tone was anxious.

Gently she was rolled to her side and an icy-cold stethoscope was placed against her bare back. "Do you hear me, Claudia?" Jim asked.

"Of course I hear you." Her voice was shockingly weak and strained.

"I want you to take deep breaths."

Every inhalation burned like fire, searing a path through her lungs. Moaning, she tried to speak again and found the effort too much.

"What is it, man?" She opened her eyes to see that Seth was standing above her, his face twisted in grim concern.

Jim was standing at his side, and now he sighed heavily. "Pneumonia."

Ten

"Am I dying?" Claudia whispered weakly. Cooper and Ashley stood looking down at her by the side of her hospital bed.

Cooper's mouth tightened into a hard line as his gaze traveled over her and the oxygen tubes and intravenous drip that were attached to her.

"You'll live," Ashley said, and responded to Claudia's weak smile with one of her own.

"You fool. Why didn't you let me know things hadn't worked out here?" Cooper demanded. "Are you so full of pride that you couldn't come to me and admit I was right?"

Sparks of irritation flashed from Claudia's blue eyes. "Don't you ever give up? I'm practically on my deathbed and you're preaching at me!"

"I am not preaching," he denied quickly. "I'm only stating the facts."

Jim Coleman chuckled, and for the first time Claudia noticed that he had entered the room. "It's beginning to sound like you're back among the living, and sooner than we expected." Standing at the foot of her bed, he read her chart and smiled wryly. "You're looking better all the time. But save your strength to talk some sense into these folks. They seem to think they're going to take you back to Seattle."

Claudia rolled her head away so that she faced the wall and wouldn't need to look at Jim. "I *am* going back," she mumbled in a low voice, though she felt guilty, knowing how desperately Jim wanted her to stay.

A short silence followed. Claudia could feel Cooper's eyes boring holes into her back, but to his credit he didn't say anything.

"You've got to do what you think is right," Jim said at last.

"All I want is to go home. And the sooner the better." She would return to Seattle and rebuild her life.

"I don't think it's such a good idea to rush out of here," Jim said, and she could tell by the tone of his voice that he'd accepted her decision. "I want you to gain back some of your strength before you go."

"Pastor Reeder introduced himself to us when we arrived. He's offered to have you stay and recuperate at his home until you feel up to traveling," Ashley added.

"No." Claudia's response was adamant. "I want to go back to Seattle as soon as possible. Cooper was right, I don't belong in Nome. I shouldn't have come in the first place." The words produced a strained silence around the small room. "How soon can I be discharged, Jim?" Her questioning eyes sought his troubled ones.

"Tomorrow, if you like," he said solemnly.

"I would."

"Thanksgiving Day," Ashley announced.

Claudia's eyes met her friend's. Ashley knew the special significance the holiday held for her. The day she'd left Seattle, Claudia had told Ashley to expect the wedding around Thanksgiving. And Ashley had teased her, saying Claudia was making sure no one would ever forget their anniversary. Recalling the conversation brought a physical ache to her heart. No, she'd said, she wanted to be married around Thanksgiving because she wanted to praise God for giving her such a wonderful man as Seth. Now there would be no wedding. She would never have Seth.

"If you feel she needs more time, Doctor," Cooper began, "Ashley and I could stay a few days."

"No," Claudia interrupted abruptly. "I don't want to stay any longer than necessary." Remaining even one extra day was intolerable.

She closed her eyes, blotting out the world. Maybe she could fool the others, but not Ashley, who gently squeezed her hand. Shortly afterward Claudia heard the sound of hushed voices and retreating footsteps.

The stay in the hospital had been a nightmare from the beginning. Seth had insisted on flying in another doctor from Anchorage. As weak as she'd been, she had refused to have anyone but Jim Coleman treat her. Jim and Seth had faced each other, their eyes filled with bitter anger. Claudia was sure they'd argued later when she wasn't there to watch.

She had seen Seth only once since that scene, and only to say goodbye. The relationship was over, she'd said, finished, and he had finally accepted the futility of trying to change her mind.

Pastor Reeder had been a regular visitor. He tried to talk to her about the situation between Seth, Barbara, and herself, but she had made it clear that she didn't want to talk about it. He hadn't brought up the subject again.

Barbara had come once, but Claudia had pretended she was asleep, unable to imagine facing the woman who would share Seth's life, or making explanations that would only embarrass both of them.

Now she relaxed against the pillows, weak after the short visit. Without meaning to, she slipped into a restful slumber.

When she awoke an hour later, Seth was sitting at her bedside. She had hoped not to see him again, but she felt no surprise as she lifted her lashes and their eyes met.

"Hello, Seth," she whispered. She longed to reach out and touch his haggard face. He looked as if he hadn't slept in days.

"Hello, Red." He paused and looked away. "Claudia," he corrected. "Cooper and Ashley arrived okay?"

She nodded. "They were here this morning."

"I thought you might want someone with you." She could tell from his tone that he knew he would never be the one she relied on.

"Thank you. They said you were the one who phoned." She didn't know how she could be so calm. She felt the way she had in the dream, lost and wandering aimlessly on the frozen tundra.

He shrugged, dismissing her gratitude.

"You'll marry Barbara, won't you?"

His hesitation was only slight. "If she'll have me."

She put on a brave smile. "I'm sure she will. She loves you. You'll have a good life together."

He neither agreed with nor denied the statement. "And you?"

"I'm going back to school." The smile on her face died, and she took a quivering breath.

He stood and walked across the room to stare out the window, his back to her. He seemed to be gathering his resolve. "I couldn't let you go without telling you how desperately sorry I am," he began before returning to the chair at her side. "It was never my intention to hurt you. I can only beg your forgiveness."

"Don't, please." Her voice wobbled with the effort of suppressing tears. Seeing Seth humble himself this way was her undoing. "It's not your fault. Really, there's no one to blame. We've both learned a valuable lesson from this. We never should have sought a supernatural confirmation from God. Faith comes from walking daily with our Lord until we're so close to Him that we don't need anything more to know His will."

Until then Seth had avoided touching her, but now he took her hand and gently held it between his large ones. "When do you leave?"

Even that slight touch caused shivers to shoot up her arm. She struggled not to withdraw her hand. "Tomorrow."

He nodded, accepting her decision. "I won't see you again," he said. Then he took a deep breath and, very gently, lifted her fingers to his lips and kissed the back of her hand. "God go with you, Red, and may your life be full and rewarding." His eyes were haunted as he stood, looked down on her one last time, turned around and walked from the room.

"Goodbye, Seth." Her voice was wavering, and she closed her eyes unable to watch him leave.

——

"Honestly, Cooper, I don't need that." She was dressed and ready to leave the hospital when Cooper came into her room pushing a wheelchair. "I'm not an invalid."

Jim Coleman rounded the comer into her room. "No backtalk, Claudia. You have to let us wheel you out for insurance purposes."

"That's a likely story," she returned irritably. Cooper gave her a hand and helped her off the bed. "Oh, all right, I don't care what you use, just get me to the plane on time." It should have been the church, she reminded herself bitterly.

Jim drove the three of them to the airport. Ashley sat in the backseat with Claudia.

"This place is something." Cooper looked around curiously as they drove.

"It really is," Jim answered as he drove. Although it was almost noon, he used the car headlights.

"I wish I'd seen the tundra in springtime. From what everyone says, it's magnificent," Claudia murmured to no one in particular. "The northern lights are fantastic. I was up half one night watching them. Some people claim they can hear the northern lights. The stars here are breathtaking. Millions and millions, like I've never seen before. I . . . I guess I'd never noticed them in Seattle."

"The city obliterates their light," Jim explained.

Cooper turned around to look at Claudia. She met his worried look and gave a poor replica of a smile.

"Is the government ever planning to build a road into Nome?" Ashley asked. "I was surprised to learn we could only come by plane."

"Rumors float around all the time. The last thing I

heard was the possibility of a highway system that would eventually reach us here."

No one spoke again until the airport was in sight. "You love it here, don't you?" Ashley asked Claudia, looking at her with renewed concern.

Claudia glanced out the side window, afraid of what her eyes would reveal if she met her friend's eyes. "It's okay," she said, doubting that she'd fooled anyone.

As soon as they parked, Cooper got out of the car and removed the suitcases from the trunk. Ashley helped him carry the luggage inside.

Jim opened the back door and gave Claudia a hand, quickly ushering her inside the warm terminal. His fingers held hers longer than necessary. "I've got to get back to the office."

"I know. Thank you, Jim. I'll always remember you," she said in a shaky voice. "You're the kind of doctor I hope to be: dedicated, gentle, compassionate. I deeply regret letting you down."

He hugged her fiercely. "No, don't say that. You're doing what you have to do. Goodbye. I'm sorry things didn't work out for you here. Maybe we'll meet again someday." He returned to the car, pausing to wave before he climbed inside and started the engine.

"Goodbye, Jim." The ache in her throat was almost unbearable.

Ashley was at her side immediately. "You made some good friends in the short time you were here, didn't you?"

Claudia nodded rather than attempt an explanation that would destroy her fragile control over her composure.

A few minutes later, she watched as the incoming aircraft circled the airstrip. She was so intent that she didn't notice Barbara open the terminal door and walk inside.

"Claudia," she called softly, and hurried forward to meet her.

Claudia turned around, shock draining the color from her face.

"I know about you and Seth, and . . . don't leave," Barbara said breathlessly, her hands clenched at her sides.

"Please don't say that," Claudia pleaded. "Seth's yours. This whole thing is a terrible misunderstanding that everyone regrets."

"Seth will never be mine," Barbara countered swiftly. "It's you he loves. It will always be you."

"I didn't mean for you ever to know."

"If I hadn't been so blind, so stupid, I would have guessed right away. I thank God I found out."

"Did . . . Seth tell you?" Claudia asked.

Barbara shook her head. "He didn't need to. From the moment Jim brought you into the hospital, Seth was like a madman. He wouldn't leave, and when Jim literally escorted him out of your room, Seth stood in the hallway grilling anyone who went in or out."

For a moment Claudia couldn't speak. Then she put on a false smile and gently shook her head. "Good heavens, you're more upset about my leaving than I am. Things will work out between you and Seth once I'm gone."

"Are you crazy? Do you think I could marry him now? He loves you so much it's almost killing him. How can you be so calm? Don't you care?" Barbara argued desperately. "I can't understand either one of you. Seth is tearing himself apart, but he wouldn't ask you to stay if his life depended on it." She stalked a few feet away, then spun sharply. "This is Thanksgiving!" she cried. "You should be thanking God that someone like Seth loves you."

Claudia closed her eyes to the shooting pain that pierced her heart.

"I once said, without knowing it was you, that the girl in Seattle was a fool. If you fly out of here, you're an even bigger fool than I thought."

Paralyzed by indecision, Claudia turned and realized that Cooper and Ashley had walked over and had clearly heard the conversation. Her eyes filled with doubt, she turned to her uncle.

"Don't look at me," he told her. "This has to be your own choice."

"Do you love him, honestly love him?" Ashley asked her gently.

"Yes, oh yes."

Ashley smiled and inclined her head toward the door. "Then what are you doing standing around here?"

Claudia turned to face Barbara again. "What about you?" she asked softly.

"I'll be all right. Seth was never mine, I'm only returning what is rightfully yours. Hurry, Claudia, go to him. He's at the office—on Thanksgiving! He needs you." She handed Claudia her car keys and smiled broadly through her tears. "Take my car. I'll catch a cab."

Claudia took a step backward. "Ashley . . . Cooper, thank you. I love you both."

"I'd better be godmother to your first child," Ashley called after her as Claudia rushed out the door.

———

Seth's building looked deserted when Claudia entered. The door leading to his office was tightly shut. She tapped lightly, then turned the handle and stepped inside.

He was standing with his back to her, his attention centered on an airplane making its way into the darkening sky.

"If you don't mind, Barbara, I'd rather be alone right now." His voice was filled with stark pain.

"It isn't Barbara," she whispered softly.

He spun around, his eyes wide with disbelief. "What are you doing here?"

Instead of answering him with words, she moved slowly across the room until she was standing directly in front of him. Gently she glided her fingers over the stiff muscles of his chest. He continued to hold himself rigid with pride. "I love you, Seth Lessinger. I'm yours now and for all our lives."

Groaning, he hauled her fiercely into his arms. "You'd better not change your mind, Red. I don't have the strength to let you go a second time." His mouth burned a trail of kisses down her neck and throat. Claudia surrendered willingly to each caress, savoring each kiss, reveling in the protective warmth of his embrace.

Epilogue

"Honey, what are you doing up?" Seth asked as he wandered sleepily from the master bedroom. Claudia watched her husband with a translucent happiness, her heart swelling with pride and love. They'd been married almost a year now: the happiest twelve months of her life.

He stepped up beside her, his hand sliding around the full swell of her stomach. "Is the baby keeping you awake?"

She relaxed against him, savoring the gentle feel of his touch. "No, I was just thinking how good God has been to us. A verse I read in the Psalms the other day kept running through my mind." She reached for her Bible. "It's Psalm 16:11.

"'Thou wilt make known to me the path of life; in Thy presence is fullness of joy; in Thy right hand there are pleasures forever.'"

Seth tenderly kissed the side of her creamy, smooth neck. "God has done that for us, hasn't He? He made known to us that our paths in life were linked, and together we've known His joy."

She nodded happily, rested the back of her head

against his shoulder and sighed softly. "You know what tomorrow is, don't you?"

He gave an exaggerated sigh. "It couldn't be our anniversary. That isn't until the end of the month."

"No, silly, it's Thanksgiving."

"Barbara and Jim are coming, aren't they?"

"Yes, but she insisted on bringing the turkey. You'd think just because I was going to have a baby I was helpless."

"Those two are getting pretty serious, aren't they?"

"I think it's more than serious. It wouldn't surprise me if they got married before Christmas."

"It may be sooner than that. Jim's already asked me to be his best man," Seth murmured, and he nibbled at her earlobe, dropping little kisses along the way.

The two men had long ago settled their differences and had become good friends, which pleased her no end. Claudia had worked for Jim until two additional doctors had set up practice in Nome. The timing had been perfect. She had just learned she was pregnant, and she was ready to settle into the role of homemaker and mother.

"I don't know how you can love me in this condition." She turned and slipped her arms around his waist.

"You're not so bad-looking from the neck up," he teased affectionately, and kissed the tip of her nose. "Has it really been a year, Red?" His gaze grew serious.

She nodded happily, and her eyes were bright with love. "There's no better time to thank God for each other, and for His love."

"No better time," he agreed, cradling her close to his

side. "When I thought I had lost you forever, God gave you back to me."

"It was fitting that it was on Thanksgiving Day, wasn't it?"

"Very fitting," he murmured huskily in her ear, leading her back into their room.

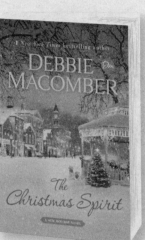